also by KJ Erickson

Third Person Singular

The Dead Survivors

the
last
witness

KJ ERICKSON

st. martin's minotaur
new york

THE LAST WITNESS. Copyright © 2003 by KJ Erickson. All rights reserved. Printed in the United States of America. No part of this book may be used or reproduced in any manner whatsoever without written permission except in the case of brief quotations embodied in critical articles or reviews. For information, address St. Martin's Press, 175 Fifth Avenue, New York, N.Y. 10010.

www.minotaurbooks.com

www.kjerickson.com

Library of Congress Cataloging-in-Publication Data

Erickson, KJ
     The last witness / KJ Erickson.—1st St. Martin's Minotaur ed.
         p. cm.
     ISBN 0-312-31468-X
     1. Bahr, Mars (Fictitious character)—Fiction. 2. Police—Minnesota—Minneapolis—Fiction. 3. Athletes' spouses—Crimes against—Fiction.
     4. Minneapolis (Minn.)—Fiction. 5. Basketball players—Fiction. I. Title.

PS3555.R433L375 2003
813'.6—dc21

                                                                        2002037137

First Edition: May 2003

10 9 8 7 6 5 4 3 2 1

Beloved Puck

the last collaboration

To suffer woes which Hope thinks infinite;
... wrongs darker than death or night;
To defy Power, which seems omnipotent;
To love, and bear; to hope till Hope creates
from its own wreck the thing it contemplates.

—PERCY BYSSHE SHELLEY,
Prometheus Unbound

the
last
witness

CHAPTER

1

No one except police had actually seen the crime-scene photos.

But everyone saw the scene in their mind's eye. Down to the most finite detail. An image that rose from rumors, bits of published fact, tabloid covers glimpsed at supermarket checkouts, and from the unrelenting speculation and gossipmongering of lawyers who spent more time on cable TV talk shows than in courtrooms.

The image was remarkably accurate.

The woman's body lying flat, facedown, on a gleaming hardwood floor.

Her long red hair was fanned out around her head, her head turned sideways in profile.

Her left arm lay at her side, twisted back so the palm turned up. The right arm was extended, elbow bent, fingers spread open, palm down. Her slim bare legs were splayed, one knee raised, as if to climb a step. One shoe, off at the heel, clung to her toes. The other foot was bare, its shoe lying at the photo's margin.

What everyone imagined remembering was the blood, shocking red against the white of her dress. *A red pool spreading out from under her body.*

Her footprints across the floor.

She'd been running in her own blood! You could tell by looking at the streaked footprints that she'd been running. You could see the dark stains on the sole of her shoeless foot.

* * *

What her father remembered about seeing his daughter's body was not the blood. Her father's mind could not associate the blood with his daughter's body. Could not accept what it would mean if the blood were his daughter's.

What her father remembered about seeing his daughter's body were two things.

First, that the person who had been his daughter was not the body lying on the floor. This was comforting, just as not accepting that the blood was his daughter's blood was comforting.

The other thing he remembered was the large bruise on the body's left arm. In such a scene a bruise was perhaps the least shocking evidence of brutality.

But not to her father. To her father, the bruise brought him at warp speed from denial to reality. Because the bruise was old, gone green and yellow with age. Like other bruises the father had seen on his daughter's body.

Bruises he had seen countless times since his daughter, Terri DuCain Jackman, had married Tayron Jackman.

CHAPTER

2

"The mistake we made," she said, "was that none of us understood evil."

Grace DuCain's face looked weathered under the harsh, fluorescent lights of Hennepin County Medical Center's surgical waiting room. Royce Olsen had known Grace for almost thirty years. She was well named. "Grace" described her character as well as her physical beauty. He'd never—not even in some pretty tough times—seen the serenity of her face disturbed.

But today her face looked ravaged. Her life, as she'd known it, had been destroyed in the space of hours. Her daughter—her only child—murdered. Her husband—unwell before the murder, shocked by his daughter's violent death—undergoing emergency surgery to save his life.

Almost as if talking to herself, she said, "Neither Duke nor I could imagine anything worse than what Terri suffered in the six years she'd been married to T-Jack. It was beyond our imagination—not just that he'd have his wife, the mother of his only child, murdered—but that he'd make us, in effect, accomplices to her murder."

She turned to face him. "Now, when I think about the agreement, it's so clear. If only we had understood evil, we would have known when we saw the agreement. It never was what T-Jack represented it to be. It was a step-by-step plan to provide T-Jack with an alibi for Terri's murder. He even made certain Duke would be the one to find Terri's body. Don't tell me he didn't know what that would do to Duke. As much as anything, what haunts me is that if we had understood evil, what happened could have been stopped."

Royce Olsen reached out, putting his hand on her arm. "This is my fault, Grace. I should have recognized that all the quirky stipulations in the agreement meant T-Jack had some sort of scheme in mind. Both you and Duke were worried about what he was up to. I was the one who said 'don't look a gift horse in the mouth.' I was the one who didn't understand evil."

Grace shook her head. "You operated in good faith, Royce. You never did know T-Jack the way we did. We should have known he was capable of something like this. It's just that what he's done was beyond our imagination. All of our imaginations."

She placed her hand on top of his, and for a moment the old Grace emerged. She even managed a smile. "Never send a corporate attorney to do a criminal attorney's job. We thought the agreement was about money. We should have hired one of those vampires who represent murderers. The sort of fellows you see barreling down the freeway, talking on their cell phones, driving one of those big SUVs that are ten feet higher than anything else on the road. I bet they understand evil."

She didn't have to add, *Not a lawyer like you, Royce, who drives a Volvo station wagon and whose life motto is "Caution is the better part of courage."*

"It would make me feel better if you'd cry," he said. "Then I could pretend to be the strong one."

"I'm not going to cry, Royce," she said, her face set in carefully controlled anger. "Not until we've proven T-Jack is responsible for what's happened. If I cry, he's beaten me. And I'm not going to let him beat me. He's taken more than I had to give. I'm not giving another inch to that man."

The surgeon was in the room for moments before they noticed him. That he hesitated in interrupting them said everything that had to be said.

"Mrs. DuCain?"

She caught her breath. Knowing what was to come didn't make the fact of her husband's death any easier.

CHAPTER

3

"How would you like one last hot case?"

Marshall "Mars" Bahr looked up from the boxes he'd been sorting in the bowels of Minneapolis City Hall. His partner, Nettie Frisch, was standing on the other side of the wire mesh walls of his storage locker.

"Why'd you come all the way down here? I've got my cell phone...."

"Because," Nettie said, "you need to be out of here now. I've arranged for a squad to take you to a crime scene. And I brought your sports coat. You're going to need it for this visit. One step down from black-tie-only."

Nettie walked with Mars to the motor pool, briefing him on what she knew. A body had been found at the Lake of the Isles home of Tayron and Terri Jackman. Terri Jackman's father had been at the scene and had suffered some sort of medical emergency. Duke DuCain was en route to Hennepin County Medical Center via ambulance—or for all Nettie knew, he might already be at the hospital.

A murder that involved Duke DuCain and Tayron Jackman definitely qualified as a hot case. DuCain ranked higher on *Forbes*'s big bucks list than any other Minnesotan. Tayron—T-Jack—Jackman, the Minnesota Timberwolves' star point guard—had been identified by more respondents in a recent *Star-Tribune* poll than either of the state's two U.S. senators.

5

As Mars ducked into the waiting squad, he said to Nettie, "Get hold of Danny Borg. He'll probably be batting cleanup on this one when we make the move to the BCA's Cold Case Unit next month. He's only got two more weeks on patrol at the downtown command before he gets his promotion. Might as well get his investigator's feet wet sooner rather than later. And call the Medical Examiner's Office. See if Doc D can handle this case."

Nettie gave Mars a patient smile as she shut the car door behind him. Through the window she said, "Doc D went out five minutes ago. And Danny's already on the scene. He was in his squad when I called to tell him you'd want him involved. Heard him hit the siren before I hung up."

It's not more than two miles from downtown Minneapolis to the Lake of the Isles. But there's no direct route. Having a gutsy squad-car driver who was willing to ignore traffic rules helped. They roared down Third, avoiding Fifth, which was torn up with construction for a lightrail transit route. They caught the tail end of a green light on Hennepin, making an illegal left turn into the bus lane, against one-way traffic on Hennepin. The driver looked to the right before making the turn, catching the clock tower on the Federal Reserve Bank two blocks down. He hissed in frustration.

"Shit," he said, "it's almost four-thirty. We're gonna be bumping rush hour...." He looked down at the dashboard's digital clock. It was not quite four o'clock. "Damn Fed clock," he muttered. "It's never right. Can you tell me why they'd put a clock on top of a building when it's never right?"

Mars shook his head. "It's an architectural *duh*? They got to the top and couldn't figure out what else to do."

The squad's flasher and siren parted the traffic coming toward them on Hennepin. As they crossed the intersection of Hennepin and Sixth, Mars looked to his right. The Target Center was a block west, the arena's graceless bulk fully exposed by a vacant square block cleared for future development. It looked like the backside of an elephant squatting to take a dump.

The sight of the arena usually set Mars's teeth on edge. Today, looking at the arena, what he thought about was the possibility that the man who brought tens of thousands of people to the Target Center during the NBA season might, at this moment, be lying dead in his Lake of the Isles home.

Mars's cell phone rang. As if responding to his thoughts, Nettie said, "I just got a call from Danny Borg. The vic is Terri DuCain Jackman. Her father found her body—but like I said, he's been taken to the hospital...."

"Where's T-Jack?"

"The DuCains' attorney talked with Danny before the attorney went down to HCMC to be with Mrs. DuCain while her husband is in surgery. The attorney, the DuCains, and T-Jack were in DuCain's office all afternoon. T-Jack was in the office with the DuCains' attorney when DuCain found his daughter's body. But the attorney is saying T-Jack is responsible...."

"This isn't making a lot of sense."

"Making sense of stuff like this is your job."

"*Our* job, Nettie. Where's T-Jack now?"

"Danny said T-Jack arrived at the house a few minutes ago. They've got a couple uniforms with him."

They went through downtown Minneapolis on Hennepin until it became two-way, headed up the hill that ran between Loring Park and the Walker Art Center, then swung right on Franklin Avenue, taking Franklin to the east side of Lake of the Isles.

A squad car speeding down Hennepin Avenue, flashers rotating, siren howling, was another day at the office. A rocketing squad car on Lake of the Isles Parkway was something else. Joggers, in-line skaters, mothers pushing strollers and buggies—all stopped cold and stared. By the time the squad rounded the north end of the lake, changing direction to the west side of the parkway, people were coming out of their houses to stare. Canoeists stopped paddling. A yellow Lab, his chin lifted as if to bay at the moon, howled in reply to the siren. Even the Canadian geese that plagued the lake's perfection took note.

They were within two blocks of the Jackman house when traffic stopped, cars lined up as far ahead as they could see.

"I can go on the grass," the driver said, looking doubtful. There were just too many pedestrians around to make that a reasonable option.

Mars shook his head, getting out of the car. "I'll hoof it from here. Why don't you call in and get some traffic-control guys out here. There must be a crowd in front of the Jackman house."

Slinging his sports coat over his shoulder, Mars started off at a slow jog. The day had started cool, but by late afternoon the temperature must have been in the upper 80s; the jog was hard work. As he rounded a curve in the road, he saw the ambulance, a couple of squads, and a crowd on both sides of the road. Mars pushed his way through the crowd, ducking under the crime-scene tape, and started up the steps to the Jackman house.

Mars had investigated his share of gang- and drug-related deaths. Those scenes looked more or less alike. A young man lying dead on the street or on a mattress in an apartment. A run-down apartment complex built around a decaying swimming pool or a trailer park.

The common denominator at all those scenes was disorder. Not from the violence of the murder, but from the way people involved in certain kinds of murder lived their lives. You knew as soon as you walked into one of those murder scenes that this was a place where death had been waiting to happen. Old carpets that hadn't been vacuumed in years. Unflushed toilets. Clothes lying all over. Unwashed dishes. Take-out food in various stages of decay. More Hardee's wrappers than McDonald's.

Six years ago, when a special unit had been set up in Homicide to handle high-profile murders, Mars had been assigned as a special detective to head the unit. Right away it became obvious that there were two differences between the high-profile cases and what he'd seen with drugs and gangs.

First, drugs and gangs were mostly handguns, stabbings, and beatings. In a high-profile case, you'd see everything from poisonings, to rifles, to strangulation. And second, there was a lot more variety in the murder scenes.

8

Mars climbed the massive stone steps leading up to Tayron Jackman's house. It was a murder scene that defied the possibility that something bad could happen. The broad steps—maybe a couple dozen from the street to the front door—were lined with planted urns. The steep lawn was terraced and perfectly cut. Around the base of the house, pruned shrubs alternated with rosebushes.

There were more planted urns on the mosaic-tiled floor under the roofed porch. Mars stood for a few moments in the porch shadows before going in through the wrought-iron front door. He turned, looking back toward Lake of the Isles. As idyllic a view as could be found in any American city within two miles of the city's urban center. The sky was blue, the sun was shining, the lake was mirror smooth.

Nothing that prepared you for what was just beyond the front door.

Danny Borg and Dr. Denton D. Mont, chief medical examiner for Hennepin County, were already in the kitchen, as was Terri DuCain Jackman's body. Along with lots of blood, lots of trauma to the body, lots of evidence that Terri had known she was in trouble, had fought hard, and had tried to escape.

The kitchen was huge—maybe thirty feet by forty feet. But the murder scene itself was relatively small. The area of visible violence was about six by twelve feet. Everything that surrounded the violence was ordered, immaculate, untouched. In a lot of ways, the order that surrounded the chaos made the murder scene that much more horrific.

Mars walked a semicircle around Terri Jackman's body, not taking his eyes from her as he walked. Some vics retained their essential character in death. Others, whatever it was that made them who they were was gone with the last heartbeat. Without having seen her in life, Mars would have guessed that the body before him was a husk of the real thing. Some vics just looked empty, hollow. Terri DuCain Jackman was one of those.

Mars, Danny, and Doc D reconnoitered in a pantry off the

9

kitchen. Danny spoke in a hushed voice. Tayron Jackman was with cops in the front of the house, but Danny wasn't taking anything for granted. He never did.

"Here's the deal. The DuCains' attorney told me T-Jack was in a conference room with him at DuCain Industries from one o'clock until he got the call about Terri. T-Jack was there to sign a divorce agreement. Twice during the meeting—and this was something T-Jack had asked for—Terri was contacted by conference call. And Doc says . . ." Danny nodded at Doc D.

"Based on what Danny told me, I think we're gonna be able to come up with a pretty tight time of death. Mostly, my physical tests are just going to support the facts of the case. I'd say—based on the facts and what I've done so far—she died no more than an hour before the time her father found her body. I did a rectal at three fifty-five and her temp was ninety-seven point two. Let's assume her temp was something above ninety-eight point six, what with the struggle and all—maybe ninety-nine plus when she died. The house thermostat's reading seventy. At that ambient temp, she's gonna lose a couple degrees every hour—so the ninety-seven point two is consistent with her being dead for less than an hour at three fifty-five. I'll check her liver temp when I get her downtown, but with the rectal and the fact that her jaw is just tightening up now, I think this is gonna be one of those cases where time of death will be a known factor. Right now, I'm inclined to call it at, say, between two fifty-five and three-fifteen. Just bear in mind that the precision comes from your case facts. All I'm saying is that my physical findings don't contradict those facts."

Mars said, "Lying like she is, what have we got on lividity?"

"Not much," Doc said. "I used my index finger on her arm—and there was a bit of compression. But she's pretty well bled out from her neck wound, so PML isn't gonna be all that reliable."

Mars turned back to Danny. "I'm not getting this," Mars said. "T-Jack is out at DuCain Industries and Terri DuCain's father is here within minutes of his daughter's murder?"

"I don't have all the details, yet," Danny said, looking embarrassed. "It was hard. Mr. and Mrs. DuCain are here, their daughter

10

is dead in the kitchen, then Mr. DuCain collapses. Mr. Olsen—Royce Olsen, I think his name was—gets here after that, T-Jack after him, and I want to get a couple uniforms on T-Jack...."

Mars held up a hand. "It's okay. You did fine. I'm just saying that we need to follow up on who was where when. And why. You said T-Jack was signing a divorce agreement. Do we know how much he saves, now that Terri's dead?"

Danny gave Mars a cynical smile. "That's not how it worked. From the little bit the lawyer said before he went down to HCMC, the DuCains were buying their daughter back from T-Jack. For a hundred million bucks. The agreement was signed—probably minutes before Terri Jackman was murdered. And the agreement is irrevocable. T-Jack gets the money, and DuCain doesn't get what he paid for. Sweet deal, if you're T-Jack."

"Might not matter much," Doc said. "I got a look at Duke DuCain before the ambulance took him. Not at all clear to me that DuCain is going to be around much longer. Wouldn't be around now if the EMT who came out wasn't Alex Gage. Gage can bring back the dead."

"There are a number of guys Gage brought back that I could live without," Mars said.

"The Lord giveth and the Lord taketh away," Doc said.

"I'm just saying the Lord should be a lot more careful about who he gives and who he takes away," Mars said. He motioned Doc and Danny back toward the kitchen. "Let's do a walk-through of the scene."

Danny began. "No evidence that the doors or any of the windows have been messed with. There's a gated drive that runs from the street to an underground garage at the rear of the house. The garage door opens on a remote control. Nothing out of order down there. Looks like she let in whoever did it through the front door. They've got a code-activated security system that was off when we got here. Whether it was off when the killer came or whether she keyed the code to let someone in—we can't say yet. You probably noticed when you came in. Nothing's disturbed anywhere but in here. So, whoever it was followed her into the kitchen. You've gotta

11

guess she wouldn't have let someone get this far into the house unless she trusted him, so we might be looking at someone she knew."

Doc D walked closer to the body. His hands were jammed into his pants pockets. Without taking his right hand out of the pocket, he made a motion in the direction of Terri Jackman's body, his eyes staring.

"See that hair thing-a-jig about four steps back from where she's lying? What I'd guess happened is the perp took a knife from that block over on the counter, came up behind her and grabbed her by the hair, which would have been in a kind of ponytail, held by that hair thing. Then he jabs her real quick, just behind her left shoulder blade. At that point, she twists around, so she's facing him. Holding on to her hair doesn't give him much control in that position, so he probably pulled her head back and went for her neck.

"There are small drops of blood back here"—Doc pointed to the floor—"that are consistent with the first stab wound and withdrawal of the knife after that wound. The hair band falls off when she turns; you can see long strands of hair attached, and there's hair on the floor. It's the neck wound that killed her. You can see the large amount of blood on the floor, her footprints in the blood from that point, blood on the cupboard doors. Blood shot out a good three feet from where her neck was cut. Arteries will do that, of course, while the heart is pumping. Especially pumping hard, which it's going to do if somebody's coming after you with a knife." Doc sighed. "Then, for good measure, he took down one of the pans that was hooked on that wrought-iron deal hanging from the ceiling. Whacked her good across the left side of her face with that. Le Creuset number eighteen. Cast iron, covered with enamel. Le Creuset puts a little die cut in the bottom of their pans with the name of the company and the number of the pan. I lifted her head some. Most of the bone structure on the left side of her face is pretty well gone—but I could see an imprint from the die cut on the skin."

Doc motioned them toward a sink set in a center island counter. "Here's what I find real perverse."

12

Mars and Danny looked down in the sink. The sink was filled with water. The water looked pink and soapy. Bits of something floated on the surface. Beneath the film of soap were a knife and a black pan.

"The murder weapon and Le Creuset number eighteen. Stick your pinkies in the water, gentlemen," Doc said.

Both Mars and Danny stepped forward, tipping fingers into the sink's water.

"It's warm," Mars said.

"Probably boiling hot when the perp stuck the pan and knife in," Doc said. "See that spigot to the right of the main faucet? One of those fancy deals that spits boiling water on demand. Damned insolent, leaving the weapons in the sink like that."

"Does it strike anybody that this perp wanted to be sure we could fix the time of death?" Mars said. All three looked toward the front of the house, in T-Jack's direction.

Mars stepped back, then walked slowly around the kitchen. In a far corner from the body, there was something red on the floor. Thinking at first that it might be more blood, he knelt down. It wasn't blood. It was a cluster of rose petals.

"What's this about?"

Danny said, "Flower petals. Don't know why. I told the Crime Scene Unit guys to bag it."

"They're rose petals," Mars said. "There are rosebushes at the front of the house."

"I noticed," Danny said. "I took one of the petals out to compare it to the flowers in front. The flowers out front, they're coral and yellow, a real bright pink, and some whites. The petals on the floor are deep red. Besides, if somebody brought flowers in from outside, where are they? I looked in the trash, thinking Mrs. Jackman might have been throwing flowers out. Which would make sense, the petals falling off and all. No flowers in the trash."

Mars nodded and continued his tour of the kitchen. From there he walked into the front hall. Danny was right. Everything was pristine. He went back to the kitchen, taking another look at the body, noticing a bruise on Terri Jackman's arm.

13

"The bruise is old, wouldn't you say?"

Doc nodded. "Looks like she got banged real hard with a blunt object. Maybe a week or so ago."

Mars drew a deep breath. He needed to talk to T-Jack. He didn't know everything he wanted to know before that conversation took place. But he couldn't not talk to T-Jack now. Mars went back into the kitchen.

"I'm going to talk to T-Jack. Danny, why don't you ride shotgun for me."

Two uniforms stood stiffly in the study at the front of the house. When Mars and Danny entered, they moved out of the room without being asked.

The study was dark, wood paneled, with a long row of leaded-glass windows facing the lake. The windows were shaded by the porch roof, giving the room a cloistered feeling. The study's bookshelves were lined with leather-bound volumes. The leather looked old. Mars guessed the books had been bought by the yard at auction. Just one of the things that made the room feel more like a movie set than a place where somebody studied.

Tayron Jackman sat on a tufted leather tuxedo couch in the center of the room. He belonged on the set. Mars had seen lots of pictures of T-Jack. You couldn't live in Minneapolis and not see pictures of T-Jack. But having seen a hundred pictures was inadequate preparation for the real thing.

The first impression that came to mind on looking at the real thing was *power*. Physical power. He was just under seven feet tall. Eighty-three perfectly proportioned, well-muscled inches. His hair was closely cropped, showing off the symmetry of his cranium. His facial bone structure was broad, but balanced. His facial expression was unreadable. That T-Jack wore dark glasses in the dim room added an ominous edge to his power.

T-Jack exuded another kind of power, the kind that comes with not giving a shit about anybody or anything. Other than Number One. His style was at once elegant and narcissistic. T-Jack was wearing a perfectly tailored black Armani suit. Mars didn't know

14

on sight it was an Armani suit. It was something he would learn after the fact: T-Jack always wore Armani. Under the suit jacket T-Jack wore a dark navy silk shirt, open at the collar. Looking at him, you could feel how the smoothness of that shirt would feel against his buff body, feel how it slipped softly every time he moved. You could tell just by looking that this man's closet was room-sized and filled with suits and shirts that hung on wooden hangers, all facing one direction, polished shoes fitted with shoe trees lined up below. You could tell just by looking that if you got close enough to T-Jack, you'd smell subtle, expensive cologne. Just like you knew that T-Jack wore cologne to please himself, not for anybody else's benefit.

"Tayron Jackman?" Mars said, as if there was some doubt. Then he flipped his badge at Jackman and sat down. "I'm Marshall Bahr. Special detective with the Minneapolis Police Department Homicide Division. I'm sorry for your loss."

Usually when Mars used that phrase it felt empty, inadequate. At this moment it felt false. Not because Mars didn't mean it, but because it didn't feel like T-Jack was particularly bereaved. T-Jack's face was calm, impassive. His right arm was extended over the back of the couch, and his right hand rose and lowered in response to Mars's words. As much as if he had said, "What of it?"

"I need to ask you some questions. It shouldn't take long. . . ."

T-Jack's right hand rose and fell again in a repeat gesture of indifference.

"Can you tell me where you were today—from one o'clock until now."

The slightest smile formed at the edges of T-Jack's lips. The parting of his lips revealed the single vulgar aspect of T-Jack's personal style: a gold right incisor tooth. Mars knew without looking that a two-carat diamond had been set dead center in the gold tooth. People said that if light hit it right, the diamond would flash bright enough to be seen in the arena's upper seats or by a beer-swilling fan at home in front of a thirteen-inch TV screen.

"At one o'clock I was in the twelfth-floor conference room at DuCain Industries. Grace and Duke were there. So were Duke's

15

attorney, Royce Olsen, and my attorney, Michael Malley. Grace and Duke left around two forty-five. I was there until DuCain's secretary interrupted my meeting with Olsen to say Grace and Duke had found Terri. Must have been three-thirty, maybe a few minutes after that. I left right away; Olsen and I drove here separately."

The black lenses of T-Jack's dark glasses stared at Mars. Even though he couldn't see his eyes, it was obvious to Mars that T-Jack was well satisfied with his efficient recital of the perfect alibi.

"And you were there for what purpose?"

"Legal business."

"Legal business being . . ."

"I was there to execute a settlement agreement. Terri and I were getting a divorce. Once I signed the settlement agreement, the DuCains could proceed with a no-contest divorce."

"Why wouldn't Terri be at the settlement meeting?"

T-Jack's right hand rose and fell again. For the first time, his voice had an edge. "She delegated power of attorney to her daddy. Terri was a daddy's girl from day one."

"And the terms of the agreement?"

T-Jack looked annoyed. He thought about it before he answered. Then he said, "It was the DuCains that wanted the divorce. Duke asked me what it would take to get Terri a divorce, and I said a number. Not really serious. Pie-in-the-sky kind of number. Thought he'd reject it out of hand. But he said 'fine.' So there I was. Situation like that, a man of his word has to go along."

"It's my understanding," Mars said, "that the agreement provided that you'd receive a cash settlement of one hundred million dollars. Would that be accurate?"

T-Jack's right hand came off the couch slowly. He took the dark glasses off, and for the first time, his eyes connected with Mars. His calm, straightforward stare was insolent.

"You wanna know more about the settlement, you can talk to my attorney. That's as much as I'm gonna say."

Mars changed tack. "When was the last time you saw your wife?"

T-Jack shrugged. "Three, four weeks ago. I was picking up Tam."

Mars thought about the old bruise on Terri Jackman's arm. How people bruised, how long bruises lasted, could vary a lot. But there was no way a bruise like that could be more than ten, twelve days old. Either Terri Jackman had been grabbed by somebody else in the past two weeks or T-Jack wasn't telling the truth about when he'd last seen Terri.

"You haven't been living here since when?"

"Since I told Duke we could go ahead with the settlement. That was two months ago."

"And you haven't seen or spoken to her for three or four weeks. . . ."

T-Jack hesitated. "Not directly."

"Indirectly?"

"During the settlement meeting today. The settlement agreement specified that Terri had to make oral confirmation by conference call twice during the meeting. . . ."

"And the times when Terri spoke by conference phone?"

T-Jack put the dark glasses back on. "Couldn't say for sure the first time. But it was shortly after the meeting began, so I'd say just after one o'clock. The second time was right before the DuCains left. Royce Olsen noted the time of the second call because the agreement specifies the time Terri has to—" T-Jack paused. Then he started again. "The agreement specified the time Terri had to be out of the house after the agreement had been executed."

"Why would the agreement specify that? Who asked for that to be included—that was something you wanted?"

T-Jack shook his head. "You've got questions about the agreement, you can talk to my attorney."

Quickly, not giving T-Jack time to think about what was coming next, Mars said, "Have you ever hit your wife, Mr. Jackman? Or used physical force of any kind that resulted in bodily harm?"

"You want to ask me questions about what happened today, I'll answer. What you just asked? None of your damn business."

Mars shook his head. "The question fits your rules, Mr. Jackman. Your wife was brutally murdered this afternoon. I need to know if violence was part of your relationship."

T-Jack remained silent. It was a response Mars grudgingly admired. Very few people appreciated the power of silence.

"Why were you getting a divorce?" Mars said.

"Like I said before. It was the DuCains who wanted the divorce. Ask them."

Mars said, "For somebody who didn't want a divorce, you don't seem real upset about what's happened to your wife."

T-Jack reached inside his suit jacket, pulling out a flat leather wallet. He pulled a card from the wallet and passed it to Mars.

"My lawyer. You have questions for me, you get in touch with him. I've said what I have to say." T-Jack rose, shrugging lightly to realign the cut of his suit jacket, then left the study.

"Nice guy," Danny Borg said.

"A prince," Mars said.

"Prince of Darkness," Danny said, then he winced. "I didn't mean it like it sounded. I meant 'dark-like-in-evil,' not 'dark-like-in-skin.' "

"I know what you meant," Mars said, used to Danny being eager to please. Used to Danny being eager to demonstrate that his tendency toward redneckness was under control. It was something Mars had brought up the first time Danny had asked about his chances of getting a spot in Homicide.

Mars had met Danny when Danny had been a patrolman working out of the Downtown Command. In their first contact, Danny had demonstrated the kind of energy and curiosity that were essential to a successful investigator. And he was ambitious. He wanted more than anything to move out of his uniform and into a suit.

Mars watched Danny in other cases and continued to be impressed. He'd encouraged him to take the necessary qualifying exams so that if a detective position opened up in Homicide, Danny'd be in line. It had been on Mars's mind that if and when he and Nettie moved to the Cold Case Unit at the state's Bureau of Criminal Apprehension, Danny would be the one to move off the street and into the Homicide Division.

Legislative funding for their positions in the Cold Case Unit had been passed in the last session of the legislature, effective September 1. Within weeks of the legislature funding the positions, Chief of Police John Taylor had left the department for a position in San Diego.

Mars and Taylor had had an ideal working relationship. Taylor was a strong chief who understood the job at a practical and a political level and who had never allowed himself to be co-opted by the city council, the mayor's office, or the police union. As much as anything, Taylor's leaving had influenced Mars's decision to leave the MPD for the new job. Never much of an organization man, Mars couldn't stomach the idea of playing the inevitable power-scramble games that followed a new chief's appointment. And though Mars didn't know who the new chief would be when he accepted the state job, he was sure whoever it was would be at least one cut down from Taylor.

Only a month after Harris McDoanagh had signed on as the new chief of the Minneapolis Police Department, Mars had revised his expectations. McDoanagh was significantly more than one cut down from Taylor. McDoanagh's only major initiative since joining the force had been to have new uniforms designed for all the command officers. Gold braid was the principal element of the new design: gold braid in double rows on the jacket cuffs, gold braid lining the shoulder epaulets, gold braid down the jacket lapels.

"They could sing backup at a Michael Jackson concert," had been Nettie's comment.

The only good thing about Taylor's leaving had been that Taylor had personally seen to it that Danny Borg got a promotion to the Homicide Division. The only bad thing about Danny getting the promotion was that through no fault of his own, Danny made Mars feel old. Still shy of forty, Mars did not consider himself old. But an hour around Danny's energy and optimism reminded Mars of how long it had been since he'd joined the MPD.

Having the responsibility of training Danny as an investigator didn't do anything to lessen the distinctions between Mars and the rookie. That Danny had developed an admiration for Mars that bordered on reverence just underscored the differences between them.

He gestured for Danny to follow him. "Let's do a walk-through of the rest of the house."

It was an old-fashioned house, probably built in the 1920s or 1930s. Solid, foursquare, carefully maintained materials. The kind of house nobody built anymore. It appeared to have been renovated recently to create a brighter, more streamlined interior. The rooms were large and well proportioned. All the furnishings looked expensive, but nothing looked like it meant something to the owners. It looked like a house that had been put together by an interior decorator who got paid to create the impression that the person signing the checks had good taste.

In addition to the study and the kitchen on the first level, there was a large living room, a separate formal dining room, a powder room just off the front hall, and a sun porch that ran across the back of the house.

Danny got it right when he said, "It looks like one of those houses they have in 'Parade of Homes.' You know, that promotional deal a bunch of builders run every fall. Fay and me have gone a couple times. Just to dream. Can't afford any of them. But those houses look like this. Ready to be lived-in, but not lived-in. They had a kid, right? Don't kids make messes?"

Mars thought about this a minute. His ex-wife's neatness had been one—only one—of the things that had driven him out of the marriage. But Danny was right. Even Denise didn't keep a house without a single piece of mail, a key ring, a jacket—anything—lying around.

From the first level of the house they went down to what Mars would have called a basement. Except it didn't look like a basement. Especially like a basement in an older house would look. There was a wide, long room. Thick, smooth carpet covered the floor, a nine-foot pool table was centered under four hanging, shaded lamps. At the far end of the room was a bar, built to look like something Mars imagined you'd find in an English pub. The walls on either side of the pool table were covered with framed pictures of T-Jack taken from newspapers and magazines. There were no signed pictures from politicians, celebrities, or other sports figures.

At the opposite end of the room was an interior-lit trophy case. The case was almost empty. The only awards were individual performance awards, no team awards. None of the kind of awards that produced big trophies. Mars hadn't followed professional sports for years. Not since professional sports had become more business than games. So he didn't remember much about T-Jack's employment history in the NBA. But looking at the trophy case gave you the feeling that however successful T-Jack might have been as an individual player, he'd missed the big, career-capping achievements that came from being a member of a championship team.

Mars turned in a semicircle, looking around. "No laundry room?"

Danny said, "You are seriously out of touch. One thing I learned from 'Parade of Homes.' Laundry rooms go upstairs these days. This place looks like it's been totally redone. Betcha anything there's a laundry up with the bedrooms. What I wish they had down here was a head. I'm gonna start leaking if I don't find a toilet in the next couple of minutes."

It was as they came up the steps from the lower level that Mars noticed what appeared to be a dull spot on the shiny hardwood floor in the front hall. He walked over, looked closer, couldn't tell what he was looking at and switched on an overhead light. Still nothing.

He lay down flat on the floor so he'd be at roughly the level he'd been at on the stairs when he'd seen the dull spot. He saw it; more than that, he smelled it.

A faint, slightly sweet smell. It smelled like chloroform.

Danny came out of the powder room to find Mars smelling the floor.

21

"Don't tell me," he said. "You're Muslim or Islamic or whatever that religion is where you gotta prostate yourself in the direction of Allah every day."

"Prostrate," Mars said, as he forced himself up from the floor, groaning slightly.

"What?" Danny said.

"Something you don't find out at 'Parade of Homes.' Pros*tate* is the gland above your balls. Pros*trate* is to lie flat."

"Oh, geez," Danny said. "I even read that in *Reader's Digest*. They had this list of the twenty-five most commonly misused words. And that was one of them."

Mars said, "Well, why don't you prostrate yourself right down where I was and tell me what you smell."

Danny dropped down effortlessly. He smelled it before he was flat on the floor.

"Chloroform," he said. Then he said, "Oh, geez," again.

"What?" Mars said.

"When I was looking in the trash for flowers? I smelled that smell. I mean, I smelled different stuff, like there'd be in the trash. But I remember now. The same smell as this. Chloroform."

They walked back to the kitchen and Danny pulled a trash basket from under the kitchen sink and knelt down next to it. He pulled on a pair of polyurethane gloves before sorting through the contents, carefully sniffing each object. He stopped at a small plastic bag. He reached into a pocket, pulling out another plastic bag, put the bag from the trash into his bag, then handed both bags to Mars.

"This is it."

"If it is chloroform," Mars said, "tell me a story about how the spot on the floor got there."

Danny pushed himself up in a single smooth action. He wasn't breathing heavily when he talked, something Mars couldn't avoid noticing. Ten years makes a big difference in stamina.

"Like we were saying before. Did Terri DuCain let somebody in or did he force his way in? How did he get from the front door to the kitchen if she didn't let him in? If he had a gun, why wasn't she shot? Not likely he'd hold a knife on her at the door. So, say she opens the door to a stranger. He forces his way in and holds something up to her face with the chloroform—he's got a rag or something with chloroform on it in the plastic bag we found in the trash. In the struggle, the container with the chloroform spills. . . ."

"And then he carries her into the kitchen and does the knife job?"

Danny stared. "Probably not."

"Put chloroform on your list of things to think about. Get the Crime Scene guys to swab the stain. Check the bag for prints. Be sure to include the area of the stain on your diagram. Photos, too. Not that they're going to get anything unless the light and angle are just right. And ask Doc D to test for chloroform when he does the autopsy. For now, let's finish the walk-through."

A broad staircase led to a split hallway on the upper level of the house. There were only four bedrooms, two to the right, two to the left, which seemed surprising for such a big house. Surprising until you saw the bedrooms, which were huge. Each bedroom had its own bath, its own walk-in closet. To Danny's satisfaction, at the far end of the left hallway was a laundry room.

If you'd expected the bedrooms to feel more personal than the rooms downstairs, you would have been disappointed. There was a perfectly decorated guest room across the hall from the kind of room an interior decorator with an unlimited budget would design for a little girl. At the other end of the corridor was a calculatedly male bedroom across the hall from a calculatedly feminine bedroom. Even when T-Jack had been living in the house, he and Terri must have had separate bedrooms. Mars noticed that the closet in the man's bedroom was bone empty. And that all the wooden hangers were facing the same way.

"Nothing," Mars said. "Let's go back to the study and scope out what we need to be doing next."

In the study, Mars stood silent for moments, hands on his hips, then began pacing, as he thought through the case facts. There were few enough of those. More than anything, what had impressed him had been T-Jack's demeanor. T-Jack had an airtight alibi and T-Jack

23

knew he had an airtight alibi. It was the perfection of the alibi, combined with T-Jack's supreme insolence, that convinced Mars that T-Jack was responsible for what had happened to Terri Jackman and that T-Jack was confident no one would be able to prove it.

Where had that confidence come from? If T-Jack was even half as smart as he was looking right now, T-Jack's confidence was something to worry about.

To Danny, Mars said, "First thing. Meaning, as soon as we're done talking, put surveillance on T-Jack. Twenty-four/seven. Until I say otherwise. I'll have Nettie take care of getting a tap on his phone."

Danny looked uncertain. "Surveillance? Taps? Now?"

"This is looking like a contract killing...."

"Yeah, but what's surveillance gonna get us now?"

Mars held up two fingers. "Two things. First, our best bet for proving T-Jack was involved, if this *was* murder-for-hire, is to track who he's in touch with. From what I know of the time line, he didn't have time to pay anyone off between the time he left the settlement meeting and the time he showed up here. For sure he didn't do a pay-off before the murder. So we need to know who he has contact with in the next few days, the next few weeks—however long it takes...."

Danny nodded. "Okay. Got it. You said two things."

Mars turned slightly, looking toward where T-Jack had headed when he'd left the study.

"Number two is the scenario we really, really, want to avoid. If T-Jack hired this hit, and if T-Jack has thought this out as carefully as I think he has, whoever he hired isn't long for this earth."

Danny looked uncertain again. He shook his head. "Hard to imagine T-Jack personally taking someone out. I mean, he's a son of a bitch. But he's a cool son of a bitch. A hands-on murder? Doesn't really seem like his style. And if he hires someone else to take out the hit man, then he's just got someone else that needs taking care of. That doesn't get him ahead of his problem at all."

Mars nodded. "You're exactly right. But right now we can't

24

worry about understanding how this fits together. We've just gotta be sure we stay ahead of the possibilities. Surveillance is number one on keeping us ahead of the possibilities."

Mars took a deep breath. "For now, stay with the CSU guys to make sure they get the photos we want. The other thing I need you to start tonight is to get some uniforms and start combing the neighborhood for anybody who saw anything. When you're finished here, head on down to Doc's and cover the autopsy. And while you're at it, ask Doc to give us something on how old that bruise on her arm might be. Tomorrow I want you out front from noon until sundown, interviewing anybody who's walking by. Find out if they walk, run, skate—whatever—here regularly and if they went by the house between noon and four today. The other thing you need to do tomorrow is get in touch with T-Jack's attorney about what went on at the settlement meeting. I'm going to start trying to figure out who T-Jack might have hired to do the job. And I'm going to follow up with the DuCains and their lawyer for their take on what happened when."

Doc D knocked on the doorframe as he walked into the study. "Thought I just heard you say you needed to talk to the Du-Cains. . . ."

"Yeah?"

"Scratch Duke. Just got a call from the OR at HCMC. Duke didn't make it."

CHAPTER

4

"The first and last time I go out with *that* guy," Sue Weck said, sitting at the dictating station in the HCMC emergency department.

The new-patient rack was empty and what they had going in the examination rooms was nothing to get worked up about. Slack time. A time to catch your breath, pee, microwave a chuck wagon sandwich from the vending machine. But most of all, to shoot the breeze.

Alex Gage sat on the counter facing Sue, his feet on a chair. His last ambulance run had been the DuCain-Jackman murder scene. It would take a week to get back in mental shape after that one. To his right, one of the docs was dictating into the automated phone dictation system. The doc seemed oblivious to everything except setting a speed record for completing his chart dictations.

Gage said, "C'mon, Sue. He's a great guy. He thought you were a hottie. Don't be so damned picky."

"Picky!" Sue said. "*Picky?* A guy takes me to Old Country Buffet on a first date? I don't think so. I subscribe to frickin' *Gourmet* magazine. There's no way I'm gonna have a relationship with somebody who thinks Old Country Buffet is a dating venue."

The dictating doc stopped, punched a button on the phone, and pulled a microrecorder from the pocket of his white lab coat. His voice rose as he said, "Note to self: do *not* take dates to Old Country Buffet."

Gage dropped off the counter, laughing. "I'm going home," he said. He stopped at a tray of doughnuts on the counter, picking up two.

Sue frowned at him. "Why is it," she said, "that health care professionals have the worst diets?"

Taking a big bite out of one of the doughnuts, Gage said, "I'm not going to eat them both. The other one's for Beth. Besides, calls usually come when you are about to eat or after you've taken the first bite. So as a matter of professional expediency, my motto is 'Eat as much as you can, as often as you can, as fast as you can.'"

As he started out, Gage saw Mars Bahr coming through the admissions door. "Hey, Candy Man," he called out. "You caught the DuCain-Jackman case?"

"Which is why I wanted to talk to you," Mars said. "I need to see the DuCains' lawyer who's supposed to be up in the OR. Thought I'd see if you were still around first."

"Mars," Sue Weck said, "would you take a date to the Old Country Buffet?"

Mars squinted at Sue. "I'm having some difficulty making a transition between a murder scene and dates at the Old Country Buffet."

"Just tell me," Sue said. "Have you ever taken a date to the Old Country Buffet?"

Mars said, "My son is in charge of restaurant selection. But I can assure you the Old Country Buffet is not on his approved list."

"Maybe I should wait for *him* to grow up," Sue said.

"Speaking of my son," Mars said, glancing at his wristwatch, "I'm supposed to be in Blaine at Chris's soccer game." He turned to Gage. "Hold on for one minute, will you."

He got Denise on her cell phone.

"Sorry," he said. "I'm going out with a bang. Tayron Jackman's wife has been murdered. Nothing's been released yet, so hold that under your hat. Just wanted you to know I'm not going to make it to the game. . . ."

"Maybe nothing's been officially released," Denise said, "but it's all that people out here are talking about. I heard it on the radio coming out to the game. Everyone's asking Chris if you're handling the case."

"The answer is yes. Tell Chris I'm sorry. I'll catch up with him tomorrow as soon as I get a break."

"Believe me," Denise said, "your being involved in the Jackman murder is worth ten dads at a soccer game."

Mars and Gage headed for a staff lounge. Mars got a Coke from a machine and plopped down on a couch. Gage was something of a legend in the law enforcement community and at emergency hospitals. After the first time Mars had seen Gage at work, he'd said a little prayer that if Chris ever needed medical attention fast, Gage would be the paramedic that showed up. He was good at what he did because he took it seriously, had great medical skills, and had a sixth sense about what was going on with patients. More than that, Gage was a decent, compassionate guy. He'd personally written a proposal for a grant that would provide paramedic training for inner-city gang members—something he'd done in the hope of providing kids with job opportunities and increasing diversity in the ranks of emergency personnel.

What Mars found particularly valuable about Gage were his powers of observation. More than once Gage had a take on a murder scene that had proved useful.

"Tell me what was going on when you got to the Jackman house."

"Well," Gage said, "not what I was expecting. We got dispatched to the Jackman house. Didn't know much about what had happened prearrival. Mrs. Jackman we called right off. Ten twentyone. Nothing, I mean nothing, we can do to make her better. Turned her over to Doc who came in right after us. We focused on Mr. DuCain, who was circling the drain. Man, what a scene. A murdered daughter in one room and a semicomatose dad fifty feet away. Mrs. DuCain was awesome. No hysterics, other than something going on between her and T-Jack about somebody named Tam. Mrs. DuCain gave me a real coherent medical history on her

28

husband. Which, by the way, was shit. Type One diabetes, kidney issues, long-term hypertension and cardiac problems . . ."

"That's what killed him? A heart attack?"

"My understanding is he had an aortic aneurysm. Stress isn't good for that kind of stuff. I thought at the scene it might be something like that. His blood pressure was nowhere, he was cyanotic, with abdominal distension. Real shocky. Figured he'd probably bled out internally. They lost him in surgery, but he was more than half dead when we loaded him in the truck."

"How much did you see of T-Jack before you took DuCain?"

Gage made a face. "Not much. Which is just fine with me. I swear to God, Mars, it was like a Roman emperor walking into the Colosseum after the lions ate the Christians." Gage shook his head. "You ever see him play basketball?"

"Couple of times on TV. Never in person. Can't stand the Target Center."

"My dad's got season tickets for Woofies games. I go every once in a while." Gage shook his head again. "He's something else on the court. I mean something to watch. But I don't know anybody who likes the guy. And after today . . ."

Gage looked at Mars. "Do you like him for the perp? Just between you and me?"

Mars thought about it. "Two answers to that question. Did he physically kill his wife? I think—and nothing's certain till I check it out, but right now—I think not. Is he responsible for his wife's death?"

Gage watched him, tense.

Mars got up. "Slam dunk *yes.*"

Royce Olsen was sitting at a desk, feet up, talking on his cell phone, when Mars walked into what appeared to be a staff surgeon's office. Olsen dropped his feet and sat up abruptly. "Someone's here," he said into the phone. "I'll get back to you."

Mars opened his badge in Olsen's direction and introduced himself. He sat down on the opposite side of the desk.

"My understanding is that you were at a meeting this afternoon that involved Tayron Jackman, his attorney, and Grace and Duke DuCain."

Olsen ran his right hand through his thinning hair. He was a carefully dressed, late-fifties guy, wearing half-framed tortoiseshell glasses. He looked harried. Mars guessed Olsen had made it a point never to be in a situation where being harried was a possibility. He'd gotten in over his head today.

"Where I was this afternoon," Olsen said, "was at an ambush."

He ran his hand through his hair again and blew air, sinking back in the chair. He removed his glasses, holding them loosely in his hand, chewing absentmindedly on the temple piece.

"I've worked for Duke DuCain for almost twenty years," he said, "and have taken a great deal of satisfaction in what I did for him personally and professionally." Olsen slid the glasses back on, letting the bridge piece rest on the end of his nose, his eyes staring over the glasses at nothing in particular.

"In the space of hours, everything I've done for Duke has been wiped out. I didn't do the one thing he needed me to do to protect what was most important to him."

Olsen's eyes focused on Mars. "It can't end like this. T-Jack can't be allowed to get away with this."

Mars said, "We have no intention of letting anybody get away with anything. But I have to tell you. We never go into an investigation assuming more than the facts can prove. And right now, I'm short on facts that prove anything. The facts I do have tell me T-Jack didn't do it. I need you to tell me about the agreement that was being signed. . . ."

Olsen nodded vigorously. "I was on the phone with my secretary when you came in. As soon as I heard you were coming here, I called and asked her to duplicate the tape of the meeting and—"

Mars flinched. "There was a tape of the meeting?"

"T-Jack specified the meeting had to be taped. Just one of several things he did to give himself perfect cover."

Mars said, "Look, that tape is material evidence. Give your secretary a call and tell her to hold on to the original. If we're going

30

to make dupes, we'll have that done by the crime lab. I'll send a squad out to pick up the tape, if you can have someone there to hand it over."

"Of course," Olsen said, looking a bit sheepish. "Yet another example of how I keep missing the boat. Grace was saying this afternoon that we should have used a criminal lawyer to deal with T-Jack. Someone who understood evil, is what she said."

From what Mars had seen of T-Jack, he was inclined to think that Grace DuCain had a point. But he didn't say that.

"A couple of other things," Mars said. "Terri DuCain Jackman spoke by conference call during the meeting?"

"Yes. Again, specified by T-Jack and documenting that she was alive while T-Jack had witnesses to his whereabouts. And not just any witnesses. Her mother, her father, myself, and T-Jack's attorney."

"And there's no doubt in anyone's mind that it *was* Terri speaking on the conference phone?"

At first, Olsen looked surprised by the question. Then he gave it careful thought.

"No. No doubt at all. I particularly remembered thinking that she sounded like the old Terri—the Terri I knew before she'd been with T-Jack. Since the separation, she's been getting stronger every time I've talked with her. The other thing"—Olsen waggled his index finger as he thought about it—"the other thing is that if you closed your eyes and listened to Terri and Grace talk, you wouldn't be able to distinguish one from the other. Grace has this little— vibrato—I'd describe it as a vibrato, in her voice. Terri has—" Royce caught himself. "Terri had the same thing. I know my judgment in this whole thing hasn't been infallible, but I feel certain it was Terri on the phone. Something else: I'm sure Grace and Duke would have recognized an impersonator. That is what you're suggesting, isn't it? That Terri might have been killed before T-Jack came to the meeting, and the voice on the phone wasn't Terri's? Maybe, *maybe* an impersonator could have fooled me. But never Grace and Duke."

"It was a long shot," Mars said, then stopped himself. He had been about to say, "But T-Jack has been so cunning, we have to consider all the possibilities." Which would have broken his own rules about not basing an investigation on unproved assumptions.

Instead, he said, "The other thing I need right now is the agreement—any chance our driver can pick up the agreement with the tape?"

Olsen nodded. "It will be at my office with the tape. What else?"

"I need to talk with Grace DuCain as soon as possible. I know what I'm asking. But time is important and sooner counts for more than later. I'm asking you to be the judge of the earliest time I can meet with her. And to make the case with her that she needs to talk to me as soon as she's able."

Royce Olsen pulled his glasses off again, a tired smile on his face.

"Grace is one step ahead of you. She asked if you could find time to see her tonight."

"Tonight?" Mars repeated, not able to contain his astonishment. "That's unbelievable—after what she's been through?"

"Unbelievable," Olsen said, "only if you don't know Grace DuCain."

CHAPTER

5

The August sun was well on its way to the horizon by the time Mars left HCMC for the DuCains' Lake Minnetonka home. Mars had turned on the radio in hopes of catching a news report on Terri Jackman. He quickly discovered that the real problem was finding anything other than weather reports and late-breaking news stories on the murder.

This wasn't really surprising. But he'd hoped for another twelve hours before things got crazy. He called Nettie to make sure the mayor and new chief of police were up to speed.

"Did Danny find you when he got back from the Jackman house?" Mars said.

"Yeah. Told me everything. I just got back from the mayor's office. Briefed Her Honor and the chief on what we've got."

"How did the chief take it?"

"He's a hot dog. All kinds of noises about wrapping this up quickly, whatever resources are necessary, blah-blah-blah. Absolutely clueless. Mars?"

He didn't like the way Nettie said his name.

"What?"

"Chief McDoanagh is having a news conference in a half hour to talk about the case."

"Nettie, there's no way. I'm not anywhere near ready to brief him for a news conference—even if I could get back downtown in a half hour, which I can't. . . ."

"Not to worry. I told him you wouldn't be available, and he said he planned on handling the conference himself."

"Oh, geezus."

"Double-oh-geezus. All the local channels are feeding live to the networks and CNN."

Mars let silence ride on the line between them for maybe five seconds before he said, "You know the one good thing about this?"

Nettie said, "I'd pay cash money to hear one good thing about this."

"Get out your purse. The one good thing about this is that it confirms that our decision to leave the MPD for the Bureau of Criminal Apprehension's Cold Case Unit was the right thing to do."

The setting sun was eye-level as Mars bore right off Interstate 94 and headed west on 394 toward Lake Minnetonka. To the south, giant thunderheads rose, carrying with them energy and moisture gathered over the Gulf of Mexico.

It was still hot. But in Minnesota, August hot doesn't have the bite of early summer heat. August hot is softer than July heat, with rounder edges, less staying power. With the sun near the horizon, Mars killed the air and opened the car windows. Fresh air blowing through the car served multiple purposes after a day like today.

Royce Olsen had given Mars detailed instructions for finding the DuCains' Lake Minnetonka estate. The detail was necessary. Located twenty miles west of Minneapolis, Lake Minnetonka isn't just one lake, but sixteen interconnected, glacier-made lakes with a labyrinth of coves, bays, islands, inlets, and peninsulas. Mars had read somewhere that if you measured all the ins and outs of the lake's shore, its perimeter would exceed one hundred miles.

Mars had few reasons for going out to the lake, which was fine with him. Settled in the mid-nineteenth century, the lake had developed from a resort area into an elite area where the Twin Cities' oldest and wealthiest families built palatial homes on the wooded hills overlooking the lake. Sometime in the mid-twentieth century, as the Twin Cities metropolitan area began its relentless expansion from two counties to five counties to seven counties to nine counties,

Lake Minnetonka became just another fixture of urban sprawl. Money could buy you a patch of undisturbed tranquility on one of the lake's nooks and crannies, but on a summer's day, boat traffic on much of the lake was as congested as a freeway at rush hour.

Grace and Duke DuCain bought their Lake Minnetonka house years after the lumber and milling barons had bought property on the lake. But the DuCains bought well in advance of the hordes that followed. And the DuCains made the smart move. They bought not for the house itself—which was fine, although nothing compared to surrounding houses—but for the land.

The DuCain property encompassed thirty acres, nearly twenty acres of which were hardwood remnants of the "big woods" that had covered much of Minnesota in centuries past. The woods rose behind the DuCain house; as you entered through the private gate you drove down a gravel road through the forest for a quarter of a mile, coming out onto an open, landscaped lawn that had an unobstructed view of one of the lake's private coves. All was quiet here. And in the late afternoon light, the waters of the lake were tranquil and semigolden.

Mars parked in the circular driveway that fronted the house. The slam of the car door seemed unnaturally loud against the stillness of the evening, and his feet crunched dramatically on the gravel as he walked to the front door.

The house was a plain but handsomely proportioned, redbrick two-story. What got called Georgian, Mars guessed. More than half the brick was vine-covered. A small, white-painted oval portico sheltered the front door. The door opened before Mars could lift the brass knocker.

Grace DuCain took his breath away.

She was maybe five six, five seven, thin and fine-boned. Her silver hair was streaked with remnants of its youthful copper color. Her eyes blazed blue. Her skin was relatively smooth, marred only by fresh strain and anguish. Mars was hard-pressed to guess her age; Terry DuCain Jackman had been around twenty-four, which would have made Grace anywhere from mid-forties to mid-sixties.

She held her hand out to him. "Mr. Bahr. I so appreciate your coming all this way. Any other time I would have stayed downtown at the Minneapolis Club and seen you there—" She stopped. "I suppose what I could have done is gone to your office. I was just trying to avoid being in a public place. . . ."

Mars shook his head. "I'm the one that's grateful. It's asking a lot for you to be available at a time like this, after today."

She held a hand up. "No condolences. I can't handle sympathy just now. There's only one way for me to get through this, and that's to resolve who's responsible for Terri's—" She hesitated again. "To resolve Terri's death and do everything I can to make sure that Tam's situation is everything it should be."

"Tam?" Mars said.

"Terri's daughter. She's four. Almost five. Tam was with her Grandmother Jackman this afternoon. Which I suppose is a good thing. Although I'd like to think that even T-Jack wouldn't have gone ahead with . . ."

She looked up at him. "We're still standing outside, Mr. Bahr. Let's go back to the porch. It's a wonderful night, and we can see the storm coming from there. Duke and I always went out to the porch to watch storms on a summer night."

As he followed her into a large foyer, she said, "I've been on the phone with lawyers for the past two hours. Trying to understand what my legal rights are as Tam's grandmother. Nonexistent is what I'm finding out."

"Your circumstances are pretty unusual. I'd guess a court would take into consideration that you're the child's only link to her mother. . . ." Mars's voice trailed off. It was too soon to be talking about Grace DuCain's dead daughter in such pragmatic terms.

Grace DuCain looked at him over her shoulder. "Yes—we've considered that." But she didn't say more as she led Mars through a long hallway to the back of the house.

She wore khaki Bermuda shorts with an oversized white silk shirt. Walking behind her, Mars couldn't help noticing that her legs were still good and her waist was trim. Unforgivable thoughts to have of such a woman on such a night.

36

As they entered the porch, a young woman emerged from a doorway.

"Grace?" she said softly.

Grace DuCain put her hand on the young woman's shoulder. "Linda Burnet, this is Mr. Bahr. He's with the Minneapolis Police Department."

Linda extended a carefully manicured hand, looking rather shy. She might have been in her mid-thirties, but her style was girlish. Perfectly cut blond hair held back with a headband, a prim, off-white sleeveless dress, expensive-looking flat shoes.

"Grace," she said, holding Grace DuCain's hand, "I've put an outline of the memorial arrangements on your desk."

Grace DuCain bent forward, kissing Linda on her cheek. "Thanks, dear. As usual, what would I do without you? Talk with Rose Bean in the morning. She'll be coordinating everything at the office. And *you* should be heading home."

Linda's presence answered an unformed question that had been rattling around below the surface in Mars's brain since Royce Olsen had told him Grace DuCain wanted to see him that night. How do you find the time to meet with a cop when you've got to make arrangements for a double funeral? Answer: staff takes care of it.

The porch was a large, screened room with a breathtaking view of the bay. And of the increasingly threatening bank of storm clouds gathering around the sunset.

There was an abundance of plants and cushioned patio furniture. On a small table between two chairs was a silver ice bucket. There were two glass bottles of Coca-Cola and a drinking glass stuck in the ice. To the other side of the ice bucket was a tea service. Grace DuCain opened a Coke for Mars, poured it into the glass, and handed it to him. She hesitated for just a moment.

"Is this all right for you?"

"Perfect," he said, watching as she poured herself a cup of tea.

"Do you mind if we leave the lights off?" she said. "It will make watching the storm better."

"Fine with me," Mars said, considering the glass. He looked

sideways at Grace. "Is this just a coincidence, your serving me a Coke—or did you take the trouble to find out that what I drink is Coke?"

"Not a coincidence, but I didn't lift a finger to find out what you'd want." An unhappy smile shaped her lips. "It was something I learned from Duke—or, rather, it was something Duke ingrained in staff. No one ever entered this house, or the offices of DuCain Industries, without staff knowing what would make that person, those people, feel comfortable and important to us. It's a small thing—but I can't tell you the number of times that little extra effort was a deal maker for Duke."

She stared away from him, toward the lake. "You'd think it would be the other way around, wouldn't you? I mean, that I would have been the one to pay attention to things like that. I was the one who was brought up in an upper-middle-class family. Duke was brought up in poverty by an assortment of relatives and semirelatives. He's one-quarter Mdewankanton Sioux. *BC Mdewankanton Sioux,* he always said. Before Casino. Before money from the Mystic Lake Casino made tribal members wealthy. His mother was an alcoholic who froze to death on a reservation up north when Duke was seven. Things like that happened all the time if you were BC Mdewankanton Sioux."

Mars noticed that Grace had referred to her husband in the present tense; Grace hadn't noticed. Who could blame her? Duke's death was only hours old. For that same reason, Mars was reluctant to interrupt her musings with his questions.

Grace said, "Do you know, Duke's background is very relevant to what happened today?"

Mars said, "Before you start—would you mind if I turned on a recorder?"

"Am I starting?" Grace said. "I'm afraid I'm having trouble focusing my thoughts. No, of course I wouldn't mind." She looked at him. "I won't mind anything, if you tell me it will help make T-Jack pay for what he's done."

Mars took the minirecorder out of his pocket and pushed the record button. Then he gave his little speech about making sure an

38

investigation began as a search for facts. That you build assumptions on those facts. Not the other way around, not looking for facts that fit assumptions.

"Yes, of course," she said. Her eyes were hard.

"Go on," he said, "with what you were saying about Duke's background being relevant to what happened today."

She took time before she started again. In the silence, the sun slipped below the horizon and Grace's face became shadowed, her silver hair glowing like a halo in the dark. Crickets were singing their late-summer song of regret. The deep awnings around the porch's exterior created a sheltered intimacy, an atmosphere of privileged security. When Grace did begin again, her voice had a hypnotic quality.

"In so many ways Duke and T-Jack were alike. They both came from hardscrabble backgrounds, neither had fathers who were involved in their lives, both were minorities. Both were handsome, intelligent young men. *Gifted* young men . . ."

She stopped. "I think where I need to start is with the way I met Duke and the way Terri met T-Jack."

"Take your time," Mars said. "The more you can tell me, the better."

"I met Duke at a state high school basketball tournament in my senior year in high school. He was the star player with a team from northeastern Minnesota. I was supposed to go to Radcliffe in the fall, but Duke was going to the U on a basketball scholarship. So I went to the U. When my parents realized what was going on, they did everything possible to break us up. They made me move out of the dorm and back home, they took away my car, they wouldn't allow Duke to come to the house. . . ."

Grace looked at Mars. "You see the pattern. Even if my feelings for Duke hadn't been based on something solid, what my parents did would have kept us together. With Terri and T-Jack—" Grace drew a breath. "Both Duke and I cringe with pain when we remember the night Terri met T-Jack. They very nearly didn't meet. Duke had been invited to a Timberwolves game by Ross Geld. Ross owned the team then. Duke wanted Terri to come with him to the game. At the last minute, to please Duke, Terri changed her plans and went to the game."

Another long sigh. "After the game, Ross had asked some of the players to come up to his box for a reception. T-Jack was one of the players that came. Usually T-Jack wouldn't participate in any of the off-the-court activities players were expected to do. That had become a real bone of contention between Ross and T-Jack. But that night, he went up to Ross's box.

"It was that close. Terri changing her plans at the last minute to go with Duke, T-Jack doing something he usually didn't do. I could tell when Terri and Duke got back from the game that something had happened. Terri was dreamy, distracted—and that wasn't typical of her. Duke was preoccupied, almost angry. I asked him what was wrong, and he just shook his head. That wasn't like Duke. We always talked about things."

Grace drew a deep breath. She balanced her elbows on the arms of her chair, folding her hands together under her chin. She stared intently across the lake. For the first time, a low rumble of thunder could be heard; sheet lightning flashed close to the horizon, illuminating the thunderheads.

"In the morning, a whole truckload of flowers came for Terri from T-Jack. It explained everything about the previous night. Terri was star-struck, infatuated. Duke was in the very awkward position of not wanting his beloved daughter to do what his wife had done—to kick over her traces and cast her lot with a fellow from a different race, from the wrong side of the tracks. Truth to be told, T-Jack was a more acceptable suitor than Duke had been. When I married Duke in our sophomore year in college, we ate boxed macaroni and cheese to survive. T-Jack was making millions when he met Terri.

"At that point, what both Duke and I did was absolutely the wrong thing. Duke did what my parents had done: he fought tooth and nail to keep Terri and T-Jack apart. I, on the other hand— trying not to do what my parents had done—supported Terri and made it possible for her to see T-Jack. I don't think without my support Terri would have kept up the relationship. She loved her father too much. But I justified her disobedience. Not to cross Duke—which I'd never done before—but because I naively thought that if the relationship were allowed to run its course, it would die a natural death."

Grace heard her words and made a sound of regret. "I never contemplated an unnatural death."

Mars said, "And in the end, Duke backed off and allowed the marriage."

"I told Duke, 'You have a choice. You can be right or you can have a daughter. And she's going to need you more than ever if she marries T-Jack.' Life without Terri was unimaginable to him. He swallowed hard and stopped fighting."

"Something I don't understand," Mars said. "I was told the purpose of the meeting today was to execute a settlement agreement that would clear the way for Terri to get an uncontested divorce and full custody of her daughter. And that the settlement agreement provided T-Jack with a one-hundred-million-dollar settlement. Why would you have to buy Terri out of the marriage?"

Even in what was now full darkness, Mars could see the change in Grace DuCain's face. She was quiet for a long time, and without even thinking about it, Mars took a package of cigarettes out of his pocket, rotating it slowly in his right hand.

"Smoke, if you want," she said. "Normally it would bother me, but tonight . . ."

Mars shook his head. "Sorry. Just a bad habit—playing with the pack. I haven't smoked since before my son was born."

As soon as he said it, it sounded wrong. It reminded them both of what she'd lost.

"You have just the one child?"

"A ten-year-old boy. He'll be eleven on October ninth. His mother and I divorced when he was four."

"Almost Tam's age," she said absently. Then she drew a deep breath. "I need you to turn the tape recorder off. And then I need you to promise me that what I tell you will remain between the two of us."

Mars hesitated. "I can't promise that. Not without knowing

what it is. What I can promise is that nothing you tell me will become public unless it needs to become public to bring Terri's murderer to court."

Grace stayed quiet for a while before she said, "I'm the one who said I was willing to do anything if it would make T-Jack pay for what he's done." She looked over at him. "And I guess I'm going to have to trust you, Mr. Bahr."

Mars said, "Somebody you trust, you should call them by their first name. Mars."

"Grace."

He nodded to her and repeated, "Grace."

"Thank you for that, Mars. It will make it a bit easier to say what I'm about to tell you. I never told any of this to anybody. Not even Duke. Terri asked me not to. I didn't know any of it myself until Terri called six months ago and said she needed our help. Both Terri and I thought if Duke knew everything that had happened to Terri, he'd die of rage. Or that he'd kill T-Jack. I know if Duke were still alive, he'd tell me the latter outcome would have been the best thing that could have happened.

"The other reason it makes sense to tell you everything is that I think it will help you understand what you're up against. I should have known after Terri told me the truth about what had been going on. But even then I didn't understand what T-Jack was capable of. It's been a long time since I realized that obsession and love have very little in common. But I always thought T-Jack needed Terri like an addict needs a fix. More than that—by controlling Terri, by abusing Terri, he had the pleasure of controlling Duke. I think that power became as important to him as possessing Terri. Even now, I think T-Jack must be experiencing a sense of loss. To be honest, it surprises me that T-Jack was willing to destroy the thing that gave him the most pleasure—controlling and degrading Terri. That it's a loss he's chosen can't make it any easier. What frightens me is how he's going to fill that void. I'm terrified that my granddaughter will become his next victim. I can't believe he's willing to live without having somebody to abuse."

Mars said, "My understanding is that you and T-Jack had a

42

conversation about Tam before you left for the hospital this after-noon."

Grace shook her head. "I'd hardly call it a conversation. I was leaving to follow the emergency people to the hospital. To tell you the truth, I didn't even notice T-Jack when he came in. Just as we were leaving, I saw him standing by the door. The look on his face—I can't tell you. And then he said, 'Too bad you didn't get a chance to say good-bye to Tam.'"

Her hand went to her mouth. There was a loud crack of thunder and a brilliant, cascading flash of lightning. For a moment, Mars could see the outline of Grace DuCain's neck, could see her swallow hard. For the first time, he felt she was going to lose her composure. She was silent for moments longer, then she spoke in an unwavering voice.

"I shouldn't have said anything. But it just—I just—reacted. I said something like, 'If it's the last thing I do, I'll make sure you're the one who doesn't get a chance to say good-bye to Tam.' The lawyers told me tonight it was a mistake, that the courts won't look favorably on granting visitation rights to a grandmother who's de-clared a vendetta against the surviving parent. I made up my mind then I wouldn't lose control of my emotions again. There's just too much at stake."

She stopped herself and cleared her throat. "I told you I'd ex-plain about the settlement. I'm going to go through this as quickly as possible. I have one favor to ask: that you not interrupt. If you have questions about anything I say, could they wait? Tonight I can't handle thinking about any of it in detail."

Mars nodded. "Tell me what you can."

Rain started before she spoke again, preceded by a gust of wind. It was instantly cooler by degrees. Mars felt chilled. Grace DuCain looked unaware of the rain or the chill.

"It started almost immediately. The abuse. The first night Terri brought T-Jack home for dinner, Terri excused herself, was gone for a few minutes, then T-Jack left the table. They didn't come back to the table for another ten minutes, at least. And when they came back, Terri's lipstick was off, her hair was a mess, her clothes were disordered. I thought, 'They've been making out.' It wasn't until six months ago that Terri told me T-Jack had followed her into the bathroom and made love to her...."

Grace DuCain turned to look at Mars. "I need to say this in a way that will make you understand exactly what T-Jack is capable of. Even if saying it the way it needs to be said is offensive. Love had nothing to do with what went on between T-Jack and my daughter. Not from the first, not until—" Her voice choked. "Not until the end. What happened is he *fucked* my eighteen-year-old daughter in the hall bathroom—maybe fifty feet from where her father and I were sitting—on the first night he came to our house as a guest. It wasn't until the separation that I knew that. Terri told me then that T-Jack had told her she should excuse herself from the table. She was acting on his instruction...."

She stopped. "I've often wondered how things would have worked out if Terri had met T-Jack when she was older. When she'd have been better able to sort out passion and love. She'd never thought she was in love before. Never even had a crush on anybody. She'd always been very analytical about the boys she met. What it was with T-Jack that changed her response, I've never understood. But whatever it was, it was immediate, it was powerful, and it changed Terri in ways that were beyond my imagination."

Grace stopped again. "I need to say something about what Terri was like before she met T-Jack. What I'm about to tell you, about why it was necessary to arrange a settlement with T-Jack—well, *that* doesn't have anything to do with the Terri who was our daughter for eighteen years. Until she met T-Jack, she didn't give us anything but joy. Not a moment's worry. She was a good student, a loving daughter. She had tremendous potential. Duke's plan was she'd take over the company. That wasn't a pipe dream. Terri had Duke's personal skills, his energy, and his analytical mind. She could do anything she put her mind to...."

Grace DuCain shivered, then rose. "It's getting chilly." She walked to a couch and picked up two afghans, keeping one for herself, handing one to Mars. "I've made it my business over the past few years to understand spousal abuse. If I'd known six years

44

ago what I know now—well, it's just another instance of if-I'd-only-known. What I came to understand was that T-Jack identified Terri as his ideal victim from day one. And he proceeded in a very methodical fashion to separate her from us, from all her friends, from everybody who cared about her.

"His technique involved degradation. He got her to do things before she really even thought about them. Then she'd feel guilty, alienated, separate from us. After they were married, she started using cocaine. And she was drinking. One afternoon—she was alone—two friends of T-Jack's stopped by the house. They said to see T-Jack. The three of them started drinking, doing cocaine and—there's no easy way of saying this—Terri had sex with both of them.

"A couple of days after that, Terri found T-Jack in the study, watching a videotape of her with the two men. Of Terri taking cocaine. He never said anything about it. He'd just watch the tape from time to time. When he knew Terri would see him watching. She found out later that he had videotaped her before. God knows what else he had on tape. The point is, he used Terri, he used his friends, for his own perverted purposes.

"From that time until Terri asked us for help, months would go by without our seeing Terri. I'd call, stop by, she wouldn't answer the phone or the door. I found out from a newspaper story—the gossip column—that she was pregnant. Duke didn't tell me at the time, but he'd hired a private investigator to observe the house. When Terri left alone—which was rarely—the investigator would contact Duke. Whatever he was doing, Duke would immediately go to make contact with Terri. He told me later that every time he saw her she was bruised. That she seemed frightened—terrified that T-Jack would find out she'd seen Duke. Duke couldn't convince her to leave T-Jack, which Duke couldn't understand. Eventually, he stopped trying to see her because he suspected his seeing Terri put her at risk.

"I noticed a change in Duke then. He was depressed. His health—which had always been bad—became a significant issue in our lives. I couldn't believe that in the space of three years, our lives had become a nightmare. Knowing that Terri had a child made everything that much worse. But the fact is that Tam gave Terri the courage to leave.

"T-Jack had tied Terri up in her closet after she'd done something that had displeased him. He brought Tam in and said, 'Your mommy has been a naughty girl. You'll never be a naughty girl, will you, Tam?'

"That did it for Terri. She decided nothing was worse than having Tam grow up in that environment. I will never, *never* forget the phone call I got from Terri. Just to hear her voice. To hear her say, 'Mom. Tam and I need help. Can you come?'

"Duke and I were there in a half hour. Terri was going to file a complaint against T-Jack—and then changed her mind. She was terrified T-Jack would use the videotape to discredit her complaint, that he'd use the videotape to get custody of Tam. She asked Duke if he could arrange a settlement with T-Jack—without ever telling Duke why she was afraid.

"Duke, to his credit, never asked. Never said, 'Why should I pay off a guy who's treated my daughter badly?' I think he knew—maybe not the specifics, but understood why a settlement might be necessary. He asked me, 'If we have to give up everything, are you prepared to do it?' There was no question. Of course I was. But it never came to that.

"T-Jack said he wanted one hundred million in advance of the divorce. Our net worth varies from day to day, but Duke could put his hands on one hundred million in a matter of hours and not know it was gone. One hundred million was not our widow's mite. T-Jack had to have known that. We both should have known then that T-Jack had something else in mind. In effect, the one hundred million was just an excuse to set up the meeting, to provide T-Jack with a perfect alibi for the time when Terri would be murdered."

Grace stopped, then said, "What you said earlier—about my legal rights to see Tam. Yes, I think you're right. My circumstances are special and a court might well take that into consideration in ordering visitation rights. But I have to be very careful. He could still use that video against Terri—against her memory. I can't risk that. Memories are all I have left. That, and the possibility that when Tam's independent, she'll want a relationship with me. That's what's going to keep me going, Mars. I have to be very, very careful in balancing my need to see Tam with what's best for her right now and what's best for both of us in the future. Just now I'm not sure what I can or should do. I think I need to hang on for a bit, until I'm feeling less emotional, before I try to force T-Jack to let me see Tam. I will file suit at some point to see her—I'm sure I'll have to do that if I'm to have any contact at all. It's just a question of timing. Until then, I can ask T-Jack's mother to give Tam messages from me. . . ."

"You have a good relationship with her?"

Grace took time to answer. Her words were slow, carefully considered, when she spoke.

"Mary Jackman has had a hard life. And her son does nothing to make it easier. I think he must be providing for her financially. But he takes every opportunity to humiliate and control her. If it isn't money, I can't imagine why she stays involved in his life. . . ."

"Even his mother," Mars said, shaking his head.

Her head came up. "This may be the only thing I'll ever say in his defense. Mary Jackman is actually T-Jack's aunt—his mother's sister. T-Jack's mother abandoned him when he was a toddler. And I think his life had been pretty bad while he was with his mother. I don't doubt it explains a lot. But Mary was always good to him. And she was always good to Terri and Tam. During the really bad years, Mary Jackman was the only lifeline I had."

Grace sighed. "I could tell you more stories, more horrors. But the point is, I don't want you to make the mistake we made. Don't underestimate T-Jack. Don't underrate his intelligence or his capacity for evil. If you're going to hold him accountable for what he's done, you've got to understand how evil he is."

She stood then. "There's something I want you to have. Excuse me for just a moment."

When she came back, she carried two videocassettes. She handed one to Mars.

"Duke had this made several years ago. It's a compilation of home movies of Terri as she was growing up and videos we made when Terri was older. Duke had everything transferred to this video after Terri was married. I can't bear that all you know of Terri is what you saw today and what I've told you tonight. I want you to know who she was before she met T-Jack." Grace held the second video in her hands for seconds before passing it to Mars. "And this is Terri's wedding video. I want you to see the wedding video because it will show you—more than anything I can say—how she changed after she met T-Jack."

Mars tapped the two videos together, conscious that he held in his hands all that remained of Grace's daughter.

"As soon as you can," Grace said, her voice urgent, raw. "I want you to *know* what's been lost." She turned her head from Mars, and he could feel the effort it was taking for her to maintain her composure.

Mars said, "What can you tell me about how T-Jack spent his time—when he wasn't at home or playing basketball?"

Grace shrugged. "What I've heard—what Duke heard through his contacts with people involved in professional sports—was that T-Jack spent a lot of time at strip clubs. Locally and when he was on the road."

Which gave Mars a starting point to track who T-Jack might have hired to kill Terri.

They were both quiet for a while. An idea had occurred to Mars, an idea that he was reluctant to suggest. But he knew it was the right thing to do, just like he knew that Grace was sincere when she said she wanted him to do whatever was necessary.

"There's something I'd like to try, as soon as possible. In the next day or two. I know it's asking a lot, but it could be important. Royce Olsen said there's an audiotape of the settlement meeting...."

"Yes," she said, as if she was just remembering. "T-Jack had insisted on the meeting being taped."

Mars spoke slowly. "It will be difficult for you. But it may bring out details that will be important. What I'd like to do is to meet in the same room where the settlement conference took place. You, Royce Olsen, and me. Play the tape and have each of you provide your memories—in the greatest detail possible—of what T-Jack was doing and saying during the call."

He heard her breath catch sharply.

"Oh, God," she said. "To be in that room again, hearing Terri's voice for the last time, before any of us—any of us except T-Jack— knew what was going to happen. Minutes before someone . . ."

Then she said, "Yes. Of course. I can understand how that would be helpful. Of course I'll do it."

CHAPTER

6

Driving back on 394 was slow going. Rain came down in sheets, reducing visibility to zero. Concerned that some yahoo, who did not consider zero visibility a reason to slow down, would barrel into him from behind, Mars got off the freeway and waited out the rain on a service road.

He looked at his watch. It was just after 9:00 P.M. Still early enough to call Chris.

"Did he do it, Dad?"

"Did who do what," Mars said, making Chris work.

"You know. T-Jack. Is he in jail?"

"No. And he probably won't be in the immediate future. I've got a pile of work to do to put this one to bed."

"Are you gonna have to wait to go to your new job?"

"Too early to say," Mars said. "If I'm not comfortable with where we are on the investigation on September first, I might stay beyond the first. But I've got Danny Borg on the investigation and if it turns out we don't wrap things up before the first, he'll stay on the case when Nettie and I move to the BCA."

"Are you gonna be on the ten o'clock news tonight?"

"Not tonight," Mars said. And when he hung up, to himself, "But unfortunately Chief McDoanagh will be."

*   *   *

Mars had lived in the same efficiency apartment in a two-and-a-half-story redbrick walk-up on the outskirts of downtown since he and Denise had been divorced. It had one thing to recommend it: It was cheap. Cheap was a virtue Mars particularly appreciated in a city where affordable housing was an increasingly scarce commodity. And cheap was necessary. Mars voluntarily paid child support three times over the state guidelines for his income.

The building's owner had not given Mars a rent increase in the almost seven years that Mars had been in the apartment. After the third year of no increases, Mars had gotten uncomfortable. He'd called the owner and asked if there'd been increases for other tenants.

"For the transients, sure," the owner had said.

"So who in the building isn't a transient?" Mars said.

"You."

Mars protested, saying he shouldn't get special consideration because he was a cop.

"Not because you're a cop," the owner had said. "Turnover in rentals costs me a lot. These guys, when they move out, they always leave a mess. And they're a hassle while they're here. Get drunk and make noise, don't pay their rent on time. You give me no grief. I'd much rather have you stay than get a few extra bucks a month."

"I just don't want to be getting a break because I'm a cop," Mars said.

"Not happening," the owner said. "But I'll say this. You park a marked squad car in front of the building every night, and I'll reduce your rent."

It wasn't until after a woman Mars had been seeing left Minneapolis to do research in England that the apartment had started to feel—what? Inadequate. Empty instead of functionally bare. Other than Chris coming over to make a meal with him in the apartment, Mars had never spent much time there. In the past few months he found himself looking for reasons to stay away.

Tonight, damp from the rain, tired from the long day, going

back to the apartment didn't feel even a little bit like going home. Mars stopped in the building's front hall to check his mailbox. Getting mail might make him feel like he lived there.

Most of his mail got delivered to the Homicide Division. That way, if he was hung up on a case and not getting back to the apartment much, mail didn't collect in the box: Mail collecting in the box, in this neighborhood, was asking for trouble.

Lifting the metal door with the key in the lock, Mars saw a single postcard standing diagonally in the box.

He smiled, in spite of himself. Only one person sent him postcards at this address.

Mars carried the card upstairs without looking at it. Counting on using the sight of the card to get him past the hollow sound of the apartment when he opened the front door.

He hadn't left air-conditioning on when he left, so the apartment was more than usually stale and hot. It was still raining too hard to open windows, so he pushed the button on the window unit, hating the sound of the machine winding itself up.

He flipped a light switch on the kitchen wall, and dropped the card on the kitchen table. Picture side up. A series of white cliffs, topped with something so green and smooth it looked like putting greens on a golf course. The white cliffs of Dover? He turned the card over. *The Seven Sisters, East Sussex, England.* He turned the card back to the front and counted the cliffs. He counted six. This was the kind of thing that had never made sense to him as a kid. The Golden Gate Bridge was orange. Most of the Rocky Mountains didn't look all that rocky. White whales looked gray. And now the Seven Sisters of East Sussex were missing a sibling.

He flipped to the reverse of the card again. There was no message, which is what they'd agreed to. But he liked to see his name, knowing she'd written it.

He put the card on the counter just below the last card he'd gotten. She'd been big on cathedrals. An interior shot of Ely Cathedral. Chapter House stairs at Wells Cathedral. Early on, Evelyn had sent a series of postcards of the royal family. Not the current crop of royals, but Henry VIII, Elizabeth I, Mary Queen of Scots,

Queen Victoria. It was impossible to see the Queen of Scot's red hair without thinking of Terri DuCain Jackman. He stared at the cards for some moments before jerking to attention. It was almost time for the ten o'clock news.

As expected, all the lead-ins bannered Terri Jackman's killing. Mars could imagine how the lawn across the street from the house looked. All three channels with their crews under klieg lights, rain casting silver threads against the artificial light, the reporters, hunched under umbrellas with microphones in hand, doing their stand-ups.

The anchors quickly cut from the crime-scene shots to the tape of Chief McDoanagh's news conference recorded earlier in the evening.

This had to be the moment for which McDoanagh's gold-braided uniform had been designed. Most chiefs of police—provided you weren't from Los Angeles, New York, or Boulder, Colorado—could expect to end their careers without having been a participant in a news conference on this scale. Lots of lights, lots of people, and an energy level that buzz-cut through the remoteness of tape and a television cathode tube.

McDoanagh was having trouble with his face. He was loving the attention and had just enough sense to know that looking like he was loving it would be the wrong look. So he concentrated on pulling his face muscles down, on forcing a serious expression. The problem was, you could see him doing it. And every so often, his mouth would escape and he'd look vaguely giddy.

He got it wrong with his first word.

"Gentlemen . . ."

Mars could see Mayor Alice Geff standing just behind and to the right of McDoanagh. Her forehead compressed momentarily at the word and then snapped back into place. She knew people would be looking at her after the chief said "Gentlemen," and she didn't want them to see that she'd heard it just the way they had.

The chief barged ahead.

"At two-thirty this afternoon, Theresa Grace DuCain Jackman, age twenty-four, was murdered in her Lake of the Isles home...."

Mars groaned and dropped his head. The chief had just made two serious mistakes in one sentence. He had given specific information that was (a) confidential at this stage of the investigation and (b) wrong. Mars knew it could only get worse, and then it did.

"I wish to assure the citizens of Minneapolis that this incident was not random and should not be viewed as a cause for general alarm. Further, I wish to assure citizens that the Minneapolis Police Department is confident that an arrest will be made shortly."

The chief removed his glasses and squinted out through the lights. "That concludes my formal remarks. I will take questions at this time."

A trickle of sweat ran down Mars's back. This was painful. The chief had, in less than thirty seconds, in a prepared statement, given factually inaccurate information, disclosed confidential information, and had made statements that would seriously compromise prosecution of the case once an arrest had been made. Not to mention raising unrealistic expectations that would dog the investigation from this day forward. And now he was opening himself up to unscripted questions from a rabid media.

Mars could barely breathe. He knew what the questions would be. But he was willing to bet after the chief's prepared statement that the chief wasn't ready for any of them.

"Is Tayron—T-Jack—Jackman a suspect in the case?"

"Everybody's a suspect in the case at this stage of the investigation."

"How can you be confident of an early arrest if you haven't narrowed the field of suspects?"

The chief's face fell into an expression of genuine dismay. He looked down at the podium, fingering his prepared statement. Then he looked up, a cocky grin in place.

"Let's just say not all suspects are equal."

An audible rumble of amazement could be heard in the room. The mayor was no longer making an effort to control her expression. Her eyebrows were knotted, and she stared hard at McDoanagh's back, as if willing him to be struck by lightning.

A chorus of voices rose up. McDoanagh acknowledged a seasoned crime reporter from the *Minneapolis Star-Tribune*.

"Is the Homicide Division's First Response Unit handling this case? And, if so, what happens when the two members of that unit take up new positions at the BCA on September first?"

McDoanagh drew himself up into a posture of righteous indignation.

"Let me just say," he said, jabbing his index finger toward no one in particular, "that on my watch there's no such thing as an 'elite' unit in any division in the department."

The *Strib* reporter came back at McDoanagh fast. "I didn't ask about an elite unit. You're saying the FRU has been disbanded? That it won't be kept in place when Bahr and Frisch are gone? That they won't be involved in this investigation?"

"I haven't said any of that. I just said I don't support the concept of an 'elite' unit. I'm expecting an arrest will be made well in advance of September first. Bahr and Frisch will be involved in the investigation up until that date, but not a day longer. That should be more than adequate to wrap this up. And we have plenty of officers in place who will be involved in the case in addition to Bahr and Frisch and who can handle the case after August thirty-first. But as I said earlier, I'm not anticipating there's going to be any difficulty resolving this case before the thirty-first if it comes to that. To hold up Bahr's and Frisch's move over to the BCA would be an indictment of the Homicide Division and the department. This isn't a two-cop shop." There was more, none of it good. The chief had succeeded in significantly complicating an already difficult investigation. And he'd backed the department into a corner as far as Mars's and Nettie's involvement went.

Mars tried to shift his mood by concentrating on what his best shot would be for tracking T-Jack's action at strip clubs. He began with a list of people he knew who were close to the strip-club scene. Top of his list was Herb Mitsch. Herb had worked Vice a hundred years ago, taken early retirement and bought out a strip club, Diamond Girls, on the north end of Hennepin Avenue.

Mitsch was that rarest of rare creatures, a clean man in a dirty business. Mars, who'd known Herb through homicide investigations that occasionally involved strippers and the men who patronized strip clubs, had asked why he'd stayed in the life after he left Vice.

A dumpling of a man, with thinning dark hair and a perpetually sad face, Herb had looked surprised by the question, then shrugged his shoulders. "You get used to it. After a while, normal feels off-center. Like, women with clothes on seem weird. Sunlight gets scary. Twenty-four-hour shifts, ice cubes clinking, and a backbeat going all the time—it's a way of life. A guy like me—what else am I gonna do? Golf? My wife, she left me two years after I went into Vice. I never did anything, but she'd lay awake at night thinking about what I might be doing. We didn't have a lot going for us before I went into Vice. After—well, going home was like landing on the moon, you know?"

Diamond Girls wasn't the kind of club where T-Jack would have hung out. But Mars thought there was a possibility Herb Mitsch might be hearing scuttlebutt that was passing through the clubs about the murder and T-Jack. So Herb Mitsch would be his first stop in the morning.

That decided, Mars stretched. He'd been tired when he'd gotten back to the apartment, but after the chief's news conference, edginess replaced weariness and sleep wasn't a possibility. He flicked through channels on the television, paced, and considered going back downtown. Then he remembered the two videos Grace DuCain had given him.

He picked them up from the kitchen counter, reading the carefully printed labels as he walked back to the television. He slipped the video labeled "DuCain Family Memories, 1977–1995" into the VCR and dropped down on his bed, propping pillows up behind his head.

The video had been professionally edited with titles introducing new scenes. The first title was "Bringing Terri Home, March 1, 1977." Mars caught his breath for the second time that night at the sight of Grace DuCain. Her hair was longer, without a trace of silver, a deep copper that became incandescent in sunlight. She and

Duke took turns holding the baby for the camera, their pleasure tangible and intense even at a distance of twenty-four years. Duke's attention was divided between the baby and his wife. There was a tenderness in his gestures, the way he looked at his wife and daughter, that was in touching contrast to his imposing presence.

The scenes that followed were predictable and distinguished from countless other family home movies only in the elegance of the settings and the joy of the participants. By Terri's first birthday, she conveyed a sense of individuality that was remarkable in such a young child. She alternated between a careful consideration of the camera and high exuberance. She was not a pretty child. Her hair was a shade brighter than her mother's, her skin very pale, and she had a good bit of her father's strong bone structure, even as a toddler. It was a toss-up if what was an interesting physiognomy in the child would mature into beauty. Pretty wasn't in the cards.

The video tracked Terri through birthday parties, Christmas celebrations, an Easter party involving an adult in a rabbit costume, parties by the pool with other children, pony rides, family trips, Terri playing tennis, Terri in a prom dress, Terri playing field hockey. From the earliest images through adolescence, there was nothing Mars saw that suggested vulnerability. There was only a happy child, an affectionate daughter, a confident teenager.

One scene particularly struck Mars. Terri must have been in her late teens. She was tall, still in limbo between interesting-looking and beautiful. She was in Duke's office at DuCain industries, standing behind his desk, Duke seated, the scene staged to show the daughter taking an interest in her father's work. Spread out before Duke was what appeared to be a blueprint, and he traced his finger over the print, turning to look up at Terri, then out to the camera with a smile. What caught Mars's interest was Terri's involvement in the scene. Within moments, she ceased to be a part of the staged scene and became visibly engaged in what her father was showing her. Her face became serious, her eyes focused on the blueprint without returning to the camera. She leaned forward, pointing and asking questions, her hair falling forward, partially obscuring her face. As she talked, her arm encircled her father's neck, and she let her own head rest against his in a movement of thoughtless adoration.

The image closed on Mars's emotions like a vise. He pushed the pause button and stared at the father and daughter, frozen in a moment of complete mutual trust and pleasure. Mars drew a quick, sharp breath. Only hours ago both lives and their unguarded optimism had been destroyed. Grace had told him she wanted him to know what they'd lost. Nothing could have done that with more power than the frozen image before him.

Mars fast-forwarded past the scenes in Duke's office. The tape appeared to have undergone editing that undid the studied perfection of the early tape. Scenes ended abruptly, pointlessly. At the same time, Terri's metamorphosis had been accomplished. The question that had existed since her birth was resolved. The awkwardness of youth had given way to beauty. Not the classical beauty of carefully arranged, balanced features, but a beauty comprised of breathtaking angles and stunning color. Her red hair had taken on a high burnish, her pale skin and dark eyes were backlit with emotion. She was decidedly tall, but her intellectual confidence had permeated her physical self. She moved effortlessly and with a compelling certainty.

Mars put the two things together—the harshly edited tape and Terri's metamorphosis. He felt certain that the two things were linked, and that T-Jack was the linchpin missing from the tape. The timing was right. From what Grace had said, Terri had met T-Jack during her senior year in high school. The change Mars was seeing in Terri was a change effected by passion. Terri had fallen in love, and the violence of that emotion had set off a chain reaction of change that had cracked the cocoon of youth.

What Mars noticed next was something he could only describe as Terri retreating from the camera. Not a physical retreat, but a retreat of her conscious involvement in family life. Scenes of spontaneous affection with her parents were absent. She was more conscious of the camera's presence at the same time she was visibly indifferent to it. Her mind, her emotions, were somewhere else.

"DuCain Family Memories, 1977–1995" ended in a noisy fuzz of gray static. Mars rewound the tape, ejected, then slid in "Wedding Bells for Tayron and Terri Jackman."

The metamorphosis had continued. No longer a physical metamorphosis, but an emotional change that introduced vulnerability and dependence. The glowing, confident young woman of the previous tape was gone. Terri DuCain as a bride was tentative, hesitant, nervous. She smiled only when conscious that the camera required a smile. Her eyes turned away from her groom only when her attention was demanded. When she looked at T-Jack, there was a beseeching quality to her expression. Mars supposed it was an expression that could be confused with love, but it bore no resemblance to the expressions of love Mars had seen from Terri in the earlier tape.

And then there was T-Jack. Arrogance personified. God-like in his perfectly tailored tux. In the tape's forty-five minutes there was not a single instance when the camera captured a gesture of affection from T-Jack to his bride. He was holding himself back from Terri even when they cut the wedding cake, when they danced alone, surrounded by guests. It reminded Mars of what he had seen of T-Jack on the basketball court when he'd caught a Timberwolves game on television. T-Jack treated Terri the way he treated his fellow Timberwolves. They were on the court together, they were in the same game, but there was no emotional connection between T-Jack and anyone near him.

The image that stayed with Mars after the wedding tape ended was a scene at the wedding reception. T-Jack sat in a chair, at ease, disengaged from the events around him. Terri sat on the floor, at his feet, her white gown billowing about her, her head leaning against T-Jack. She had reached for his hand, which he'd pulled back without looking at her. At that moment Terri turned full face toward the camera. It was her expression that startled Mars. For the first time her eyes connected with the camera. What Mars saw in her eyes was awareness. Mars felt certain that at that moment, Terri DuCain was aware of what her future held.

He froze the image again. Grace's words were on his mind.

59

I want you to know what's been lost.

The image before him guaranteed he'd not be able to forget what had been lost, what T-Jack had done to Terri.

Mars walked over to a calendar that hung on the end of one of the kitchen cupboards. He hadn't turned the months since June.

He flipped the pages to August, and counted from today's date, August 23, to August 31. As of today, he had nine days to establish T-Jack's connection to Terri DuCain's death. He scribbled three words on tomorrow's date.

T-Jack minus eight.

CHAPTER

7

Hennepin Avenue is the crotch of downtown Minneapolis. City leaders have stuck sequined pasties on the crotch—renovating old theaters and hanging banners designating Hennepin as downtown's theater district. But even in the middle of the day, Hennepin is damp, hairy, and excremental.

Diamond Girls was one of the last strip clubs left on Hennepin. Most of the hard-core sex businesses had moved a couple of blocks west where rents were lower and customers felt less visible. Apart from the renovated theaters, what was left on Hennepin, north of Seventh Street to Fourth, was a mix of shabby restaurants, empty storefronts, and a lot of people waiting for a bus.

Mars pushed through the padded door entrance to Diamond Girls, leaving behind the bright sunlight of an August morning. He stood, blinded, in the club's neon-hued darkness. The air smelled like melting ice cubes and dirty carpet.

A tall woman with jet-black hair and bare breasts was working hard at making a pole look interesting. Mars considered the woman. The light in the club had a smoothing effect that made her younger, prettier, than she would be on the other side of the padded door. But even in the semidark you could tell there was nothing behind her black-lined eyelids and that her half-open, fat red lips were a mime of passion.

She danced on a small stage in the center of a circled bar. Barry White was voice-humping "Love to Love You, Baby," but nobody,

61

including the dancer, believed him. There were maybe half a dozen guys sitting on stools around the bar, nursing drinks and smokes and making it look like hard work to be there. At the far end of the bar, Herb Mitsch was talking on the phone. He lifted one finger toward Mars when their eyes met and Mars walked around the bar toward Herb.

Herb hung up, shaking his head. "Tell me any other business," he said, "where the boss has gotta know when the help have their periods. More to the point, any other business where the help think it's a reasonable thing to call up the boss and say, 'I can't do my shift because I've got the curse.' Why do these women think God invented tampons?" He motioned Mars to follow him out of the bar to the back, where he had an office.

"Maybe lifeguards, at the ocean," Mars said.

"What?" Herb said, over his shoulder as they walked.

"I've heard that female lifeguards that work ocean beaches have to tell their supervisors when they have their periods. Puts them— and probably other swimmers—at greater risk of shark attack."

Herb stopped, tapping Mars on the chest. "That's the first good news I've had in a long time. Gives me a retirement option. I give this up, I can apply to work as a lifeguard supervisor at some ocean beach. 'Extensive experience managing work schedules affected by menstruation.' That's me. C'mon in to my office."

It could have been the office of a used-car salesman. Maybe eight by twelve feet, veneered wood paneling halfway up the wall, a couple of filing cabinets, harsh lights, and an adding machine on the desk. No girlie calendars on the wall, no family photos on the desk.

Herb sat down on a chair that rocked back on a spring. "Like I told you on the phone," he said, "T-Jack never came in here. Everything I know about the guy is secondhand, at best, from other guys in the business."

"That's fine," Mars said. "What I'm looking for is a starting place. I'm looking for somebody who can give me a lead on people T-Jack hung out with in the clubs. From there I want to find somebody who would have been up to do a hit for a price."

Herb nodded slowly, not surprised by the suggestion that a strip-club patron would kill for money. "In the clubs, you see three types of guys. You've got the boys'-night-out crowd: guys getting married, boys in town on business tonight, home on the plane tomorrow. Revenuewise that's maybe twenty, twenty-five percent of my business. Then you've got players, flashy guys who show up now and then, spend money, move on. Don't see much of that type at Diamond Girls; they tend to hit the high-end clubs, which we're not. You couldn't keep the business going with either the boys'-night-out crowd or the players. It's the regulars we depend on. The guys who show up every day, spend big on paydays. And paydays for those guys don't tend to be Fridays. They have a good day at the track, at the blackjack table, that's a payday for a regular. Sell something that fell off the back of a truck. Have a good run at a poker game and get out with something more than they anted. They're always hustling some way to make a buck. The clubs aren't recreation for the regulars, the clubs are home. All their social contacts are through the clubs; anytime they aren't out making a buck, they're here. Hell, we take phone messages for them, some of them have mail delivered here. One guy listed Diamond Girls as his next of kin. He died in bed and we got the call. I ended up paying the funeral expenses myself. Still came out way ahead on what he spent here versus what I spent to bury him."

Mitsch pointed a finger at Mars. "If T-Jack hired his wife's hit, he did it through a regular. Now I've got any number of regulars who might be up for that kind of action. Guys who've been living on the edge since the first time they stole a car. Thing is, like I said before, T-Jack never hung out here. But I have breakfast every now and again with a bunch of other club owners. A couple run high-end clubs. Regulars' action in the high-end club is gonna be higher-end trouble, if you know what I mean. But if the price is right, there'll be guys who'd take on a hit. Or at least negotiate a hit if they didn't want to handle the action themselves. One of the guys I have breakfast with, Royal Bergh, opened up Dames! Dames! a couple years back. . . ."

"The place over on Washington everybody calls Double Ds?"

Herb nodded. "That's the place. I've heard Royal say T-Jack hung there. I can get in touch with Royal, see what he knows."

"Not to put pressure on you or anything, but could you get around to it sooner rather than later?"

Herb raised the receiver on the phone. "I'm making the call as we speak."

Herb's conversation was semicryptic. Lots of "uh-huhs," and "yups." Herb's eyes darted up, down, and sideways while he listened, scribbling now and again on the back of an envelope, his head bobbing occasionally as if in agreement with something that was being said. At one point, a small smile passed Herb's face.

Herb gave Mars a tired smile as he hung up.

"Royal's out of town, be back tomorrow. I talked to one of his managers." Herb's smile widened to a grin. "But you're gonna love this. Remember when you were in Narcotics a few years back? A big mean mother? Mr. Jerome Hebb?"

Mars groaned. "Hebb? Jeez. My lowest—lower than lowest—moment on the force. The city's number one biggest narcotics problem, and I had to punt a charge because my partner violated a search in collecting evidence. I left Narcotics after that fiasco...."

"What I heard," Herb said, "is that you got froze out in Narcotics after you refused to back up your partner's story about the evidence."

"That would be a true version of the same story," Mars said. "But it's history. What I want to know is, what's Hebb got to do with T-Jack? He never did anything directly, just had a stable of goons he'd let loose when something aggravated him—that's what you're saying? That one of Hebb's goons took the Terri Jackman hit? I don't think so ..."

Herb was shaking his head. "Not what this guy said. He said a couple of Hebb's goons were looking for a guy who hung out at Double Ds sniffing T-Jack's butt every chance he got. The manager personally eighty-sixed the guy a few months back because the two goons made a scene at Double Ds while they were looking for the butt sniffer. *Rude* guys, from what Royal's manager says. Not his type of clientele at all. He figured the butt sniffer had been dealing

64

from Hebb's stock, and hadn't paid his bills with Hebb. The manager guy figures that, because he suspected the butt sniffer had been dealing at Double Ds before the goons showed up. Said Royal could probably tell you more about the butt sniffer when Royal gets back in town."

"The butt sniffer, Herb. Does he have a name?"

Herb looked thoughtful. "Yeah. Paul Tanney." He continued to look thoughtful. "Where've I heard that name before?" He shrugged, and passed the envelope he'd been scribbling on over to Mars. "Anyways, there's the name. The manager said your best shot at finding Tanney is to talk to Hebb's goons, see what they've dug up. Says Tanney is a mighty elusive type of guy, but if anybody's gonna find him, it'd be Hebb's boys."

Herb's grin returned. "You remember how to find your way to Whiskey-Tango-Tango-land, Candy Man?"

Oh, yes, Mars remembered his way to Whiskey-Tango-Tango-land.

When he'd been in Narcotics, he'd thought more than once that the most efficient way to eliminate drug felonies would be to nuke the Garden Trailer Park on the city's northwestern border. Jerome Hebb's trailer was at the center of Garden Trailer Park, with four smaller trailers nearby occupied by his band of merry men.

Long before Mars had been assigned to Narcotics, it was an accepted fact that Jerome Hebb was at the center of a drug importing and distribution ring in the Twin Cities. Mars had worked for almost a full year to establish Hebb's link with a chain of rural meth labs. What Mars wanted was to prove not only that Hebb was involved in meth production, but that he was the primary distribution point for the illegal drugs. After months of tedious tracking and surveillance, they'd nailed down a major shipment of meth from a rural factory to Garden Trailer Park. They knew when the shipment would be arriving, had a description of the delivery vehicle, and a search warrant in hand for Hebb's trailer and the four other trailers. The trailer park was too insular to allow them to stake out near the trailers, so they had surveillance all around the perimeter of the park, and as soon as the delivery vehicle arrived at the park entrance, the code was called.

"Mail has been delivered at Whiskey-Tango-Tango-land. Pick up in ten minutes."

"Whiskey-Tango-Tango" being code for "White Trailer Trash." Pickup delayed for ten minutes to allow Hebb's boys to put hands on the shipment and start stashing it in the trailers.

Which was as good as it got. Where it went wrong was that the drugs had been stashed in an abandoned trailer, not one of the trailers listed on the warrant.

Mars realized what had happened even before they'd completed the search of the last trailer. His partner had it figured, too. Mars saw his partner corner one of Hebb's guys outside, holding his service revolver against the guy's temple, shouting at him.

By the time Mars got outside to intervene, his partner had kneed Hebb's guy in the groin and started to the abandoned trailer.

"It's over here, Mars."

Mars caught his partner by the shoulder as he started to bash in the trailer's door. "What did you say to him? When you had the gun to his head?"

Breathing hard as he'd bashed against the door, his partner said, "I told him . . . he had . . . a choice. Tell me . . . where the stuff was . . . or have his brains blown out."

His partner had looked over his shoulder at Mars, a big grin on his face. "He made the first smart choice of his life."

"We can't do it," Mars said. "You used unreasonable force to coerce the admission. No court—"

"You fucking turd," his partner had hissed as he'd spun around to face Mars. "You, me, and that piece of shit are the only ones who know what I did or didn't say. It'd be his word against us. Look at him. Who's gonna believe anything he says? My story is I saw him going in here while we were conducting the search and it was—"

"I don't want to hear your story," Mars said. "And I won't back you up in court."

66

Which was how a year's work had gone down the drain and Mars had decided Narcotics was not where he belonged.

Now, making his first return appearance at Whiskey-Tango-Tango-land, Mars was about to reap the long-delayed rewards of his clear conscience. Mars's altercation with his partner over the search had become known to Jerome Hebb. Hebb was not a generous man, nor was he a man who much cared about rewarding virtue. But he'd made note of the fact that Mars Bahr had not lied to protect his partner or the bust. What that got Mars was a free pass to enter and leave Garden Trailer Park intact.

The high, electrical whine of cicadas rose and fell over Mars's head, adding an appropriate score of tension to the scene as he walked toward Hebb's trailer. The trailer looked more dilapidated than it had during the failed search. And it had looked pretty bad then. Nobody who had a reasonable guess about how much money Hebb made could figure why the guy lived like he did. The trailer was only marginally habitable and its furnishings barely functional. Except for the two giant-screen, rear-projection TVs that filled an entire wall of the trailer and took up a good third of the space in the trailer's largest room.

Mars could see the light from the TVs behind the screen door. The few windows in the trailer were blacked out, and there didn't appear to be any lights on.

Mars rapped on the screen door. "Jerome Hebb? Marshall Bahr of the Minneapolis Police Department. I'd like to talk to you, if you've got a minute."

A woman appeared at the door. Skinny, fried hair, shorts and a halter top that hung on her frame.

"Jerome says to come on in," she said, pushing back the door.

Hebb looked like he hadn't moved since Mars had been there the last time. He was on a couch opposite the TVs, staring at the sets, both of which were on, with the sound muted. Monster trucks were doing tricks in an arena on one set, while a NASCAR race spun in circles on the other set.

Hebb held the remote in one hand, but didn't move his eyes. He didn't smell any better than he had the last time Mars had seen him, and Mars considered that it was entirely possible that Hebb had not bathed in the intervening years. Hebb had the kind of beard that made him look, to Mars, like a religious fanatic: a clean-shaven face except for a fringe that ran along his jawline up to his sideburns. His pasty skin was grayish, like the undershirt he wore, his face slick with sweat. While the temperature had cooled after last night's storm, the unventilated trailer had held the thick, intense heat.

"I'm looking for a guy named Paul Tanney," Mars said. "I understand you've been looking for him, too."

Hebb's eyes didn't move from the TVs.

"I don't care why you're looking for him, Jerome. I just need to know if you've found him, and if you did, where I could find him."

Moments passed before Hebb spoke. Then he hollered, "Lyle!"

A tall, thin guy became a silhouette against the screen door. "What?"

"Get in here. Don't make me holler out at you."

Lyle stumbled in, having a hard time adjusting to the change in light. He was a weasly, bug-bitten guy, whose eyes shifted with years of accumulated guilt.

"What's going on with you and Matt finding Tanney?"

A different smell mingled with the smell of layers of dried sweat that came from Hebb. This smell was fresh and sour and it came from Lyle. Lyle shifted, moving like a man who wanted to be somewhere else.

Mars looked at Hebb. He saw Hebb move his eyes from the TVs to Lyle. Saw Hebb smelling the same smell Mars smelled that came from Lyle. Then Hebb's eyes moved to Mars. When their eyes met, Hebb looked back at the TVs.

"I told you this morning," Lyle said. "Nothing. Matt thought he was onto something, but nothing. I think Tanney left town. Nobody's seen him for a while. If Matt shows up this afternoon,

68

we'll go out again. Even if Matt doesn't show, I'll go. If Tanney's still around, I'll find him."

Hebb said, without looking at Mars, "Now you know what I know."

Which was exactly right, Mars thought as he walked back to his car. *Hebb and I both know Lyle knows something he isn't telling. And both Hebb and I think it's worth knowing.* As he pulled out of the park, Mars noticed Lyle skulking away from Hebb's trailer, looking like he couldn't get out of there fast enough. *Something,* Mars thought. *I don't know what, but something.*

Mars had almost an hour before he was scheduled to be at DuCain Industries to reenact the settlement meeting. He found a parking spot in the parking lane on Third Avenue and entered city hall through a side entrance.

Mars was becoming sentimental about city hall. The cavernous red granite building represented the best parts of being a cop. It had its own sense of drama and public purpose. Working in the building made you feel like what you were doing was important. Unlike most modern public buildings—including the one where he and Nettie would have offices with the BCA—which made you feel like an easily replaced cog in a creaking machine.

Nettie was at her computer when he walked into the division office. He sat down on her desk, butt on the desk edge, legs stretched forward.

"You saw the news conference last night?"

Nettie smiled a sweet, false smile. "I'm still seeing spots from the lights reflecting off all that gold braid."

"It was," Mars said, "a disaster."

"It sounds like we've got eight days to wrap this up. That a possibility?"

"I don't know. I've got a line on a guy that hung out around T-Jack from Herb Mitsch that's a possibility. Finding him isn't going to be a cakewalk. But at least I've got something to follow. And who knows? Maybe the BCA wouldn't agree to let us stay beyond the end of the month, anyway."

"McDoanagh could offer a hundred yards of gold braid in exchange for us."

"Which is about what we'll be worth if we can't get this one sorted out." Mars shifted to a chair next to Nettie's desk.

"It annoys me," Nettie said. "I mean, how many dead wives and girlfriends have we zipped into body bags in the last couple of years who'd been abuse victims before they were killed? It's an epidemic."

Mars nodded. "Yeah. But they don't get killed like this. It usually happens in a—hey, you've got fifteen seconds: 'It happens in a rit of gishus fage.'"

"I don't think you've got the quote right," Nettie said. "But Peter Sellers said something like that in *A Shot in the Dark*."

Mars sighed. "Bingo. Whatever. My point is, think back on the wife/girlfriend murders we've had where past abuse was involved. It's the husband who commits the murder. And it does usually happen in a fit of vicious rage. It's not cool and calculated like this one. The perp doesn't hire it out."

"How about—oh, what was her name? The woman who'd left her husband and was living in the Towers condo downtown. Got shot in the elevator by a hired gun. Hired by her husband."

"Yeah, but there was a financial motive there. She had insurance and her husband was the beneficiary. There wasn't any history of abuse—"

"Other than the routine, jerk-husband kind of shit."

"What do you know about jerk husbands, Nettie?"

"You don't have to be married to know about jerk husbands. You could probably make a case that it's because we know about jerk husbands that women stay single."

"You're too young to be so cynical."

"And you're too old to be so sarcastic."

"Don't start on old. I spent most of yesterday with Danny Borg, who makes me feel like Strom Thurmond."

70

Nettie made a face. "Strom Thurmond was born a dirty old man. Age doesn't have anything to do with who he is. Just like age isn't what Danny is about. Danny won't live long enough to become cynical or sarcastic. Danny was born young and will die young. It's why you like him so much. Chris is maturing at a rate of five years per minute. Danny will be your kid for the rest of his life."

"This conversation is getting seriously off-track."

"Oh. That reminds me. Herb Mitsch called while you were out. Said he'd be hard to get hold of until tonight. Nothing important, give him a call when you can."

The phone on Nettie's desk rang just after Nettie had walked away to get her bottle of semifrozen Evian water out of the department fridge.

"Can you get that?" she said over her shoulder.

Mars winced when he heard the mayor's voice asking for him.

"Can you come to the office now? I've got a meeting in another half hour, but I need to talk with you as soon as possible."

Alice Geff was standing behind her desk, pulling things from the desk and putting them into a briefcase. As soon as Mars came in, she said, without saying good morning or looking at him, "Did you see McDoanagh on the news last night?"

Without being asked, Mars sat down. Alice Geff looked tired, like she hadn't slept much. The kind of tired look you get when you don't sleep because you're worried. She was at an age when the juice and heat of youth were irrevocably gone and when carefully cut hair, carefully applied makeup, expensive clothes, and staying fit weren't enough to cover that you were tired and worried.

Mars hadn't answered, which was an answer. For the first time she looked at him.

"I appreciate your not saying 'I told you so.'"

Mars shrugged. "I understand why you did what you did. Maybe I just had a better idea of what the practical consequences of your deal might be."

She sank into the big leather executive chair behind her desk.

One manicured hand went to her forehead, the gleaming red nails pressing into the skin, leaving marks when she dropped her hand and looked at him again.

They were both thinking back to a discussion that had taken place when she'd received the Police Union's three choices to replace John Taylor. She'd been in a tough spot. The union had accepted Taylor's nomination only with the promise that when Taylor left, the mayor would make her next appointment from a list submitted by the union.

On paper, the appointment of the chief of police was one of the few real powers the Minneapolis mayor had. In reality, the mayor's appointment had to be approved by the city council, and the Police Union almost always had enough influence with enough members on the council to make an appointment the union didn't support difficult, if not impossible.

Hiring John Taylor had been a coup. Before coming to Minneapolis he'd been deputy chief of police in a major eastern city where he'd handled riots, citizen complaints, police brutality charges, and a major crime increase that had voters moving to the suburbs in droves. In five years' time, Taylor had put the department to rights and citizens' confidence had been restored. Most significant, to Mars's way of thinking, Taylor had done that without making a lot of friends among police ranks. What he did earn was their respect. At the end of the day, that's what you want in a chief of police. A city where the chief is loved by the ranks is a city with a problem. A city where the chief is respected by the ranks is a city citizens are lucky to live in.

The other thing about Taylor had been that he was black. Which meant, with his track record, he could write his ticket. He started getting job offers the first week he'd been on the job in Minneapolis. When he got an offer from San Diego, where his wife had family, he told the mayor he'd be leaving at the end of his contract.

That put the mayor on the Police Union's hot seat. The union would call in its chit on the next appointment. Neither Mars nor the mayor anticipated the extent to which the union would stick it to her in the process. The three names they sent forward were spectacularly unqualified. A division chief in Vice who was in the union's pocket and who was the union's preferred choice, a black deputy chief of campus police for an East Coast Ivy League school, and McDoanagh. McDoanagh had been chief of a metropolitan force in a homogeneous, conservative city one-third the size of Minneapolis.

Alice Geff had gone ballistic when the union's list had come to her. Mars had been in her office with Taylor when the list came up, and he and the chief had been a captive audience to her anger for more than a half hour. When she finally calmed down she threw the list in the direction of her desk and said, "I won't honor the agreement. They haven't acted in good faith—sending me names like that. All they want to do is assure that the internal candidate will be the choice. That doesn't leave me a choice."

John Taylor had argued with Geff that failing to honor the agreement would assure she'd spend the rest of her term putting out fires with the police department. And a police department has a hundred different ways to sabotage a mayor they feel has betrayed them.

"All right," she'd said, her eyes going steely, "I'll appoint McDoanagh."

Taylor had argued as strongly against this option as he had against Geff's rejection of the entire list. "I don't know the man personally," Taylor had said, his usually reasoned voice showing strain, "but I know enough to know he's not up to this job. Whatever faults the internal candidate has—and I share your concerns about him—he's a competent man and he knows the department. It's a two-year appointment, you can make a change after that. You can talk to the union about your expectations if you make the appointment. . . ."

Geff said, "I won't let them pen me in this way. It's a travesty of the process we agreed to. I'm going to appoint McDoanagh. They can eat their own offal."

Appointing McDoanagh is what Alice Geff had done. Problem was, it was Alice Geff eating the union's offal.

"What I need you to tell me, Mars," Geff said, "is that wrapping this case up by the end of the month is a possibility."

Mars tapped his fingers on the arm of the chair and thought about it.

"Not impossible," he said. "But not likely. All indications are that T-Jack has been planning this over the past several months. If we get a break, if we can find who he hired to do this, then we've got a shot at establishing and proving a connection between them. But I won't kid you. Just finding who did it could take a lot longer than the end of the month. Proving T-Jack's connection could be a life's work. And there's another potential problem. That whoever did this has a big red bull's-eye taped to his back. I've just got to hope we find him before someone hits his mark."

Geff stared. "I had a call from the public information office just before you came in. All the networks, CNN, Fox, will have crews here by this afternoon. You know what my problem is. I can't have McDoanagh meeting with the local, much less the national media. . . ." She hesitated, looking at Mars like she wanted him to say something. Mars made it a point to stay quiet.

"I'm thinking," Geff said, "that you should handle press communications on this case."

"No," Mars said. "That wouldn't be a good idea. For all the usual reasons and for the additional reason that I'm only here until the end of the month. If we don't have this thing wrapped up by then, my leaving will just draw that much more attention to the failure if I've been media liaison. . . ."

"Which brings me to my second point," Geff said. "What would it take to get you to stay? I don't mean just through the Jackman case, I mean *stay*."

This surprised Mars. There'd never been any bad feelings between Mars and the mayor, but he'd had the distinct impression that the mayor was indifferent to police personnel below the level of the chief, provided they didn't do anything to embarrass her.

74

"It's time for me to go. And I've made commitments. I'm not leaving because I didn't get a better offer from the department. I'm leaving because—well, it's what I said. It's time. I'll do everything I can to make the transition as smooth as possible. I've already brought Danny Borg in on this case. You'll get what you need from Danny and the others in Homicide. As for press coverage, have the department's PIO be the direct liaison. That's the usual drill."

"The public information officer—you mean Dana Levy?"

Mars nodded. "The chief trusted her—Chief Taylor, that is—and so do I. Just keep her in the loop so she can maintain credibility. She's got good judgment, she takes care of the media in ways they care about, she understands police work. She'll do fine for you."

The mayor sighed. "Losing Taylor has been about more than losing a chief of police. I didn't know that until he left. He was a moral center for me in many ways. I miss that anchor."

Mars said, "It's been the same for me."

Geff looked at him. "It's what the chief said about you, Mars. That you were a moral center for the department. I didn't appreciate that until John Taylor was gone. Now, with you going too—well, I'm just starting to appreciate what I'm losing."

She sat up straight abruptly. "Well, so much for self-pity. I've got to get over to the convention center. Let me end with this. You said proving T-Jack's connection to this case could be a life's work. If you're right about that, I'm going to hope that your life span isn't any longer than the end of the month."

CHAPTER

8

DuCain Industries had been one of the first major Twin Cities employers to build its headquarters in the suburbs. They'd saved money on taxes and land costs, but the big advantage had been in attracting employees who'd moved to the suburbs and wanted free parking when they drove to work.

The company had expanded over the years, and now there were four towers on what had been a vast, empty acreage. Parking lots had expanded with the buildings and all that remained undeveloped was a marshland to the west of the original tower.

Mars had been instructed to park in the only gate-controlled lot on the property. Getting out of his car, he picked up the copy of the recording from the previous day's meeting and the settlement agreement that Nettie had had ready for him. When he looked up, he found a golf cart waiting for him, driven by a uniformed young man who greeted Mars by name.

"I'll be driving you to Tower One," the young man said. "It's a long walk on a hot day."

It wouldn't have been more than a couple blocks and the temperature was at least 10 degrees cooler than it had been yesterday. The storm of the previous night had left the air fresh. But Mars figured his arrival had been carefully planned and refusing a ride would likely set off a scramble of administrative regrouping. So he rode.

The next link in his ascent to the conference room greeted him by name and led him to an elevator. They traveled in silence to the twelfth floor.

The conference room covered the entire level, with floor-to-ceiling windows that provided a 360-degree view of the horizon. To the east was downtown Minneapolis, to the west the marshland and glimmers of what was probably Lake Minnetonka. The north and south views were of suburban sprawl as far as the eye could see.

There was a copy of the agreement at each of the three places at the table. The agreement on the table was covered with a memorandum from Royce Olsen; the memo summarized the points in the agreement that Olsen considered to be relevant to the murder investigation. Each of the relevant points had also been highlighted in the agreement.

This was helpful. Mars felt reviewing Olsen's memo would give him a good structure for listening to the tape without desensitizing him to the interpersonal details of the meeting. But before he could begin to read, Royce Olsen and Grace DuCain stepped off the elevator into the conference room.

"Mars, I'm sorry we're late. The entire company is in mourning, and it was impossible not to . . ."

Mars took Grace DuCain's offered hand, then shook Royce Olsen's hand.

"I was early," he said. He waited, expecting that something might be said about the chief's news conference.

Royce Olsen said, "Special Detective, I'm sure you can appreciate how difficult this is for Mrs. DuCain. I don't want to seem inhospitable, but if we can move through this as quickly as possible, it will spare Mrs. DuCain . . ."

"I'm prepared," Grace said. "I'll be grateful when it's over, but if I have to go through this, I want you to have the time you need to do it right. So don't worry about me."

Either they hadn't seen the news conference or they didn't want to talk about it. Mars knew he had to say something to Grace, but he was grateful not to have to start the meeting by making up a defense for the chief's comments.

Mars said, "What I'd like is for each of you to sit where you were sitting yesterday."

Grace DuCain took the chair to the right of what would have been the head of the table. Olsen sat down directly across from her at the left of the table's head. In a soft voice, Mars said, "Duke was sitting at the head of the table?"

"Yes," Olsen said. "T-Jack's attorney was to my left, next to T-Jack at the opposite end of the table from Duke."

"Okay. What I want out of this exercise is to bring to the surface any thoughts, observations, impressions you might have had during the meeting yesterday. Especially those things that we're not going to hear on the tape or read in the settlement document itself. However vague, however insignificant. Anything you can remember about how T-Jack looked, any action he took—anything that will give me insight into what was on his mind during the meeting."

Looking directly at Royce Olsen, Mars said, "Before we start, I'd appreciate your giving me some background on how the agreement came into being." He nodded to Grace DuCain. "And I'd like to know the verbal process between you and T-Jack prior to there being a written settlement agreement."

"I think I can speak to both points," Olsen said, taking off his half-framed glasses. "Duke contacted me before he made a formal settlement offer to T-Jack...."

Mars said, "Something that isn't clear to me. Did T-Jack raise the subject of a settlement, or was it Duke who initiated the discussion?"

Olsen gave the question a bit of thought, chewing on the earpiece of his glasses.

"There were two phases to the discussion. Grace told me she had shared with you that at one point—and this was perhaps three years ago—Duke had arranged for Terri to be under surveillance. Through information provided to him in that process, Duke saw Terri on several occasions. He observed that she didn't appear to be well. More than that, it was clear she'd been abused. She was bruised. She declined help at that time, but Duke did have me contact the man who was T-Jack's attorney. I broached the subject

78

of a divorce on Duke's behalf. Duke hadn't wanted me to be aggressive or threatening in raising the subject, he was concerned that Terri would bear the brunt of any anger a threatening approach might produce. The attorney got back to me the same day. He said his client had no interest in further discussions on the topic.

"Then—it was last February—around Valentine's Day—when Terri called Grace and asked for help. At that time, Duke contacted T-Jack directly. He did consult with me first—Duke was shrewd about things like that. For the most part, Duke was his own best counsel, but he always listened to other people, always considered what they had to say before he took action. In this instance, when Duke told me he wanted to offer T-Jack a cash settlement in return for granting Terri an uncontested divorce and full custody of Tam, my position was it wouldn't be necessary."

Olsen hesitated, looking at Grace before he continued. "I had the strong impression that Terri had grounds for divorce. Based on information that had come out of the surveillance, and—well, frankly, there were always a lot of rumors about T-Jack. I just didn't think T-Jack deserved, or Terri would need to make, any concessions. But Duke was adamant. He wanted the divorce and custody matters to be settled as quickly and painlessly as possible. I was astounded when Duke said he was going to offer T-Jack a hundred million dollars. But at that point, the money was moot. Duke got back to me shortly after talking to T-Jack and said T-Jack wasn't interested. . . ."

Mars said, "And it was Duke who suggested one hundred million?"

"Oh, yes," Royce said. "A number like that, you remember who says what."

"And T-Jack rejected Duke's offer when?"

Olsen hesitated. Grace DuCain said, "It was early March, Royce. A couple of days before my birthday."

"Yes, I think Grace is right. I'd say sometime around early March."

"And it was T-Jack who came back to Duke? Duke didn't go back to T-Jack with an offer of more money?"

Royce shook his head. "No. It was a little surprising, really. T-Jack called Duke here at the office. I specifically remember now, it was April fifteenth. Tax day. I was in Duke's office the morning of our April board meeting. T-Jack asked Duke if the offer was still on the table . . ."

"And he mentioned the one hundred million specifically."

"Yes. Well, what he said was, 'one hundred mil.' "

Mars nodded slowly, taking out the pocket-sized spiral notebook he'd taken to carrying around on cases. He flipped it open to the first page where two words were written, each with a question mark following the word:

Roses?
Chloroform?

On the line below "chloroform?" Mars wrote, *What changed T-Jack's mind about the money?*

Royce Olsen said, "I haven't had a chance to say this to you, Grace, but I had breakfast at the Minneapolis Club this morning before coming out here. One of the partners in Daniels Winton followed me into the men's room. He told me he'd heard that T-Jack's financial advisor had taken a very substantial position in the IPO for Deltron Medical before Deltron tanked. This fellow told me he was quite certain that the advisor had put his investors into the stock heavily."

Olsen tipped his head down, putting his glasses back on the end of his nose. "In short, what with his lifestyle, his gambling, and then a possible bad investment involving a substantial portion of his assets—T-Jack may well have needed the one hundred million. I haven't had a chance to follow up, but Deltron went into receivership around the end of March. That fits nicely with T-Jack's change of mind."

Mars said, "But his income is—what? Three million a year? He must have endorsement income in addition to that."

Royce said, "T-Jack has never had the really big endorsements.

His personality and lifestyle have made him a no-man's-land for high-end advertisers. On the basketball court he's a god, but a god who was feared rather than liked by his peers, a god who was admired rather than worshipped by fans. People came to see him play. They didn't come to cheer him."

Mars said, "So T-Jack got back to Duke in mid-April and said he was interested in moving forward with the settlement. Why didn't the agreement get executed then? Did T-Jack ask for more money at that point?"

Royce shook his head. "No. But he did have a number of stipulations with respect to the agreement itself. He jerked us around on details for months. There was nothing that seemed significant at the time...." A grimace passed his face. "In retrospect—well, what he was up to seems painfully clear."

Grace DuCain spoke. "Royce blames himself for not seeing the agreement for what it was. But that's ridiculous. Duke and I didn't read it that way and we knew T-Jack better than Royce. And as clear as it seems now what T-Jack was up to, I'd have to say that when I first saw the agreement, I thought I understood almost everything he was asking for."

"Explain what you mean by that," Mars said.

Grace took a moment to think through what she was going to say. "There were four things. That T-Jack wanted the meeting to be here, that Terri wouldn't be at the meeting—but she'd participate by conference call at the start of the meeting and when the agreement had been executed. What I find most perverse is that the agreement specified that Terri had to be out of the house after the agreement had been executed. He knew that meant we'd find her...."

Grace stopped, closing her eyes. She held fingertips to her lips for a moment, then started again. "He knew we'd find her the way we did. Duke sheltered me from seeing everything he saw—he'd gone in first. I think T-Jack even knew that. And I think he knew how finding Terri would affect Duke. I think T-Jack knew that finding Terri would kill Duke."

Mars gave her time before he pressed his question. "You said you thought at first that there was a reasonable explanation for the conditions stipulated in the agreement. . . ."

Grace nodded. "T-Jack always accused us of ruining his marriage. He wanted the meeting to be between us, to be held in Duke's office, to make the point that this was something we wanted, not something Terri wanted. If Terri had been here—well, it would have made the point that T-Jack was losing her. Another thing. He always needed to *defeat* people. I think completing the agreement on Duke's turf, so to speak, was a source of satisfaction to him. Our removing Terri from the house made the point that Terri was still a daddy's girl. T-Jack always taunted Terri with that accusation."

"I told Grace yesterday," Royce Olsen said, "that I think we have a basis for voiding the agreement. No contract is binding if it involves fraud—and T-Jack was clearly perpetrating a fraud . . ."

Grace shook her head hard. "No, Royce. This isn't about money. It would just gratify T-Jack to think that we cared about the money. I don't want one ounce of energy expended on the money. I want to be completely focused on putting T-Jack in jail for Terri's murder. And in getting Tam back. Let the money go."

She glanced at Mars, looking almost embarrassed. "It's self-indulgent for me to say that. I can afford to let the money go. But if it were every dime I had, I'd say the same thing. The only money that has value for me now is money that can make a difference where T-Jack and Tam are concerned."

"So," Royce Olsen said, dropping his glasses to the table. "There you have it. A plan to murder, to protect the murderer, and to cause maximum pain to the victim's loved ones. Am I right that the agreement alone might give us a basis for prosecution?"

Mars drew the tips of his fingers back and forth across the grain of the table as he considered Olsen's question. It was a reasonable question, one that had occurred to him as they'd discussed the agreement's stipulations.

"I think," he said, "that it's a question that should be considered. But my first reaction?" He looked to Grace and Royce. "It's not unlike Grace's response to the possibility of challenging the settlement payment. It's not what's important here, and it runs the risk of diverting resources from what we're all committed to doing. . . ."

"I couldn't agree more, Mars," Grace said. She focused a hard stare on Mars. "Last night you said that the investigation would be based on facts and that you didn't yet have facts that established T-Jack was responsible for my daughter's murder. Do you still believe there's a possibility T-Jack isn't responsible for what happened to Terri?"

Mars smiled at Grace. "It is an increasingly reasonable assumption that he's involved." He paused before asking her, "Are you ready to listen to the tape—or would you like to take a break?"

"I want to go ahead," she said, lifting her chin slightly.

Mars could see Grace brace herself as the tape player buttons were pushed. She put both elbows on the table, both hands clasping her forehead, partially covering her eyes, as if to concentrate. Mars recognized the pose for what it was: a defensive gesture to shield herself from the first sounds of her dead husband's and daughter's voices.

At first, all that was heard was Olsen talking, reviewing the meeting's purposes, Olsen reading the agreement. Suddenly, another male voice. It took Mars a moment to realize that the second male voice was T-Jack's.

"Make the call."

Mars pushed the stop button. "T-Jack?"

Royce nodded. "He was asking me to make the first of the two required calls."

"And the time would have been?"

Royce considered. "I don't remember exactly, but it wasn't more than three or four minutes after the scheduled start time of one o'clock." He stretched forward, looking at the counter on the tape machine. "We're three minutes into the meeting, so we would have called Terri at around one-oh-six, one-oh-seven. Something like that."

Mars started the tape player again, listening to the modulated beeps of a phone being dialed, the dull buzz of the ringing phone, then a woman's voice.

"Terri DuCain speaking."

Grace DuCain visibly flinched. Mars hit the stop button again.

"I need to ask. Terri said, 'DuCain,' not 'Jackman.' Did you notice how T-Jack reacted to that?"

Grace said, "I couldn't bear to look at him. I saw him when he came in, but I never really looked him in the face even once."

Royce lifted both hands, turning the palms up. "I have to admit. I avoided looking at him too. And he was wearing dark glasses. I made it a point to address my questions and comments to his attorney. It would have been very difficult to gauge T-Jack's reaction to anything, even if I had looked at him hard."

"I had an *impression* of him during the meeting," Grace said. "You could feel his contempt. He seemed very calm. Triumphant. He projected that feeling. Which is why I didn't want to look at him. It was hard enough, feeling those things. I didn't want to have to see them as well."

Mars hit the play button again and heard Olsen speaking to Terri. T-Jack's voice interrupted again.

"The recorder is on?"

Royce's voice continued on the recording, explaining to Terri the agreement's requirement that she confirm her delegation of power of attorney to her parents to act on her behalf.

Terri interrupted Royce. Her voice was strong, confident. And for the first time, Mars heard the vibrato in Terri's voice that sounded so like her mother's.

"Royce, I confirm that I've given power of attorney to my parents to act on my behalf in executing the settlement agreement."

Mars glanced at Grace. Her hands shadowed her face. She was trembling slightly. He hated asking her, but the question needed an answer.

"Grace? Do you have any doubt—any doubt at all—that it is Terri's voice on the phone?"

She started, drawing her hands down, away from her face, looking slowly at Mars. "Are you asking me if someone pretending to be Terri was on the call?"

Mars nodded.

She drew a breath, taking in what he was saying. "Reverse the tape. Let me hear again what she just said."

"Royce, I confirm that I've given power of attorney to my parents to act on my behalf in executing the settlement agreement."

Grace drew herself up, shaking her head. "It's Terri," she said. "I don't have any doubt of it. Royce?"

"I agree, Grace. What especially strikes me is that it's the way Terri's been sounding since the separation. The confidence . . ."

"Exactly," Grace said.

"Let's keep going, then," Mars said.

Royce's voice, reminding Terri that they'd be calling again, to confirm execution of the agreement.

Then T-Jack's voice, interrupting, more insolent than usual.

"Ask her if she got the flowers."

Mars slammed the stop button.

"What's he talking about?" he asked Grace and Royce.

Royce said, "I had no idea. I tried to cut him off. He'd been very specific about the agenda for the meeting, and we'd accommodated all his requests. He hadn't said anything about flowers until the call. But Terri said—well, just play the tape."

Royce Olsen's voice followed, tight with annoyance, and then Terri spoke.

"It's all right, Royce." Terri's voice was soft, patient. When she spoke again, her tone had changed. *"The flowers were delivered. I didn't bring them in. They'll be outside the door when you get back to your house."*

In a small, sad voice, Grace said, "The day after T-Jack and Terri met, T-Jack sent Terri dozens of red roses. After they were married, red roses became a symbol of terrorism. T-Jack sent her roses after he'd beaten her. Once, when she'd thrown them in the trash rather than putting them in water, T-Jack took them out of the trash and beat her with them. Can you imagine how it would hurt to be beaten with thorns?"

Mars said, "It's a small thing—but it explains in part something at the scene that we couldn't figure. There were red rose petals on the floor in the kitchen. If Terri left them on the porch, were they

85

there when you arrived? Or did you see them in the house? We couldn't find flowers anywhere inside the house, not even in the trash."

Grace shook her head. "I didn't even think of it. It's possible I overlooked them—I was very preoccupied when we went into the house. And then, within seconds, Duke found Terri's body and collapsed. After that, I probably wouldn't have noticed. But I do think I would have noticed the roses on the porch—and knowing what they meant to Terri, if they'd been there, I would have moved them.

"Talking about the roses reminds me of one thing," Grace continued. "When Terri told T-Jack she had left the flowers outside, I glanced at T-Jack. It was really the only time I looked at him directly. I was afraid something like that would send him into a rage. That he might back away from the agreement. But I remember he looked—I don't know. Disdainful. But not upset. I'd expected him to look upset."

"Remembering that kind of detail about T-Jack's behavior could be important. Keep thinking in those terms," Mars said. "Are we ready to start the tape again?"

For almost an hour, Royce Olsen's voice droned through the agreement. Occasionally T-Jack's attorney would interrupt to question or emphasize a point. Even on a tape, you could hear in the guy's voice that he was in over his head. You could tell just by listening that he wasn't used to sitting down at the table with billionaire businessmen and world-class athletes. Mars made another note in his little book:

"Where'd T-Jack get this guy?"

It wasn't until they reached the point where the DuCains and T-Jack were to execute copies of the agreement that T-Jack's voice was heard again.

"Give me a minute."

"Oh, God," Grace said. "I'd almost forgotten this part."

"I thought he was playing the scene to extract the last possible ounce of pain from Duke and Grace," Royce said. "I was wrong, wasn't I? He was pulling our chains. Making us sweat right up to what we thought was the bitter end."

Mars said, "What was going on?"

"As you heard, just at the point where the agreement was to be signed, T-Jack puts everything on hold. Spends several minutes 'reflecting.' "

"My heart stopped," Grace said. "I thought, 'This is it.' When he got up, I thought he was going to walk out."

"He got up?"

"Yes," Grace said. "Walked over to the window, stood there for a minute, then came back to the table and sat and stared for—I don't know—five minutes?"

Mars stood. "Walk me to exactly where T-Jack stood at the window. Show me what he did when he was at the window."

Royce rose, looking uncertain. "Well, from his chair, he moved this way. . . . I'd say he stood right about here? Wouldn't you, Grace?"

"I think he was standing just to the right of the credenza— that's all I remember. I didn't want to look at him, not even his back."

"And he just stood at the window?"

"Well," Royce said, "at one point he more or less leaned against the window."

"Leaned how?" Mars said. "Put yourself in the position T-Jack was in. As close as you can."

Royce raised his right arm, placing the palm against the window. Then he leaned forward, head down slightly, as if in thought.

"What was the time when T-Jack did that?" Mars said. "As close to the minute as you can say."

"I remember exactly," Royce said. "I looked at my watch when T-Jack got up from the table. It was two twenty-four. It wouldn't have been more than one or two minutes after that when he put his hand on the window."

Mars said, "I need to go down to the ground level. While I'm doing that, call your head of security and have him here as soon as possible. Royce, as soon as you see me below, take that position. Then stand straight, and take the position again. Do that a couple times, until I wave from below for you to stop."

It took Mars a few minutes to find the position in the parking lot from which he could see the twelfth-floor window where Royce would be standing. Royce was not distinguishable as an individual, but his form was visible. As was the raising and lowering of his arm, particularly his hand as it went flat against the glass. Mars walked to a border of shrubs on one edge of the parking lot and scooped up a handful of landscaping rocks. He took his handkerchief out of his back pocket as he walked, dropped it on the ground where he'd watched Royce, and covered it with rocks. Then he went back to the building.

Grace and Royce were standing, arms folded, when Mars walked back into the conference room. Two men were also in the room, one middle-aged and squarish, the other in his twenties, blond and pink-cheeked. Royce introduced the men as the director of facility services and as building supervisor for Tower One.

"I need two things," Mars said. "I need someone to put spray paint or something on the spot on the lot where I've left my handkerchief anchored by rocks. The second thing I need—and this is a two-parter—I need to know if you've got a security cam on the lot directly below these windows, and, if you do, if you have the tape from the camera for yesterday."

The squarish director of facility services looked perplexed. The pink-cheeked building supervisor of Tower One lifted a cell phone from his belt and spoke into it.

"I'll have someone out on the lot putting paint down in five minutes," he said. "We've got a twenty-four-hour camera on each lot. They're on the building, level with the third floor. Easier to do maintenance that way and we avoid vandalism to the cameras. The tape in the camera automatically rewinds after it runs its cycle. . . ."

"And the cycle starts when?"

"It restarts at eight A.M. every day. But I've gotta tell you, even with the parking lot lights, night tapes aren't worth much." He stopped, looking guilty. "That, and we've had some problems with the recording units sticking on the Tower One lot. I've talked to the other tower supervisors, and they've been having trouble too. I've put in for new equipment, but..." His eyes darted nervously toward the director of facility services. It was clear to everyone in the room who had not approved a request for new recorders on the security cameras.

Mars said, "What you're saying is, the tape for yesterday—August twenty-third—would have begun at eight A.M. yesterday and rewound itself at eight A.M. this morning?"

"Unless it stuck."

"Let me know the status of the tape ASAP, will you?" Mars said to the young supervisor. "And I'll need a tape that shows the spot on the lot that you're going to paint too."

It was Grace who spoke first after the building people had left the conference room. "What you're thinking is, the man who killed Terri was in the parking lot during the meeting. Waiting for a signal from T-Jack that it was okay to go to the house."

Mars sat down, leaning back in the big, comfortable conference room chair. He rocked slightly, swiveled a bit, before he answered Grace.

"Not exactly. I think what happened is this. I think T-Jack had someone waiting for a signal in the parking lot. But I don't think that person drove to the house and killed Terri. The timeline is just too tight for that. I think the person in the parking lot called the killer after getting T-Jack's signal. I think the killer was waiting near the Jackman house. Think about it. At this point in the meeting you and Duke are—what?—at the outside, twenty minutes away from leaving to pick up Terri. A twenty-minute jump on you is just not enough time for the killer to drive from here to Lake of the Isles, find a place to park his car—and remember, there's no street parking in front of the house, so he's going to have to park almost two blocks away, provided he can find a spot that close—walk to the house, climb up the steps, get into the house, do the job, get out of the house, down the steps, and away before you show up."

Mars shook his head. "T-Jack had somebody near the house, ready to move as soon as he got the call from the parking lot. That would give the killer the twenty minutes before you left plus the half hour it would take you to drive to the Lake of the Isles." He looked at Grace and Royce, both of whom looked crestfallen by further evidence of their unintended complicity in the previous day's events.

"This is *good* news," he said softly. "The more people T-Jack had involved in this deal, the more witnesses we have to his involvement. The more witnesses, the greater the chance that we'll find someone who can link T-Jack to Terri's killer."

He motioned them to sit down. "We need to finish listening to the tape of the meeting. I'm hoping we'll get something back on the security-camera tape before I leave. Royce, I'm going to send a couple guys out to interview staff who might have noticed someone in the lot yesterday. Can you coordinate that with whoever is in charge of personnel?"

The Tower One supervisor knocked on the door just as they were finishing up.

"Good news or bad news?" Mars said.

The supervisor hesitated for a moment. "Am I right in guessing from what you said that it would help you out if the tape didn't rewind at eight this morning?"

"Provided it ran through, say, three o'clock yesterday afternoon."

A broad smile broke across the young man's face.

"Good news, then. The tape stuck at eight forty-five last night. Cold weather and rain are what have been giving us problems. And it was raining like crazy out here from about seven-thirty on last night."

"Nothing I like better than to have God on my side in a murder investigation," Mars said.

CHAPTER

9

Too much luck made Mars nervous. Especially when good luck started piling up early in an investigation.

They were on the second day of the Terri DuCain Jackman investigation and they already had a couple of major breaks. First, the stuck tape, and then, when Mars got back downtown from the meeting at DuCain Industries, there was news from Danny Borg that they'd found a jogger who'd seen Terri DuCain Jackman yesterday, on her porch, with a guy, at about two thirty-five.

Danny and the jogger were in an interrogation room on the third floor of city hall when Mars walked in. The jogger, Mike Zimmerman, was a young guy, late twenties, early thirties. He said he was a financial analyst who lived in an apartment building east of Lake of the Isles. He was a stereotypical Uptown resident: expensive haircut, expensive casual clothes, expensive watch. Mars would put money you'd find a BMW that belonged to Zimmerman parked within walking distance of city hall.

"I run around the lake three, four times a week," Zimmerman said. "From the front door of my apartment building, around the lake and back is just under four miles. On a good day, I can do it in, oh, thirty-two to thirty-five minutes. Yesterday was hot, and I was kind of low on energy. Which was why I left the office early. Felt like I needed to get some oxygen to my brain. So I was slow. I've got a couple of points on the lake where I check my time.

Down at the north end, by the canoe rack, in front of T-Jack's house, then at the south end of the lake..."

"You knew the house was T-Jack's—or you found out after you noticed someone on the porch?" Mars said.

"I knew," Zimmerman said. "It's no secret that's T-Jack's house. It's one of the reasons I picked it as a checkpoint. I always kind of watched the house when I went by, in case he'd be around. He never was, but I always looked."

"You said you saw T-Jack's wife with a man on the porch."

"Well, I saw a woman who looked like the pictures I've seen of T-Jack's wife. I've never seen her around the house either. But I saw this thin, red-haired woman, white dress...."

"And the time you saw the two people on the porch?"

"I'd looked at my watch just before I noticed them. It was two thirty-five. I've got a digital."

"Did you have any impression of what was going on between the two people on the porch?"

Zimmerman thought about it. "I didn't stop or anything. But I'd say they were talking. She looked like she was about to go into the house. His back was to me, but he turned kind of sideways once."

"Can you describe him?"

"I'd say he was about my height—just under six foot—he had on dark glasses and a baseball hat, brim forward. So I couldn't say much about his face. That, and the porch was shadowed, so it was hard to say for sure. But he had on a T-shirt, running shorts..."

Like every other guy around the lake on a summer afternoon, Mars thought.

"One thing," Zimmerman said, "and I didn't notice this until I walked past the house coming back..."

Mars and Danny jerked to attention, in an identical motion, and said simultaneously, "You went by the house twice?"

"Yeah," Zimmerman said. "I just wasn't cutting it. The heat was bothering me, so when I got to the south end of the lake, I sat down on a bench for a while, then I turned around and started walking back. I wanted the exercise, but I just didn't have the juice to keep running. When I passed the Jackman house again, the same guy was coming down the steps. Except he'd taken off his T-shirt, he was carrying it in his..." Zimmerman squinted, trying to remember the guy on the steps. "In his left hand. I'd taken my shirt off too. That wasn't what struck me as odd. What I thought looked odd was he had on dark shoes and socks. Hard to figure with the running shorts and hat—but I guess there isn't a dress code, even for Lake of the Isles."

Mars said, "Do you remember the time when you saw him coming out of the Jackman house?"

Zimmerman shook his head. "No, I wasn't timing myself at that point. But I'd checked my time at the south end of the lake, when I started back. It was three-oh-three. I would have been slower walking than I'd been running. So, I'd guess it was around three twenty-five, something like that."

"What do you think?" Nettie asked after Zimmerman left. Danny Borg had returned to Lake of the Isles to interview residents with a description of the guy Zimmerman had seen.

Mars was tossing his cigarette box from one hand to the other. "It doesn't give us a lot, other than nailing down the timeline. And soft stuff—like I'd guess he took his shirt off because it was bloody and that he wore dark shoes and socks because they wouldn't show blood. It does seem pretty clear at this point that Terri knew him."

"Maybe she knew him through T-Jack."

"Also possible," Mars said, not sure of much of anything. "When did you say Doc wanted me to come over?"

Nettie looked at her watch. "Ten minutes. Which reminds me. Denise called. Wanted you to call her back."

"Carl wants me to go to Cleveland with him tomorrow. It came up kind of sudden. Could you take Chris?"

Mars drew a breath. Her timing wasn't good. But Denise made few time demands on Mars and if she asked for something it was important to her. He gave a moment's thought to what he'd be doing on the investigation over the next few days, decided there wasn't anything where Chris couldn't tag along—or hang out with Nettie in the division.

"Sure," he said. "I'll pick him up tonight."

The Hennepin County Medical Examiner's Office was below ground level at HCMC, a couple of blocks east of city hall. Mars waved to the receptionist who buzzed him past the waiting room into the inner sanctum of death-in-a-drawer.

He smelled Doc D's cigarette smoke before he saw him. Doc was standing over a stainless steel autopsy table, peering down at the smooth, well-nourished body of a young black man.

Mars stood across the table from Doc D and looked down at the boy. He'd never get used to how benign a small-caliber bullet wound looked. Even three small-caliber bullet wounds.

"Gangs, drugs?" he said to Doc.

"Probably a little bit of both," Doc said. "A goddamn waste. You want to talk about the Jackman girl, right?"

Calling Terri DuCain the Jackman girl, caught Mars off guard. He thought back to her voice on the recording. Thought back to how strong her voice had sounded when she'd said, "Terri *DuCain.*" He couldn't call her Terri Jackman anymore.

They walked back into Doc's office. In his person, Doc was slightly disheveled; the kind of guy, when he got a haircut, you always noticed. When he wasn't in his green scrubs, his street clothes were clean, but nondescript. They looked like they got washed in a machine, dried in a machine, and had never seen the inside of a dry cleaners or the flat, hot side of an iron.

Mars had never seen Doc in a suit. When Doc had to testify in court, he'd put on a sports coat that had been hanging behind his office door for as long as Doc had been in the ME's office. The tie he always wore was in the jacket pocket, and he'd tie it on as he walked to court.

There was nothing disheveled or seat-of-the-pants about Doc's office. It was pin neat. Which was the kind of medical examiner he was. Efficient, reliable, organized—and something else. He was a man who found drama in his work, who told himself stories about what had brought the bodies to his stainless steel butcher block. A man who could get emotional about the waste of death but who never let emotions get in the way of judgment.

"No surprises," Doc said as he opened Terri DuCain's file. "It was the neck wound that finished her—if she'd survived that, Le Creuset number eighteen would have given her serious problems...." He read through the file, turning pages slowly. Then he tapped his finger on a page. "You asked about chloroform."

Mars explained about what they'd found on the floor and the bag in the wastebasket.

"Well," Doc said, "I'm not gonna be able to help you out much. Didn't find any evidence of chloroform in blood or tissues—at least, not in preliminary analysis. The way chloroform works, it can enter the bloodstream from the lungs or intestines—from the intestines if you pick it up from something you eat. From what you describe, I'd expect it to enter the bloodstream via the lungs. And that happens fast. A matter of seconds. Once it's in the bloodstream, it travels all through the body. Usually collects in body fat. The lab can run more sophisticated tests than what I've got to work with, so it's possible something will come back that didn't show up here. But I wouldn't count on it."

Mars sat back and thought about it. Terri DuCain had been on her front porch with somebody it appeared she knew. She had been there within minutes of speaking on the conference call. Why had she gone out to the porch if she knew the guy, rather than having him come in? Mars could think of only one reason. She didn't want to get hung up with the guy. She wanted to get rid of him. Her parents were going to be there within a half hour; she wanted to get rid of whoever it was, didn't want him hanging around.

So when he came to the door, she stepped out onto the porch rather than asking him in. But why would she do that? Why wouldn't she just say, "This isn't a good time for me," and close the door on him? It had to be somebody who, for some reason, she felt she had to show some courtesy. And he, whoever he was, must have followed her back into the house—with her reluctant consent or without Terri knowing that she was being followed. Once in the house, behind her in the hall, he must have taken out the plastic bag with the chloroformed cloth. Had he brought along a bottle of chloroform and attempted to pour more on the cloth, spilling on the hall floor in the process? Or had he dropped the cloth on the floor? In either case, based on what Doc D was telling him, it seemed certain that Terri had gotten away from him before he'd had a chance to cup the cloth over her face.

"How about the bruise?" Mars said. "Can you give me an idea of how old the bruise on her left arm is?"

Doc grimaced. "Contusions are the pits to age. I can tell you with maybe fifty percent certainty if it's occurred within twenty-four hours—after that?" He shook his head. "I can tell you it was old. Like I said at the scene, my best bet would be ten to fourteen days. I checked recent research that's been done on aging contusions in battered-children cases. But the way kids bruise and heal is so different from adults, I didn't find much of anything that was helpful. How elastic your skin is, body fat, muscle tone, blood flow, hemoglobin levels, venous structure, nutrition deficiencies—any or all of those things can make a big difference."

"Would you be comfortable saying the bruise is no more than a month old?"

"No problem with that. Don't think I've ever seen a bruise last more than two, three weeks—other than in automobile accidents or injuries involving something like a baseball bat, where there's bone and tissue damage. What Terri DuCain Jackman had on her arm looked like somebody'd socked her hard. Probably with a closed fist, from what I can tell of what's left of the bruise impression. A contusion like that's not going to leave marks longer than a month. Hell, a month is way too long. Couple weeks, tops."

Doc D sat back and looked at Mars. "If a fella believes what he sees on the TV, you're on a kinda short string for wrapping this one up. Doesn't strike me these are the kind of questions you ask if you're close to clearing a case."

Mars stood up to leave. "A fella shouldn't believe what he sees on TV, Doc."

96

Nettie had reviewed the Tower One security tape at fast-forward, cueing it up to start at 1:00 P.M. on the twenty-third. As always, Mars was appalled by the quality of the security tape. Its images were in shades of gray and very grainy. Mars couldn't count the number of times a murder could have been solved in a matter of hours with a decent-quality security tape. But he was able to pinpoint the area where someone waiting for T-Jack's signal would need to be.

It was especially helpful that the tape included a time counter that showed minutes and seconds on the screen image. As the counter approached 2:20 P.M., Mars and Nettie sat closer, afraid to blink. But the time counter passed 2:30 and eventually 2:45 without Mars and Nettie seeing any action other than a car backing out of a parking space at 2:28:37.

"Reverse to the car backing out," Mars said. "I don't remember seeing anyone get into that car and the time is right. Olsen said T-Jack got up and went to the window between two twenty-four and two twenty-six. Maybe someone was watching the twelfth floor from inside the car."

"Or," Nettie said, as the tape reversed, "maybe it was just someone sitting in the car waiting for someone else. If someone had gotten in on the passenger side, we wouldn't have seen it. The passenger side of the car isn't visible until it . . . here it is. Look. We see the rear end of the car that backed out at 2:28:37, and we would have seen someone getting into the driver's side, but the passenger side is obstructed by the van on the right."

"Slo-mo it here," Mars said, just before the car started to back up. As the car backed up, then moved forward and away from the camera, Mars and Nettie peered at the screen. "Can't tell if there are two people in the car," Mars said. "Do you think the lab can get a license plate from an enhanced image?"

Nettie stared. "I can't even see a license plate on the rear of the car. And look . . ." Her finger touched the screen. "On this car, the other side from the car that pulled out—I can't make out the numbers, but I can tell there is a plate with numbers. The car that's pulling away doesn't look like it has a plate on the rear. And something else, Mars." She paused the tape and touched her finger to the departing car. "Here—there's a sunroof, and it looks like it's open. I don't think anyone parked in that spot could see the twelfth-floor window from inside the car. But from an open sunroof? Maybe."

Mars said, "Send the tape over to the lab. See what they can come up with on make, model, a plate—and anything on occupants, driver or passenger."

CHAPTER

10

"Why doesn't she write on the cards?"

Chris stood at the kitchen counter in Mars's apartment, bent forward, butt out, elbows on the counter, chin resting on one hand, the other hand picking up each of Evelyn Rau's postcards, putting them down in an order that wasn't clear to Mars. Only a couple of years before, Chris's chin would have been at counter level. Just one of the changes that hit Mars between the eyes every time he looked at Chris.

"She sends *me* letters," Chris said. There was nothing behind these words other than genuine puzzlement that Mars was receiving blank postcards from Evelyn Rau.

"It's not an easy thing to explain," Mars said. "We talked about it before she left. She said she wanted me to know she'd be thinking about me, but she didn't want to write. I know that doesn't make a lot of sense, but I do understand it. Can't tell you why I understand it, but I do."

"Do you send her postcards with nothing on them?"

Mars shook his head. "I think because you and Evelyn write, she feels like she knows what's going on with me."

Chris nodded. "Yeah. I suppose." He pushed himself away from the counter and went to the bag of groceries he'd brought with him. Mars watched him as he took things out of the bag. For reasons beyond understanding, Chris Bahr had been born knowing and caring more about food than Mars and Denise combined. Maybe it was biology, but it had always felt to Mars like metaphysics—that the union of two subhuman particles could produce a human being who was, in important ways, like both parents and completely original.

"So," Mars said. "What's for supper?"

"Garlic soup. With green salad and the bread we got at Surdyks'."

"Garlic soup," Mars said, working hard to sound optimistic.

"Forty cloves of garlic with potatoes, onion, some mushrooms, chicken stock, and cream. After everything's cooked, I'll mush it up in the blender."

"Forty cloves of garlic?"

"About. It's okay. It doesn't taste like forty cloves of garlic. Oh, and butter too. And it tastes real buttery, more than garlic. Especially 'cause I'm gonna use Yukon Gold potatoes."

Mars held up both hands. "Whatever. What do you need me to do?"

"Cut the onion and peel the garlic."

They didn't talk much while they worked; Chris was getting quieter as he got older. But tonight there was a difference in the quiet. Chris had seemed preoccupied—maybe a bit unhappy about something?—since Mars had picked him up. Mars knew the best way to find out what was going on was to wait. Chris would find his own way of bringing up whatever it was that was bothering him.

The soup tasted like a heart attack waiting to happen. Thick, rich, and—Chris was right—buttery. The garlic was subtle, while the soup was in your mouth. The aftertaste was sharp and breathtaking.

"Do you like it?" Chris said, chewing on a crust of bread, watching Mars's face.

"It's delicious," Mars said. "A bowl of this once a week and you could be pretty sure you'd die young."

Chris grinned. "Too late for you, Dad. But you've got a shot at dying middle-aged."

Mars tapped Chris on the head with what remained of their sourdough baguette.

"Tell me again when classes start for you."

"Tuesday after Labor Day . . ."

"And you're through with algebra and soccer camp when?"

Chris made a face. "One more week of algebra. Soccer camp is over this week. I'm *never* gonna do advance placement math again. I don't even feel like I've had vacation. Dad? Is it true about T-Jack getting a hundred million to divorce his wife?"

Mars nodded. An article in the morning's *Strib* had reported details on the settlement agreement and it was the topic of the day.

"Why do you think he asked for a hundred million?"

"Right now, I'm guessing the money was the means to an end. I think he wanted the money. He may even have needed the money. But what he really wanted was to set up a reason for meeting with the DuCains, leaving Terri DuCain alone and giving himself a great alibi for the time when Terri was killed. He wanted to ask for enough to make the deal look serious, but not so much the DuCains wouldn't agree to the settlement."

"How much do you think they would have given T-Jack?"

"As much as they had," Mars said.

"Didn't T-Jack know that?"

Mars thought about T-Jack. About what T-Jack knew and what he didn't know. "I think T-Jack is plenty smart," he said. "But I don't think he understands people who care about someone else more than they care about themselves. So, no. I don't think T-Jack knew he could have asked for everything the DuCains had."

Chris dropped his chin down, resting it on top of his hands, which were folded on the table. His eyes moved back and forth in deep concentration as he thought about what Mars had said.

"But he was already rich."

"Right, but he lived well, spent big, and with athletes, it can be over in a split second. So if he'd blown his investments—which might have happened—he could have been one knee injury away from living like the rest of us. Well, maybe some better than that,

101

but not how a guy like T-Jack would want to live. So it's possible he needed a hundred million. I just don't think that's the only thing that motivated him."

Chris tapped his fingers on the table. Not saying anything, and still looking to Mars like something was bothering him.

Then Chris said, "So, what do you do next?"

"I need to find who T-Jack hired to kill Terri DuCain."

"How're you gonna do that?"

"That reminds me," Mars said. "I've gotta make a call," he said, heading to the phone.

"Herb," Mars said when Mitsch picked up. "Nettie said you called, that you had something . . ."

"*Maybe* something."

Mars let the line stay quiet while Herb made up his mind what he wanted to say next.

"This may be nothing, but I'll pass it on for what it's worth."

"I'll take anything you've got."

"When Royal Bergh mentioned Paul Tanney, it, like, rang a bell. Like I'd heard of the guy before. Came back to me after you left this morning. Few years back I used to have dinner at a steakhouse out on Highway 55. Owned by a guy named Ralph Gerber. Ralph had a pile of money. Not just from the restaurant. Married a gal probably twenty years younger than him. Yvonne Gerber. Vonnie is what everybody calls her. Real good-looking, smart as a whip. I'd guess she had her eye on the bottom line when she married Ralph, but thing is, she was good to him. He died of cancer couple years back. Reason I bring it up, I ran into Vonnie, oh, maybe late spring, early summer. Must be in her early forties now. Still real cute. What surprised me was I ran into her at the Shoreview Lodge. She was hostessing. I called her up for a drink after that. She said she'd gone kind of wild after Ralph died. Rolled over for the first good-looking guy that put the moves on her. If I'm remembering right, the name she said was Paul Tanney. Said Tanney took everything Ralph left her and landed her in debt besides.

I'll give you her number. She might be able to tell you something about Tanney that would be helpful."

Which told Mars what he needed to do first thing on T-Jack minus seven.

CHAPTER

11

"Come out right away," Vonnie Gerber had said when Mars called her. "I'll have a half hour or so before the lunch rush starts."

The Shoreview Lodge was ten miles northeast of downtown Minneapolis. A flat, sprawling building with a big parking lot to the front and side, it was a last bastion of what used to be called continental cuisine. Inside, the tables were covered with pink or white tablecloths, which in turn were covered with a clear plastic top cut to fit the table. There were small vases of plastic flowers on each table that changed with the season. Daffodils and lilies of the valley in the spring, daisies and roses in the summer, mums in the fall, and poinsettias and holly leaves November through February. An electronic organ in the corner provided live music every evening from six-thirty until ten, and a big salad bar ran down the center of the restaurant. A banner hanging outside the Shoreview Lodge read, "Home of the Twin Cities' Biggest Salad Bar."

Mars spotted Vonnie Gerber as soon as he walked into the reception area of the Shoreview Lodge. She was on the phone at the receptionist podium, the phone tucked between her left ear and shoulder as she turned pages in a reservation book on the podium. Her red talon-nails traced pages on the book as she talked in a voice that was both friendly and authoritative.

Herb Mitsch had gotten it exactly right. Vonnie Gerber was real cute. Bright blond hair swept into a little topknot, soft, perky features, deep violet eyes, a small waist and a voluptuous bosom.

There was something slightly retro, past the buy-by date, about her that fit the Shoreview Lodge. Mars guessed she was older than she looked, and she looked late thirties, early forties. Whatever—she was at least fifteen years older than she needed to be to get what she wanted out of life.

"Yvonne Gerber?" he said as soon as she hung up the phone. He held up his badge. She gave him a careful look and called out, "Sheila? Cover the desk and phone for the next half hour, will you?"

To Mars she said, "Let's go into the bar. I'll have them comp you a drink." Gathering up her cigarette pack and lighter, she slid her butt off the high stool she'd been sitting at, landing on spike-heeled sandals. She gave a tug to each side of her skintight Capri pants, wiggling her hips as she tugged, and motioned Mars, with a tilt of her head, to follow her.

"What are you drinking?" she said as they walked into the bar. She dropped her cigarettes and lighter at a booth in a far corner and lifted a finger toward the solitary bartender.

"Coca-Cola will do it for me, and I'll need to pay for my drink. Department rules."

"Like anybody's gonna know," she said. But she didn't argue when he handed her two bucks. When they were settled in the booth, she said, "Why are you interested in Paul Tanney?"

Deciding how much to tell someone you're interviewing about why you're interviewing them is one of the fine arts of interrogation. Nine cases out of ten, the less you said, the better. Every once in a while, it paid off to level with the person you were questioning. Mars's instincts told him that the more he told Vonnie Gerber, the more she'd tell him. And he had a gut feeling that Vonnie could be trusted not to be indiscreet about their conversation.

"I'm involved in the Terri DuCain Jackman murder investigation," Mars said. "Herb Mitsch told me that Paul Tanney knew Tayron Jackman and that you knew Tanney."

Vonnie Gerber rolled her eyes. "Hope you don't mind if I smoke," she said. She drew a cigarette out of her pack and lit it with her lighter. Then she took a deep drag on the cigarette,

105

blowing smoke in a sharp, steep line, extending her full, pink lower lip to direct it away from Mars's face.

"You want me to talk about Paul Tanney, you've got to listen to a story."

"It's what I came to hear," Mars said.

"I need, for what's left of my pride, to explain how I got involved with Tanney." She looked up at Mars. "I'm not stupid, but I acted like I was stupid."

Mars said, "Herb Mitsch said you were a smart lady."

She looked up at Mars quickly. "Herb said that? Well, Herb's always been a sweet guy." She played with her lighter before she spoke again.

"I married my husband, Ralph Gerber, for his money." She looked at Mars to see how he took what she said. Then she shrugged. "He was crazy about me, and I was sick of being alone. He'd been married before, but his wife had run around on him. When he met me, he hadn't been married for more than twenty years. Me, I'd been married twice. To losers both times. Ralph said if I married him, he'd treat me like a princess. I could have anything I wanted. I just had to be faithful. I was so fed up with guys that didn't have anything to offer other than what you had to unzip to get at, I was more than happy to go along with Ralph's rule."

Vonnie sighed and lit another cigarette off the end of her previous butt. "We were married nine years when Ralph got diagnosed with lung cancer. They said they'd got it early and he'd be fine. Couple years after the surgery, he had recurrence. Eventually it was in his spine, his brain, his liver. I can't tell you how awful it was. I kept him at home, had round-the-clock nurses, and ran the businesses out of the den. Three years of that. And anytime during those three years a trip to hell would have been a vacation. The only good thing that came out of it was that when Ralph died, I was grateful. Not just for me, but for him. The bad thing was, I went wild. I sold the house Ralph and I had lived in—the house he had died in—and bought a condo, got a whole new wardrobe and a Cadillac convertible."

Vonnie looked at Mars. "Enter Paul Tanney."

"How'd you meet?"

Stubbing out her cigarette, Vonnie said, "First mistake. I met him at a bowling alley. Crissakes. Bowling alleys and pool halls. My mother was right. Wrong kind of people at bowling alleys and pool halls. Some gal pals coaxed me out a few months after Ralph had died. I met the gals at the Stardust Alleys over on Twenty-sixth and whatever. Just north of Lake Street. Paul was standing outside when I pulled into the parking lot. I noticed him noticing me, but I didn't let on. He was a doll. Absolutely to die for. Then he came in and stood behind our lane. Just stood there, watching me bowl. Last ball on the last line, for the first time I looked at him, let him know I knew he had his eye on me. I held my ball up, balancing it, and winked at him. Then I threw a strike."

Vonnie shook her head and shrugged. "He got hard and I got dumb." She shrugged again, making clear that being dumb for the right reasons wasn't worth losing sleep over. "He followed me out to the parking lot, made small talk for maybe three minutes, then got into the Cadillac with me. Knew how to work the electric seat controls and a lot of other things besides."

Vonnie took out another cigarette, but didn't light it. "I suppose you could say I was flat-out stupid. But the thing is, I was attractive. Why shouldn't he be crazy about me? If I'd been rich and ugly, well, I might have asked myself: What's this guy about? But I don't think I was altogether crazy for believing he was interested in me.

"And he was so slick. The first three, maybe four months we were together, we went to the best restaurants, he bought me the loveliest gifts. One day, he said he needed to borrow the Cadillac. He'd never done that before. Had this little smile on his face when he asked. I knew he was up to something. When he came back, he had a high-end Mercedes for me. Worth at least twenty thousand more than the Cadillac. Said the Mercedes was a class car, and I was a class lady. What I didn't know was that he had forged my name on the title to the Cadillac, sold it, pocketed the money, and gotten the Mercedes on a six-month lease. I'm not a bad business-woman. All I would have had to have done to call his game was to ask for the title to the Mercedes. Lord help me, I didn't even consider it. I was just thrilled he wanted me to be driving a Mercedes. The other thing that should have occurred to me was that he had to have known where I kept the title to the Cadillac. Which meant he knew where all my financial records were. But by then he'd done a lot of things that made me trust him. When I look back on it, I realize how clever he was. And not just clever. This was a guy who had practice doing this stuff. I wasn't the first person he'd conned, and I doubt I'll be the last."

"The other things he did?" Mars said.

"Oh, like after we'd been together maybe half a year, he started acting different. Quiet, kind of preoccupied. Like something was bothering him. I pushed him about it and he said he had a temporary cash flow problem. Not a big problem, something that would be resolved in time. My heart kind of sunk when he said that. I've heard about guys conning women with a line like that. You know, starting out spending big to gain a woman's confidence, then saying they need money for a short time. That it made me worried when he said it tells me I wasn't totally numb from the neck up; it must have been in my mind to start with. So I pretended to bite. I said, 'Can I help?' If he'd said yes, I would have been on to him. But he said absolutely not. That he didn't believe in mixing money and personal relationships, and besides, it wasn't worth worrying about. He apologized for letting it affect the way he treated me. I kind of held my breath for a couple weeks after that, half expecting him to come back and say, 'Sorry, but maybe I do need to take you up on that offer.' It never happened. A few weeks later, he came home with a big bouquet of flowers. Said everything had worked out, even better than expected. Thanked me for being so patient and understanding. Smart move. I see it clear as anything now."

She paused and signaled the bartender for a refill. She noticed Mars noticing and said, "Yes, two gin and tonics are a bit much for the middle of the morning, but when I talk about Paul Tanney, I need it."

When the bartender set the drink down in front of her, he said,

"You keep this up, Vonnie, you're not gonna clear your tab out of this week's paycheck."

"Not a chance. What I do need to do less of is puff on these death sticks," she said, shoving the pack and lighter away from her. She put her elbow on the table and leaned forward, resting her head on her hand. "I know I'm going on. But you can tell a lot about Paul Tanney from the things he did to me...."

"I'm not complaining," Mars said. "You're absolutely right. This is telling me a lot about Tanney. When did you find out you'd been conned?"

"Just after I got the big bouquet of flowers, he told me he wanted to celebrate our first year together in a big way. Wanted to sign us up for a six-week, first-class cruise. The Mediterranean, Tunisia, Malta, the Greek Isles. Trip of a lifetime. More than twenty-six thousand dollars per person. I was dying to go—but I was still managing the restaurant and Ralph's other properties. I just didn't see how I could go away for that length of time. Which was when Paul said he knew someone who'd be interested in buying me out. A client of his who'd been looking for something to invest in since he'd sold his company . . ."

"What was it Tanney told you he did for a living?"

She shook her head. "That was the thing about Paul. He never said something simple, like, 'I'm an investor.' What he told me was he'd cashed out his stock in a software firm where he'd been an employee. That he'd reinvested that money and done well and friends started asking for advice on investments, so he started advising them informally. Then, friends of friends asked for help, so he turned it into a business. He said he charged a one-percent commission against investments and was netting almost a million a year. It was the first time he mentioned T-Jack's name, actually. He said he'd met T-Jack through friends and T-Jack and he were working on a deal together that would be huge."

Maybe the one time he told the truth, is what Mars thought.

"Anyway, I was reluctant at first. I enjoyed managing the businesses. Paul said he wanted me to be free to travel with him—on business and pleasure. Said I could always use the money from selling the business to start something new, something that really excited me. So I said, sure. Wouldn't hurt to see if Paul's friend made an offer, what the offer would be. Well, the 'offer' was double what I was expecting. And when you consider that the main property, the restaurant, would need major capital improvements in the next couple years, the offer looked even better. Twenty-five words or less—I signed on. Which is when the con went into high gear.

"About a week and a half before we were to leave on the cruise, Paul comes back to the condo in a panic. We were due to close on my sale of the properties two days before we left. Paul said the buyer has a family emergency and has to be out of town until the week after we leave. There's no question of delaying the closing because—this is what Paul is saying, remember—it doesn't work out taxwise for the buyer. Paul says the only thing to do is to cancel the trip. At that date, he'd lose fifty percent of the cost of the trip. I said it would be a crime to lose that much money for nothing, we'll just have to find another buyer. And he says, that doesn't make any sense because finding another buyer on the same terms just wasn't very likely. That we'd lose more on changing buyers than we'd lose on canceling the trip. Then he said I should go, he'd stay for the closing and come later. He said to take a girlfriend on the trip. I say, how is that going to work? My friend is going to have to fly home alone from God knows where? I said if he really was prepared to stay for the closing, I'd go by myself until he could join me. Paul says, no way. He'd book another spot for my friend and she could stay for the whole trip. I argued with him for a while, but he made me feel like canceling the trip would be the biggest disappointment he'd ever had. So I said okay. Then it occurred to me he'd have to have my power of attorney at the closing. Immediately he says, well, that won't work. And I argue with him until he agrees to let me give him power of attorney. I didn't even read the document he brought me to sign. I was packing, getting ready to go, I signed it blind. It was not a limited power of attorney— limited just to the sale, that is. I gave him full power of attorney over all my assets. Remember, it still hadn't occurred to me that he knew what my assets were or how to get to them."

"And when did the light go on?"

"Two things happened on the trip. The first was a small thing, but it just sat on my brain like a rock. My friend and I had been out on the deck one night—watching shooting stars for luck, is what we were doing—and she said, isn't it funny how things work out? If that creep John Sater who'd bartended at the restaurant hadn't known Diane Lee, you'd never have met Paul. I didn't have a clue what she was talking about. Diane Lee was one of the women I'd gone bowling with the night I met Paul. And she had been going with a bartender at the restaurant named John Sater. We'd fired him, because we found out he'd been making book with customers. But I never knew until that night, in the middle of the Mediterranean, that Paul and John Sater had known each other. And for sure I didn't know that it wasn't an accident that Paul was at the bowling alley that night. It was a blind date, except I didn't know it. What I know now is that John Sater had more or less suggested to Paul that I'd be an easy mark.

"Anyway, knowing that our meeting wasn't accidental was the first time I had real doubts. Nothing very solid, but I felt uncomfortable. Then, a couple days later, I got a cable from Paul saying there were problems with his clients' investments, he wouldn't be able to join us, we'd do the whole trip over next year, blah, blah, blah. If I hadn't had a girlfriend along, I probably would have gotten off the boat first chance and gone home. Paul had figured that out, too. Which, I'd bet, was why he suggested the girlfriend in the first place. I mean, the guy was seriously good at this con.

"But the cable was the last thing I heard from him. When I got back from the trip, all his stuff was out of the condo and I was broke. My credit cards maxed out, a second mortgage on the condo at eighty percent of assessed value, my accounts empty—the sale? The properties had been sold, all right, but for about twenty percent of what they were worth. It was how he made the deal work so fast. And the money from the sale gone. The first phone call I got when I was back was from the leasing agency. No payments had been made on the Mercedes lease for the past two months. By the end of the month I'd lost the car."

Vonnie Gerber drew a deep breath. "But the worst was yet to come. A month ago, I was coming into the lobby of the apartment I was renting, and two guys pushed in behind me. They practically carried me up to my apartment by my neck. They were looking for Paul and John. These goons both had Magnums or whatever you call those big, black pistols you always see in movies. One of them pushed me down on the couch, sat over me with his knees on either side of me, a gun to my head. The other guy tore the place apart looking for financial information. It seemed like what they were saying was that Paul had been dealing for their boss, but had gotten behind—substantially behind—on paying for inventory. Paul told them I was good for the debt, that I was loaded. I was lucky that I'd put my records in order after Paul left. I was able to show them what I had. More to the point, what I didn't have. They were furious. And this next part you need to know. It will explain why I'm gonna have some limits on what I will and won't do for you in this investigation. Before they left, they pissed and shit all over me. Smeared shit on the walls, the furniture, rubbed it in my hair. Said that wasn't half what they'd do if I ever filed charges against them. What I'm saying is, I'll never go into court against those guys. If what I tell you helps you find Paul, great. But I don't ever, ever want to see those two guys again. Can you understand that?"

Mars nodded, then said, "Describe the guys."

Vonnie Gerber drew her shoulders up and rubbed her hands together as if she were cold. She shook her head.

"You give me your word this won't tie back to me?"

Mars held up one hand, palm facing Vonnie. "Word of honor."

She smoked and thought. "Okay. One was big—tall, but thin. Your height, maybe. Around six one, six two." She paused, squinted, thinking hard. "The other guy was six inches shorter. At least. He had a whitish bandanna tied around his head. You know. Straight across his forehead, tied at the back."

112

"White, Black, Hispanic?"

"Red and white," Vonnie said.

"Red and white?" Mars said. "You mean, one Indian and one white?"

"No. 'Red' as in 'redneck.' And 'white' like in 'white trash.'"

"You didn't get any names, didn't hear them call each other by names . . . ?"

She shook her head, then hesitated. "The big guy. When he was looking at financial records. He said something to the shorter guy. Called him . . . Mutt. I remember, because they looked like Mutt and Jeff. You know, real big and real little."

"Could it have been Matt?"

Vonnie snapped her fingers. "Yes! He did say Matt, and I thought, 'More like Mutt and Jeff.' Mutt kind of stuck. But what the tall guy called the other guy was Matt." She looked at Mars, her eyes narrow. "You know these guys?"

"I may have met one of them," Mars said. "But what you've said has been very helpful. I'm going to try to find photos of the two of them—I'm guessing they've both got some kind of police record. It would help if you could identify them."

She was shaking her head violently. "I don't want to be seen near the police department. Couldn't you come here again? Just let me know when, and I'll schedule some time. But I don't want to be seen near the police department." She looked up at him, her tough exterior pierced by genuine terror. "I live alone, Mr. Bahr. I've only just started to sleep for more than a half hour without waking up in a sweat."

"I'll work around whatever feels right to you. But one thing I want to be clear about. 'Mutt' and 'Jeff' were looking for Tanney and Sater—not just Tanney?"

"Yes. They talked about both Paul and Sater. I'd guess any problems they had with Paul, Sater was involved. I certainly found out the hard way that Paul and Sater did deals together."

"Okay. Just a couple of questions about T-Jack. Did Tanney say anything specific about what he was doing with T-Jack?"

Vonnie lit another cigarette, then looked off in the distance,

113

thinking about Mars's question. "The first time he mentioned T-Jack was when he was having the cash flow problem. That was last—I don't know exactly. March, April maybe? He never said specifically what they were involved in, just said it was big." She tipped her cigarette in the ashtray, and a small crease formed between her eyebrows. "Now that I think about it, it was the one time he didn't go into a lot of detail. I guess you could say when he was lying, you got a big story. When he was telling the truth, he didn't say anything or said very little." Vonnie blew smoke. "Too bad I didn't figure *that* out a lot sooner."

"Did you ever meet T-Jack?"

Vonnie shook her head. "Oh God, no. Paul was real tense about T-Jack. I'd say he was afraid of the guy. Which was part of why I thought he wasn't telling me anything specific about what they were doing. Anytime he did say anything to me about T-Jack, he'd always swear me to secrecy. Even though he never said anything important—just that they were doing a big deal. Looking back, my guess is he didn't know what T-Jack's deal was. T-Jack had probably just asked Paul if he was interested in making some big money."

She tapped the ash on her cigarette again and said, "You're thinking T-Jack hired Paul to kill T-Jack's wife, aren't you?"

The question brought Mars right back up against the fundamental problem of how much to say.

"I'm considering it as a possibility," Mars said. "Do you think he could do it? That Tanney could murder somebody for money?"

"For money?" Vonnie said. "Especially for big money? You bet. Right after I got back from the cruise and got hit with what had happened—well, I kind of fell off the edge. I was in bad shape, and a friend insisted I go see a shrink she'd been seeing for more than twenty years. I mean, I ask you, how good could this guy be if she's still seeing him after twenty years? But I went, just to shut my friend up, really, and the shrink actually told me something useful. I'm describing Paul to him, and the shrink kind of shakes his head like he knows what I'm gonna say before I say it. He wheels around on his chair, pulls a book out of the bookcase, opens it up in front of me and taps his finger on the page. 'Antisocial personality,' the shrink says. 'Commonly called a sociopath.' He showed me the list of personality traits—charming, manipulative, nonstop lying, doesn't give a shit about anybody other than themselves. Whoever wrote that must have known Paul personally. 'You never had a chance,' is what the shrink said. 'These guys spend their lives using other people and they don't lose any sleep doing it.'"

"You have any pictures of Tanney?"

"Snaps," Vonnie said. "Couple table shots when we went out to Vegas. You know, Paul and me sitting cheek to cheek in a padded booth, drinks in hand, sappy true-love smiles on our mugs. And a picture of both of us standing by the Mercedes."

"I'd like to send someone out to pick them up, if that's okay."

"I'll have them here tomorrow."

Mars said, "Who other than T-Jack and Sater did Paul spend time with?"

"No one other than Sater, far as I knew. Where Paul hung out—where he met T-Jack—was Double Ds. I didn't know that until after the cruise." A hard look crossed Vonnie's face. "And of course, there were women at Double Ds. Another thing I found out after the fact. If I were still looking for Paul, Double Ds would be where I'd start."

"Vonnie?" The young woman who'd been covering the phone and desk for Vonnie stood two booths away. "I've gotta start waiting tables, people are coming in for lunch."

Vonnie Gerber raised her eyebrows at Mars, scooped up her cigarettes and lighter and stood up.

"Time to make a buck," she said.

In the parking lot, Mars opened both front doors of the car and cranked the air conditioner up to high. While the car cooled off, he leaned against the front fender, took out his notebook and started to write down the things he needed to remember. He could add John Sater to the list of people that needed to be tracked down. He needed to check narcotics files to see if he could come up with photos of Lyle and Matt—just saying their first names, that they worked for Hebb, and the physical description should be enough to get the photos. And Mars needed to bring Vonnie photos of Lyle and Matt to confirm they were the jerks who'd roughed her up. Nettie and Danny could take care of getting their witness at the Lake of the Isles to look at Tanney's photo once Mars had picked the photos up from Vonnie.

Because Mars was thinking that had to be the way this deal worked. Tanney had to be the guy that had killed Terri, and John Sater had been the guy in the parking lot, waiting for T-Jack's signal.

More than what Vonnie had given him to follow up on, was what Vonnie had confirmed: that Tanney was working on a big deal with T-Jack, that Tanney needed money, and that the timing of T-Jack and Tanney's deal fit with when T-Jack would have been planning Terri DuCain's hit.

It was a lot. It took him farther in the case than where he'd had any hope of being two hours earlier. Mars needed to put hands on Tanney or Sater, and he was guessing that Vonnie Gerber had been right. The best way of doing that was to pay a visit to Double Ds.

Mars was underdressed for Dames! Dames! Even early afternoon, there was a substantial crowd of young to middle-aged, warm-faced men in expensive suits, silk ties loosened, chomping on cigars and eyeing the half-dozen naked dancers on an elaborately lit stage.

A cocktail waitress with blond hair so bleached it stood on its own power approached Mars. "Something to drink?" she said, sizing Mars up in a single glance and expecting the answer she was going to get.

"No. Thanks. Is Royal Bergh in?"

She blinked hard and slow, which was to be expected with that much liner and mascara on her lids and lashes. Then she pointed toward the back of the room, in the direction of a lighted hallway. Mars followed the hallway to a door marked Private and knocked.

Three things made the sex trade a lousy business: the owners, the staff, and the customers. If Herb Mitsch was an exception to the rule that all sex club owners were coldhearted, money-grubbing, lewd guys, Royal Bergh proved the rule. In violation of any number of city ordinances, another cotton-candy-headed blonde, nude from the waist up, was sitting on one end of the couch in Bergh's office. From the waist down she wore a gold lamé thong and heels with several inches of platform. She was chewing gum while she smoked a blue-papered cigarette.

"Honey," Bergh said to the woman as Mars flashed his badge. She rose gracefully and left the room, smoking, chewing, and walking on the platforms, all at the same time.

"A very talented young woman," Bergh said, his eyes glittering in a face heavy with dead flesh.

"Just what I was thinking," Mars said. "Herb Mitsch talked to you?"

"Said you'd be stopping by."

"I'm looking for two guys, Paul Tanney and John Sater. Herb talked to one of your managers yesterday who said he knew Tanney. Your guy said Tanney hung around Tayron Jackman, when Jackman was in the club."

The light went out of Bergh's eyes. He sat forward, the loose flesh of his face tightening.

"Trouble. The both of them. And the dancer Tanney was shtupping. Trouble. All three of them."

"Tell me why you say that."

Bergh shrugged. "Gail Pearce—danced by the name of Barbie Bush—was dumb. Tanney and Sater were dishonest." Bergh shrugged again. "Maybe she was dishonest too. Sometimes it's hard to tell dumb from dishonest."

"Dishonest how?"

"Tanney was dealing. Didn't pay his supplier. Hung around here hitting on the girls and hanging on the high-end customers until we barred him from the club. Which we did after a couple of lowlifes showed up here looking for him and Sater. Gail—she'd stick anything up her nose, in her arm, down her throat. Any hole she had, you could put whatever in it. Which is how I think she started with Tanney. He was her connection. Not sure what his interest was in her. My guess is she was turning tricks for him before we cut her loose. She was caught pickpocketing from customers twice. Said they'd agreed she could take her tip from their wallets after a lap dance. Not the way they saw it. And in our business, the customer is always right. Dancers are easy come, easy go. A customer who spends a thousand a night gets the benefit of the doubt. The regular customers Gail had stayed with her for a while because she'd get downer and dirtier than the other girls. She was your basic place-to-put-it. But at the end of the day, it's not all that hard to find another place. With a lot less hassle."

"The guys that came looking for Tanney and Sater. What did they look like?"

"Wouldn't know," Bergh said, pushing a button on his phone. When the phone rang, he picked it up and said, "Tell Horst to come back to the office." He dropped the phone back to its cradle and said, "I wasn't around. Horst was the manager on the shift they showed up."

Horst looked more like a bouncer than a manager. Big, stuffed into a sports coat, brush cut. Horst moved as if his arms were pistons, pulling his massive body forward against the drag of gravity.

"What?" he said to Bergh as soon as he walked into the office.

"The guys that came looking for Tanney and Sater. The ones that caused all that trouble, what'd they look like?"

Horst got a look that suggested there was a brain behind his face. "Your regular white trash. Nothin' fancy. One short, one tall. The short one had a bandanna tied around his head. More than that, I couldn't say. I personally picked the both of them up by the collars and put them out the back door. Told them, they had business with Tanney or Sater, they don't do it at Double Ds."

"You see them after that?" Mars said.

Horst smiled. "Not on my watch. All the door people had the word on them. Easy to spot a pair like that...." Horst stopped. "Now that I think about it, one of the door guys told me a pair of losers had shown up asking for me. Probably wanted to make sure

I wasn't here. They didn't get in, but they gave the door guy a twenty and a phone number and told him to call if Tanney or Sater showed up. Dumb. Like the door guy is gonna do anything other than take the twenty."

"He still have the number?"

Horst guffawed. "Not a chance. The number or the twenty— long gone."

After Horst had left, Mars said to Bergh, "When's the last you saw Tanney or Sater?"

Bergh raised his eyes to the ceiling, grimaced, then said, "Tanney? I don't know, maybe a couple months ago. Sater? I couldn't say."

"Could you give me anything on names of people Gail Pearce knew—I may need to find her to find Tanney and Sater. Any records on where she was living?"

Bergh gave him a narrow look. Then lurched forward in his chair and opened a bottom file drawer in his desk. His fingertips walked through the tops of the file folders, stopped, and pulled one of the folders out of the drawer. He dropped it on his desk, turning back the folder, and sorted through the contents. He pulled out a photo, then, after copying something down, passed the photo and an address to Mars.

"That's the last picture we had of her. Looks better in the photo than she ever did in the flesh. Wouldn't count on her still being at that address," Bergh said. "Not the kind of girl that stays put. With men or apartments."

Mars looked at the photo, finding it hard to see much different in Gail Pearce from any of the other women Mars had seen in the club. You would need X-ray vision to see what Gail Pearce really looked like under layers of makeup. He folded the paper with the address carefully. "What was Tanney's relationship with T-Jack about?"

Bergh's face closed. "Mitsch shoulda told you. I don't discuss customers. Especially customers who make me money."

Standing, Mars said, "So T-Jack spent money here? On the girls?"

119

Bergh stood to open the door for Mars. "This much I'll tell you. Doubt I ever made a dime selling T-Jack a drink or taking a cut from the girls. T-Jack made me money because he brought in guys who spend big. Those guys, they like to be where a guy like T-Jack hangs. Next day, they go into the office and make like a big deal. Had a drink with Tayron Jackman. Which would be a lie. T-Jack never drank with anybody."

"Why'd he come?" Mars said.

Bergh started to close the door behind Mars. "He liked the attention," Bergh said. "Never responded to it, but he'd just kinda sit and let people fawn over him." Bergh looked like he regretted what he just said. He changed the subject. "I'll tell you this. Even after everything that's happened, with his wife and all, when he comes back, there'll be twice as many—ten times as many—guys who'll want to say they had a drink at Double Ds with Tayron Jackman. He might not be welcome anywhere else, but he'll be welcome here."

Mars looked at his watch as he left Double Ds. He probably could get over to the address that Bergh had given him for Gail Pearce and still make it back to City Hall by late afternoon.

Gorgeous Georgia Ventura had been ironing when Mars knocked on the door of her south Minneapolis apartment.

She was wearing a cutoff sweatshirt, with cutoff jeans. Barefooted. Her blond hair was stringy, unwashed. She asked to see his badge when he explained why he was there, then let him in, becoming self-conscious about how she looked.

"All the makeup I wear at work, when I'm at home, I really kick back." She looked over her shoulder at him. "You been to Double Ds when I've been dancing?"

Mars shook his head. "Not my scene."

Georgia made a face. "You want something to drink?"

"No. Thanks. Okay if I sit down?"

She made an expansive gesture with her arm. "Mind if I keep ironing?"

The smell of the hot iron on fabric was pleasant, reminding

Mars of vague childhood memories. Mars chose to ignore Georgia's frequent suggestive gestures of touching a finger to her tongue, then to the iron to make a hissing sound.

"Gail was here how long?"

"Too long."

"Which would be . . ."

Georgia put the iron on its end and gave the question some thought.

"Well, she moved in before Thanksgiving last year. She didn't pay her share of the rent for two months, so I told her she had to go. Then she paid. Next thing I know, she's bringing guys home. Middle of the day, someone else after work. Didn't take a rocket scientist to figure out what was going on. And she had a regular guy too. Paul Tanney. A real jerk. He just sorta moved in at one point last spring. Ate the food, used my towels. Then, these two creeps show up looking for Paul. Lucky for me, I had a friend over, or I have an idea they would have been real nasty to deal with. The good thing was, when I told Paul these two guys had come around, he was gone. Never saw him again. Gail broke up with him around the same time. That's what she said, anyway. If she did, it would have been good. He was using her. I think he took some of what she was getting from the guys she was bringing home. She had plenty of problems of her own. And he was real hard on her. Criticized her nonstop. She was too thin, she was too fat, her hair was too blond, she had shit taste in clothes. Like that. He promised all kinds of stuff that never happened. . . ."

"Do you know where she went when she left here?"

"I know where she *said* she was going."

"Which was . . . ?"

"She said she was going to Hollywood to get into the movies. Ha."

"And you haven't seen her around since she moved out?"

Georgia shook her head. "One of the girls that started dancing at Double Ds after Gail left said she'd run in to Gail in Reno. Said Gail was working at one of the real low-end clubs there. Still talking about going to Hollywood."

"Tanney with her?"

"She didn't say. But I could give you the gal's name, and you could ask her. That, and I've got Gail's sister's phone number. She called a couple times, and I hung on to the number. Thought I might need a way of tracking Gail down if she ran out on me without paying the rent."

Back in the car, Mars did a quick check on the number Georgia had given him for Gail's sister. It was a Northfield number, a small college town thirty-five miles south of the Twin Cities.

He called from the car. A man who sounded like a husband answered the phone. Mars asked to speak to Marta Rockwell, then heard an extension phone pick up. He didn't hear the husband's line click off after Mars had introduced himself.

Mars could feel Marta Rockwell tighten up while he explained why he was calling.

"I'm sorry," she said, not sounding sorry. "I don't have a relationship with my sister. I can't tell you anything. . . ."

"I can appreciate that, Ms. Rockwell, but it isn't your sister I'm interested in. I'm trying to find a man she knew—a Paul Tanney. Just a few questions—"

"I can't—I won't—talk about my sister." And the line went dead.

Mars sat with the receiver in his hand for moments after Marta Rockwell hung up. Her reaction was not unusual, especially given what Mars knew about Gail Pearce. Pearce had probably strained limits in their relationship at least once too often. When you investigated homicides, it was common to find relatives who didn't want to know anything about family members who'd made their lives hell-by-association. With a sister like Gail Pearce, Marta Rockwell's heart probably skipped a beat every time the phone rang, every time there was a knock at the door.

He considered pushing it with Rockwell, maybe driving down to Northfield. When he thought about the time that would take, he gave it up. Better to spend time trying to find more recent connections to Tanney, Sater, Lyle, and Matt.

* * *

Danny was sitting next to Nettie when Mars got back to city hall.

"How we doing on T-Jack's surveillance?" Mars asked.

Nettie turned around, looking like she was going to say something, but she didn't.

Danny said, "No action at all. They've seen some lights go off and on, but no T-Jack coming outside the house or out of the garage in his car—I got vehicle descriptions and license plate numbers from the DMV. It's been tough, because there's no parking in front of the house. I could get by with a park patrol vehicle or some kind of dummy service van intermittently. But if we've got something there twenty-four/seven, he's gonna figure it out."

"So?"

"So I put a car across the lake with binoculars. Then I've got two cars parked on Dean. One backs up the other for potty breaks. The Dean stakeout is the cushy job. They've just got to sleep, read, whatever, until they get a call from the car on the other side of the lake. But I had to put two guys, one car, across the lake. Tough duty staring through binoculars nonstop, infrareds after dark. The stakeout will run twelve-hour shifts."

Mars frowned. "I'd prefer eight-hour shifts, at least for the guys that have to use binoculars. Twelve is fine for whoever is sitting on Dean."

Danny shook his head. "Couldn't get the support. Moved the request all the way up to the deputy chief, and he said four guys on a twelve-hour shift was the best we could do."

Nettie said, "I'll take care of it." She looked over at Danny. "Not your fault. You're still one of them. They're not afraid of you yet. They know I'm trouble."

Danny said, "Well, more power to you." A smug smile passed his face. "I found them to be pretty in-core-a-guble."

Both Mars and Nettie looked at Danny, and in unison said, "*In-*what?"

"I-n-c-o-r-r-i-g-i-b-l-e. It means somebody who can't be changed. I'm doing the *Reader's Digest* vocabulary builders every month. Figure it will help me when I write up investigation reports."

"You need to learn how to pronounce the word after you find out what it means," Nettie said.

"But 'incorrigible' is one you should keep near the front of your book," Mars said. "You'll have a lot of opportunities to use it. Not to stifle your intellectual development, but have you had a chance to connect with T-Jack's attorney yet?"

Danny nodded. "Yeah. Was out there first thing this morning. I was just telling Nettie. It doesn't make any sense."

"Like how?"

Danny shrugged. "T-Jack's got an agent, a financial advisor, an accountant—all high-powered guys—and he goes into a hundred-million-dollar deal with a guy he's never seen before who runs a one-man office in the suburbs. Decent enough guy, maybe even a decent attorney. But I don't get it."

Mars squinted at Danny. "T-Jack had never met the attorney who represented him at the settlement meeting?"

"That's what the guy said. I was trying to sound him out on his part in writing the settlement agreement. Which was tricky, as it's all privileged. He knew that and didn't give anything away, but he did say even if privilege wasn't an issue, he couldn't have told me much. He'd talked to T-Jack on the phone a couple of times, they'd exchanged a couple of faxes—but the first time he'd met T-Jack was at DuCain Industries. I think he was as surprised as anyone to find himself involved in the deal."

Mars blew air. "I think we know maybe a quarter of what T-Jack has going. Seven days aren't looking like very much time. But I have made some progress."

He walked them through what he'd found out about Tanney, Sater, Gail Pearce, Lyle and Matt. He asked Nettie to follow up in Reno to see if they could find out anything about Gail Pearce there.

"I'll have Vonnie Gerber's photos of Tanney tomorrow, Danny. I'll want you to have the witness see if Tanney's picture looks like the same guy he saw with Terri DuCain on the porch."

Nettie picked up a message slip and passed it over to Mars. "Grace DuCain called. Wanted you to call her back, not urgent."

There was something in Nettie's tone, in the way she wasn't looking at him when she talked, that reminded Mars that Chris had never said what was bothering him. He looked at his watch. He'd need to pick up Chris from advance placement algebra in another couple hours. He swung around in his chair and called Grace DuCain.

Grace's assistant, Linda, answered, but Grace came on the line immediately.

"Mars—I'm so sorry to bother you. But there are two things. . . ."

"You should call anytime. I mean that. If I can't talk, I'll say so, and get back to you. But if anyone in this case has the right to call, it's you."

"Thank you. It means a lot to have you say so. In fact, it was one of the reasons I called. I don't want to be a bother, calling at the wrong time. Would it be possible for us to just set a time— maybe once a week if you think that's reasonable—when we could sit down, and you could tell me what's been happening. Bad news, good news, no news. I don't care. I just find it helps to know what's going on."

"Of course. I should have told you what to expect. I always get back to families on a regular basis—just like you said, bad news, good news, no news. And if something big comes up, something I think you should know about right away, I'll call right away. As for scheduling something regular—let's play that by ear. I can try to take a run out later this week—" Mars hesitated and checked his pocket calendar. "Sorry, I've got my son on my own this week. His mother won't be back until Sunday, so . . ."

"Couldn't you bring him along?" Grace said. "Have him bring a swimsuit and we could have lunch by the pool—" She stopped. "I'm sorry. I'm being presumptuous. Where would it be easiest for you to meet?"

"Your place is fine," Mars said. "Chris has a soccer game in the afternoon in Blaine, which means we'll be out west anyway. We'd need to leave around one-thirty to get to the game, but if that works for you. . . ."

"Noon, then?" Grace said.

"We'll be there at noon. You said there was something else you wanted to ask?"

"Guy Corson," she said, "the new owner of the Timberwolves. He called to say how sorry he was. He and Duke were good friends. Duke had known the previous owner of the club, Ross Geld—but they weren't close. Duke was impressed with the direction Guy was taking the club. More than that, I think Duke felt that Guy brought some real principles to the team. Not easy when there's so much pressure on winning at any cost, when twenty-year-old players are paid millions of dollars a year . . . anyway. Guy called and mentioned that if he could help—specifically he said if you needed to talk to him—you should call. He'd make a point of being available."

Mars wasn't at all sure what Corson might know, but that he'd indicated an interest in talking to Mars was promising.

Corson's assistant put Mars on hold when he introduced himself, explaining his reason for calling. She was back on the line in moments.

"Mr. Corson wondered if there was any chance you had time this afternoon? He apologizes for the short notice, but he would like to see you."

They agreed Mars would be over in a half hour. Which would just give Mars enough time with Corson before leaving to pick up Chris.

He hung up and looked at Nettie. "I wonder what that's all about."

"What?"

The sharpness in Nettie's voice reminded Mars that something seemed to be bothering her. But he didn't have time to go into it with her now.

"Guy Corson wants to talk to me. Obviously, I'd like to talk to him, but I really didn't hold out much hope he'd have anything to say. I assumed he'd have a conflict of interest—T-Jack being a star

126

player on the Timberwolves. But he's really going out of his way—"

The phone rang again, and Nettie reached for it as Mars started out. She called him back. "Mars? It's for you. Corson's office."

Corson's assistant said, "Mr. Bahr, sorry to change plans so soon, but Mr. Corson was wondering if you'd mind meeting him down by the river—there are some benches on the river path just below the post office. It's such a beautiful day, and Mr. Corson's been on airplanes for the better part of the past two weeks. He said he'd love to get some fresh air—if you don't mind."

Mars stood silent for a moment after agreeing to meet Corson by the river. Then he said, "Now I know something's going on."

"He's canceled?" Nettie said.

"No. Wants to meet down by the river, instead of in his office. His assistant said he 'wanted some fresh air.' Ha."

"Why not?" Nettie said. "If I could work by the river today instead of in this tomb, I'd be there in a flash."

"If Guy Corson wants fresh air," Mars said, "he can afford to have it trucked into his office. I'm beginning to think what I'm going to be getting from Corson is hot air."

The river paths just north of downtown had been developed in the past four years, giving the Mississippi long overdue recognition from a city that owed its existence to the river. Up until the time the paths had been built and the Stone Arch Bridge had been opened for pedestrian traffic, you could have been in downtown Minneapolis every day of your life without ever getting close to the river or St. Anthony Falls, which fell just upstream from the Stone Arch Bridge.

For Mars, the river near downtown had been the site of more than one murder investigation. In the river's derelict days, homeless people who lived under the river's four downtown bridges would freeze to death, set themselves on fire, bludgeon each other with whatever was at hand, or—most surprising of all—die from what passed as natural causes. Whatever the cause of death, most ended up as floaters in the Mississippi.

A couple of years earlier, a teenager from suburban Edina had been murdered on the Father Hennepin Bluffs, just across the river from downtown, and Mars had spent months chasing blind leads until a witness had come forward. That witness had been Evelyn Rau. She of the Blank Postcards. A chance meeting between the two of them after the investigation closed had led to a friendship and then to what, in Mars's life, could loosely be described as a relationship. Evelyn's leaving a few months back to do academic research in England had, as much as anything, revealed to Mars that his life was lopsided.

It was as he'd looked at his watch that he caught sight of Guy Corson approaching.

You wouldn't know from looking at him that Guy Corson was one of the wealthiest men in Minnesota. Corson looked more like the guy he had been thirty years ago than the self-made multibillionaire he had become since he'd left professional basketball. He was tall, maybe six feet one or two, which is what you'd expect of a guy who'd played college and pro basketball back in the days when basketball was a still a game at both levels. He probably wouldn't have been tall enough to play in today's NBA. But among ordinary mortals on an August afternoon he looked big.

Corson carried a suit jacket, his tie loosened, wearing large sunglasses. Mars recognized him from newspaper photos—most of which had appeared around the time Corson had bought—with his own hard, cold cash—the Timberwolves. Before that time, the business community knew who he was, but your average Minnesotan wouldn't have given him a second look. Even now, when his picture turned up regularly in the paper, especially in the sports section, he wasn't the kind of guy who drew attention to himself.

Corson paused, noticing Mars looking at him. Mars nodded in Corson's direction, and Corson moved toward him.

"I appreciate your coming down here," Corson said. "It's too nice a day to be in the office. . . ." He dropped down slowly on the bench, bracing himself with his left hand. "What guys my age got from playing pro ball was bad joints," he said. What he said next went a long way with Mars toward establishing Corson's credibility.

"To be honest, I thought it would be better if you didn't come to my office."

Mars turned his eyes out toward the river, giving Corson the opportunity to take the conversation where it needed to go.

"I have a problem," Corson said. "I want T-Jack off the team. But I need to have a solid legal basis for breaking his contract, or he'll take us to the cleaners in a wrongful termination suit. With punitive damages, we could end up being liable for several multiples of his contract value. And if he proves wrongful termination, our insurers aren't going to cover the loss...."

"Why don't you just trade him?" Mars said.

Corson gave Mars a look of deep regret. "Exactly what we were in the process of doing when Terri was murdered. The people who were interested in T-Jack before the murder have backed off. No surprises there. He never was an easy sell. Now? He's a pariah."

Mars said, "What I don't understand is this. You pay a guy millions of dollars a year, he's your star player, highest scorer in the division, and keeping T-Jack a Woofie isn't your priority?"

Corson winced. "We hate it when people call the team Woofies."

"Sorry. Look. I understand your legal issues. I'm just not clear on why you're so anxious to have him off the team. Everything I hear, T-Jack is your ticket to the championship. Without T-Jack, the team isn't going to break five hundred for the foreseeable future."

Corson stretched his legs. He took his dark glasses off and instantly looked ten years older. He had dark circles under his eyes, deep wrinkles down his cheeks, drooping eyelids.

"You don't read the sports pages regularly, do you?"

Mars shook his head. "I go through the paper every day, but the sports pages don't get a lot of my time."

Corson's glasses went back on. He said, "You know that I paid for the team with my own money?"

Mars nodded. "I remember hearing that. Not sure what it means, the way these deals get cut."

Corson grinned. "You're right to be skeptical. The important point is that I put at least five times more capital—my own money—into this purchase than any other owner in the league. I did that for a lot of reasons, only two of which are important to this conversation. Number one, I didn't want the hassle of going to the city or over to the legislature, hat in hand, crawling all the way, to beg for financial backing. Number two, I wanted to run the team my way."

"Meaning?" Mars said.

"Meaning I wanted the game to mean what it meant when I played. When players had a real connection to each other, to their communities, to the whole idea of sportsmanship. Where a winning team was the natural outcome of having that connection in place. Players today join a team as individuals, play as individuals, and get paid as individuals. It's ruining the sport. Not to say what it's doing to twenty-year-old kids who go from having nothing to having everything. And I do mean everything. People hanging on them, women lined up outside the garage when they leave stadiums in their seventy-five-thousand-dollar vehicles. All they have to do is open the passenger-side door. And I'm sorry to say a lot of passenger-side doors get opened...."

Mars said, "T-Jack opened the passenger-side door regularly?"

Corson leaned forward, elbows on his knees, balancing his chin in his hands. "Not T-Jack. Situation like that, he might have to talk to the woman once she was in the car. For the younger guys, the girls outside the garage are like Halloween candy. There for the asking. Guys that never got anything without a struggle can't resist a setup like that. Some of them actually start relationships with the girls—if you count letting the same girl in the car more than once as a relationship. My guess is T-Jack stuck to high-end call girls. Probably had somebody else make the call for him."

Corson straightened himself up again, wincing slightly as he did so. It was obvious he had a hard time finding a comfortable position. And that he was used to dealing with physical discomfort. He held both arms straight out in front of him, stretching his muscles.

He dropped his arms abruptly, then he said, "Here's where I'm going with this. I want the ability to build a team that is a team. To build a team where character counts for something. To do that I have to play hardball with star players. I'd have to ax some guys who are important to winning—at least in the short term—essentially because of attitude problems. My theory is, with guys that make it to the NBA, they've all got the basic goods to be outstanding ballplayers. With a few exceptions—Michael Jordan, Charles Barkley, Magic Johnson being the obvious examples—the difference in players is largely confidence, discipline, and attitude. If you start rewarding players for a good attitude, I expect to see a performance improvement. And eventually, when the team is really in synch, we should start winning games a team of equivalent ability would lose." He looked over at Mars. "Basically, I'm saying I'd rather have five guys on the floor, with 75 percent of Michael Jordan's ability, playing at 110 percent of their ability, than five guys with 90 percent of Michael Jordan's ability playing at 50 percent of their ability. I call it my five times 110 objective. And my theory is, the way you get a guy to play at 110 percent is to develop and reward character and team play. Not just individual performance. Which is how we reward now."

Corson sighed, looking a little sheepish about how emotional he'd gotten talking about what he wanted to do with the team. "You ever see the movie *Chariots of Fire?*"

Mars nodded. "Liked it a lot. One of my kid's favorites. Kids love heroes."

"Exactly," Corson said. "The Scottish guy that ran better than his physical ability? That's the kind of player I'm looking for. And I can tell you from personal experience, there's nothing more rewarding than playing on a team that is a team. Where players care about each other as much as they care about how many points they've scored at the final buzzer. Right now, you give most players a choice between scoring thirty points and winning the game, they're gonna go for the points. They won't say it, but actions speak louder than words. Points are the name of the game. And playing the game that way just isn't any fun. The points? That's about another couple million a year in contract negotiations, a shot at endorsements, the best-looking girls lining up by your car down at the garage—not about loving the game."

Corson started making movements like he needed to be leaving. Then he sat back down again and said, "The truth is, T-Jack represents everything that's wrong with the team right now. The other players don't trust him, are afraid of him—they'll never play at 110 percent with T-Jack on the floor. With T-Jack on the team, we will go as far as one star player can take us and no further. We'll never win a division title and for sure we will never win an NBA championship. To build my dream team, T-Jack's gotta go."

Corson stood up, pushing off the bench with his arms and shoulders rather than using his legs to stand. "I've enjoyed talking with you. If you can think of anything I can do to help, I'm more than willing. Apart from what I've told you about the team, Duke DuCain was a friend. What happened to Duke, his daughter..." Corson shook his head.

Mars rose, shaking Corson's hand. He'd enjoyed meeting Corson and, more than that, he liked the guy. But ending this way felt a little incomplete. It was hard to understand why a man like Corson would take forty-five minutes out of a busy day to come down to the river and tell Mars his strategy for building a better basketball team.

As Corson started to walk away he turned back. "You don't read the sports pages much, but you said you do read the *Strib*?"

Mars tilted his head, trying to understand the question. "Sure, I read the *Star-Tribune*."

"Sunday, Wednesday, and Fridays?"

"Pretty much every day."

Corson nodded. "Good. And I meant to ask. You're pretty sure there's no way T-Jack could have murdered Terri?"

Mars stared at Corson without saying anything. Corson didn't look like he expected an answer. Then Corson did leave. Mars watched Corson walk toward the road, noticing a black Mercedes pull out farther down the river road. The Mercedes pulled up at the curb, and Corson opened the back door, eased himself into the back seat, and pulled the door shut. The Mercedes was gone in the blink of an eye.

Now Mars knew what Corson's agenda had been. He just didn't know what it meant.

CHAPTER

12

"Two Jucy Lucys and we'll share a basket of fries. A Coke for me and . . . ?" Mars looked at Nettie, raising his eyebrows. The noise level in Matt's Tavern was so loud that Nettie leaned toward him, cupping her ear.

"What do you want to drink?" Mars said, exaggerating the pronunciation of each word.

Nettie said to the waitress, "You don't have Evian, right?"

The waitress looked at Nettie like she was crazy.

"Okay. Give me a bottle of lemonade." To Mars, after the waitress left their table, Nettie said, "I might need two Jucy Lucys, just for me."

Mars took his wallet out and laid a twenty, a ten, and two ones on the table between them. "This is what I've got to get me to payday. Plus some change in my pocket. Payday, in case you don't remember, is three days from now. And I've got Chris until Denise comes back. So I've got to hold to my original offer, which was to buy you *a* Jucy Lucy. Meaning one."

Nettie frowned at him. "So why did you call and offer to buy me a Jucy Lucy at Matt's? Would have made more sense if you'd asked me to take you out to dinner."

"Because," Mars said, "you were one of two people in my life who seemed to have a burr under their saddle. Chris being the other one. He's doing a sleepover at a friend's, so you got the call."

Nettie's eyes dropped to the table. Absentmindedly, she picked up the twenty, then dropped it down again. "You made a lousy deal on your divorce agreement. Chris being the age he is, you and Denise should work something else out. I don't know how you live on what you've got left after child support."

Mars leaned back in the booth, stretching his legs out under the table diagonally across from where Nettie was sitting. The waitress came with their drinks and an empty glass for Mars. As she put the glass on the table she gave Mars a second look and said, "No ice, right?"

"You got it," Mars said. Mars popped the Coke can and poured most of it into the glass. He sat forward again, trying to find a voice level just under the din of the bar.

"The agreement isn't really the problem. It's the extras that are killing me."

"Like what?" Nettie said, hunching forward to hear.

He twisted the glass between his hands. It was the first time he'd said out loud that he had problems with the way things were working financially between Denise and him. More than that. He hadn't really thought about it himself at a conscious level. Saying it aloud made him realize he'd been feeling edgy about money and how he and Denise were handling money for the past several months.

Thinking as he spoke, he said, "Well, it started with the stipulated support agreement. I wanted it in the agreement that Chris would have new clothes. That sounds—I don't know—like a picky point, maybe. But I grew up in foster homes, and I remember how it felt never to have new clothes. Never to be able to have something to wear that was cool. The closest I got was something that had been cool maybe two years before it came to me. And believe me, that isn't cool."

"With what you're giving Denise, Chris should be able to have new clothes every day of the school year."

Mars shook his head. "The thing is, Denise balked at that point. She is—God love her—tight as a pin when it comes to money. It's an emotional thing with her, just the way new clothes for Chris is an emotional thing for me. So to resolve it, I just said I'd buy Chris's clothes. . . ."

"In addition to the child support?"

Mars nodded. "Which wasn't that big of a deal when Chris was four. But I can tell you it's getting to be a big deal now that Chris is almost eleven. Clothes for preteens are, like, twice as expensive as what he's been wearing, and he's changing a full size every six months."

"I can't believe this," Nettie said. "I mean, I like Denise, but Mars, any rational person looking at this deal would say you're getting robbed. You know what else, Mars? When you were first divorced, Denise probably did have Chris most of the time. But now, he's with you as much as he's with Denise."

Mars stared at his Coke. Having brought the subject up, a flood of nagging injustices took over his consciousness. He swallowed long on the Coke, put the glass down, and exhaled. "What's really aggravating me is I have this gut feeling that some of the money things are related to this guy she's seeing. Carl."

"Like how?"

Mars tapped the bottom of the glass lightly on the table while he thought about it. "Small stuff. Like when she first started going out with Carl, Chris was too young to mow the grass. I'd always paid to have the grass mowed when Denise and I were married, so I gave her an extra ten bucks a week to have the neighbor kid keep mowing the grass, shoveling the snow. . . ."

Nettie put both elbows on the table and dropped her head into her hands. "This is just beyond belief. You are the world's biggest sucker."

"I know I didn't have to do that, Nettie. It just felt better—to me—to do it that way. I found out a year or so ago that Carl had been mowing the lawn. So I said to Denise, does it make sense for me to pay Carl to mow the grass? I kind of thought she just hadn't been thinking about it, and when I raised the question, she'd say right away, 'Of course not.' But she got real tense, and said Carl said it was only fair if he was doing the job that Denise should be able to keep the money. Carl told her it wouldn't be fair for Denise to lose money because Carl was helping out. Never mind that Carl was storing all of his cabinet inventory for his business in the basement of the house I pay for or that he was eating two, maybe three meals a week at Denise's—meals I paid the groceries for. There are a bunch of other things like that. . . ."

"For instance?"

"Well, year before last, Denise had a cash flow problem. So I paid for soccer camp. She said she'd pay me back, but I told her to forget it. Last year, she didn't say anything about paying. Just assumed I'd pay. And last January Chris earned some money taking care of the neighbor's dog. Denise made him put aside—I don't know—like, ninety bucks toward soccer camp. But when Chris's fees were due, the whole bill came to me again. So, I said to Denise, 'What's the deal? I thought Chris put some of his dog money aside for camp.' And Denise said Carl said it made more sense to put that money in Chris's college fund. Like this is Carl's decision? That, and Denise and Chris are covered on my health insurance. When the coverage started requiring a co-pay on doctor visits, Denise said Carl said, because the insurance was my responsibility under the agreement, I should reimburse her for the co-pays. And it wasn't just that she was asking for the money, it was that she'd bring Carl into it at all. She didn't look at me. She seemed almost embarrassed. Which made me think he'd really given her a hard time about it, or she wouldn't have asked. And it made me realize how much I've appreciated that whatever our differences have been, we'd always been respectful of each other. For the first time, I felt like I couldn't exactly trust Denise. That bothered me more than the money."

Mars shook his head, annoyed with himself. "Talking about this is starting to feel like scratching an itch until it bleeds. It feels real satisfying at first, but in the end, all you do is damage. And it's just what I said I'd never do when Denise and I were divorced. That I'd never let money get to be an issue between us."

"From where I'm sitting," Nettie said, "you're not letting money become an issue. Denise is *making* money an issue. Here's the bottom line, partner. When you got divorced you voluntarily paid child support three times over the state guidelines, right?"

"Yes, because I wanted Denise and Chris to be able to stay in the house. Denise didn't want to work when Chris was young, and I wanted her to be able to stay home. Better for all of us. And you know as well as anybody, with my job, I couldn't be counted on to be around on a regular basis to take Chris."

Their waitress came up to the table fast, dropping the big red plastic basket of fries in the center of the table and putting a tissue-wrapped Jucy Lucy in front of each of them. To Mars she said, "You I don't have to tell how to eat a Jucy Lucy." She nodded toward Nettie. "Has she been briefed?"

"I've brought her here a couple of times before," Mars said. "I'll refresh her memory before she bites."

"Not necessary," Nettie said. "The first time I had a Jucy Lucy, nobody warned me. I had a blister on the roof of my mouth for three days after. . . ."

In a singsong voice, the waitress said, "Start eating around the edges while the cheese in the center cools. . . ."

Nettie waved her off. "I know, I know." She turned back to Mars. "All I'm gonna say is this. Go back and calculate what you'd be paying Denise under current state guidelines against your current salary. I'm willing to bet you're still at least twice over what you'd be obligated for. . . ."

"That's not the way it works," Mars said. "The state guidelines are set as a percentage of net monthly income. I pay three times the state percentage guideline for my income."

"Except," Nettie said, "for all these ridiculous 'extras' you're tossing in gratis. As long as you're significantly over the guidelines, Denise should not be taking you to the cleaners on all this other stuff. She should be handling that out of what you give her. And for crissakes, don't feel guilty about it. You've been a saint about this. A stupid saint, but a saint."

Mars felt a mixture of relief and guilt. It wasn't until now that he realized how much the situation with Denise had been bothering him. And he felt a little embarrassed. True confessions weren't re-

138

ally part of his relationship with Nettie. To change the subject, he said, "This dinner—modest as it is—wasn't supposed to be about my problems. Have I been imagining it, or has something been bothering you?"

Nettie pursed her lips, looked up at Mars quickly, then looked away. "It's just that I'm not used to working as a threesome. Sometimes it feels like the communication lines are out of whack."

Mars didn't know what to say. He had felt that having Danny Borg on the case had been a luxury. It had made a huge difference in how much they could get done quickly.

"You don't like Danny?

Nettie shook her head. "Danny's fine. A bit of a toilet seat, but fine."

"A *toilet seat*? You call somebody a toilet seat in the same breath that you say he's just fine?"

"It's a line from *Catcher in the Rye,* Mars. Holden Caulfield describes somebody as being as sensitive as a toilet seat. It's just another way of saying what you've said all along: that Danny isn't very sensitive. But I do like him and I think he's good at what he does. I trust him to do his job right. Which is more than I can say for a lot of other people in the department."

"Give me an example of what you mean about communication lines being out of whack."

Nettie came back at him quick. "Surveillance on T-Jack's house. I didn't even know that was happening until Danny said something about it when we were all in the squad room. . . ."

"The last thing I meant to do was make you feel bad."

Nettie reached up with both hands and pulled at her hair. In a tense hiss, she said, "This isn't about my feelings, Mars. And it makes me damn mad that you think this is about my feelings. It's about keeping the investigation organized. What has always been good about the way we work together is that each of us does what we're best at. I'm best at keeping everything organized, coordinating, managing the data. You're good at the hands-on, street-level, intuitive stuff. But if you go off doing things with Danny that I don't even know about, the investigation is going to start falling

139

apart. What I think would work best would be if you'd have everything go through me. Same as always. You want surveillance on T-Jack's house? You call me, and I'll call Danny. Or whoever needs to be called. Then I know it's going on and I can track what's happening with surveillance. Like that."

Mars said, "You're right. I've always been a lousy manager."

"So let me manage. And speaking about keeping me in the loop, you haven't said anything about how your meeting with Corson went. Did he do more than blow hot air?"

"I think so. But he was being real coy. He'd like to be rid of T-Jack. Thinks T-Jack is what's wrong with the team. The problem is, the team could have significant liability issues if they terminate T-Jack's contract. Corson spent most of the time talking about where he wants the team to go. Then, just as he was leaving, he said a couple of things that I think were his way of telling me what he wanted me to know without telling me."

"What did he say?"

"Corson asked me if I read the *Strib*—Sunday, Wednesday, and Friday. He said that with real emphasis. Like there was more meaning than just the words."

Mars paused, taking a big bite out of his Jucy Lucy. It was the perfect cheeseburger. Rich beef flavor, crisp, seared meat, and melted cheese stuffed between two meat patties. He nodded as he chewed, swallowed hard, and said, "The thing he said that really sent a chill down my spine. He asked if I was sure there wasn't any way T-Jack could have committed the murder. He said it the same way he asked about my reading the *Strib*. Like he meant a lot more than he was saying."

"Does he know about the meeting with Grace and Duke?"

"I assume he does. It's been in the paper."

"The comment about reading the *Strib* on Sunday, Wednesday, and Friday?"

"Yeah?"

"Those are the days that Melanie Gonzales-Robb's column runs."

"The gossip column? I've never read it."

Nettie nodded. "Mostly stuff on local media personalities. But she does stuff on sports types too. I don't remember ever seeing anything on T-Jack, but maybe I missed it. I'll do a search on the archives and see what I can find."

"So what you're thinking is Melanie Gonzales-Robb might have run something on T-Jack in her column that'll tell us something we should know. That's what Corson meant."

Nettie shrugged. "Like I said. It won't be hard to check online."

"Worth checking," Mars said. He scooped up the check, pulling one last French fry from the basket. "You ready to go?"

"Let me get the check, Mars. You've taken me out a lot. I've never bought you dinner. And this is cheap."

Mars held the check away from her. "Look at it this way, Nettie. Money that I spend on buying you a Jucy Lucy is money Denise doesn't get."

Except it didn't work that way when Mars tried to pay at the cash register.

"Your bill's been paid," Mike said. "Need to keep you stoked up to put that son of a bitch behind bars."

"Mike, I can't accept free meals. It's against department rules."

Matt's owner came up behind Mike.

"This isn't a free meal," Scott said. "Someone paid your check." He folded his arms across his chest and looked stubborn.

Mars shook his head, then walked back to the booth he and Nettie had been sitting in. He dropped a ten on the table in addition to the two bucks he'd already left.

"You are such a sucker," Nettie said as they left.

"Saved me five bucks over what I would have paid if I'd gotten the check," Mars said. "In my budget, five bucks is a big deal."

The red message light was glowing on Mars's answering machine when he got back to the apartment. It was Chris, telling Mars when he could be picked up in the morning at the Ziemers'.

141

The wall calendar was next to the phone. Mars's blood ran cold as he looked at it. Three days down already. Lots of birds out of the bush, nothing but a bunch of feathers in hand.

And tomorrow would be T-Jack minus six.

CHAPTER

13

"Danny. What've we got from surveillance and neighborhood interviews?"

Mars, Nettie, and Danny were in the department lounge. Mars and Nettie were on the big leather couch, Nettie with her feet tucked up under her, a partially frozen bottle of Evian water at hand, Mars leaning back, legs extended, his first Coke of the day on the table next to the couch. Danny was on the leather chair, sitting forward, looking like an eager bird dog, even at 7:00 A.M.

"Nothing worth anything." Danny's eyebrows tightened. "One thing that seems weird. T-Jack has hardly left the house at all since we put surveillance in. From what I know, he's not a homebody. Now he hardly ever leaves."

"He's got the kid to take care of, right?" Nettie said.

"Yeah, but his mother's been there a lot. She's probably the one taking care of the kid."

Mars said, "Find a reason for having something delivered to T-Jack. Something for him to sign—from us, the medical examiner's office, whatever. Have that happen when we haven't seen anything of him for a few hours. Make sure he is there and hasn't found some way of slipping out."

Nettie said, "Can't be any fun for him to go out. Nobody much liked him before. Now everyone thinks he killed his wife."

"That's probably part of it," Mars said. "But let's be sure. Nettie.

Where are we on enhancing the videotape from the parking lot at DuCain Industries?"

"Should have something back today. What I'm hearing isn't encouraging. But the lab has sent it out to another lab that has new equipment they think may be able to squeeze a few more pixels out of the image. So, we're still trying."

"Danny, I'd like you to touch base with..." Mars hesitated, trying to remember the name of the *Strib*'s gossip columnist. "Who you said last night, Nettie—the woman who writes the gossip column..."

"Melanie Gonzales-Robb."

"Melanie Gonzales-Robb," Mars said. "When I met with Guy Corson, he made an indirect reference that Nettie and I think might have something to do with Gonzales-Robb's column. Have you found anything on-line, Nettie?"

Nettie shook her head. "I checked the *Strib*'s archives as soon as I got home last night. T-Jack shows up twice in her column—once after his kid was born and then in connection with references to the team. Nothing very interesting. For sure nothing that tells us anything about Terri DuCain's murder. I printed them out. They're on my desk. I'll give them to you, Danny, but they're not going to be much help."

"Talk to Gonzales-Robb," Mars said to Danny. "Find out if there's anything about T-Jack that Gonzales-Robb didn't print. Corson was making a point, I'm sure of that."

As they walked out of the lounge, Danny said, "This may not be revelant to what we've been talking about, but I'm curious..."

Nettie said, "*Rele*vant, Danny."

"Whatever. And I don't mean to get too personal here or anything, but I've wondered. Do you ever wear anything that's got colors, Nettie?"

"I've seen her wear denim from time to time," Mars said. "Other than that, she lives by a black-and-white-only rule."

"Gray," Nettie said. "Sometimes I wear gray."

"Why only black and white?" Danny said.

"Keeps my life simple," Nettie said.

144

"Not a bad idea," Danny said. "I like it."

"Monochromatic," Nettie said.

"What's that?"

"One color. Or variations thereon."

"Hot damn," Danny said. "I get a great idea for simplifying my life and a new word in one deal. Fantastic."

Nettie said, "Where are you headed, Mars?

"I'm going to pick up Chris, then head out to the Shoreview Lodge to get Vonnie Gerber to take a look at the photos I picked up from Narcotics of Lyle Venema and Matt Weber. And I'm going to get her snapshots of Tanney. I should be back here in a couple hours. Maybe less."

"Iceberg lettuce," Chris said.

Chris had considered the restaurant's salad bar banner and rendered the two-word judgment. "You know what else? I bet over half the stuff in the salad bar comes out of a can."

"You're on," Mars said, relieved that Chris was talking. Even Chris's food-snob persona was preferable to the silent kid of the past couple days. "But I can't afford to lose more than a quarter."

Chris looked sideways at Mars, as if he might ask a question, but he got out of the car without saying anything and followed Mars toward the restaurant.

Vonnie Gerber gave Mars a little wave from the reception podium, signaling him to follow her toward the back of the restaurant.

"Okay if my son checks out the salad bar while we talk?"

"Oh, sure," Vonnie said. "Does he want a hamburger or something?"

"No, thanks," Chris said.

"What a cutie," Vonnie said, watching Chris head off toward the main dining room. "Let's go back to the office. "I've got about twenty minutes before the lunch crowd starts."

It didn't take twenty minutes. Vonnie recognized Lyle Venema and Matt Weber within thirty seconds of starting to turn the picture ID pages Narcotics had given Mars based on the description that Vonnie had given Mars.

She shuddered as she looked at them. "What are their names?" Then she held up both hands. "No. Don't tell me. I don't want to know names. It's enough that you know. What happens now?"

"You've given me what I need to know. And your pictures will make it easier to find Tanney. You've been a big help."

"Canned beets, canned button mushrooms, canned peas, canned olives—green, ripe, and pimento—canned corn, canned pearl onions. . . ."

"You win the quarter. Iceberg lettuce?"

"Of course." As they got into the car, Chris said, "What do you have to do now?"

"Good question." Mars sat in the driver's seat, clutching the steering wheel, tapping his fingers against the molded plastic. With what he'd gotten from Mitsch and Vonnie Gerber, he was feeling confident that Tanney was who he needed to find. Tanney and Sater. Even one of them would be good.

He could always go back to Whiskey-Tango-Tango-land and put the screws to Lyle Venema. Squeeze him until more of that sour stink oozed out of him. But that felt like a waste of time. The last sight Mars had of Lyle Venema, Venema looked like he planned to be hard to find. Which meant it would take time and effort to find him, with no guarantee Venema would have more to say than he had when he'd been leaking flop sweat in front of Jerome Hebb.

No. Mars's priority had to be Tanney. He'd have Danny talk to Narcotics about keeping an eye out for Venema, finding an excuse to haul him in on something. Then Mars would have some leverage for getting Venema to talk about Tanney, and Mars wouldn't have wasted his time looking for the bug-bitten creep.

"I need to do two things," Mars said. "I need to see if I can find any phone records that link our suspects and T-Jack. And I need to hope that the video we've got from the parking lot at DuCain Industries tells us something solid about who it was that T-Jack signaled."

Mars looked over at Chris. "You okay hanging out in the squad room for a few hours? Have your algebra book with you?"

146

Chris frowned. "Yeah. What am I gonna have for lunch?"

"Whatever you want as long as it costs a quarter."

"Ha," Chris said. Then his face brightened. "Dad? Can I go to Different Noodle on the skyway?"

The Different Noodle was a displaced New Yorker's attempt at a real delicatessen in the heart of downtown Minneapolis. Mars had taken Chris there the first week it opened, and Chris had become an instant fan. Mars liked the place for its seat-of-the-pants atmosphere. In Mars's mind, the Noodle was what a deli would look like if you'd overslept, waking with no clean clothes, sitting on the side of the bed in your underwear, scratching your head while you decide what you want to do that day. Then the light bulb goes on, and you say, "I'm gonna open a deli and have it up and running by noon today." *Voilà!* The Different Noodle.

Mars considered his wallet. "Yeah. You can go to Different Noodle on two conditions. You've got a seven-fifty spending limit and you've gotta be off the skyway and back at city hall before one o'clock."

"Seven seventy-five, counting my quarter," Chris said. "Dad? Could James come downtown and go with me?"

Mars frowned. Adding James to any equation always made things more complicated. On the other hand, Chris had been spending more time at James's over the past month than James had spent with them.

"I don't have time to pick him up," Mars said.

"You don't have to pick him up. He can take the bus. Then we can walk over to the Different Noodle together."

Mars gave in. "Okay. But your budget stays at seven-fifty and you've both got to be back at city hall by one."

"Seven seventy-five," Chris said.

It took Mars twice as long as it should have to bully his way past three Qwest gatekeepers to the person who not only knew what Mars needed to know, but had an appetite for working through the questions he raised.

Stewart Jedrezek was a hustler. High energy, born to take responsibility and make decisions. He liked problems.

"Here's the deal," Mars said. "I know a guy's name. I need to find out if he made a cell phone call on a specific date and who the call went to. I know just enough about cell phones to know if the guy had a cell phone in his name, we can get that information. What gets tricky is we'd like to pinpoint the location from which the call was made and the location for the receiving cell phone. Last time we tried to get cell phone evidence that identified the location from where the call was placed, we got nowhere. What I was told maybe a year ago was that you can pinpoint where a call is being made from while the cell is in use. But when the connection's been broken, all you've got is a record of the sending cell phone number, the time and date the call was made, and the receiving cell phone number and time and date. I'm hoping in the past year you've come up with better technology. . . ."

Jedrezek shook his head. "Sorry. Once the connection is broken, the information evaporates into the Ethernet. Totally different technology to create the record of the call and to pinpoint the location of an active call. I think it's probably technically possible to create some kind of mapping system that would generate and retain the precise location of every call made. Thing is, where's the market for that kind of thing? The cost would be huge, and other than cops and wives that are getting cheated on, who wants the information? Nobody who's willing to pay the freight, I'll tell you that."

"So we're still where we were a year ago."

"Yup. But getting the customer cell numbers shouldn't be a problem. The caller's phone may not be on our database—what I mean is, he may not be a Qwest subscriber—but that information is only technically proprietary. The way things work, every cell provider knows every other cell provider's customers. So you get me the name, and I'll get you the cell phone number. Problem we're going to have is access to the Customer records. Which will get you to calls made from that number. But you know that."

Mars sighed. "Yeah, I do know that. But if you can get me the number, that's a place to start. That and the service provider. I'll have to work through the County Attorney's Office for a phone record warrant."

"Okay. So the next thing you've gotta hope is that your customer name is unique. Or at least unusual."

"John Sater," Mars said. "S-a-t-e-r. I'm looking for a cell number for a John Sater. And, while you're at it, if you can get me a cell number for a Paul Tanney—T-a-n-n-e-y—that would be great."

As Mars drove back to city hall, he thought through the justification for a search warrant for Sater's phone records. It was pretty thin. T-Jack at the window at DuCain Towers and Sater's relationship with Paul Tanney were, at best, circumstantial details. He need to get together with Glenn Gjerde from the County Attorney's Office to talk through a warrant.

There was a message from Nettie on his desk when he got to the squad room: *Turn your cell phone on, daddy! Your son and his pal James are being held in the Juvenile Division. James was shoplifting on the skyway.*

Mars saw Chris as he walked into the Juvenile Division. The door to the interrogation room was partially open, and Chris was sitting opposite the door. He looked green with anxiety. Even without seeing James, Mars could hear him talking.

"I know what I was doing was wrong. But I guess getting caught doing something like this when you're young is good, huh? I mean, like, I've learned an important lesson. What if I hadn't gotten caught until I was twenty or something? By then, maybe I'd be robbing banks—or convenience stores. Which would be worse for everybody . . ."

Mars walked into the interrogation room. Nettie had been leaning on the wall, facing James. Chris was silent, but he was literally shaking with a combination of fear and emotion. A Juvie officer sat at the head of the table, staring at James with an expression somewhere between fascination and disbelief.

Nettie pushed away from the wall. To the Juvie officer she said, "Before I go, I just want to say two things." She pointed at Chris. "This is real." Then she pointed at James. "*That* is an act."

As she left, rolling her eyes in Mars's direction, she said, "You coming up to the division before you leave?"

Mars nodded. Then he said to the Juvie officer, "We need to talk."

To the boys he said, "Can I trust you to stay here for five minutes without getting into trouble?"

"Mr. Bahr," James said, his face contorted into seriousness. "This wasn't Chris's fault. . . ."

"What is and isn't Chris's fault is between Chris and me, James. I'm asking if I can trust you for five minutes?"

"No problem," James said, an angelic smile on his face.

"Your kid called nine-one-one from a skyway phone," the Juvie officer said as they stood in a hallway outside the interrogation room. "He turned in the motormouth. But the officer who responded to the call picked them both up. I've listened to the tape myself, Mars. It was Chris on the nine-one-one call. He even described his pal as the 'perpetrator.' " The Juvie officer paused, grinning. Then he shook his head. "What I would give some thought to, if I were you, is keeping Chris off the skyways on his own. Better yet, not letting Chris go anywhere with the Ziemer kid without adult supervision."

Mars nodded. "You're right. It was sloppy of me to turn the two of them loose on their own. Sorry for the trouble. Have James's parents been called?"

The Juvie officer looked at his watch. "Yeah. More than an hour ago. I can release Chris to you. He won't be facing charges. The Ziemer kid I'm gonna have jump through some hoops. He needs the lesson. But as soon as a parent shows up, he can go too." The Juvie officer gave Mars a wave and headed out.

Which was when Rona Ziemer showed up.

She came at Mars fast. "You let those two boys go off on the skyway by themselves?"

"A mistake, Rona. Just like your letting James take the bus downtown was probably a mistake. I've talked to the Juvenile officer. James is going to face some charges—but that's going to be pretty much a scare tactic. He won't have any permanent record—"

"*James* is going to face some charges? Not Chris?"

"The officer said Chris wasn't involved."

"Oh, *right,*" she said. "Cops take care of their own is how that works."

Mars thought about how good it would feel to stuff something down Rona Ziemer's throat. He let the thought pass, then said, "Have your attorney look at the investigating officer's report, Rona. Chris doesn't get any special breaks because he's a cop's kid. But he doesn't get any undeserved knocks because he's a cop's kid either."

Mars started to move away. Rona Ziemer had never been easy to deal with, and their present circumstances brought out all her worst qualities. More talk wouldn't get them anywhere, and Mars was just tired enough to say or do something intemperate if he didn't move on.

Behind him, he heard her say, "You've got some responsibility in this, even if you pull strings to get your kid off. . . ."

Mars and Chris took the elevator back to the squad room in silence. What Mars minded more than anything was that Chris was back in the emotional hole he'd climbed out of before he and James had become embroiled in their skyway adventure. If anything, the hole seemed darker and deeper than it had before.

He put his hand on Chris's shoulder as they walked into the squad room, giving it a light squeeze. "Wait for me in the lounge. I've got a couple things to sort out with Nettie, then we'll plan something for dinner. We can talk back at the apartment."

Chris looked so forlorn that Mars changed tack.

"Maybe rent a video. Think about what you'd like to see."

"Could we get *Good Will Hunting*?" Chris said, sounding a little brighter.

A buddy flick, Mars thought. Appropriate.

Nettie made it a point to be busy as Chris walked past her to the lounge. Then she looked over at Mars. "He okay?"

"My working assumption these days is that things could always be worse."

They picked up a pizza after stopping at the video store. Chris still silent and unhappy.

Back at the apartment, as they ate, Mars said, "There's a difference between making a mistake and being responsible. What happened with you and James this afternoon—you weren't responsible. But you made a mistake. I need to know that you know how to avoid making that mistake again."

Chris poked at his pizza with a finger. "I can't trust James," he said, his voice low.

"Which means?"

Chris didn't answer.

Mars waited.

"He's been my best friend since first grade, Dad."

Mars waited.

Chris dropped his eyes down, leaning his head to the side. "I guess I can't do some things with James—I mean, like going over to his house when his parents aren't there. Or going to the mall or downtown. . . ."

"You've gone to his house when his parents weren't there? I thought that was one of our rules, Chris. You don't go to friends' houses when their parents aren't at home. Right?"

Chris looked exhausted by the complications of his life. "They've always been there when I went. But then, sometimes, they'd leave. . . ."

Mars backed off. "Let's just leave it at this. If you're going to spend time with James, it's got to be at soccer, or when I'm with you. That keeps it simple. Okay?"

Chris nodded, but didn't look any less worn out.

"Let's watch the movie. We both need a break."

Saturday Night Fever meets *Ordinary People*," Mars said when the credits started to roll at the end of *Good Will Hunting*. He rose, stretching. Being stationary after a busy day had left him groggy. "I don't know about you, but I'm ready for bed."

"You didn't like the movie?" Chris said.

"It was okay." Mars started to say that for all their talent, Ben Affleck and Matt Damon needed another twenty years before they'd have any deep insights into life's mysteries. He stopped when he looked at Chris and realized from Chris's dreamy expression that he'd completely bought into the movie's half-baked romanticism. It took only a moment's reflection to grasp that any eleven-year-old would want to be Matt Damon's character, a guy with a great group of buddies who leveled pompous adults with his intellect.

By the time they'd cleared their pizza dishes and hit the sack—Mars on the bed, Chris on the floor on the futon he'd used since he'd been four—Mars had shaken off the deep sleepiness he'd felt after the movie. He lay on his back, staring toward the ceiling, aware that Chris wasn't asleep either.

Chris's voice rose toward him in the dark. "Why is it easier to tell someone's awake when the room is totally dark?"

"Haven't really thought about it. But I could tell you weren't sleeping either. Must have something to do with sound. That how a person sounds when they're sleeping is more important than what you can tell with your eyes."

"What are we doing tomorrow?" Chris said.

"I almost forgot," Mars said. "Mrs. DuCain, Terri DuCain's mother, invited you to come out and swim in her pool. I need to brief her on the investigation. We'll go for lunch, and then from there to soccer. But I won't be able to stay for the game. I'm going to have to follow up with Nettie on what we've got from the lab on the parking lot video and run down some people I'm looking for."

"What's their pool like?"

Mars looked down at Chris. "I didn't see the pool the once I was there. But I think you can count on its being pretty nice."

The darkness filled the space between them again. Mars said, "Whatever it was that was bothering you—before what happened with James—it's still bothering you?"

153

The darkness stayed heavy and empty for moments after Mars spoke. Then Chris said, "It isn't mine to tell. I mean, the thing that's been bothering me. It's about somebody else. They should be the ones to talk about it. I can't say anything until they tell."

"What I said before, Chris. I respect your right to privacy. I just want to feel sure that when you're ready to talk, we'll talk."

Mars could feel Chris's nod of consent in the darkness. He hesitated, then said, "I'm feeling like Mom and I kind of pushed you this summer. You went right to Gramma and Grampa's after school was out, then you've been doing soccer camp and advance placement algebra all summer. Hasn't left you much space just for yourself."

"It's been okay," Chris said. His voice lacked conviction.

Mars thought about summers when he was a kid. No ambitious parents setting an agenda. Just endless days of doing whatever you felt like, when you felt like it. By mid-August, you were ready to get back to school.

"The thing I miss most about not being a kid," Mars said, "is the last day of school. Maybe the night of the last day of school. You knew when you woke up the next morning the day belonged to you. What you did, what you wore—your choice. All your responsibilities were over. You got a fresh start. You never get that when you're an adult. Responsibilities keep rolling over on each other. What was great about the last day of school was that it was a full stop. The only time you get that is when you're a kid. I don't want you to miss that."

"But you clear cases. A case ends..."

"Not the same. For every case you clear, two more pop up. And some don't clear clean, or clear at all. Those stay with you. They're never out of mind."

"Like if you don't clear the DuCain case before you go to your new job?"

"Don't even think about it," Mars said. He yawned. The relief of talking to Chris, of having broken through his silent misery,

154

relaxed Mars, made him sleepy again. He fell into a deep sleep without knowing it was happening.

It was a sleep so deep that Mars didn't know that Chris stayed awake for hours.

CHAPTER

14

T-Jack minus five was a good day to go swimming.

They'd walked on a flagstone path away from the house, through a forested area, coming out into broad sunlight on a terrace overlooking the lake. Chris looked over his shoulder at Mars, unable to contain his pleasure. As Mars and Grace sat down in chairs around a glass-topped table, Chris dove into the sparkling water with the casual elegance only young bodies have.

Grace DuCain smiled as she watched Chris. Without looking at Mars she said, "With some children, you can tell on sight. Everything is as it should be. They have good lives ahead. Your son is like that. He's a special boy."

"Apart from my bailing him out of jail, yesterday, it's how he looks to me," Mars said.

Grace turned toward him sharply, looking alarmed. Mars grinned. "He was with the wrong person, in the wrong place, at the wrong time. And I'd given him too much responsibility. It was a learning experience. For both of us. Nothing to worry about."

Mars glanced over at Grace. He was in awe of her self-discipline. And, wearing a pale blue silk shirt and matching trousers, her blue eyes glowing, she was more beautiful than he remembered. In the sunlight, the copper streaks glinted in her silver hair. For the first time he noticed the wedding ring she wore, an old-fashioned setting crowned by an infinitesimally small stone. The

156

kind of ring a guy would buy when he was years away from being able to afford being married. That Grace still wore the ring Duke gave her years ago, that it hadn't been replaced by a rock that represented Duke's achievement since then, was only one of the many things about Grace DuCain that Mars liked.

"The past few days have been interesting," Mars said, feeling bad about having to spoil the beauty of the scene with the sordid details of the investigation. "On the plus side, I think we have a good idea about who T-Jack may have hired. Finding him isn't going to be easy, but I've got some leads that look promising."

"The person who killed Terri." Grace focused hard on Chris in the pool. "The person you think T-Jack hired. What do you know about him?"

"He'd met T-Jack at a place called Dames! Dames! downtown. Not much more than a hanger-on, really. Your garden-variety sociopath—which is to say he doesn't have much of a conscience. Useful if you're going to take money to commit murder."

"Why do you say it will be hard to find him?"

It was Mars's turn to stare in silence at the pool. Then he said, "I think T-Jack is going to make sure that anyone who was involved is going to be hard to find."

"You mean T-Jack would have murdered anyone who was involved in Terri's murder? To protect himself?"

So much for subtle. "I think that's one possibility. Just hard to figure how he'd have done that. We had surveillance on him right off the bat. It's also possible T-Jack would have arranged to have the person leave town, with a new identity. Anyway, we're looking at every angle. I should know in the next few days if finding our perp is going to be hard or easy."

"And if you find who you called the perp, what you said before is that would make proving T-Jack's involvement easier."

"Easier, but not necessarily easy."

Two people from the house came toward the pool, carrying trays.

"I hope Chris likes chicken salad," Grace said.

* * *

Chris was changing into his soccer uniform after lunch as Grace walked Mars out to the car.

"I can't tell you," she said, "what it means to me that you came out. It got me through the end of the week and it's given me the energy to start a new week." She looked up at Mars. "We're having the joint memorial service tomorrow. I've always heard that the police like to attend services—did you plan on coming?"

Mars shook his head. "Overrated, in my estimation. I mean, as an investigative tool. Especially in this case. I don't think there's any possibility our perp is going to want to be anywhere near the memorial service." Mars saw something like disappointment on Grace's face. It had been insensitive of him to talk about the memorial service in terms of its value to the investigation.

"I'd come for your sake," he said in a softer voice. "But time is too important. I need to be working the case." This was the perfect segue to the last thing he'd wanted to tell Grace. "I don't know if you're aware—but I'm leaving the Minneapolis Police Department at the end of the month. The legislature funded an expansion of the state's cold case unit—nothing I'd like better than to charge T-Jack before I make the move. Or at least have the charge within reach . . ."

With an involuntary motion, Grace gripped his arm. "But you won't leave—not if you haven't resolved—"

Mars put his hand over Grace's hand. "It's like I said. I think we have a shot at wrapping this up before I leave. And worst-case scenario, even if it's not where I'd like it to be by September first, this is a high-profile case. It'll have the department's best investigators picking up where I left off. They won't miss a beat. We're going to get this done, with me or without me."

Grace's jawline set. "I was more involved in my husband's business than most people knew, Mars. And if there was one thing I learned by being involved, it's that nothing matters more than having the right people. And keeping the right people. You're the right person for this investigation. And I will pull out all the stops to see that you stay with this job until it's done. You may not know

158

me well, but you know me well enough to know that I'm a determined woman."

Mars put his arm around Grace's shoulders and gave her a quick squeeze. "That I do know. Let's just concentrate on wrapping this thing up by the end of the month. And let me warn you. This is one instance where pulling strings could hurt rather than help. We've got a new police chief who's already pretty sensitive about anyone thinking I'm the only guy who can solve this case. He gets pushed, he's just going to dig his heels in harder than ever."

Grace looked no less determined.

In the car, Chris said, "I didn't think that I liked chicken salad. But I liked *that* chicken salad. I went into the kitchen when I came downstairs from changing, and the cook gave me the recipe. You know what makes it really good? The chicken is baked in cream. That and those little grapes. The cook said they're called champagne grapes. I'm gonna make it for Mom's birthday." Chris frowned. "Carl will probably say something snotty about me making a salad."

Mars gave a quick, sharp glance at Chris. "Like what will Carl say about you making a salad?"

"When I made a Caesar salad on Fourth of July, he said men who liked to cook had lace on their britches. What he meant was, that I was gay. Like I care. I said, 'Guess what? You don't *cook* a Caesar salad.' He said I had to apologize for talking back, and I said I was sorry, I forgot he had balls where his brains were supposed to be."

Mars suppressed a grin. But a question quickly came to mind. "Do you think about that? I mean, whether you're gay?"

Chris made a face. "No. Some kids do, though. I don't think I'm gay. But it may be too soon to tell." Chris looked sideways at Mars. "Would you care? If I was gay?"

Mars hadn't considered it. He knew his feelings about Chris well enough to be certain that whoever Chris became, whatever choices he made, would be acceptable. But he had to acknowledge that even in the new millennium, being gay was harder than being straight. In his heart, he wanted everything to be easy for Chris.

159

What he said was, "Not if that's who you are."

Mars's mind shifted to a more immediate problem. What Chris had just said about Carl wasn't funny. It was just one more piece of evidence that Denise's involvement with Carl was bad for all of them. He didn't know how he was going to convince Denise of that, but it had to be done.

Three of the soccer moms—any one of whom would have, with justification, killed Mars for calling her a soccer mom—were in the parking lot when Mars pulled in. Ginny Piccard, Jane Belzer, and Judi May waved Mars over as Chris got out of the car.

"We're going to have a barbecue at Jane's after the game," Ginny said as Mars pulled up next to them. "All right if Chris comes?"

Mars glanced at his watch and made a face. It would take him a half-hour to drive back downtown, he'd have two hours at the department before he'd have to turn around to pick Chris up, and there'd be more time spent picking up stuff for the barbecue and going to the barbecue. He'd planned to bring Chris back downtown with him after soccer so he could keep working.

"Can't make it," Mars said. "I've got to spend as much time as possible in the department today."

"Not a problem," Judi said. "We can take Chris to the barbecue. Could you pick him up by six-thirty?"

"If you don't mind, that would work great for me," Mars said.

"Just so you promise to put T-Jack's ass in jail," Jane said.

For the first time since Terri DuCain had been murdered, there was no gauntlet of television crews lining the driveway into the garage at city hall. Mars took the elevator to the ground floor, got out and walked through the empty, cavernous lobby, past the statue of the Father of the Waters, then up the marble stairs. He couldn't say exactly why he wanted to walk rather than stay on the elevator. It was a little like passing through a decompression chamber between the outside world and the soul of the investigation. He stopped for a moment on the second-floor landing and looked down at the top of the Father of the Waters' head. A twinge of pain flashed in his gut. How many times had he leaned against that statue during past investigations, Chief of Police John Taylor at his side? He realized for the first time how much he was missing Taylor—not just as a man, but as someone who made a difference on an investigation. It wasn't that Taylor had ever mucked around in an investigation. He had just been there, adding ballast.

Mars hadn't met with McDoanagh even once since the investigation had begun. He knew only as much about McDoanagh's take on the case as anybody who watched the nightly news.

Nettie and Danny were in front of the computer monitor, each hunched forward. The lab had significantly enhanced the image of the DuCain Industries video. They were able to establish the make and model of car, and confirm that there was no license plate at the rear of the car. "There," Danny Borg had said, pointing at the screen. "Plain as day. No rear plates."

Nettie stopped the image and zoomed in on a small blip over the car's right rear taillight. BestRentals it read. "It's a regional rental car company," she said. "I've got a call in to them, checking for all rental agreements for this make and model car for the month of August. Here's the other thing. . . ." She fast-forwarded to the point where the car turned and briefly proceeded toward the camera before it disappeared from the camera's range. "Definitely a male," she said. "But the sun visor and shadows keep us from seeing his full face. You're thinking this guy could be—what was his name? John somebody?"

"Sater," Mars said. "John Sater." He stood up and started to pace, tossing his cigarette pack back and forth between his two hands. "We're going to go with the assumption that John Sater was the guy in the parking lot. If we can tie him to the car rental, it'll be solid. And if it was Sater in the parking lot, that strengthens the assumption that it was Paul Tanney who was waiting for Sater's call near the Lake of the Isles house."

Nettie said, in an aside to Danny, "In case you haven't noticed, he starts fooling around with the cigarette pack when he's thinking big thoughts."

"But you don't smoke, right?" Danny said.

Mars gave the pack a little toss, caught it midair, then dropped it back in his pocket. "Nope," he said. "Not for eleven years. Look. I want you to keep working this thing with Venema and Weber. What have we got on T-Jack's whereabouts? Has surveillance picked up anything at all?"

Danny shook his head. "He's picked his kid up at his mother's, he's dropped his kid off at his mother's twice when he's gone to a gym. Gourmet Express has made three deliveries. He's kept a very low profile. I think it's like we said before. He gets a lot of negative attention if he goes out. So he's staying in."

Mars sat forward and rubbed his eyes. An idea had popped into his head moments before as he'd talked to Danny. But it was gone. Then his phone rang, and he remembered. He needed to check back with Qwest to see if Jedrezek had the phone numbers Mars needed and he needed to meet with Glenn about a warrant to get access to the records for the phone numbers.

Mars reached for the phone on the second ring. "Special Detective Bahr, Minneapolis Police Department."

"Dad? Can I stay at the Mays' until nine-thirty?"

"Did Mrs. May invite you to stay?"

"Yeah. And she said she could bring me home if you wanted."

Mars thought about Judi May driving into his neighborhood in her sleek new Volkswagen Passat station wagon after dark.

"Tell Mrs. May thanks, but I'll pick you up at nine-thirty."

Mars looked at his watch. Nettie and Danny had left an hour earlier and the squad room was empty. A moment like this, when John Taylor had been chief, Mars would have walked down the hall to see if the chief was around. If a light had been on, Mars would have gone in, slouched down in a chair in front of Taylor's desk and talked out loud about what was going on in the investigation. It was the way Taylor had structured Mars's assignment: Mars reported directly to him. They'd never formalized how they met; one or the other of them would just turn up when they had something that needed discussion. It had worked perfectly. As he thought about it, Mars realized it was possible that McDoanagh didn't know that Mars reported directly to the chief. He picked up the phone and punched the four-number extension for the chief's office. Then he left a message on the chief's assistant's voice mail.

"Marlene. Marshall Bahr. Can you get me fifteen minutes with the chief? Thanks."

Mars sat in silence after he'd hung up. Now that he thought about it, the fact that the chief hadn't asked for a briefing by now was troubling. Was it simple stupidity, laziness, or something more ominous?

"Probably all of the above," Mars said to the empty squad room.

"You didn't have to spend anything on food today," Chris said as they drove back to the apartment from the Mays'.

Mars was startled. He kept his eyes on the road as he said, "Why do you say that?"

Chris shrugged. "No reason. Except, sometimes it seems like you're worried about money. So I just thought it was good you didn't have to spend anything today."

Mars drove in silence for a bit, then said, "How does it seem like I'm worried about money?"

"Well, like when we're shopping or eating in a restaurant. When you pay, you always look at the money in your billfold for a long time. Then you take each bill out real slow. And you never used to leave change for tips. You'd always just leave dollar bills, even if it meant you left a bigger tip than you should."

Mars was overwhelmed with pride and regret. Pride because Chris had just demonstrated impressive powers of observation and insight. More than that. Chris's mind worked exactly the way Mars's mind worked, which touched Mars more than he could say. But he also felt regret that an eleven-year-old had to worry about whether his dad was worried about money.

"It's not your problem, Chris. Money has been tight. My salary hasn't been keeping up with inflation, and I haven't been getting the overtime that I had when the department had a pile of murders. Good news for the city is bad news for my paycheck. But I'm getting by. I just have to be careful."

Chris's face was clouded. "Will you get more money at the new job?"

"A bit more—I do get a new salary structure that's higher, and that means I can make more over time. For now, it doesn't give me much of a bump."

"Did Mom give you my dog-sitting money for soccer camp?"

Mars hesitated. He'd never lied to Chris. But not causing tension among the three of them was as much a priority for Mars as being straight with Chris. "We talked about it," Mars said. "We put it in your college fund, instead." Which was true without being the whole story.

"I don't know why you have to pay for soccer anyway. Mom should use the money you give her for that. You give her a lot more money than other divorced fathers do. You give her more money than Eddie Kleinfelter's dad gives his mom. And Eddie's dad earns a lot more money than you do." Chris paused, then looked at Mars. "Carl is always hassling Mom about money. Especially about the money she spends on me. Anytime she spends money on me, he says, 'You spoil that kid.' I've heard him."

Blood rushed in Mars's ears. His anger went in two directions: at Carl for thinking it was okay to interfere in Denise's management of anything connected to Chris—and at himself. He'd been angry at Carl for putting pressure on Denise about money based on how it affected Mars. He hadn't stopped to consider how Carl's pressure might be affecting Chris.

"Is this what's been bothering you?" he said, looking closely at Chris's face.

Chris shook his head. "No. I mean, this isn't what has been

bothering me. But Carl has been bothering me. I don't know why Mom likes him."

They drove in silence before either of them said anything. Mars broke the silence and said, "I could tell you why I think Mom likes him. But it's Mom who should tell you. You should ask her. And you should tell her—in a nice way—when Carl does something that bothers you. And if things don't get better after you've talked to her, then you need to tell me. You shouldn't be in the middle on this."

Chris's face tightened. "I liked our family the way it was before. Before Carl, I mean." He looked up at Mars, a shy smile on his face. "I didn't even know you and Mom were divorced until I was in first grade."

"You serious?"

"Yeah," Chris said. "James told me in first grade. He said his mom and dad fought more than you and Mom, and his parents weren't even divorced like you and Mom. So I asked Mom if you were divorced, and she said you'd told me all about it when I was four. Except I didn't remember."

"But you knew I lived in a different place."

Chris shrugged. "I thought that was because you were a cop. I thought all cops had their own apartments." He shrugged again and they both laughed.

Later, in the dark apartment, they once again lay awake in the darkness.

"I can pick two classes that I take this year. Anything I want to. I think Spanish and filmmaking."

"Both good ideas. You can take filmmaking in fifth grade?"

"Yeah, with a videocam. We learn to edit and stuff."

Mars's first thought was that he'd have to buy Chris a video camera.

"We check out videocams from the media center," Chris said quickly, "so you won't have to buy one."

More dark silence until Chris said, "What was your favorite

165

class?" His voice was slower, sleepiness starting to take hold.

"I liked science, history. I liked the phys ed classes that were individual skills more than team stuff. And I liked math until math became calculus."

"What was the best thing you learned?"

An interesting question. Mars thought about it. When he thought about it, the answer was easy.

"Eighth-grade math. Teacher's name was Miles Smart. He started the first class of the term by saying, 'My name is Smart, and I am.' Then he said he needed to survey where the class was in math. So he said, 'I assume you all learned your multiplication tables through twelve.' The whole room was quiet. We'd all learned multiplication tables through ten. But he was intimidating. So nobody said anything. Just as he started to go on to something else, I raised my hand, and said, 'I only learned my tables through ten.' I did it because I was sure if I didn't, he'd spin around, point a finger at me, and say, 'You! Seven times twelve.' It was sheer self-preservation on my part. Nothing to do with honesty.

"Smart looked around the room and said, 'Marshall gets an A this term, because he's learned the most important thing I can teach him: that admitting what you don't know is the most important part of learning.' And he was right. Remembering that has served me well. Maybe especially as a homicide investigator. Being certain about what you do and don't know is what it's all about, really . . ."

From the futon on the floor the slow, deep breathing of a sleeping boy rose toward Mars. Mars sighed. His great life lesson had gone unheard. He rolled over and tried to relax himself into sleep. But all he could think about was how little he was sure he knew about the DuCain investigation.

That, and tomorrow's date on the calendar.

T-Jack minus four.

CHAPTER
15

Nettie was at her desk, on the phone, one hand clasping a clump of her shiny black hair into a topknot when Mars walked into the squad room.

She leaned backward, looking at Mars upside down. "You're in luck," she said into the phone. "He just walked in." She held the phone toward him. "Denise," she said, in a neutral voice. But she rolled her eyes.

"How was the trip?" Mars said.

"Fine. Actually, I need to talk to you about something. Could I meet you downtown for lunch?"

"Downtown for lunch?" Mars repeated the phrase in astonishment. Denise didn't like coming downtown because she didn't feel safe in parking ramps. And she didn't like to spend money eating out. Recovering himself, Mars agreed to meet Denise at one. It was a good opening for him to raise his issues about money and how Carl was treating Chris. It would work better fitting his agenda into her request than to have Mars initiate something on his own.

"Denise wants to meet for lunch," Mars said to Nettie after he'd hung up.

"Make sure she picks up the check." Nettie looked at him. "She's gonna marry Carl."

Mars returned her look. "She told you that?"

Nettie shook her head. "No. We haven't really talked about anything lately. I don't want to get in the middle, so I've made it a point not to chat. But why else would she want to talk away from the house? She's gonna marry Carl. The relationship's definitely been heating up, right?"

Mars thought about it. He'd expected that Denise and Carl were going to get married at some point. Nettie was right. Carl had been around a lot more in the past six months, which was part of the reason the problems with Denise had intensified.

Observing his silence, Nettie said, "I think you're jealous."

Mars's head came up fast. "No way. I mean that, Nettie. One of the problems with my marriage was that I never cared enough about Denise to be jealous." He thought about the way that sounded, then said, "What I mean is, I didn't care about her in a way that would make me jealous. I always liked Denise. I've always respected her. There just wasn't the kind of emotional attachment you need to keep a marriage going. Not for either one of us. What I do mind is the way Carl has affected our relationship. I mean, Denise and Chris and my relationship. We were getting along great. Better than a marriage. I'd be happy for Denise—except I don't think Carl is good for Chris. And I'm not liking Denise much, now that Carl is a big part of the picture. So it's probably good we're going to talk."

"Like I said. Make her pick up the check."

Mars shifted in his chair. "Right now, I don't have time to think about that stuff. Danny was going to push Narcotics on picking up Matt Weber and Lyle Venema. You know if he's found anything out?"

"I was going to say. Danny went out himself. Narcotics had some uniforms checking for Matt and Lyle, which made Danny crazy. Said if they found out the police were looking for them, they'd be impossible to find."

"He's right. If any division should know the value of keeping a low profile, it's Narcotics. What's with those guys?"

"Anyway," Nettie said, "Danny's doing the gumshoeing himself."

"Have we heard anything from the chief's office? I called Marlene to schedule a briefing, but I haven't heard anything. . . ."

"Nada."

"Maybe I'll track Danny down for breakfast. If we hear anything from the chief's office, let me know."

"They've disappeared," Danny Borg said. "Eviscerated into thin air, as far as I can tell."

He shoveled scrambled eggs onto toast and pushed the whole schmeer into his mouth. Mars and Danny had met for breakfast at a Keys on the east side of St. Paul, less than a ten-minute drive from Minneapolis City Hall. Mars kept looking at his watch. He was expecting to hear from the chief's assistant about a meeting time.

"*Evaporated,* Danny. They've evaporated into thin air."

"That's what I meant," Danny said, talking through the eggs and toast. " 'Eviscerated' is a word I learned yesterday. So it's been on my mind. Whatever. The point is, the last time anyone saw Lyle Venema and Matt Weber was last week."

"Be specific. What was the last date anyone saw them?"

Danny pulled out a notebook and dropped it with a slap onto the table, next to his plate. He turned pages with one hand and forked in food with the other. "August twenty-first. Just Lyle, not Matt. Lyle was hot-wiring a buddy's car. The buddy caught him. The buddy remembers the date because the buddy had a court appearance on the twenty-first, which was why he was going out to his car at eight o'clock in the morning."

"I saw Lyle on the 24th. And Matt?"

Danny turned more pages in his notebook. "Narcotics picked up a kid on possession. The kid said he bought the stuff from Matt earlier in the day. That was the sixteenth. Narcotics has a warrant out on Matt, but they haven't gotten close to picking him up. It's like, if they're walking down a dark alley and trip over him, fine. But no one's gonna put out any special effort. Nettie tell you? That Narcotics had uniforms out looking for Matt and Lyle in response to our request? It's no wonder we can't find them. I went over there personally and raised hell."

"You talked to Melanie Gonzales-Robb yet?"

"Tomorrow. She's been out, but her phone message says she'll be back in town tomorrow."

Mars's cell phone rang. He took the call, then shoved himself up and out of the booth.

"I've gotta get downtown. Let me know if Matt or Lyle turns up."

"You got your meeting with the chief," Danny said.

"Not exactly," Mars said.

Keith Narum looked uncomfortable sitting behind his desk in the small, open-topped box that was his office. Mars didn't understand these offices: two sidewalls, glass halfway up; the front wall had glass halfway up, none of the walls reaching the ceiling. This was the office division commanders got, and Keith had become a division commander shortly after Mars had joined the First Response Unit. The offices—if you could call them that—ostensibly recognized that division commanders had to deal with personnel matters that required some degree of confidentiality. It wasn't clear to Mars how glass walls that didn't reach the ceiling served confidentiality.

Keith Narum must have agreed. "Let's move back to the conference room," he said, as soon as Mars came into Narum's office. "You want coffee?"

Mars thought he knew why Narum was uncomfortable. McDoanagh's assistant had said in her call that the chief wouldn't be available to meet with Mars, but Narum was available to meet at Mars's earliest convenience. If Mars hadn't reported to the chief, Narum would have been his reporting officer. It was clear that McDoanagh was going to have Mars report through Narum for the duration of Mars's tenure in the MPD. Narum didn't understand that not reporting to McDoanagh wasn't a problem for Mars.

Narum held the conference room door open for Mars, shutting it gently behind them. He kept his eyes down as he moved to the head of the conference room table, pulling out a chair for Mars.

"I've talked to the chief," he said, "and he's asked me to make some changes in your work assignment through the end of the month. . . ."

170

"It's okay, Keith," Mars said, anxious to relieve Narum of his anxiety. "I don't view reporting to McDoanagh as a perk—or as necessary to the case. I'm more than happy to report to you until I leave."

Narum's expression lightened slightly, but something was still bothering him. He nodded his head thoughtfully in response to Mars, but still didn't look at Mars. "Good," he said. "Good. I'm glad you're okay with it." His right hand moved back and forth over the table. He had more to say, but was obviously finding it difficult. He cleared his throat. "The other thing the chief said is that he wants to restructure the DuCain investigation. Just in case you're not able to wrap it up before the end of the month."

Everything in Mars shut down. He held his breath and kept his eyes on Narum, feeling sweat rising on his back. "Like what?"

To Narum's credit, he raised his eyes and looked at Mars directly. "What the chief wants is to have someone in charge of the investigation who will be here after you're gone. . . ."

"Which is why my reporting to you makes sense. That, and Danny Borg knows the case backward and forward."

Narum shook his head. "What the chief has in mind is more than just the reporting relationship. He wants another lead investigator. And he thinks having some fresh blood involved may be helpful. So he's bringing in a senior investigator from another division. . . ."

Mars's voice was hoarse when he said, "I'm off the investigation?"

"No, no," Narum said, relieved to have something positive to say. "You're still on the case. But you won't be the lead investigator. You can keep doing what you're doing, you'll just need to coordinate what you're doing through a lead investigator. . . ."

"Who will report to you. . . ."

Narum's eyes dropped again. "Yes," he said. Then he looked up. "I won't pretend to be happy about this, Mars. I can agree that putting in another senior investigator for the sake of continuity makes sense, but I'd prefer that individual to report to you. And I think we've got plenty of good people in Homicide who could do the job. I don't see that we gain much by bringing in someone from outside Homicide. I said as much to the chief. But he felt strongly..." Narum hesitated. "To be honest, Mars, he had a bee in his bonnet about this. Are you aware that Grace DuCain has been pulling strings to keep you on the case past the end of the month?"

Mars groaned. "I knew she was upset about my leaving. She told me she was going to do what she could to keep me on the case. I was real clear with her. I told her that pressure to keep me on the case could be counterproductive. I thought she understood that."

Narum sighed. "Too bad she didn't take your advice. A woman like that—well, she probably doesn't understand that there are things money and connections can't fix."

"She's learning the hard way," Mars said. "What she hasn't figured out is that there are things that money and connections can make worse."

"Exactly," Narum said. He looked to the side, then lowered his voice. "It makes no sense to make a change like this when you've just got a couple days left. McDoanagh's the worst kind of executive. Doesn't pay attention to the important stuff, mucks around where he doesn't know what he's doing. Which brings me to more bad news. He doesn't feel Danny Borg has the rank to be involved. He wants him started off on smaller cases—" Narum held up a hand to keep Mars from interrupting. "I trust your judgment on this, Mars. But at least on the face of it, the chief is right. Borg is fresh out of his uniform. Rookie investigators don't get broken in on high-profile cases. If it were up to me, I'd leave it your call. But it's a point I can't argue."

Mars knew Narum was right. But taking Danny off the case was the worst of the bad news Narum was delivering. It would demoralize Danny, and without him on the case, Mars would lose a key link to the case after the end of the month. One more reason why he had to put this one to bed before September 1—an ambitious objective even before Narum had delivered the chief's latest orders. Now that Mars had lost his slot as lead investigator, it got harder. Which reminded him.

"So who's coming in to Homicide to lead the investigation?"

"Clayton Freize. Narcotics and Vice."

Just when you thought you'd heard the worst. Mars groaned. "That lazy, lying, brown-nosing, ass-kissing jerk. A living, breathing testament to the damage the union has done to the department. Taylor tried twice to fire him, and the union protected him. You suck up to the right people in the union, and there's nothing you're gonna do that'll get you fired."

Mars stood up and paced, crunching the Marlboro box in his pocket in one quick, lethal motion. "I'll tell you something else. When you were talking about the chief saying Danny Borg was too green to be on this case—something about that didn't square. Now I know what it was. The chief doesn't know, doesn't care who Danny Borg is or what he's doing. Somebody got to him about Borg. Let me be more specific. Clayton Freize told the chief I was using a junior investigator on the case and told the chief to tell you Borg was off the case. And the reason Freize did that is Danny criticized Narcotics for using uniforms to look for witnesses on the case. Freize was getting him back."

"It happens, Mars. Look: I'm not happy about Freize coming over to Homicide. Makes my life a lot tougher. I had it good when you were working the high-profile cases, reporting to Taylor. Let me carry on the rest of the division's business in peace. But Taylor's gone and you're a short-termer. And like I said before. McDoanagh gets a bee in his bonnet, pushing him isn't going to accomplish anything. You're just gonna have to suck it up and do the best you can."

Mars couldn't bring himself to sit down. "You know about Freize, don't you? He filed false overtime reports, drugs he'd confiscated were missing. There were all kinds of problems with case documentation. Glenn told me there were dozens of cases that didn't get prosecuted because Freize's paperwork was so sloppy they couldn't use it. And he was lazy. I was in Narcotics and Vice for maybe six months while Clayton was there. He came late and left early. Always said he was working cases—but nothing ever got done on the cases he was working. This bit with him having uniforms go looking for Venema and Weber? No reason that shouldn't have been handled by the undercover guys in Narcotics. Just keeping their ears and eyes open on their assignments, knowing who they could ask questions without it getting around. Just like Clayton to pass it off to someone else."

"You're not telling me anything I don't know, Mars." This time it was Narum who stood up, making clear that there wasn't anything he could say that would change the way things were. "I'd give anything to have you handling this. But the chief has made up his mind. It's what you said. Freize is a world-class brown-noser, and we've got a chief who's open to having his ass polished. Freize saw an opportunity, he understood his target, and he went for it. The chief was a big enough fool to bite." He stopped again. "If you run into problems with Freize, let me know. The one thing we've got going for us is he does report to me."

Mars was relieved that neither Nettie nor Danny was around when he got back to the squad room. He wasn't ready to tell either Danny or Nettie what had happened. Nettie would be pissed but indifferent. She was, first and foremost, practical. And of the three of them, she was the least affected by the change. For Danny, the change would be a body blow.

As he sat, his mind worked through options. The best option was to go over the chief's, Narum's, and Freize's heads to the mayor. It had been on his mind when he'd been with Narum. His impulse then had been that was a card he should wait to play. A card he should save if things got even worse than they were now. How could things get worse? Why not see if the mayor would intervene with the chief while Mars still had time to close the investigation?

He called the mayor's office and got fifteen minutes with her at noon. Then he called Narum's number. He was relieved when he got Narum's voice mail. Briefly, he left a message to let Narum know he'd decided to go to the mayor, making clear that he'd be sure the mayor understood Mars's problem was with Freize and McDoanagh, not Narum.

"I can't get involved in this, Mars. Not at this stage. If I start telling the chief which officers he should assign on which cases, he'd be justified in calling foul."

The mayor's face was calm. If she was going to say no to Mars's request that she intervene on his behalf, she could at least look like she felt bad about it.

"It's not just about me. I can handle reporting to Freize for the time I've got left. But taking Danny off the case is stupid for a lot of reasons. You'd better be prepared. The PD and the city are going to take a lot of heat if we mess up on the DuCain case."

"You're not telling me anything I don't know. Which is why I was counting on you to wrap this up before you leave."

"And what I'm telling you is that was a tough job before I got pulled as the lead investigator. With Freize on lead, there's no hope."

"It's just not something I can do, Mars. I tell McDoanagh you stay as lead investigator and you don't wrap this up, he's got a fall guy. Two fall guys. And I'm one of them. That's not going to happen." Her face was still smooth, untroubled. This wasn't costing her anything.

He understood her then. Her agenda had changed. She wanted McDoanagh to fail. She wanted his handpicked investigator to fail. It would be Exhibit A in her case against his reappointment. She was going to win her battle with the police union even if it meant she had to cover herself in mud on the DuCain investigation.

"You're playing a high-risk game," he said as he left her office.

"I'm not playing and it's not a game," she called after him.

Denise was already in a booth at Peter's Grill when Mars arrived. She held the menu with her left hand, propped up in front of her on the table, the tips of the fingers on her right hand resting lightly on her lips as she read. It was a gesture Mars recognized. It meant Denise was about to do something she wasn't comfortable doing.

In this case, she was going to spend money in a restaurant. More likely, that Mars was going to spend money in a restaurant. It didn't make any difference to Denise. Anyone spending money in a restaurant made her uncomfortable.

He slid into the booth across from her. "Don't worry about it, Denise. You can't spend more than seven dollars on lunch at Peter's. Not even if you try."

"I'm not hungry anyway," she said, dropping the menu. "I'll just have a chicken salad sandwich." Her hand went out and touched a manila envelope that was on the table to her right.

"Where'd you park?"

Her eyes, which had not yet met his, moved farther away. "I didn't drive. Carl dropped me." She glanced down at her watch. "Which is why we've got to hurry. He's picking me up on the corner of Seventh and Second at two."

Mars had considered as he'd walked from city hall to Peter's Grill if today was the day to talk about Carl. He was still upset about what had happened with Narum and Freize, and he didn't want to taint his words about Carl with the sour emotion of his concerns about work. Now, Denise saying she was in a hurry cinched it. His problems with Carl would have to wait.

"That's fine with me," Mars said. "I'm under the gun on the DuCain case. The sooner I get back, the better. You said you had something you wanted to talk about. . . ."

She nodded, pulling the manila envelope in front of her. "I have something I need you to sign."

Mars held out a hand for the envelope. Denise pulled the envelope closer to her.

"It needs to be notarized. Which is part of the reason we need to hurry. There's a notary at Wells Fargo, so as soon as we've eaten, we can go there."

"*What* has to be notarized, Denise?"

"I have to explain first," she said, both hands smoothing the envelope. It gave her a place to look, other than at Mars.

Mars looked at his watch. "I'm listening."

176

"The thing is," Denise said, "Carl and I are thinking about getting married. . . ."

If Mars had any doubts about his feelings for Denise, his response to those words provided absolute clarity. Given that he didn't much like Carl, he felt concern. And his earlier feelings that Carl had disrupted the comfort of his relationship with Denise intensified. But there was no emotional wallop, nothing that felt anything like jealousy.

"It's what Nettie said. She said you and Carl were going to get married. I've got some issues with Carl, Denise, and I'm going to want to talk to you about that at some point, especially if you and Carl are going to be married. But if you care about Carl, I'm happy for you. What I still don't understand is why you and Carl getting married means I have to sign something that needs to be notarized."

Color flushed across Denise's face. "We've found a house we want to buy. But we've got to make an offer by the close of business today. Carl's brother knows the builder, and he's giving us first option to buy. But if he doesn't get our bid by six o'clock—Eastern time—he'll accept offers from other buyers, which means the price will go up. . . ."

Mars was missing something. "Eastern time?"

Denise's voice was low. "Cleveland. The house is in Cleveland. Carl and his brother are going to go into business together, so we'll be moving to Cleveland."

Mars sat speechless. Ideas moved on wild tracks in his head, colliding, bouncing, turning in circles. "You and Carl are moving to Cleveland?"

"Well," Denise said, her face looking hot, "Carl and me—and Chris, of course."

A high, numbing sound started in Mars's head. He lost his ability to breathe without making a conscious effort. The sounds and motions of the world around him seemed remote and out of synch. If he'd needed to stand at that moment, he wouldn't have known how to find his feet.

As he sat, dumbstruck, Denise started talking. "We've conditionally qualified on the loan—but the underwriter says because your current level of child support payments are voluntary and not set by state guidelines—and because the divorce stipulation specifies that you're obligated at that level only until Chris is twelve—you need to provide a notarized statement that the payments will continue as stipulated until Chris is eighteen—"

Mars held up both hands. "Stop. You're sitting here telling me—without once having looked me in the eye—that *(a)* you're taking my son away from Minneapolis, and *(b)* you want me to continue child support payments that we put in place to let you stay in the house. . . ."

"What's the difference, Mars? The house that we're building in Cleveland is a hundred times better than our house here. It's got an attached garage and atrium windows in the living room—"

"Denise. I'm not interested in financing your dream house in the Cleveland suburbs. The idea when we signed the divorce stipulation was that we wanted to provide a stable home environment for Chris. The only way we could do that was for me to give you enough money so you could stay in the house. Your marrying Carl—who, frankly, is a problem for Chris—and moving Chris away from the only home he's ever known—moving Chris away from *me*, Denise—doesn't work. Does Chris know about this?"

Reluctantly, Denise looked at him. Face on, Mars could see the shadow of the Denise he had known for almost fourteen years. A scrupulously honest, fair woman. Short on imagination, low on spontaneity, small-minded about life goals—but someone he had trusted for most of his adult life. But that was Denise's shadow self—submerged under the red, emotional face of the woman sitting across from him in Peter's Grill.

"I haven't said anything to Chris," she said, her voice angry. Then, the shadow self briefly wrested control. "He may have heard me talking to my sister on the phone, before we went to Cleveland. He seemed upset about something after that. But he hasn't said anything. . . ."

It isn't mine to tell. Chris's words to him in the dark. It was unconscionable that Chris had lived the past several days with the

178

burden of believing Denise was moving him away from Mars, to a strange city, with a man Chris deeply disliked.

"He knows," Mars said, his voice unexpectedly hoarse. "And I'm not signing anything. The first issue is your legal right to move Chris without my permission."

"You are so selfish!" Denise's voice was like a hiss.

They were, Mars realized, having an argument, something that hadn't happened between them before. In the past, when they'd disagreed, each had hastily retreated from the other. Each disagreement and retreat taking them to a more distant place. Something Mars knew at a conscious level was that their retreats had been a tacit recognition that their relationship was too fragile to withstand direct confrontation. Denise, who did not think abstractly about anything, was not conscious of the reasons they never fought; her retreats were instinctive. So for both of them, sitting in a booth at Peter's Grill, what was happening between them was not only surprising, but it carried the weight of years of unspoken resentments.

Mars knew he hadn't been much of a husband. But it was shocking to him to be accused by Denise of being selfish. It was the one thing in their marriage and in their postdivorce relationship he hadn't been. He had been sel*fless*. To a fault.

"Selfish!" he said. "Find another ex-husband who has been as generous as I have . . ."

"Everything you've done, you've done for yourself. From day one. The day I told you I was pregnant? You didn't ask me what I wanted to do. You just said, 'We'll get married.'—Not because you wanted to be married to me, but because you wanted the baby. You quit smoking the day I told you I was pregnant! We'd been living together for almost a year, and you'd never given a thought to how your smoking affected *me*. Did you stop to think how it made me feel that a person you'd never met, that you'd never touched, was more important to you than I was? Tell the truth, Mars. Before I told you I was pregnant, you were thinking about breaking up, weren't you? You *only* married me because I was pregnant. And that was a selfish thing to do. I felt like the mother in *Rosemary's Baby,* that horrid video you made me see."

For the second time in minutes, Mars had to concentrate to breathe normally. He remembered the day Denise had told him she was pregnant. Remembered her sitting next to him on a flower-printed couch in their apartment, unfallen tears defying gravity, brimming in her eyes. Her skin pink around her nostrils, around her lips. As he remembered, he felt a wave of shock. She was right. What he remembered was the extraordinary rush of joy he had felt at the idea of being a father. He didn't remember any special feelings toward Denise. Not toward Denise as an individual. Denise had immediately become important to him—more important than she'd been at any prior point in their relationship—as the *container* that held his child. The shock of that realization was overtaken by guilt.

"You could have said...you could have said you wanted to think about other options." He couldn't say more than that. The idea that one of those options could have been not having Chris, giving Chris to other parents, was too painful to imagine.

Denise shook her head. "I wanted the baby. It was never that I didn't want Chris. But I wanted you too. And you only wanted the baby. You got what you wanted. I got half of what I wanted. And when Chris was born, it's always been he's ninety percent your son. It's like the two of you belong to a private club. Those movie games you play. With Chris, with Nettie—you've been closer to Nettie than you've ever been to me."

"Jeez, Denise. The movie games? You don't even like movies. I thought we were each of us being parents in the best way we knew how. I thought we were doing what we chose to do when we were divorced."

Denise brought both hands up to her face, pressing them against her skin. "But you got everything and I had the leftovers. I took care of the house. I cooked and cleaned and shopped. I did Chris's laundry. I took him to doctor appointments. He had all his fun with you, you were the one he talked to. I mean, really talked to. He loves me because I'm his mother, just like you married me because I was his mother. It's never felt like he loved me for me."

"So taking him away from me now—without even talking

180

about it—is going to make Chris love you for yourself?"

Her face set. "That's not what this is about. I just feel like it's my turn. Carl is interested in *me*. We want the same things. He enjoys being home with me—you did everything you could to find excuses for not being home. Carl helps with the yard, he can fix anything in the house, he goes to church with me on Sunday. Maybe I'd like to have another baby. . . ."

"So let me take Chris."

Panic crossed Denise's face. "I'm not giving up my son. I got custody, Mars. You agreed to that. . . ."

Their waitress, a delicate young Asian woman, approached the table, her eyes darting between Mars and Denise. "You ready to order?" she said, pretty sure from looking at the two of them that her timing was bad.

"Give us a couple minutes," Mars said.

"No," Denise said. "We don't have a lot of time." To the waitress she said, "I'll have a chicken salad sandwich. You can bring it right away."

The young woman looked at Mars.

"Nothing for me." He waited until she was out of earshot, then said, "I don't expect you to care about how taking him will affect me—not after what you've just said. But how's it going to affect Chris? You're willing to make him miserable—why? We could work something out. He could come to you holidays, summer when he's not in soccer camp. . . ."

Denise was losing emotional control, the color in her face waxing and waning. "It's not what I've planned. What we're counting on. The house and everything . . ."

Mars stared at her. "Tell me you aren't saying you don't want to give up Chris because you don't want to give up child support. . . ."

Denise shook her head, more in frustration than to say no. "You're confusing this whole thing. Yes, we need the child support money to afford the house. But it's wrong of you to say that's the only reason I want Chris. I will not be one of those mothers who gives up their children. That's not who I am."

Mars stood to leave. "How you get your house in Cleveland is your problem. Chris stays."

He bumped into their waitress as he strode blindly toward the door. She was carrying Denise's chicken salad sandwich.

"I'll take that," he said, walking back to Denise. "Don't say I never played the movie game with you." Then he dumped the sandwich on her lap.

"Hold that between your knees, Denise. And I'll save you the effort of trying to come up with the answer. Jack Nicholson. *Five Easy Pieces.*"

CHAPTER

16

The first person Mars ran into in the squad room was Danny Borg.

Danny started to say something about the rental car in the parking lot at DuCain Industries, looked at Mars's face, and stopped.

"We need to talk," Mars said. "Is Nettie in?"

What he told them about the changes in their assignments gave him an excuse for why he was upset. He wasn't ready to say anything to Nettie about lunch with Denise.

They responded as he'd anticipated. Nettie was ticked but remained on track. Danny was heartbroken.

"Eviscerated," Danny said. "I knew there was a reason I needed to know that word. I feel like I've been eviscerated."

"Emasculated," Nettie said. " 'Emasculated' would be a better word in this instance."

"You always do that," Danny said, his usually unflappable self too raw not to be sensitive. "It doesn't matter what I say. You've always got a word that's better." To Mars he said, "Would this have happened if I hadn't mouthed off about how Narcotics handled things with Venema and Weber?"

Mars sighed and stretched out his legs. "Yes and no. I think the reporting changes would have happened regardless. You being off the case is probably because you irritated Freize."

Danny's face crumpled in grief.

"It was still the right thing to do, Danny. Maybe, in hindsight, it would have been better if you'd talked to me about it, and I'd talked to Narcotics. Freize already hates my guts. It's not a question of being right or wrong, it's a question of understanding how the department works, where the minefields are. That just takes time and experience. Like I said, you did the right thing. This time, doing the right thing wasn't the right thing to do."

Mars straightened up, pulling energy from the day's ashes. "Here's how we're gonna operate until someone tells us otherwise. I assume Freize hasn't showed his shitface around here yet?" He looked from Danny to Nettie. Both shook their heads and shrugged their shoulders.

"So the three of us are gonna keep doing what we're doing until we have orders from Freize to do something different. . . ."

Danny looked worried. "I'm not gonna get in trouble staying on the case after Narum told you I was off?"

Mars smiled a serene smile. "Narum told me what the chief told him. I'm still waiting for orders from my new reporting officer. Until he gives me an order to the contrary, we keep doing what we're doing. If someone gets upset about that, they've got a problem with me, not you. And whatever they're gonna do to me, they've got four days to do it. I can tell you for sure that nothing, absolutely nothing, related to personnel happens in four days." Mars shifted in his chair. "Danny? When I came in, you said something about the rental car that we think John Sater was driving at DuCain Industries on August twenty-third."

It was the best possible moment for Danny to have good news. "The rental car we *know* John Sater was driving at DuCain Industries on August twenty-third. The dumb turd rented the car in his own name. And it hasn't been returned. The car company has filed a stolen vehicle report with MPD. I checked just before I came up here. Nothing's been reported yet. . . ."

"That's fantastic," Mars said. "Danny, go after that angle hard for as long as you can stay upright and keep your eyes open. It'll mean liaising with the city precincts and state patrol, which I assume you're comfortable doing?"

"Absolutely," Danny said, buoyed by Mars's enthusiasm.

184

Nettie shook her head. "What else is going on, Mars? I had the distinct impression when you first got back that there was something seriously wrong. I mean, something that happened with Denise at lunch. . . ."

Mars didn't want to start on lunch with Denise. "You going to be around later tonight?"

Nettie looked at her desk. "I need to get out of here before seven."

"Right now, we've got to talk to Glenn."

Glenn Gjerde did not like uncertainty, ambiguity, or doubt. This was probably an occupational hazard for a prosecuting attorney, but Glenn's reluctance to take a flyer on prosecutions was renowned. The truth was, anything that got past Glenn's skepticism was a sure thing to get past a judge or jury.

Sitting on the edge of Nettie's desk, Glenn chewed on a pencil, spitting out bits of wood and yellow lacquer as he and Mars argued back and forth on the logic of Mars's argument for why they should have access to John Sater's and Paul Tanney's phone records. Then, surprising Mars and Nettie, Glenn gave up the fight in a matter of minutes.

"Hell," he said. "I really want to nail this guy. Doing that is gonna take a stretch." He picked up the phone, checked judge's schedules, hung up and said, "If I can get the warrant drafted in the next half-hour, I can get Penner. She's pretty good on victim's rights and she's got guts. She's not gonna pull her hair out worrying about potential reversals on a high-profile case."

Mars and Nettie sat in stunned silence after Glenn left.

"Well," Nettie said, "that's a first."

Mars sighed. "It tells you something about this case. Everybody wants to nail T-Jack. I heard Jill is getting hammered about the case every time she sticks her head outside her office. She's probably been pushing Glenn on what he's getting from us. Jill's running for reelection. She doesn't want to be campaigning for county attorney while T-Jack is shooting three-pointers at the Target Center."

185

Mars rocked back and forth on his chair for a bit. "Danny and I have the hot items covered for now. What I'd like you to do before Freize is hanging around is to duplicate the case files." He looked at her, knowing that she wouldn't miss why he was asking.

"I take it," she said, "you're thinking this is going to be our first cold case?"

Mars continued to rock. "Things are going okay. But I'm superstitious. I'm betting if we have the files, we won't need them."

"I'm transferring stuff over to our new office every day," Nettie said. "I'll just start including copies from the DuCain file."

"The DuCain stuff I'm taking back to the apartment," Mars said.

Nettie looked over at Mars, but let what he said pass without comment. "So. We were gonna talk about lunch with Denise."

In a nanosecond, all the bile and grief of his conversation with Denise returned, carrying off the distraction of working the DuCain case.

Watching him, Nettie said, "She's marrying Carl. And you're having a hard time with it. I was right."

Mars let his chair drop hard on all four legs. "She's marrying Carl, and I am not having a hard time with that. What I'm having a hard time with is that she's moving to Cleveland with Carl and plans on taking Chris with her. And she wants me to sign a notarized statement that my child support payments will continue at their present level until Chris is eighteen. She needs that so she and Carl can qualify to buy a house with atrium windows."

For maybe the first time since Mars had known Nettie, he had shocked her into silence. She stared at him, her lips slightly open. When she started talking, her words came in a sputter.

"You—you *didn't*—you *couldn't* have signed it. . . ."

"You're right on both counts. I didn't sign it because I couldn't." He sat forward, dropping his face into his hands, elbows on his desk. He rubbed his face hard. "I'm gonna go for custody. Which is going to be bloody. How I'm going to afford the kind of lawyer who can win this case for me is an unresolved question . . . guess I

186

better look into borrowing from my pension fund."

"Well, thank God you're talking sense. You need to talk to Karen Pogue. She'll know a lawyer...."

Karen Pogue was a psychologist who specialized in criminal sexual deviancy. Mars had worked with her for years, and they'd become friends, as well as colleagues. Her husband was an attorney with one of the city's powerhouse firms and the Pogues knew everybody who counted.

"The Pogues are up at their lake place until after Labor Day."

"Do you need to do something before then?"

Mars thought about it. He and Denise had started to argue before they'd gotten into the specifics of Denise's plans. What he did know was that the house they wanted to buy was in the process of being built. So they had maybe six months before a move. Maybe longer, given that Mars had refused to sign the child support commitment.

"No," he said. "I think I can wait until Karen gets back. Which is just as well. I need to be less emotional about this than I'm feeling right now. I'll just screw things up if I go after her now." He looked at Nettie sheepishly. "I dumped Denise's chicken salad sandwich on her lap at lunch."

Nettie stared at him, slack-jawed. "You didn't."

Mars smiled. "I did. And I fulfilled a long-delayed wish. I had a situation where I could use Jack Nicholson's line from *Five Easy Pieces,* the one in the restaurant, when he can't order toast."

"Hot *damn!*" Nettie said. "Except what Nicholson did was, he swiped all the dishes off the table...."

"I know, I know. But I wasn't looking to cause problems for the waitress. My target was Denise. Even without broken dishes on the floor, it felt real good."

"Denise must be in shock."

"That's the plan," Mars said. "The other thing about waiting to start the legal stuff—it leaves me free to concentrate on the case. If we can tie Sater, Tanney, and T-Jack together, we've got a real shot at wrapping up the investigation before the first."

*　　*　　*

Mars stayed in the squad room after Nettie left. Waiting to hear if Glenn had gotten a warrant for Sater's phone records from Judge Penner. Glenn's call came just after 7:00 P.M.

"Got it," he said. "Penner gave me a hard time. But I could tell right away she wanted to do it."

"Let's keep our fingers crossed that we'll find a call from Sater's number to Tanney's number on August twenty-third between two-fifteen and two-thirty. We get that, and we've got the connection between Tanney and T-Jack, Tanney's character and financial situation, a witness at the Jackman house who saw someone who resembled Tanney within the time frame of the murder, T-Jack at the window with Sater's rental car leaving the lot within minutes of that event. All we need is the phone call to link the thing together. Then it's just a question of breaking Tanney and Sater down to flip on T-Jack. Start tracing financial records for payoffs. . . ."

Glenn narrowed his eyes. "You talked to either of these guys yet?"

"Can't find them. But we're working on it. We're following the rental car Sater was driving and the two goons who were looking for Tanney. We find the goons, we're probably going to be able to find Tanney. Or at least get a line on where he might be."

Glenn's question brought Mars back down to earth. Mars still had serious doubts that anyone associated with Terri DuCain's murder was still alive, and each day that passed without finding Sater and Tanney intensified his doubts. What he was counting on was that T-Jack hadn't had an opportunity to take either Tanney or Sater out.

Glenn interrupted Mars's thoughts. "Are we gonna be willing to let Tanney off easy to get T-Jack?"

Mars allowed himself the luxury of slipping back into a scenario where Tanney and Sater were alive. "Depends on how you define 'easy.' He's gotta do ten to fifteen. Minimum. And only if T-Jack gets life without parole."

Glenn nodded. "Jill will be willing to put Tanney up at the Hilton for the length of his term if he'll roll on T-Jack. We take

T-Jack to trial before the general election and she's home free."

"And if we don't?" Mars said.

Glenn sighed. "I get a new county attorney to train, is my guess. You just get one broke in good and they're gone. What happens at city hall if we don't bring T-Jack to trial? My guess is Her Honor will blow a gasket."

"Or jump for joy," Mars said. "I think Her Honor is running a different agenda from the rest of us."

"The warrant's got today's date on it?" Jedrezek asked when Mars called to set up a time when he could bring the warrant over for Sater's phone records.

Mars gave a quick glance at the warrant. "Yup. Signed by Judge Penner." Mars could hear Jedrezek clicking something against his teeth.

"Tell you what," Jedrezek said. "I'll pull this one myself. Fax me the warrant. I don't do this stuff much anymore, so it may take me an hour or two. But that's quicker than waiting until tomorrow and having staff do it. I'll give you a call as soon as I have the records, then you can come over with the original warrant and I'll give you what I've got."

"That's great," Mars said. "I'll wait for your call. Really appreciate your willingness to put in the extra effort."

There was another silence until Jedrezek said, "This is for the T-Jack case, right?"

"Possible," Mars said.

"Hell," Jedrezek said. "I'd do this standing on my head on Christmas Day if it meant putting that guy away."

Mars went back to the lounge while he waited for Jedrezek to call back. He stretched out on the leather couch. The couch had been a gift from the Feebies who'd worked a case with Mars and Nettie earlier in the year. They'd had the couch and a matching club chair and ottoman shipped out after the furniture had been surplused from a retiring FBI assistant director's office. It was a vast improvement over the battered and unbalanced piece of plastic and metal that had previously served the lounge.

Since Evelyn had left, Mars had spent more than one night sleeping on the leather couch in the lounge, waking before people started coming in, heading back to the apartment to shower and change, after which he'd drive back downtown to city hall. With what had happened at lunch with Denise, and with the case where it was, Mars anticipated spending every night until the end of the month in the lounge.

His cell phone rang as he was leaning back on the couch.

"Detective Bahr? Stewart Jedrezek. I've got the records you need if you want to come over."

Jedrezek was gone when Mars got over to Qwest, but he'd left the envelope for Mars to pick up, with a number where he could be reached if Mars had questions.

Mars forced himself to leave the records in the envelope until he got back to the squad room. He did stuff like that a lot. Made a bargain with himself that if he did x, y would happen. Stupid, superstitious shit. But he couldn't stop doing it. The bargain he'd made with himself on the phone records was that if he waited to go through the phone records until he got back to the squad room, he'd find the call on August 23 from Sater to Tanney.

He started opening the envelope as soon as he walked into city hall. He took the records out of the envelope before he walked into the squad room. It took every bit of willpower to keep from reading the record dates before he sat down at his desk.

Finally at his desk, with the records square in front of him, his finger traced down the left-hand column of calls made from Sater's cell phone on August 23. There were seven calls.

Mars's heart stopped on the sixth call. It was made at 2:24 P.M.

Only problem, it wasn't made to Tanney's number.

"Damn," Mars said out loud, his voice echoing in the empty squad room. He slapped the records down. "I should have waited to open the envelope until I sat down at the desk." He clasped his hands behind his head and stretched his legs, staring mindlessly, his eyes catching the wall clock.

In another hour and thirty-five minutes, they'd have seventy-two hours left.

CHAPTER

17

Mars didn't make it back to the couch or his apartment. He spent the rest of the night and early morning hours finding out as much as he could about the seven numbers on John Sater's cell phone call records for August 23.

Judging by the area codes, all but one of the seven calls were cell phone to cell phone. Of the seven numbers, two were repeat calls. Which left Mars with five numbers to identify. Of those five, it appeared that two numbers were in fact one number that Sater had misdialed. The number was dialed seconds before the following number and was different by only one digit.

By dawn, Mars had names and addresses for three of the four numbers. Predictably, one call Sater had made less than a half hour before he'd made the 2:24 call was to a phone sex line.

"You meet the nicest people investigating murders," Mars muttered as the velvety recorded voice answered the 1-900 number. Mars guessed that the time of the call marked Sater's arrival in the parking lot at DuCain Industries. The 1-900 call was something to do while Sater waited for T-Jack's signal from the window. Sater's pants had probably been unzipped while he'd sat there, one hand on the cell phone, the other inside the open zipper.

Also predictable: the single number that remained a total mystery was the call placed at 2:24 to another cell phone. Mars called the number repeatedly, getting the same recorded answer: *The person you called is not available.*

He'd pass the three calls—including the phone sex call—for which he had names and addresses on to Danny for further investigation. The question now was how much time he should put into trying to make sense of the 2:24 call.

Which was what Mars was thinking about when Nettie arrived. She gave Mars the once-over.

"You slept in the lounge last night?"

"No."

She continued to look at him. "You were here all night, but you didn't sleep."

"Right." He slid the phone record information toward her and explained his night's work.

"This is good," she said slowly.

"But not good enough," Mars said. "We still don't have anything that ties the three of them together. Damn, damn, damn, damn."

"Professor Higgins to Colonel Pickering," Nettie said.

Mars did a half-turn toward Nettie. "What?"

"*My Fair Lady.* Rex Harrison is about to sing "I'm An Ordinary Man." That's not what you're about to do?"

"Not likely. Here's a question for you. Name the top three things that have changed police investigations in the last twenty years."

"This is what you think, or it's some kind of established fact . . . ?"

"What I think."

Nettie gave the question a moment's consideration. "Okay. Computers, of course."

"Agreed. That's one."

"DNA."

"You're two for three."

She tapped her fingers on her desk, thinking.

"Cell phones," Mars said. "And those damn calling cards. Calling cards are the worst."

"You're telling me this because?"

"Because I've decided any time we spend on trying to figure

out who Sater called at two twenty-four on August twenty-third is going to be a waste of precious time. It's gonna be a stolen cell phone or a phone booth. Either way, it's going to be a waste of time."

"Can't say I disagree. So what do we do instead of chasing our tails looking for a stolen cell phone?"

A question that got answered when Danny showed up with Melanie Gonzales-Robb. And an answer that changed everything.

"I never was sure where the tip came from," Melanie Gonzales-Robb said. "Not until now."

They were in the squad room lounge. Danny had brought Melanie back to the department after talking to her. He knew Mars would want to talk to her himself.

"Start at the beginning," Mars said.

Gonzales-Robb, a handsome Hispanic woman, kicked her spike heels off and stretched her legs out on the coffee table in front of the couch, like she was getting ready to tell a long story.

"Six months ago I had an anonymous call on the tip line. I get them all the time, and most of the time it's crap. Somebody doing a dirty on someone they're mad at. Not even worth following up. But this one was interesting. I kept the tape."

Danny sprang forward, pushing buttons on a tape recorder on the side table.

A slow, muffled voice said, *"Was that really T-Jack at the Children's Hospital fund-raiser last Saturday, or was it his double wearing shades and an Armani suit?"*

Mars said, "And now you think you know who the tipster was?"

"I'm coming to that," Melanie said. "After I got the tip, I went over and talked to one of our sports reporters. Asked him why T-Jack would have had a double at a community event. He said probably because T-Jack didn't want to do the event himself. And I said, if he didn't want to do it, why go? And the sports guy said because T-Jack's contract required him to do a certain number of community events. I called the PR person over at Children's—she

193

used to be a reporter at the *Strib*—and asked her if T-Jack had been at the event. She said he had been there—but said he could just as well have stayed home. He'd signed a couple of autographs, but hadn't said two words to anyone, including the kids. Kept his dark glasses on the whole time he was there. Left after about a half hour. I checked with the community relations office at the Timberwolves to find out when T-Jack was scheduled to do another community event. It was a visit to Courage Center, the rehab center out in Golden Valley. So I went. Just showed up. About fifteen minutes after the thing got under way, 'T-Jack' shows. Dark Armani suit, dark glasses, stone-faced, silent. Signed some autographs for some of the kids, started to leave. I went up behind him and said, 'Tayron?' Figured if it was an imposter he might be primed to respond to 'T-Jack,' but might not respond to 'Tayron.' He just kept walking. So I said, 'T-Jack?' and he half-turned as he walked. Just for the hell of it, I said, 'Oh, sorry. Thought you were Tayron Jackman. My mistake.' He looked real confused, said, 'I *am* T-Jack,' and left fast."

Nettie looked doubtful. "You're saying some guy is passing himself off as one of the most famous sports figures in the country just by wearing an Armani suit and sunglasses?"

Melanie Gonzales-Robb gave Nettie a cynical smile. "More like by being big and black. That's what people see. The suit and the glasses are props." She looked around at the others. "Take my word for it. If you're Asian, Hispanic, black—it doesn't take much for Caucasians to confuse you with another Asian, Hispanic, or black. All people see is the color. We all look alike, don't you know?"

Nettie, Danny, and Mars were silent. As cops they'd seen lots of cases of mistaken identity that had essentially been based on color. Mars knew Gonzales-Robb was right. A witness might not be able to tell you a suspect's age, height, or what the suspect was wearing. But they could always tell you color.

"Well," Gonzales-Robb said, "I thought it would make a great item if T-Jack was using a double. But I knew I couldn't run it unless I gave T-Jack a chance to comment. So I called the Timberwolves' flack and asked him. He wouldn't touch it. Said he'd have T-Jack call me back if T-Jack had a comment. Within a couple of hours of my making that call, my editor got a call from T-Jack's agent. Said if we ran anything that even suggested T-Jack hadn't been at the event, he'd sue our asses."

Melanie made a face. "If this had been a story one of the news reporters had been working, I can tell you my editor would have told T-Jack's agent to go fish. What my editor told me was that an item in a gossip column wasn't worth a lawsuit. He put a lid on it. I asked that the tip be referred to another reporter. I was willing to have it go to the sports desk, if that was the only section that was interested. But nobody would touch it. Not because they were afraid of getting sued, but because no one wanted to admit picking up a story from the gossip column. Talk about ghettos...."

"So you think the tip came from . . ."

"I started thinking about it when I was talking to Danny. Just going through the story again, some things seemed obvious that I hadn't thought about before. If the only reason T-Jack would have gone to the fund-raiser was because his contract required that he go, someone in the Timberwolves organization must have been putting pressure on him. Otherwise, a guy like T-Jack isn't going to bother. Another thing. When I called the Timberwolves' flack? I didn't get a call back from anybody in the Timberwolves organization. This is their star point guard I'm calling about. I'm saying I'm going to run something that's gonna make their star point guard and the organization look like jerks. They don't even bother to respond. They pass the call on to T-Jack's agent. Like they're putting the screws to T-Jack, instead of trying to resolve the problem. Something I know about a guy like T-Jack: He doesn't like being told what to do by anybody, but especially by some flunky. The only pressure T-Jack would pay attention to is pressure that came from the top. It's a guess, but it's what I'm guessing. I think if Corson didn't make the call to the tip line, somebody who worked for Corson did. It would be dirty work for the Woofies to run that story down, and if they got caught doing it, maybe T-Jack could play them for chumps and claim they're setting him up to break his contract. So Corson sets me up to do his dirty work for him."

195

Mars stared at Gonzales-Robb, working at not showing his admiration. Maybe other reporters didn't have respect for Gonzales-Robb, but she had just thought through a fairly complex problem without breaking a sweat. And she'd come up with the right answer.

She stood to leave, looking around the lounge as if seeing it for the first time. "Nice furniture," she said. "But it's too big. Barely room to walk."

"It was a gift," Nettie said. "From the FBI."

"That sounds like an item," Gonzales-Robb said. She looked at Mars. "Can I assume that you're thinking the same thing I thought when I read about Terri Jackman's murder? That maybe it wasn't T-Jack at that meeting with Terri's parents?"

Mars said, "On or off the record?"

"Don't worry about it. No way I'm going to write anything that would compromise this investigation. I want the guy to burn as much as anyone else."

"Let's just say," Mars said, "you've given us a lot to think about."

The three of them sat in silence for moments after Gonzales-Robb left, feeling like they'd had the wind knocked out of them.

Nettie said, "We were so close when we considered that it wasn't Terri on the phone."

"It'd be just like something T-Jack would do," Danny said. "And it explains about his lawyer. Why he'd want some guy he'd never seen before."

"But it doesn't explain how the DuCains—and their attorney—could have been in the same room with a double and not know it wasn't T-Jack," Nettie said.

Mars said, "Something Grace DuCain said more than once when I asked her what T-Jack's reaction had been to various things that were said in the meeting. She said, 'I couldn't bear to look at him.' Their attorney said the same thing. And they'd hardly seen T-Jack over the past couple of years." Mars straightened up, looked at the wall clock. "I think you know what we need to do next.

We've got to figure out who was at the meeting in DuCain Towers on August twenty-third."

Skeet Russell, an assistant sports editor at the *Strib,* knew Mars from Skeet's days on the city desk. Mars held a handful of chits he'd never called in on Skeet, which meant he could trust that his questions wouldn't get passed on.

Skeet thought about what Mars asked for a while, with his hands folded on top of his head, feet up on his desk, then said, "Davon Els."

"Who's Davon Els?" Mars said.

"He'll be a sophomore linebacker on the Gophers football team this coming season. Built a lot like T-Jack. Put him in an Armani suit, with shades—maybe. Maybe. Can't think of anyone else, but Davon Els would be a definite maybe. He should be in training at the U by now. Kid's from Cincinnati—maybe Cleveland? I'd start with Davon, if I were you."

Mars tracked Davon Els to his dorm room at Wilkens Hall on the university's East Bank campus. Which was after Mars had called the athletic department and talked to a retired cop who now worked part-time in university security. The cop checked and told Mars where the team was working out. Mars had gone over to the field just east of Dinkytown and stood on the sidelines, watching the team doing exercises. In a scrimmage, Mars could have checked out the linebacker positions. But scanning the players running through tire line-ups and ramming into weighted obstacles didn't give him any clues as to which of the players Davon Els might be. The only thing he had to go on was someone who looked like T-Jack. That he figured out in less than thirty seconds. Davon was a definite maybe.

Then Mars walked the half-mile to Wilkens Hall and found the dorm's resident manager. If Mars had to pick one job of all jobs that offered the fewest rewards and the most headaches, resident manager of a dormitory housing maybe two hundred eighteen to

197

twenty-two-year-olds would be very near the top of his list. Wilkens Hall's resident manager looked like he would agree with that assessment—especially when Mars flashed his badge and said he needed to speak with Davon Els.

"Look, if there's a problem, I've got to call the coaching staff. Davon's here on a football scholarship, and we're required to advise the coaching staff of any problems that come up with scholarship kids. That's hardwired."

Mars closed his badge. "I don't think that's going to be necessary. I need to talk with Davon about something that involves him indirectly. If it looks like there's a problem, I'll give you a heads-up. All I need at this point is information. He's over at practice now—can I expect he'll come back here from practice?"

The resident manager nodded. "He's got to be back here within a half hour of practice. Those are the rules. And his tutor comes at six-thirty. Davon's better than most about sticking to his schedule." He looked at his watch. "He should be showing up in another twenty, thirty minutes."

Mars sat in the lounge, reading a stale newspaper, facing the dorm's front door. Davon Els came in with a group of shorts-clad, tank-topped football players, all still shining with sweat from practice.

Mars gave it another fifteen minutes, enough time for Davon to shower, before he walked to the elevator and punched the button for the fourth floor.

Davon Els was sitting on a bed in his dorm room, back against the wall, a towel wrapped around his waist. Half-naked and close up, the resemblance to T-Jack held. But there was a difference. Two other towel-wrapped guys sat on the bed opposite Davon. The three of them were in high spirits about something. Davon's connection to the other two was unguarded, genuine. His capacity for pleasure and sociability was unmistakable. At least in temperament, he was unlike T-Jack.

Just how unlike became even clearer when Mars asked if he could speak to Davon alone. Mars didn't want to contaminate Davon's social relationships by identifying himself as a cop. But even without Mars saying he was a cop, a complicated range of human emotion flashed across Davon's face in response to Mars's request: curiosity, fear, guilt, uncertainty, and what Mars read as Davon's basic instinct to be polite and responsive to another human being. Nothing like T-Jack's self-centered, iron mask of a face. If Davon had doubled for T-Jack, it must have taken every ounce of Davon's willpower to control his own good-natured, spontaneous personality.

"Do you mind if I sit down?" Mars said, pulling a straight-backed wooden chair away from a desk. As he sat, he pulled out his badge, and explained his purpose in wanting to talk to Davon.

Davon gulped hard. A sheen of sweat gathered instantly on his forehead. His eyes darted away from Mars. "I can't talk about that," Davon said, still not looking at Mars. "Coach says we can't ever talk with cops or reporters without his knowing about it. He told me to never say anything about T-Jack. That if anyone asked, I should say to talk to Coach."

"Davon," Mars said, "I'm not interested in nailing you for any-thing. My only interest is finding out if you ever doubled for Tayron Jackman at public events and, if you did, when that happened. You tell me what I need to know about doubling for Jackman and we can leave it there. And, just so you're clear, you can have a lawyer present when we talk, if that's what you want. But your coach doesn't tell the Minneapolis Police Department who we talk to, when we talk, or what we talk about. He tries to keep you from talking to us, 'Coach' can end up in jail on an obstruction-of-justice charge."

Mars let his advice sit for a minute before he said, "How about it, Davon? You want a lawyer?"

The sheen on Davon's forehead had turned into beads of sweat. "I don't guess," he said, looking deeply unhappy. "Coach says I didn't do nothing wrong anyways. Just said it could look bad. Wasn't an NCAA violation or nothin'."

"What *did* you do, Davon?"

"NCAA rules," Davon said, "say we can't take money from anybody. You know, like gifts and stuff. But we can get paid for jobs we do. You know what I'm saying? Like, I could work at

199

Burger King or something and get paid for that. But if one of the team boosters hands me a-twenty, that's a rule infraction. With T-Jack, I was, like, working for him. He didn't have time to do stuff around town. Go to hospitals and such . . ."

"How did he contact you?"

"I met him at a sports banquet last spring. He was real nice. Friendly and all. Said I could help him out and make some money at the same time. Said he'd pay me five hundred dollars for each public appearance I did for him. That, and I'd get some real sharp clothes, designer shades. Class stuff. Got fitted for the suit and all. . . ."

Mars resisted asking Davon if receiving five hundred dollars for what was probably about an hour's work didn't constitute a violation of NCAA rules. He guessed that it was when "Coach" found out how much Davon was being paid that "Coach" decided Davon had an appearance problem.

"And how many times did you double for T-Jack?"

"Only the two times," Davon said, eager, his eyes turning to Mars in a beseeching expression. "First time at a fund-raiser for a homeless shelter, then out at Courage Center. At the Courage Center, some woman started bird-dogging me, seemed to want to find out if I was T-Jack or not. Got me scared. Knew it would look bad for T-Jack if someone found out. So I was gonna quit doin' it anyways. I called T-Jack up as soon as I got back to the dorm and told him what happened."

Davon's face grew troubled. He looked twice at Mars before saying, "T-Jack got real nasty with me, then. Nothin' like how he'd been when I met him."

"Nasty how? He wanted you to keep doubling?"

Davon shook his head. "Not that. I guess he agreed right off that it would be bad for him if someone found out I was doubling. But he started, like, kind of threatening me. Said I'd better keep my mouth shut about what I'd done or I could lose my scholarship. That I'd get the whole program in trouble. But what really bothered me was he said if I did anything to embarrass him, if I told anyone

T-Jack had been involved in the doubling, that I'd regret it. That's what he said. The way he said it, well, it kinda scared me. That's when I talked to Coach. Coach said to give T-Jack back any money he'd given me, give him back the suit, the shades, everything, and not say anything more about it."

Mars didn't say so, but he was impressed that Davon had had the sense and character to talk to someone about what he'd done. "What did T-Jack say when you gave him back the money?"

Davon looked half embarrassed. "I gave him back the suit and the shades. He'd never paid me, anyways. Always said he was going to. Never did."

The jerk! Mars thought, but did not say. "Davon, two more questions. And I need your word on this. You only doubled for T-Jack twice? And you don't know of anyone else that doubled for T-Jack—or that T-Jack asked to double for him?"

Davon looked at Mars straight on. "On my word, sir. Just the twice. After that, I don't even want to see the guy again. Not even to see him play basketball. As for anybody else doin' it—I couldn't say for sure. But if they did, I didn't hear about it."

Mars's stomach churned as he walked back to his car. His gut was telling him chasing down Davon Els had been a waste of time. But he couldn't leave it without being sure.

He considered calling Grace DuCain and asking her if she was confident that it had been T-Jack at the settlement meeting. It would be an unsettling question for her, probably best dealt with when they met face to face.

Then it occurred to him that what he knew about Davon Els gave him leverage to force a face-to-face meeting with T-Jack. The question was, should he go through T-Jack's attorney or just show up at T-Jack's front door?

It didn't take more than a moment's thought to conclude that where T-Jack was concerned, you needed every advantage you could get. The worst that could happen was that T-Jack would blow him off. Mars opted for the surprise visit.

*   *   *

He was winded after climbing the steps to the entrance of the Jackman house and took his time before ringing the buzzer. The one thing Mars didn't want to be when—and if—T-Jack came to the door was winded. So he stood in the shadows of the porch until his breathing was back to normal, then pushed the bell.

Mars hadn't been sure who would open the door, but when it opened, he was looking in the wrong direction.

Tam Jackman stood in the open door, mature-looking for someone not yet five, barefooted, dressed in a sleeveless black leotard. In appearance she was both her mother's and father's child. Her thick, wildly curly black hair was burnished with copper. Her skin was darker than her mother's had been, but lighter than her father's. And like her mother, there was no promise of prettiness in her strong, mature features. Unlike her mother, whose physical presence had passed through a long phase of awkwardness, Tam was already beautiful in a special and unusual way.

"Who are you?" she said, the ripple of a vibrato in her voice echoing her mother's and grandmother's voices and sending a chill through Mars. The question had a child's hesitancy, underlaid with a strong will.

Before Mars could answer, an older woman came up behind Tam, breathing heavily.

"Tamara Jackman! What are you doin' opening the door like that? And you heard your daddy say you were to get dressed. You know he doesn't like it when you walk in your bare feet on the floors. . . ."

Tam's face settled into obstinacy. "I want the shoes Mommy bought me."

Then, suddenly, without Mars seeing him coming, T-Jack loomed behind the older woman and his daughter.

"What's going on?" He barely had the question out before he saw Mars. T-Jack's face changed, the muscles flattening as if it were taking effort to control his reaction. It seemed he was going to say something to Mars, but he stopped himself. Instead, he pushed the

202

older woman back without looking at her. "I told you to get Tam dressed. She's been runnin' around in her ballet clothes since she got home." He looked at the child—without affection or interest, but critically. "I've told you before, Tamara. You don't walk around on the floors in your bare feet. It leaves marks."

Tam stood her ground. She wasn't being mindlessly obstinate the way a child can be, she was making a choice to be defiant, her chin set and her back straightened. "I want the shoes Mommy bought me."

Mars could feel the sense of risk between the father and daughter. Could feel T-Jack making a quick calculation about which attack to confront first: the intruder or his daughter.

Fastening his eyes on Mars, he said, "Ma. Take Tam upstairs. I don't want to see her down here again until I say so. And she'd better be dressed when she does come down. Then, before you leave, I want the floor damp-mopped. Anywhere Tam walked barefooted."

Tam's extraordinary self-control broke. She let out a child's wail of rage and disappointment as her grandmother physically pulled her toward the stairs. *"I want the shoes my mommy bought me!"*

"Little girl!" T-Jack said, turning toward his daughter, extending his right arm, his finger pointed directly at Tam. "I don't ever want to hear you talk about those butt-ugly shoes again. Not ever. You hear?"

To his mother, his voice a sneer, T-Jack said, "Get the child upstairs and don't take any shit from her. She's gonna grow up as spoiled as Terri. Won't be fit for nothin'."

Mary Jackman's eyes were down. She put both hands on Tam's shoulders. "You heard your daddy, Tamara. Don't be a bad girl, now. You c'mon."

Tam continued to cry, but she moved to Mary Jackman's side, and followed her toward the staircase. Her wail could be heard even behind the door that closed upstairs.

T-Jack stood silent, eyes down, hands resting loosely on his hips, until the child's cry was muffled by the closed door. Then he raised his eyes toward Mars. Not another part of T-Jack's body moved, but Mars had a deeper sense of physical threat at that moment than he'd had in all his years of police work.

T-Jack's voice was low, hoarse. "What are *you* doing here? I told you. You've got something you want to know, you call my lawyer. I ever have to tell you that again, you'll have harassment charges brought against you. Understand?"

Mars let the words settle. Then, casually, he said, "I wanted to talk to you about Davon Els. Thought you might prefer that conversation to be just the two of us." He shrugged. "If not, I can call your lawyer. . . ."

T-Jack controlled his response. But Mars knew him well enough by now to see that it took effort. An effort below the surface, but effort, nonetheless.

T-Jack looked away from Mars. His left hand began tapping slowly against his thigh. Still not looking at Mars, he said, "What about Davon Els?"

"You tell me," Mars said.

It was moments before T-Jack said anything. Then he straightened up, arrogance filling his face again. "If this conversation is gonna be anything other than a complete waste of my time, I'm gonna go downstairs and shoot some pool while we talk."

T-Jack shooting pool was like everything else he did. Graceful, effortless, and to the point. With Mars standing to one side of the table, T-Jack racked the balls, then, using the black eight ball as the cue ball, he began shooting balls into the pockets.

"Black ball on yellow, corner pocket," he said, bending forward, pausing for a heartbeat before his right elbow cocked and moved forward. The black ball moved sharply, purposefully, cracking smartly against the yellow, then stopping. The yellow ball moved with a soft hiss across the green tabletop, dropping without hesitation into the corner pocket.

"What about Davon Els?" Mars said.

T-Jack shifted around the table, not taking his eyes off the balls.

"Black ball on green, center pocket," T-Jack said. After the shot, he straightened and looked at Mars.

"I've met Davon Els," T-Jack said. "Met him at a sports dinner last winter. Just like I meet a lot of guys. What about it?"

Once again, Mars had cause to admire T-Jack's judgment. T-Jack had made the smart move, and not just on the pool table. To deny knowing Davon Els would have been a serious, incriminating mistake. A denial Mars would have had an easy time refuting, and once refuted, a denial that would have forced T-Jack to play defense.

There wasn't any sense in playing cat and mouse with T-Jack. Mars went right to the point.

"Davon Els says you paid him to attend events you were obligated to attend under your Timberwolves contract. Paid Els not just to attend the events in your place, but to represent himself as Tayron Jackman."

A slow smile passed T-Jack's face. He shot a couple more balls without calling the shots. Then, as he considered the remaining balls, he said, "He said that, did he? He tell you about the clothes I bought him?"

T-Jack had just acknowledged the most significant evidence Mars could produce to support Davon Els's story.

"An Armani suit and expensive sunglasses, is what he said."

T-Jack nodded slowly, then made another perfect shot. What was left on the table were the most difficult shots. But T-Jack was picking them off with no apparent effort.

"Didn't say anything about the shoes?"

"Didn't say anything about shoes."

T-Jack shook his head as he chalked the cue, his eyes still fixed on the table. Then he knocked off the orange ball, spinning if softly between two balls with a hair's margin on each side.

"Damn," T-Jack said. "The shoes cost more than the suit and shades together. He didn't even *mention* the shoes?"

Mars didn't answer.

"I call that ungrateful," T-Jack said.

"You're acknowledging that you hired Davon Els to impersonate you?" Mars said, certain that T-Jack had something else in mind.

"Not what I said," T-Jack said.

"But you did buy him the suit and shades. And a pair of shoes."

"Sent him to my personal tailor," T-Jack said.

"And you did that because . . ."

"Felt sorry for the kid. Showed up at the banquet in a sweater and khaki pants. Said it was all he had. Looks bad. Black kid shows up lookin' sloppy, looks bad for all black athletes."

"Even though you knew it would be a violation of NCAA rules for him to accept a gift—especially a valuable gift."

T-Jack shrugged. "I started playing pro ball right out of high school, you know? Don't know about NCAA rules and such. Davon didn't say it worried him any. He could've said if it was a problem."

"And you didn't ask him to attend events impersonating you?"

T-Jack made another shot, almost carelessly, but it went just where he wanted it to go.

"What I heard was, he was showing up places saying he was me. I don't think he meant any harm, probably thought it was a joke. When I heard that, I called him. Said I wanted the clothes back. I couldn't have him goin' around saying he was me, could I?"

It was close to perfect. Which isn't the same as perfect.

"Let's see if I have this straight," Mars said. "You're saying Davon Els showed up at public events dressed like you and you heard about it from someone else."

"That's it."

Mars nodded, as if he was considering that T-Jack's answer was a reasonable possibility.

"Which means you weren't at the events where Davon was showing up dressed like you?"

For the first time since Mars had met T-Jack, T-Jack was lagging Mars's thought processes. T-Jack looked wary before he said, "That's right." Then he waited, uncertain where Mars would go next.

206

"Here's what I'm wondering," Mars said. Then Mars lied, with absolute confidence that what he was saying was true. "The Timberwolves keep records of team members' participation in public activities—because of players' contractual obligations to do a certain number of events each season. "When I checked with the Timberwolves' front office about the events Davon told me you'd asked him to attend as your double, they said you'd reported attending both events. Why would you do that when you'd know how easy it would be for the Woofies to confirm you hadn't been there? Unless you'd arranged for a double to make it look like you had been there. . . ."

T-Jack's face went sour. He stopped acting like the pool game was the only reason he was there.

"What is it you want, anyway?"

Mars said, "I need to be sure it was you at the settlement meeting at DuCain Industries on August twenty-third. Not a double."

T-Jack continued to stare at him. "How do you make sure of that?"

"I'm not interested in making it public that you used a double. I'm especially not interested in exposing Davon Els. Not if there's another way."

"So what's the other way?" T-Jack said. His voice worked hard to make it sound like Mars's problem, not his.

Mars said, "Your fingerprints. If you give me your prints today, and I can match the prints you give me to the settlement agreement you signed on August twenty-third, I'll leave it there."

T-Jack thought about it.

"Let's do it this way." He turned to the table, and picking up his cue, gave Mars a pointed look.

"Black on red, corner pocket," T-Jack said, a nasty smirk twisting the corner of his lips.

Then he gave his stick a brutally precise thrust that sent the red ball spinning across the table before it disappeared into the corner pocket. The black ball back-spun after hitting the red ball, then stopped well short of the pocket.

T-Jack walked slowly around the table, retrieved the red ball from the pocket, then carried the ball to the bar at the other end of the room. He leaned across the bar and pulled a crystal tumbler from a shelf, impressing his fingers on both the red ball and the glass, dropping the ball into the glass, then walking back toward Mars.

"That should do it," he said, as he handed the glass to Mars. "Now get out of my house."

As he left, Mars passed Mary Jackman in the front hall. She was damp-mopping the floor. She glanced at Mars without speaking, he nodded to her.

When he got out to his car, he drove past T-Jack's house and then pulled over, keeping his eyes on the rearview mirror.

Within ten minutes, a cab pulled up. Mary Jackman came down the front stairs and got into the cab. When the cab passed him, Mars pulled out and followed it to a high-rise apartment a couple miles south and east of Lake of the Isles. He parked and went into the apartment's lobby before Mary Jackman had paid the driver and gotten out of the cab.

If T-Jack was supporting Mary Jackman, he wasn't doing it in style. The apartment building Mary Jackman lived in was one of many HUD buildings in the city, most of which provided subsidized, Section 8 housing. Some, like this building, were open only to senior citizens. Most of the buildings were fairly well maintained, but there was nothing fancy or luxurious about them.

She saw him as soon as she came into the lobby. She drew back a bit, startled, but then regained her composure. As she walked past him toward the elevators, she said in a quiet voice, "I guess you'd better come up, then."

Mary Jackman's apartment—with the exception of a few religious works of art on the walls—came close to being as spartan as Mars's. After she'd put down the things she'd carried with her, she sat in a chair and looked at Mars directly.

"What is it you want?"

Mars sat opposite her, on the edge of the chair, trying to look like he wasn't settling in. "Is there anything you can tell me that would help me find who murdered your daughter-in-law?"

208

She took her time answering. "You may not believe me—you may think I wouldn't say anything about my own boy, but I need you to believe this. If I knew anything—anything—that would help you answer that question, I'd tell you. Regardless."

"There's nothing you can tell me . . ."

"This is what I can tell you. That one life has been lost in that house. And my granddaughter is at risk . . ." She saw Mars start, and held up a hand. "No. Not like that. He won't physically take her life—just as I'm sure he didn't physically take Terri's life. But he'll take Tam's soul. It's already begun. He's trying to break her, just the way he broke her mother. Does Grace DuCain know that, Mr. Bahr? Is she going to do anything to help?"

"She'll do what she can. She's afraid if she pushes Tayron, it will be worse for Tam. And, I'm sorry to say, the courts haven't been very strong on grandparent rights."

Mary Jackman looked away from him. "It's why I stay in that house. People think he gives me money. It isn't true. You saw the way he treated me today. I stayed to be a comfort to Terri. I never told Grace that. I didn't want her to know how bad things were. I stay now to try and save Tam. But there's only so much I can do. If I fight him, I'll be out. And that little girl will fight him—you saw that today, didn't you? The more she fights, the meaner he'll get." She shook her head and looked up at Mars. "What you're doing—don't think it's justice for the dead. What you're doing is the only hope there is to save Tamara. If she's not taken from him, he'll ruin her just the way his mother—my own sister—ruined him.

"You remember that, Mr. Bahr. You remember that it's not the dead, it's Tamara depends on you."

Mars left Mary Jackman's apartment weighed down with disappointment at the time they'd lost pursuing the possibility that T-Jack had used a double to attend the settlement meeting. More than that, Mary Jackman's warning about Tam's future carried the force of certainty. And Mary Jackman was right. At this point, Tam's future was more important than justice for Terri.

* * *

Mars pulled out the tumbler, wrapped in his handkerchief, that contained the red billiard ball. He put both on Nettie's desk, letting the handkerchief fall away from the glass.

"Direct to you from Tayron Jackman's billiard table. His right-hand fingerprints should be on the ball and the glass. Get it over to the lab, will you?"

"Any doubt it's going to match the prints on the settlement agreement?"

Mars shook his head, sinking down into his desk chair. "No. It was a flutter. I don't believe he used a double at the meeting and I think his prints on what's on your desk and what we're going to pull from the agreement are going to match up. The light at the end of the tunnel is growing mighty dim."

"It would have been satisfying, wouldn't it? To be able to prove he'd actually murdered her himself, not just arranged for her murder."

"It would have explained everything. Too good to be true. We're back to our usual suspects."

"Those being Paul Tanney and John Sater?"

Mars smiled. "Here's a soft ball into center field. You've got fifteen seconds. The first character says, 'Do you know a dealer named Ruby Deamer . . . ?' and the second guy says, 'Do you know a religious guy named John Paul?'"

Nettie blinked. "I can't remember who said what, but it was *The Usual Suspects.*"

"You got it—or, more to the point, I gave it to you."

"Do *you* remember who said what in that movie? I didn't like it much. I liked the characters, but I never knew what was going on. Not even at the end."

"That's because figuring out what was going on was mostly intuitive. *You* are fact lady."

"Which makes you intuit man. Sounds like something you'd dig out of a glacier. What I asked before—ruling out that T-Jack used a double means what we've got left is Sater and Tanney?"

"Dem's it. Or having Narcotics pick up and charge Weber and Venema and getting one of them to talk. But the light at the end of that tunnel isn't just dim. It's pretty much burnt out. Time is not on our side."

"Any progress on finding Sater's rental car?" Mars asked Danny after Nettie told him what Mars had found out about T-Jack's "double."

"I'm drawing blanks," Danny said. "Think he must have left the state right after they did the job."

What Mars thought was the reason Sater and his rental car had gone missing was because somebody had dumped Sater and his car in a lake.

Mars's overcharged brain refused to crank on those questions. He was, in fact, so tired that the thought of going back to his apartment didn't fill him with dread.

Driving back to the apartment, he concentrated on there being a postcard from Evelyn in his mailbox. But even after two days, the box was empty. He pulled himself up the stairs, considering an immediate flop on his bed. But he knew if he lay down without a shower, without taking off his very stale clothes, he'd wake in a couple of hours, still tired but unable to get back to sleep. So he took a shower.

He looked at himself in the mirror as he was toweling off. After the brutal day he'd had, he felt bruised. That his skin looked untouched was somehow startling.

With a towel wrapped around his middle, Mars went to the calendar to make a notation on tomorrow's date, but stopped himself. He'd do it in the morning. If he wanted to sleep, he didn't need to remind himself that tomorrow was T-Jack minus two.

CHAPTER

18

Clayton Freize made his first appearance in the squad room a couple hours after Mars, Nettie, and Danny had arrived the next morning.

Clayton stared at the three of them, letting his look send a message before he spoke.

"So. This is the Homicide Division's elite First Response Unit at work," he said. "Nice work, if you can get it."

"And you can get it, if you try," Mars said, not moving. He'd shot a look at Danny that said, *Don't move.* Nettie didn't need to be told. "I've been wondering when you'd wander over."

Clayton jerked his head away from the squad room. When he spoke, it was clear he was talking only to Mars.

"We need to talk."

They sat at opposite ends of the conference room table, neither man happy to be there. On the face of it, Freize should have had the upper hand. He was now officially Mars's reporting officer. But there is such a thing as moral superiority. Mars was holding aces on that point. So, under present circumstances, and with the weight of a shared history between the two men, Freize was more uncomfortable than Mars.

Freize tried to gain ground by being belligerent. "What's Borg doing around?"

"He works here."

"Not until September first, he doesn't. Besides. I told Narum I wasn't using a rookie on a case like this."

"The unit has always had the authority to pull in resources to work a case. I've worked with Danny before and he's first-rate. I needed someone to oversee the street side of the investigation and he's done just fine on that, rookie or not—"

"What I'm saying, *Candy Man,* is that I'm the lead officer on this case, and I said Borg wasn't supposed to be involved. So why is he?"

"I was told I report to you, Clayton. I was waiting for your instructions."

"Narum said he told you."

"Narum told me I report to you. I assumed you'd want to give me your orders directly."

"Smart-ass," Freize muttered, but he looked away from Mars. "Well, I'm telling you now. Borg is off this case. You need more resources, you ask me and I'll make a decision about who gets assigned. That order direct enough for you?"

Mars stared at him without answering.

"In the meantime," Freize said, "I've gotta give the chief a briefing on the case status this afternoon. And the chief wants the presentation done professionally. He wants a PowerPoint presentation. He let me know he hasn't been happy with the department's informal style. I'll want you to run the machine or whatever it is you use for PowerPoint, but I'll do the talking. Same if we do the show for the mayor."

Mars continued to stare at Freize. "You reduce my investigative resources at the same time you want me to spend time putting on a dog-and-pony show?"

Freize scraped back on his chair and stood up.

"It's what the chief wants. And I'm gonna want to look at what you've got before we meet with the chief. I'm not having my ass hanging out there on something I haven't seen until the chief sees it."

*   *   *

"He wants *what?*" Nettie said.

"A PowerPoint presentation, is what he called it. Summarizing the case status. I was hoping you would know what it was and how to do it. I don't have a clue."

Nettie blew air. "I know what it is. I've never done one, but it isn't rocket science. I'm pretty sure I have the software. . . ." Nettie turned and clicked through screens on her monitor. "Yeah, it's part of the package we've all got on our hardware. You create a disk that can be played on a computer screen or through a special projector—I think we could reserve a projector through support services. I mean, sure, I can do it—if you give me the content. But Mars, why should either one of us be spending time on what is essentially a slide show at this point in the investigation?"

"Because my reporting officer has ordered us to do it." An impish grin passed Mars's face. "Any way we can put gold braid on the PowerPoint screens?"

Nettie said, "I don't feel like making jokes. This is awful. Freize and McDoanagh are idiots, but even they have to know what they're doing isn't going to help the investigation. What do they get out of sandbagging us?"

"It makes them feel like they're doing something," Mars said.

Mars was getting ready to leave the squad room when his cell phone rang.

"Mars," Danny Borg said, "something interesting from the surveillance at T-Jack's house. That witness coach Fritz Mercer uses to prepare his clients before trial? Hal Flison? He's shown up at T-Jack's. Is Jill's office gonna charge T-Jack anytime soon?"

Mars hissed. Fritz Mercer was the Twin Cities' most formidable criminal defense attorney. He was renowned for the thoroughness of his case presentations, and Hal Flison, a behavioral psychologist, was one of his most effective consultants. Mars had seen defendants evolve from fang-toothed monsters into lovable humanitarians under Hal's guidance. Except it wasn't that simple. Anybody can alter

214

their behavior. What Hal did with the clients he coached was to make the change believable.

Mars said, "I need to talk to Glenn."

Glenn wasn't in his office, so Mars paged him, then sat on his desk waiting for the return call. It came three minutes after Mars had left the page.

"Glenn. Danny says Hal Flison's been showing up at T-Jack's. Two questions. Has T-Jack retained Fritz Mercer? And is Jill planning on charging T-Jack on what we've got so far?"

It was Glenn's turn to hiss. "Hal Flison, huh? Well, geez, not that I've heard. About T-Jack retaining Fritz Mercer. But Fritz has Hal on an exclusive contract. He pays Flison big bucks to keep it like that. So, if he's working with T-Jack, Fritz is working for T-Jack. As for Jill charging T-Jack anytime soon—she'd like to. We both know that. God knows she's pushing. But that's gonna be my call, and based on what we've got in hand right now, it's not happening. You don't need to worry about that, Mars. Jill tries to push a charge through for political reasons, I'll play my trump card. . . ."

"Which is?"

"I'll tell her I'll quit and let the press know why."

Mars exhaled. "That should do it."

"Yeah," Glenn said, "but a trump card is something you get to play only once. I hope it doesn't come to that. On Mercer and Hal? I'll do some checking and get right back to you."

Glenn got back to Mars in a half-hour.

"I'm not sure how all this fits together, but I've found out that T-Jack *has* retained Fritz Mercer. Just picking up on scuttlebutt— and I can't tell you who scuttled whose butt, so don't ask—Grace DuCain is going to be filing suit to get visitation rights for her granddaughter. . . ."

"That doesn't surprise me. It's something she's always known she'd have to do. It was just a question of when. What I'm not getting is how that fits with Fritz Mercer and Hal Flison."

"Let me spin this out a bit," Glenn said. "When you paid your visit to T-Jack about Davon Els—I'd bet T-Jack was in touch with Mercer while you were walking down the front steps. Probably the first time since August twenty-third T-Jack saw himself as being remotely vulnerable. Mercer being Mercer, the first thing he's going to be thinking about is he's got a client who has what can be described as a major image problem. So Mercer puts out the hook for Flison. In the meantime, Mercer probably hears from the same source I hear it from that there's going to be a visitation battle over the grandkid. More image trouble. The big, bad black guy who's getting away with murder is going to try and keep the dead mother's mother from seeing her only grandchild. Mercer decides to go on the offensive. Prep T-Jack for a major media appearance. . . ."

"Has he lost his mind? What possible chance is there T-Jack can pull that off?"

"C'mon, Mars. You've seen what Hal Flison can do. Worst case, people who hated T-Jack before will still hate him. Nobody likes him to start with, so what's to lose?"

Mars blew air. "I can buy your analysis up to the point where Mercer wants to put T-Jack on TV. Worst case, best case, I think that's a long shot."

"It was until about an hour ago. T-Jack is gonna be on a special edition of *60 Minutes* tomorrow night. CBS will be running promos starting on their morning show tomorrow. Bryant Gumbel's doing the interview."

The air-conditioning in city hall had gone out two days earlier, just in time for the building's southwest windows to catch the afternoon August sun.

When the interior of a granite building gets hot, it stays hot. The air thickens, goes stale, and accumulates the worst odors of its occupants. By late afternoon, the division conference room where Mars, Nettie, and Freize were meeting was fetid. Fans had been set up, but the blowing air's only effect was to make it impossible to ignore how uncomfortable you were.

Mars's and Freize's body heat—higher than normal—fed the

room's temperature. Nettie was, as usual, cool and unflappable in a crisp black tee and a white cotton skirt.

"The presentation with the chief," Freize said, "is just you and me." He nodded toward Nettie. "She's not invited."

Nettie continued setting up the presentation projector. Mars said, "Unfortunate. Because I don't know how to run the machine. And I have no plans to learn. Without Nettie, we've got no Power-Point. I could, of course, just talk us through. . . ."

Freize loosened his tie and stared at Mars. "I told you I expected you to be ready to do this presentation today. You forget how to take orders from a superior officer?"

"I can't believe you want me to take time in the middle of a high-profile investigation to learn how to run a video projector. The presentation is ready. Nettie knows as much about the investigation as I do. . . ." Mars paused before he said, "More about the investigation than you and the chief put together. And she can run the machine. There can't be any reason for her *not* to be there. In fact, if things come up that she needs to follow, it'll save time to have her there."

Freize slumped back in his chair, chewing on the side of an index finger. "Something you've gotta understand. Things aren't like they used to be. McDoanagh wants a tight ship. No prima donnas, no flush resources."

"We're good to go," Nettie said, sounding like she hadn't heard anything Mars and Freize had said.

Freize watched the presentation in silence, until they came to the section on the settlement agreement.

"Shit," he said, "we've got enough on the agreement alone to charge T-Jack. What're you doing fucking around with all this other stuff? Bring him in on the agreement evidence, put the other stuff together after he's been charged. It'll take some heat off us and put some heat on him. Who knows what he'll give up once he's charged. . . ."

Mars took his time before he answered. Losing his temper on this point with Freize would be dangerous. He worked at keeping his voice level, slow, when he said, "The problem with the agree-

217

ment is that it's totally circumstantial. I—we—need to be able to tie it to some element of the crime. Like we outlined in the presentation. If we can establish a link between T-Jack, Tanney, and Sater on the twenty-third, then the settlement agreement becomes powerful evidence. Or, if we can establish that T-Jack gave Tanney or Sater money, it supports that the settlement agreement was part of T-Jack's murder strategy. . . ."

"What do we know about T-Jack's financial records?"

"Pretty much what I suspected. They don't tell us anything about a transaction involving a significant withdrawal of cash around the time of the murder. They do indicate that T-Jack might have been experiencing some cash flow problems for most of this year. But to come up with a solid handle on that is going to take time. And I'd like to work with a forensic accountant we use—"

"You're not listening, Candy Man. Fat City is going thin. You're actually gonna have to do this work yourself."

Mars ignored him. "The point is, T-Jack could have hired out a job like this for as little as ten thousand—at least up front. It would be no problem for T-Jack to come up with ten thousand in cash—even if he was having cash flow problems—without leaving an account transaction record. Which is my point on why we can't rely on the settlement agreement by itself. Without a direct link between the agreement and specific action by T-Jack to have his wife murdered, a defense attorney is gonna tear the agreement apart—"

"I don't care shit what a defense attorney is gonna do. I care how this is gonna sound to a jury. And a jury's gonna hear what I just heard: T-Jack set a scene to give himself an alibi and make big bucks while he was at it. And remember. Nobody likes this guy. Christ, guys who buy season tickets to Woofie games hate his guts. Your average juror is gonna have his tongue hanging way out hoping we give him anything—anything—that'll let him put this guy away. Maybe what we've got is circumstantial, but it all fits. And the settlement agreement is the clincher. And that's what I'm gonna tell the chief. We should have pulled T-Jack in the day you had the agreement in hand."

218

Mars stood up and began a quick, tight pacing on his side of the table. He kept his hands in his pants pocket, crushing the cigarette box he'd bought that morning.

"Clayton," he said, his words measured, "I can understand how you'd see it that way. But you've never put together evidence on a homicide case that's going to trial. I'm telling you, what sounds good between us, just sitting around, looking at what we've got in a real linear fashion, seeing the case just from our perspective—that's gonna get blown away in a courtroom. You have to develop the evidence defensively as well as offensively. I mean, you've got to anticipate what the defense is going to come up with and have something that counters that. You don't have to take my word for it. Talk to Glenn Gjerde..."

Freize shoved back on his chair, put one leg up on the edge of the table. He sputtered, a condescending smile on his face. "Gjerde. Mister There's-no-such-thing-as-good-evidence. I don't need to be an old hand in Homicide to have Gjerde's number. He's a joke. You listen to Gjerde, nobody goes to trial."

Mars felt desperate. He didn't have any doubt that given half a chance, Freize could sell this line to the chief. There wouldn't be any way Glenn would buy it, but if the chief went over Glenn directly to the County Attorney's Office, Jill might be willing to take a flyer and go for it. Especially because the charges would get filed in advance of the general election.

"Clayton, even Grace DuCain came up with benign explanations for T-Jack's terms in the settlement agreement. If Grace DuCain could come up with justifications for why T-Jack wanted what he wanted, T-Jack's defense attorney can do a lot better."

Freize said nothing, examining at close range the index finger he'd been gnawing. Looking satisfied with the damage done, he straightened up. Then he pushed up from the table. As he left the conference room he said, "McDoanagh's office at three."

Gold braid and a ruddy complexion don't mix, and the chief's face was red and sweaty above the heavy blue jacket of his uniform. Air-conditioning units, clearly jerry-rigged for the occasion, rattled

219

in two of the windows. The window shades were drawn, creating an aura of doom in the large office. Even with the window units blasting, Mars could feel no difference in temperature between the chief's office and other areas of city hall. The room was simply too big for air conditioners designed to cool a room a fraction of the size and height of the chief's office.

"You should take your jacket off, sir," Freize said to the chief, making it sound as if the chief keeping his jacket on was an act of heroism too great to be expected of a public official.

"Somebody's got to set a standard for decorum around here. Even this problem with the central air. What excuse is there for that? Somebody's not been doing his job . . ."

"The building administrator's request for funds to overhaul the building's heating and AC systems has been turned down in the last two budget cycles," Nettie said.

"Whatever," the chief said, mopping his forehead. "Let's get going. I'm leaving as soon as this is over."

Nettie had the video projector in place as Freize started to talk. "In the interest of conserving your time, sir, I'd like to cut to the chase. I've personally reviewed the case file and concluded there's no reason why we shouldn't be asking the County Attorney's Office to prepare charges against Tayron Jackman. Not to say there isn't more work to be done, just that I'm satisfied there's plenty to support the charge. We do that and we gain the advantage of creating pressure which may well cause Mr. Jackman to be more coopera-tive. . . ."

Mars and Nettie were too stunned to speak. Even the chief looked surprised, but a fool's optimism quickly overcame any sense of skepticism that was justified under the circumstances.

"Well, of course I'm delighted, if that's the case . . ."

Sharply, Freize said, "Projector on, now. Move directly to screen seven."

Before them was Royce Olsen's summary of the settlement agreement's main points, including Olsen's interpretation of how the points served T-Jack's strategy. A skin-tingling warmth was spreading over Mars's body, kind of like how you feel after a wound turns from numbness to pain.

He opened his mouth to form an argument against what Freize was saying, but the chief quickly cut him off.

"Any differences between the two of you should be resolved within the department. My time isn't going to be spent umping pissing matches. I will say this. From what I see here, I'm inclined to take Clayton's side. In any event, Clayton's the lead officer on this case. I'm a firm believer in supporting my line officers. And am I correct, that this is the county attorney's call? Which is to say, if they don't agree we have a solid basis for filing the charge, it won't go anywhere?"

Freize stood. "Appreciate your support sir. We won't take any more of your time. And you're exactly right. It'll be the county attorney's call. I should say that it's going to take me another week or so to get the case in shape to go to the county attorney. But from my review, I'm convinced we've had in hand what we need to charge since day one. So it's piss-or-get-off-the-pot time. One thing I would appreciate. A point that would require the prestige of your office, if it comes to that. The assistant county attorney who typically would review our case is well known for being a logroller. Churns cases and eats up resources, delays going to trial as long as possible. I'd like your permission to say that you've asked the county attorney to personally review our request."

McDoanagh nodded. "Yes. Of course. I've already made clear to you how I feel about running a tight ship. I'm not going to spend our resources satisfying some attorney who's not prepared to do his job. Given the high profile on this case, I think asking for the county attorney's personal involvement is appropriate. Is that all?"

Freize motioned for Mars and Nettie to stand. "Yes, sir. Thank you, sir. Again, it's a pleasure to have your support and leadership."

"Well," McDoanagh said, "in my judgment, too many in my position mistake leadership for meddling. I'm a believer in delegating. And once I've delegated, I'm the kind of man who believes in supporting the delegatee. That's my definition of leadership."

"Do you think Freize knows what a delegatee is?" Nettie asked. They were back in the squad room, sitting shell-shocked at their desks, uncertain what to do next.

"I'm not sure *I* know what a delegatee is," Mars said.

"We should ask Danny," Nettie said. "I think it's a word he's gonna need to know."

"Have you noticed," Mars said, "that people who constantly describe themselves—like, 'I am the kind of person who'—are always the world's biggest jackasses?"

"Now that you mention it." Nettie sighed. "So. What next?"

Mars leaned back. "Chris is sleeping over at my place tonight. We were going to make dinner. I can't put that off. I've got to talk through with him what's going on with Denise. Why don't you and Danny come over for dinner? We'll figure out what to do next. Chris and I can talk after you leave."

Nettie raised an eyebrow in his direction. "So, Danny is still on the case?"

Mars gave Nettie an innocent smile. "We can't talk about a case over dinner?"

Before he left city hall, Mars called Glenn Gjerde. Glenn wasn't in, so Mars left a message on his machine.

"Heads up, Glenn. Freize has concluded we're ready to charge T-Jack. Based on the settlement agreement terms. And the chief is going to ask Jill to personally review the charge request. So get out your trump card—"

"Shit!" Glenn said, picking up. "Forget about it. That dog's not gonna hunt. Not gonna get by me, not a chance."

"That's what I wanted you to say, Glenn. Do what you can."

"I've been reading this book," Chris said. "It's about how chemistry changes what you cook. So I'd like to buy something for dinner where I can test different chemical reactions."

Mars frowned as they pushed their grocery cart down the aisle at Cub Foods. "I can't say I much like the idea of eating a lab test."

222

Chris rolled his eyes. "It's not gonna taste like a lab test, Dad. It's gonna taste like dinner. I'm the only one who'll know about the chemical reactions." He looked up at Mars with a canny expression on his face. "Besides. What I was gonna make was pasta with pesto sauce. Which is real cheap. We just need the pasta, some pine nuts, walnuts, and the basil leaves. And bread. We'll need baguettes. I think we've got everything else. Then I'm gonna make the sauce two ways. Half I'll make with walnuts and the stems and bottoms of the basil leaves on, and the other half I'll make with pine nuts and the stems and leaf bottoms off. The sauce without the stems and bottoms and pine nuts should be a brighter green, instead of that muddy color, than the other sauce. Oh. And half the pasta I'm gonna cook with lemon juice in the water and half without because acid in the water'll keep the basil from turning the pasta green. . . ."

Mars said, "I used to like pasta with pesto. I'm not so sure anymore."

"It'll be fine. Dad?"

Mars looked down at Chris, which was a shorter distance every day. "What?"

"Can we stop at Video Update and get a video to watch after Nettie and Danny leave?"

Mars hesitated. "We have things we need to talk about after Nettie and Danny leave."

"There'll be time to talk. Can we?"

"Something special you want to see?"

"I've been thinking about *Alice Doesn't Live Here Anymore*. The one we rented with Evelyn. I'd like to see that again. I really liked the kids in that movie."

"Oh, great," Mars said. "The two juvenile delinquents who end up in jail. A little too close to home for me."

Chris gave Mars a soft punch. "They were really good. Both you and Evelyn said so."

What Mars didn't say was that he knew when Chris brought up something that was connected with Evelyn, it meant Chris was missing her. Renting *Alice Doesn't Live Here Anymore* was Chris's way of invoking Evelyn's presence. The other thing Mars didn't say was that he wanted to watch *Alice Doesn't Live Here Anymore* for the same reason.

"Oh, cool," Chris said, staring down into one of the two pots boiling on top of the stove.

"Not cool," Nettie said. "Hot. Or, maybe it's not the heat, but the humidity. Is there a reason you've got two pots of water boiling for the pasta? It's starting to feel like city hall in here."

"Don't ask," Mars said.

"Because," Chris said, "I'm doing a chemical experiment. I've got lemon juice in the water in one of the pots, and the pasta cooked in that water is supposed to stay white after I put the pesto sauce on. And what the book I'm reading says is that pasta cooked in acidic water might clump up more. Look. It's clumping up."

"That's supposed to be good?" Nettie said, her eyebrows drawn together.

"It means my experiment is working," Chris said.

Nettie looked closer into the pot. "But why does it do that?"

"Don't ask," Mars repeated.

"How come," Danny Borg said, "I'm the only one with green noodles?"

A huge grin spread over Chris's face.

"Don't ask," Nettie said.

"Because," Chris said, "you got the pasta that wasn't cooked in lemon water."

Danny stared at his plate.

"You had a choice," Nettie said. "You could have clumped white pasta or unclumped green pasta."

Danny continued to stare at his plate. "I guess I'm not a gourmet." He said "gore-met." Nettie opened her mouth to correct him, caught Mars's eye, and stopped.

"I mean," Danny said, "I thought all pasta was cooked in just plain water. What difference does lemon juice make?"

"Don't ask!" Mars and Nettie said in unison.

Chris said, "It's about how phenolic enzymes—"

Danny held up both hands. "Skip it. Sorry I asked. Green or white, I don't care. Clumped or unclumped. It's tastes the same. Never mind."

Mars, Nettie, and Danny moved into the apartment's single room after dinner, while Chris cleaned up in the kitchen. Nettie and Danny each took an end of the single bed that doubled as Mars's couch. Mars folded the futon in half, leaning one end against the wall, dropping down on the part that was flat against the floor.

"The first thing that needs to be said, Danny, is that you have the option of staying out of this altogether. No hard feelings if that's your choice. With Nettie and me gone, you're going to be vulnerable. The only thing I can say is that I don't think Freize is gonna notice much what you do or don't do. He's too damn lazy to really manage the investigation."

Danny shook his head. "To tell you the truth? With you and Nettie gone, I'm not even sure I want to be in Homicide. Especially with somebody like Freize running the show. What I'm saying is, the way things stand, I don't care if I do get in trouble. I want to do anything I can on this investigation. I just need you to tell me what I do if I find out something that I think is important. I can't go to Freize. He'd just be pissed I was on the case, wouldn't matter what I'd found out."

"You let me know, you let Nettie know. What we do depends on what it is you find."

Nettie said, "Does this mean we're assuming we're going to leave with everything pretty much the way it is now?"

Mars shook his head. "It's not over until it's over. We're going to use all the time we've got. All it takes is one break. If we can put hands on Tanney, Sater, Weber, or Venema—even one of them—that could unravel the whole thing. Danny? Anything at all on Weber or Venema—even somebody who's gotten a phone call or seen one of them across a crowded room since the twenty-third?"

"Nothing," Danny said. "I can find any number of people who saw them before then. After the twenty-third, the last person to see Venema is you, Mars. After that, it's like they've dropped off the face of the earth." He hesitated. "Any chance T-Jack would have murdered them too? I mean, assuming he got to Tanney and Sater."

Mars stared. He'd given thought to this early on and concluded that T-Jack wouldn't have had time to dispose of Tanney and Sater, much less Weber and Venema. More than that, he was increasingly sure that T-Jack wasn't going to personally murder anybody. He said as much to Danny and Nettie.

"So," Danny said, "you think he hired somebody else to take those four guys out?"

"No, I don't think that," Mars said. "What would that get him? An ever-widening circle of people that needed to be taken care of. If Tanney, Sater, Weber, and Venema are dead, I'm pretty sure that T-Jack is responsible, but I'm also guessing that whoever actually did the deed doesn't know that T-Jack is responsible."

"I don't follow," Danny said.

Nettie sat up and started to put a sandal on. "Figuring out what we need to follow is our first order of business. Geez," she said, pulling on the second sandal, "you know it's hot when a sandal with two half-inch strips of leather make your feet sweat. I'm gonna go home."

Mars said, "I'm meeting Grace DuCain tomorrow. I want to drive the route between downtown and DuCain Towers anyway— time it. See if it tells me anything about what T-Jack might have done between the settlement meeting and the murder scene. So, if I drive that far west, I might as well go out to the DuCain house. She said she still feels like a freak show when she's in public. . . ."

"So I'll see you in the squad room when I see you," Nettie said. "Where are we gonna watch T-Jack and Bryant tomorrow night?"

"Back here at eight?" Mars said.

Mars noticed Danny giving a look around the apartment as he left.

"This is what you've got to look forward to if you do good and stay around long enough," Mars said. "A real motivator, huh?"

Mars and Chris sat on the bed to watch the movie. Evelyn had given them an important tip about watching *Alice Doesn't Live Here*

Anymore. Skip the first two minutes. The first two minutes of *Alice* proved that even great directors like Scorsese are capable of making serious errors in judgment.

"Why do you think he did it that way?" Chris asked as they fast-forwarded past the sepia-tinted scenes of Alice as a little girl, fantasying about her future as a singer.

"Don't you remember? Evelyn said she thought it was both a tribute and a satire on *The Wizard of Oz. . . .*"

"Yeah, but when Evelyn said that, she hit herself on the head right away and said it was saying stuff like that made her hate being an academic."

Just in the nick of time, the movie's color and sound track got real, dropping Mars and Chris out of Alice's sepia-hued past into her crappy Technicolor life with a Coca-Cola truck driver in a New Mexico town.

Everybody in the movie was great. Harvey Keitel put a face to domestic violence that was as terrifying as anything Mars had seen on film. Then there was a young and androgynous Jodie Foster, who blew everybody else off the screen every time she was in a scene. Most remarkable was Alfred Lutter, a woeful, dead-on-real kid who played Ellen Burstyn's son. Watching them, Mars thought he could see the movie once a month for the rest of his life, just for the pleasure of seeing those two kids.

After the movie, they sat side by side, silent, as the VCR rewound, semihypnotized by the machine's soft whirring. Watching the movie—remembering watching it with Evelyn—had left a texture in the room neither wanted to disturb by speaking. Then Chris said, "What do you think happened to the kid who played Alice's son? We've never seen him in any other movies, have we?"

Mars stretched, holding both arms out straight in front of him, twisting his wrists. Then he said, his words distorted by a long, slow, yawn, "*Bad News Bears*—wasn't he in *Bad News Bears*? If he was anything like his character in *Alice,* I'd be a little worried he got himself into deep water once Ellen Burstyn wasn't his mom anymore."

"Do you think Alice was a good mom?"

Mars thought about Ellen Burstyn's character: unfocused, unrealistic, badly educated, inconsistent.

"I think," Mars said, "she was a great mom. In all the ways that really count."

"Like how?"

"Great sense of humor. Loved the kid a lot. Let him see that she wasn't perfect."

Chris nodded. "I think so too. That she was a great mom. But she's not at all like Mom, right?" Chris turned his head toward Mars.

The perfect segue to the conversation they needed to have.

Mars clasped his hands behind his head and took time before he answered. "Your mom is a great mom in a completely different way. She shows you she loves you by making sure you're taken care of. She's put her own life on hold to make sure she's there when you need her to be there." He hesitated for a heartbeat. "Chris, I'm sorry you found out about your mother's and Carl's plans before your mom and I had a chance to talk to you. It was too much for you to have to think about on your own. Something like that happens again, I want you to talk to your mom or me right away."

Chris's voice was small when he said, "I was afraid if I said it out loud, it would be real. I don't want it to be real. I want everything to stay the way it is." He looked over at Mars again. "Except for Carl. What would be good would be for Carl to go to Cleveland and for us to all stay just the way we are."

Mars put his arm around Chris's shoulder. "It's like I said. Your mom has put her life on hold for a long time for your sake. Now she has a chance for something that's important to her, to her future. If she doesn't take this chance now, I think she feels like she might not have another chance. And you're almost eleven. You'll always be the most important thing to Mom and me, but we're not always going to be the most important things in your life. Your mom has to have things in her life where she is the most important thing."

Chris said, "Why can't I stay here, with you?"

A wave of relief washed over Mars. He realized in that moment he hadn't been sure that Chris would choose to stay with him if that were an option. But the pleasure of the moment was quickly overtaken by reality. It might be his choice, it might be Chris's choice, but that didn't change that Denise wasn't considering it as a possibility. A fact which took Mars to another segue. A difficult segue.

"I would like it if you stayed with me. The thing is, your mom isn't going to want you to stay. I've talked to her a little bit about it, and she was pretty definite. She wants you with her. That's the problem. We both want you with us."

There was a deep frown on Chris's face. "So she decides?"

Mars nodded slowly, feeling like he was moving out on thin ice. "I can challenge this, Chris. In fact, what I wanted to talk about was that I am going to see a lawyer and see what my options are. But if I do that, it's going to create a lot of bad feelings. Between me and Mom, you and Mom—whatever happens in the future, if I fight Mom on this, it could make things worse. What I'm saying, Chris, is that it's up to you. If you want me to fight this, I will."

Chris's frown was deeper. Mars knew he could trust that Chris understood all the issues. But understanding what the issues were made it harder, not easier.

"I don't want to hurt Mom's feelings."

"I don't either. But I also want what's best for you. And I think what's best for you is to stay with me. I don't think I'm being selfish when I say that. But if you decide the best thing for you is to go with Mom, then I won't fight."

There was a long, troubled silence before Chris said, "So if you go to the lawyer, the lawyer might tell Mom she has to let me stay?"

"Not the lawyer," Mars said. "There'd probably be a court hearing. A judge would probably decide. Mom and I would both have lawyers."

"But I wouldn't have to say anything? I mean, I wouldn't have to tell Mom I wanted to be with you instead of her?"

Mars's heart sunk. He knew what Chris meant and he knew that at Chris's age any judge would want Chris to say what he wanted.

"I think you probably would be asked to speak at the hearing.

The judge would want to know what you wanted. You'd have to say who you wanted to be with."

Tears welled in Chris's eyes. "I can't do that," he said. "I can't tell Mom I'd rather be with you." Chris looked up at Mars. "The thing is, if I said that, Mom would be really hurt. She'd be more hurt than you would if I said I'd rather be with her. You'd understand. She won't. There are lots of ways you and me show we love each other. With Mom, she shows me she loves me by cooking and cleaning and making sure I have clean clothes. And I show her I love her by keeping my room clean and getting good grades and putting my dishes in the sink after we eat. Stuff like that. If we didn't live together, she wouldn't have any way of showing that she loved me. And I wouldn't have any way of showing I loved her. And it would be worse if we didn't live together because I'd *said* I didn't want to live with her. It would be like saying that all the things she does for me don't count. If I didn't live with you, you'd still know I loved you. If I didn't live with Mom, I think she'd feel like I didn't love her anymore."

"I think you got that exactly right," Mars said.

They sat in a miserable silence for minutes.

"Can you just talk to the lawyer, Dad? And see if he has any ideas?"

"Yeah," Mars said. "I can and I will."

CHAPTER
19

It took Mars twenty-four minutes to drive from the Jackman house on Lake of the Isles to the exit for DuCain Industries off Highway 394. Mars would have to go over the time line again, but he remembered enough about when T-Jack had left DuCain Industries and when he had arrived at the house to know that—at most—T-Jack might have squeezed a spare five minutes out of the trip.

Not enough time under any scenario to murder Tanney and Sater and dispose of their bodies, much less Tanney, Sater, Weber, and Venema.

Which was no surprise. But Mars remained troubled by the idea that if John Sater and Paul Tanney were dead, T-Jack had to have done something to cause their deaths within that small window of time. T-Jack was plenty smart enough to know that once he went back to the murder scene, he'd be under a microscope. If he was going to do something to cause Sater's and Tanney's deaths, T-Jack's best shot would be between the time he left DuCain Industries and before he arrived at his house.

It was another fifteen minutes to Grace DuCain's front door. Linda Burnet opened the front door, her expression more serious than usual.

"How's Grace?" Mars said as he followed her through the house in the direction of the back porch. "Will somebody be with her tonight?"

"I'm staying—and Royce is coming over. She's all right," Linda said. Then she stopped, and in a low voice said, "I'd feel better if she weren't all right—do you know what I mean? She hasn't broken down once since all this has happened. I worry that this television program T-Jack's doing tonight..." Then she shrugged. "I guess we all just have to hope for the best. She's been looking forward to your visit." Then, before Linda led Mars through to the porch, she said, "She's counting on you. Maybe too much. Don't just give her good news. *Prepare* her for the worst, even if you don't think it will come to that."

Linda hadn't said anything Mars didn't already know, but her having it said so pointedly didn't make him feel good, especially with everything he knew about where they were on the case.

"Mars!" Grace said, rising from a chair as he walked into the porch. "I was just saying to Linda that the days you come are a real bright spot...."

Grace stopped, and the pleasure on her face evaporated. "What is it? You look—I don't know—wounded. What's happened?"

Mars shook his head, fudging the truth. "Nothing to do with the case. I'm tired, there've been some personal problems. Nothing that should concern you."

Grace's face remained uncertain, her eyes fixed on him.

"Can we sit?" he said, moving to a chair, the same chair he'd sat in the first night they'd met. It seemed like a hundred years ago. He started talking to distract her.

"We've made some progress. We've identified the car in the parking lot at DuCain Towers that we think T-Jack signaled during the meeting. We've identified the individual who rented the car and confirmed that he made a cell phone call at the time T-Jack's signal would have been received. What we haven't been able to do is tie his call to the individual we think murdered Terri—or to T-Jack, for that matter."

"And you haven't been able to find him? Or the individual you think actually killed Terri?"

Grace had, of course, put her finger on the key unresolved questions.

"No. What I'm most concerned about is that neither of those

individuals may be alive. If we can find either one of them alive, we've got a good chance of putting together a solid case. Without either one of them . . ."

"You're saying if you can't find one of these men—the man T-Jack signaled from the window during the meeting, or the man who murdered Terri—that you won't be able to send T-Jack to jail?"

Mars could hear the tremble in Grace's voice as she spoke those words. He shook his head. "No. But that's our best shot. And to be honest, it's my only shot before I leave. Today and tomorrow are all I've got. Developing other angles will take time. It can still happen, but it will take time."

"And you *will* be leaving?"

Mars nodded without speaking.

Grace turned her face from him. "I tried to change that. Obviously without success. If Duke had been alive, you'd be staying put."

"I doubt it," Mars said. "Politically, these are very deep waters."

Grace sighed. "I'd asked Royce to do what he could. He knew someone who knew the city council person who chairs the public safety committee. I knew from the sound of it that we didn't have a chance. Royce is very good at many things. But this is the second time I've made the mistake of asking him to do something that wasn't in his line. And both times the mistake has cost me dearly." She turned her head back toward Mars. "You know I'm going to be filing suit to allow me to see Tam?"

Mars nodded.

"All of this would be so much easier if you were going to be involved. . . ."

It took energy for Mars to sound encouraging. "I mean it when I say it will be proven that T-Jack's responsible. It's just that I'm going to feel like I've let you down if I leave without accomplishing that. Personal vanity."

They sat in silence for moments before Mars rose to go. He was startled when he looked at Grace straight on. She looked older.

Impulsively, he reached out and encircled her neck with his

arm. To the top of her head, he said, "It won't matter where I am, Grace. This isn't over."

It was when he passed the exit for DuCain Industries, headed back to town, that the idea began to take shape. He thought about it as he drove back east toward downtown. Take out of the equation the certainty that T-Jack didn't have time to deal with Tanney and Sater between the time he left DuCain Industries and when he arrived at the Lake of the Isles house. Just think about Tanney and Sater. What would they do, when Sater left DuCain Industries, when Tanney left the murder scene. Mars took himself back to August 23, imagining John Sater leaving the parking lot at DuCain Industries. What they both had to be thinking about was getting paid.

Where would the pay-off happen? Double Ds? If so, they would have been seen. Someone would have remembered seeing them there together on the afternoon of the twenty-third. And no one remembered seeing them together anywhere after the twenty-third. Besides, would Tanney have chosen to meet Sater in public minutes after he'd murdered Terri DuCain?

"I don't think so," Mars said out loud. He took the next exit off the freeway and pulled over on a side road. He found a map of the metro area on the floor of the back seat and spread it open across the steering wheel. He traced 394 with his right index finger, paying close attention to areas on either side of the freeway that would have offered T-Jack a private meeting spot with Sater and Tanney.

He found what he was looking for approximately a mile west of downtown Minneapolis. The Elouise Butler Wildflower Garden and Bird Sanctuary. It was a hilly, sheltered area of hardwood trees, ponds, and bogs. The sanctuary was often deserted in spite of its proximity to the urban population—or maybe because of its proximity to the urban population. There was a nature center, but staff at the site was too small to patrol the park. When Chris and Mars had visited two years earlier to collect pictures of wildflowers for a

234

Cub Scout project, theirs had been the only car in the parking lot at 9:00 A.M. on a Saturday morning.

Mars knew from past cases that the sanctuary's parking lot and environs had been the scene of drug deals and the occasional murder. There were higher-risk park areas in the city, but none that offered the same degree of accessibility combined with tranquil isolation.

An idea popped into Mars's head as soon as he pulled off Theodore Wirth Parkway into the sanctuary's parking lot. Before he got out of the car, he called Nettie.

"Check Park Police records and see if they ticketed and towed a car from the Elouise Butler Sanctuary that matches Sater's rental car."

Once again, the parking lot was empty. Within a couple of strides outside of his car, Mars realized why. The air was thick with clouds of mosquitoes. There probably wasn't a better breeding site for the pests in the metro area. It was unlikely that the nature preserve's many stagnant ponds of water would be sprayed for mosquito control and the park was uniformly shaded.

Mars had felt the first *ting* of possibility when he'd sited the preserve on the map. It was the perfect site in terms of privacy and that it was in a direct line between DuCain Industries and the Lake of the Isles. The *ting* had increased in volume as he'd driven into the parking lot. Now, heading into the sanctuary on a narrow dirt path, moving from bright sunlight to dim daylight, all of his senses were ringing with recognition.

They'd been here.

It was then that he saw it. Off the path, in high weeds. At first sight, a scrap of paper. As he moved closer to it, it confirmed his guess. It was half of a hundred-dollar bill. Battered, soiled, but unmistakably, half of a hundred-dollar bill.

Mars cursed himself for not having a plastic bag with him. He pulled a clean handkerchief out of his back pocket and delicately picked the bill up, folding it gently into the cloth, which he tucked into his shirt pocket. He moved on, following posted maps that showed a bog near the sanctuary's center.

Within a hundred yards, the path forked. He went to the right, moving slowly to allow him time to scan each side of the path for more bills, or anything that tied to Sater and Tanney having been here. There was nothing, but the vibes continued to feel right.

Within ten minutes he came out into an open area, the path leading on to a narrow wooden bridge that crossed an algae-covered bog.

Ting, ting, ting!

Mars stood on the bridge for minutes, his heart pounding. The water was too murky, the bottom would be too deep with soft mud, for divers to have an easy time of it. He'd need to get cadaver dogs down here. And what he was certain the dogs would find would be Sater's and Tanney's bodies.

Any elation Mars felt was quickly eroded by basic facts. Although it made sense that the sanctuary would be the perfect spot for T-Jack to reconnoiter with Sater and Tanney, there was no way T-Jack would have had time to meet them here, kill the two of them, dump their bodies into the bog, and make it back to the Lake of the Isles house in less than thirty minutes. There was still something that Mars was missing.

His cell phone rang.

"Mars?" Nettie said. "Sater's rental car was tagged by Park Police and towed from the parking lot of the Elouise Butler Wild Flower Garden and Bird Sanctuary at eight-thirty the morning of August twenty-fifth. I've arranged for the car to be transferred and examined as a crime scene—it should be in our custody within the next hour. Annoys the hell out of me. Don't know why we have so many problems integrating Park Police records with our records. Another thing—they didn't even file the paperwork on the tow until yesterday."

Mars stared out across the bog, holding the cell phone to his ear, swatting bugs with his other hand. He thought back to what he knew about Sater in the parking lot at DuCain Industries to Sater's drive to the sanctuary parking lot to meet—who? Tanney for sure. Then he remembered something else that he knew about Sater waiting for the signal in the parking lot at DuCain Industries.

He remembered the 1-900 call to the phone-sex line.

"Nettie? We need cadaver dogs at the bog in the sanctuary. And send a Crime Scene Unit. One other thing. When the car comes in, be sure someone checks the front seats for seminal fluid."

"Semen?" Nettie said. "Why do you think there's going to be semen on the front seat?"

"Tell you when I get back."

"If they're there now," Clayton Freize said when Mars asked him to approve overtime to begin the search of the bog that night, "they'll still be there tomorrow."

Which was why, at 8:00 P.M. on August 30, Mars was not at the sanctuary's bog, but was in front of his TV set with Nettie and Danny, waiting to see Bryant Gumbel's interview with Tayron Jackman.

"Fritz Mercer made a mistake picking Gumbel," Danny said.

"He's black and he's a sports nut," Nettie said.

"That's the mistake. Gumbel's a tough interview. He's not gonna cut T-Jack any slack because he's black or because he's a jock. You ever see Gumbel on that HBO sports program, *Real Sports*? He blows people away."

"Missed it," Nettie said, not convinced.

60 Minutes ticking clock interrupted them. The ticking clock and Mike Wallace's face were all that were familiar of the program's format. Wallace sat in front of a black background, against which giant red letters read: T-JACK TALKS. And in smaller letters, A CBS News Exclusive Interview.

Wallace's urbane, leathery, carefully groomed face stared at the camera. You could smell a faint, citrusy-aftershave just looking at him. Wallace's voice was deep, vaguely severe, as it rolled over his script, his eyes not leaving the camera's eye.

"Tonight, we depart from our usual time and format to bring you an exclusive CBS News interview with Tayron Jackman, star point guard for the Minnesota Timberwolves and"—here there was the slightest lift of incredulity in Wallace's tone—"according to

T-Jack, the bereaved husband of Terri DuCain Jackman." Wallace stretched out the pronunciation of "bereaved," drawing his chin in. He let the statement hang for the barest moment before going on.

"Terri DuCain Jackman was found brutally murdered in her exclusive Minneapolis home on August twenty-third. Since that time, speculation has run rife that T-Jack—if not directly responsible for his estranged wife's death—arranged to have her murdered. T-Jack has refused public statements since that time. But tonight, on the eve of what is certain to be a bitter legal battle between T-Jack and Terri DuCain Jackman's mother over visitation rights for the Jackmans' only child—T-Jack has agreed to speak with *60 Minutes*. In arranging this interview, CBS made no concessions to Mr. Jackman regarding format or the questions that would be asked. He did ask that our colleague Bryant Gumbel conduct the interview. Bryant is a respected newsman in his own right and we were happy to accede to this single request."

"Ed Bradley must be biting bricks," Nettie said.

"Bradley would have been good, too," Danny said. "Not a jockstrap sniffer, but he would have been tough."

"Ed Bradley and Barbara Walters and Diane Sawyer and Katie Couric *and* Mike Wallace," Mars said. "They're all biting bricks about now."

CBS went to a commercial break directly after Wallace's intro. Mars paced, deeply curious about how T-Jack was going to handle the interview, but acutely aware of how Grace DuCain, sitting in front of the television, would be feeling as she waited.

The interview began immediately after the commercial break, with the camera tight on T-Jack.

Simultaneously, Mars, Nettie, and Danny howled. T-Jack was wearing a khaki suit, a blue oxford-cloth button-down shirt, and a red and blue striped rep tie.

"Where's the black Armani?" Nettie yelled at T-Jack's image.

"In Hal Flison's closet," Mars said.

Bryant Gumbel came out of the blocks fast and straight.

"Tayron Jackman. Did you murder your wife."

T-Jack looked directly at Gumbel. His body posture was re-

238

laxed, his expression benign—not hard and arrogant as it had been every time Mars had seen him. Then, T-Jack blinked: slowly, purposefully.

Mars and Nettie howled again, Nettie falling to her side, pounding the bed she was sitting on with clenched fists.

"What?" Danny said.

"It's a classic Flison-coached move," Nettie said. "If his client can't generate real tears, they blink just like that. As if they're holding back emotion. . . ."

"Shhhh," Mars said.

T-Jack spoke in a soft voice.

"I did not. I couldn't have. Not physically, not emotionally. I love Terri. Loved her from the first moment I saw her. She's the mother of my only child." T-Jack hesitated, then the slow blink came again. "She *was* the mother of my only child."

Nettie stuck her fist into her mouth. "Thith ith making me nuths," she garbled over her knuckles.

Gumbel narrowed his eyes, drawing his head back slightly as he looked at T-Jack.

"You said you couldn't have 'physically' murdered your wife. What do you mean by that?"

T-Jack lifted a hand in a motion of helplessness. "I mean that I couldn't have been in two places at once. I was somewhere else when Terri was murdered. Terri's mother knows that, the DuCains' lawyer knows that. The police know there's no way I could have murdered Terri."

Gumbel's expresssion changed, became less neutral. "You're a smart man, T-Jack. You know what people are saying. They're saying even if you didn't actually murder Terri, you arranged to have her murdered. They say the terms of the settlement agreement you were signing when Terri was murdered make your agenda clear."

T-Jack shook his head slowly, did a Flison-blink twice before responding.

"The whole settlement thing. That was never something I wanted. It was something the DuCains wanted from the day I married Terri. They did everything they could to make our marriage fail."

"It's rumored," Gumbel said, "that you asked Terri's father for a hundred million to divorce Terri. You're a wealthy man, T-Jack. Why would you give up a woman you say you loved for money?"

Again, the slow headshake. "Duke was always offering me money to divorce Terri. Just to say how much she meant to me, I said, a hundred million. I never thought he'd take it serious. When he did—well, I consider myself to be an honorable man. I said a hundred million, not meaning it, he said okay. There I was. I think the question is, what kind of man would offer money to break up his daughter's marriage? If I could change one thing in all of this— one thing more than Terri not being murdered—it would be that I never said a hundred million when Duke asked me how much I wanted to give Terri up."

The program went to commercial break.

"He's doing it," Nettie said. "He's not looking evil and what he says makes sense."

Mars was silent. Grace DuCain's reaction to what was happening in the interview was filling his mind.

Gumbel shifted tack in the next segment of the interview.

"The Timberwolves' first exhibition game of the season is early this year. Less than six weeks away. You going to be suiting up when they hit the court?"

For just that moment, there was a flash of the black Armani T-Jack. His face set, glimmering with hostility. Then it was gone. He managed a look of remote amusement.

"Why wouldn't I?"

"If I were Guy Corson," Gumbel said, "I'd have to be more than a little worried about having a player associated with his wife's murder playing ball for me. Gotta be a distraction for the team and for fans."

T-Jack made an open motion with his hands. "Corson's a businessman. He understands costs and benefits. All I've got to say on the subject is my lawyers tell me that the Timberwolves have no reason for not honoring my contract. Even the police acknowledge

240

it's not possible that I murdered my wife. The Wolves try to keep me from playing because my wife was murdered, I call that kicking a man when he's down. Playin' ball and my daughter—that's all I've got left now. Besides, they don't let me play, I take that as a kind of slander, don't I?"

"Do you?" Gumbel said, not taking his eyes off T-Jack.

T-Jack met Gumbel's stare. "You bet I do."

Gumbel began a series of questions about T-Jack's basketball career which seemed to Mars to break the flow of what the interview was about. But as he watched T-Jack loosen up as he answered questions unrelated to Terri's murder, Mars began to suspect that Gumbel was working a strategy.

Gumbel confirmed Mars's suspicion with a sharp question that followed Gumbel asking T-Jack how he saw the Timberwolves' season shaping up.

"If you aren't responsible for Terri's death, who is?"

T-Jack appeared to be startled. Then you could see him regrouping, finding the flap he could slip under into his Flison-ized personality. But his rhythm was off. For the first time in the interview, he seemed something less than in control.

"I have some ideas. But there are things I can't talk about. Like I said, I loved Terri. She was the mother of my only child. I can't talk about things that would hurt that memory or that would hurt my daughter."

Gumbel let T-Jack's answer sit for a moment, then he said, "But you have shared those ideas with the police."

T-Jack's answer demonstrated that he had recovered from the surprise of Gumbel's shifting focus. "Let me put it this way. I think the police have what they need to solve this case. Whether they choose to pursue everything they know—that's a separate question. The truth is, I'm constrained in what I can say by the agreement the DuCains had me sign. There are things I can't talk about, even if I, personally, weren't concerned about Terri's reputation."

"The shit," Mars said.

The rest of the interview involved Gumbel pushing T-Jack on questions asked earlier, shifting field, changing lines of attack.

T-Jack, having been surprised once, was not taken by surprise again. Not even at the end of the interview.

"T-Jack," Gumbel said, "You've refused any comment on your wife's murder until now. Why talk now?"

T-Jack took his time to answer. Mars could see him settling deeper into his Flison-ized persona, physically and mentally. He sat farther back in his chair, he composed himself. If you didn't know better, you'd say he was feeling something emotionally and wanted to get that under control before he spoke.

"I'm going to be doing something that people are going to have a hard time understanding. I'm going to try to keep Terri's mother from seeing my daughter. If people think I'm doing that because I'm selfish, because I'm mean—well, I might not succeed. I lost my wife because Mrs. DuCain poisoned Terri against me. I can't trust her not to do the same with Tamara. I'll do whatever it takes to preserve my relationship with my daughter.

"It's what I said before. She's all I have left."

The words sent a chill down Mars's spine. He could only guess how they'd made Grace feel.

"I've got to leave," he said.

Mars slapped the flasher on the dash and hit the siren as he pulled out of the apartment parking lot onto the street. He ripped through downtown, onto 394 going west, driving like a madman. There was an accident just east of the Highway 100 exit, backing traffic up for almost two miles. Barely slowing down, Mars sped along the shoulder, raising false hopes in fellow drivers that he was on his way to untie the traffic knot.

When he got within a half-mile of Grace DuCain's house, he turned the siren off. She didn't need to hear the siren. He parked at a crazy angle in front of the house, knocking on the door and pushing it open in a simultaneous motion. He ran directly into Linda Burnet.

Linda started to shake her head, then said, pointing, "Royce just left. She's alone. In there."

Grace DuCain was standing at a window, her back to Mars.

242

Without seeing her face, he could tell she was crying. She knew it was Mars without looking. She didn't turn around as she said, "He's done it. He's beaten me."

Mars stood behind her. Both hands on her shoulders, squeezing hard.

"It's not over, Grace. I'm not done."

She didn't answer him.

Driving east on 394, headed back toward downtown, he took the exit for the Elouise Butler sanctuary. He sat in the car in the parking lot, wanting to stay close to the only chance he had left to close the case before he left.

He was still there when the search crews arrived the next morning, August 31.

CHAPTER

20

"Bog people," Doc D said, flicking ashes from his cigarette into the green pudding of the pond.

Two rowboats moved slowly on either side of the bridge, each occupied by two officers and a dog. One officer rowed, while the other held a dog on a short lead.

"What?" Mars said.

"There's almost no oxygen in a bog. That, and vegetation in the water, has an alkalinizing effect. So a body in a bog remains relatively well preserved for long periods of time. I remember reading about a bunch of people pulled out of a swamp in Florida. Thousands of years old. Discolored, but more or less intact. I'm looking forward to seeing what we'll fish out of this soup." He gestured toward one of the boats. "What sort of reaction from the dog indicates a find?"

Mars said, "I've never seen a dog working under these conditions. Normally, the dog becomes agitated, will have a focused gaze, will keep looking back to his handler. They do everything short of pointing with a paw. One of the handlers was telling me before they started that he was concerned that under these conditions— where there's normally a lot of decay, both vegetative and animal— the dogs might have a hard time distinguishing a single decay site. So they both seem a little hyped, without the focus they might have in fresh water, where the only source of decay would be what you were looking for."

"That," Doc D said, lighting another cigarette, "and the fact that—like I said—I'm not expecting your guys to be decaying much if they got dropped in this muck right after dying."

Mars frowned. "They've pretty much covered the surface of the bog now. And I haven't seen anything that gives us a place to start searching."

"Looks to me," Doc D said, "like you're going to have to pull a net across the bottom. That should be interesting."

Mars gave a short kick to a rail on the bridge. "This could take forever. Our first problem was that Freize wouldn't approve overtime for the cadaver dogs last night—no, that's not right. Our first problem was I *asked* Freize to approve overtime. Didn't think for a minute he'd say no. I was just giving him a chance to get involved in what might be the most significant part of the investigation. Thought he'd like to see his signature on the authorization form. So we lost time getting started."

"What's he up to, anyway?" Doc said. "He wants to delay resolving this thing, so he can take credit after you leave?"

Mars shrugged. "That would suggest Freize has the brains to think strategically. I just think he's stupid. Saying no feels more like being boss than saying yes, so he says no more than yes."

Doc sighed. He stubbed out his cigarette and twisted his wrist to look at his watch. "We know where we're gonna get dental records on these guys once we pull them out? I'm betting they're not going to be carrying drivers' licenses and birth certificates."

"Nettie's running that down," Mars said. "And Tanney's got fingerprints on file from a prior arrest. Provided the hands are in good enough condition to allow us to pull prints." Mars grinned. "For Sater, we've got a possible DNA source. There was seminal fluid on the front seat of the rental car he drove here—at the front edge of the driver's seat and along the left side of the passenger seat, like he rubbed his hand on the side of the seat after he shot his wad. So, if we can match the DNA from the fluid with what we get from a body, we've nailed Sater."

"Oh, you'll be able to pull prints on Tanney, all right. If he went into the bog right after he died. It's what I was just saying.

245

Somebody in a bog is gonna turn a funny color, but they're gonna be in good shape." Doc squinted at an increasingly clouded sky. "So, the other guy jacks off while he's waiting to get a signal to murder someone? Damn. I figure any lousy thing a woman wants to think about men is more or less justified, wouldn't you say? The power of lust. Give a guy a minute with nothing better to do, and he'll figure it's time to raise the flag."

"In this case, we're lucky he did." Mars looked at the sky. "It's gonna rain." He signaled to one of the boats to come over to the bridge.

"What do you think?" he said as the boat came alongside.

The guy handling the dog shook his head. "Bad environment for the dogs. They're frustrated. You've probably had a pile of critters slipping in here over the years and the vegetation that's decayed creates a strong odor overlay. It's overwhelming the dogs." He looked up at the sky. "And it's going to rain, which will intensify all of the environmental odors they're dealing with. I mean, normally there isn't any problem for a dog to separate scents. It's just there's a lot of general decay in the area."

Mars nodded. "Look, talk to the other handler. If he feels the same way, I think we'll call off the dogs. We're gonna have to go for a drag. I'd like to find our bodies and get out of here before Christmas."

Mars called Nettie to ask her to put in a request with the Sheriff's Department to send out the Hennepin County Water Patrol Unit. He apologized for not having thought of putting them on stand-by earlier.

"Not to worry," Nettie said. "I gave them a standby request at the same time I scheduled the cadaver dogs. Just in case."

Doc snapped his fingers when Mars told him Nettie had already arranged for the water patrol to come out. "Thank you for that. For years Nettie has reminded me of someone, and I just figured out who. Radar on *M*A*S*H*. Feels good to put a name to that one."

"I hope it doesn't follow," Mars said, "that I'm Colonel Klink or whatever his name was."

"Colonel Klink is *Hogan's Heroes*. And no, it doesn't follow. Nettie makes everybody look like dim bulbs. Doesn't matter how smart you are, Nettie's gonna be two steps ahead."

Which, Mars thought, didn't make him feel less like Colonel Klink.

A light drizzle had begun by the time the water patrol showed up. The water patrol set up a tarpaulin at one end of the bog which gave everyone at the site some shelter from the wet and increasingly cold day. There was a stack of camp chairs under the tarp, and Mars and Doc each set a chair up.

As the temperature dropped, the rain intensified. "Feels like September is upon us," Doc said, blowing on his hands. "At least it keeps the mosquitoes down."

"September is tomorrow," Mars said.

"You know, everyone talks about how cold it is in Minnesota. How much snow we get. That's not what makes our weather so miserable. It's days like today that are hard to take. Mid-morning today it was, what? High eighties, low nineties? Right now it's gotta be low fifties. A thirty- to- forty-degree drop in a matter of hours. That's Minnesota weather for you. And you never know. I remember I was flying somewhere on April 14, 1983. I wake up to go to the airport and there are seventeen inches of snow on the ground. Took me longer to get to the airport than to fly wherever it was I was going. Remember the day Gorbachev came to Minnesota? June of 1990, wasn't it? The wind was blowing and there were snowflakes in the air. Poor guy must have thought he'd landed in Siberia. Three years ago on December first? I went home for lunch and picked greens from the garden for lunch. A week later, it was below zero. That's Minnesota weather. It's got nothing to do with the temperature or how much snow we get. It has to do with never knowing what the weather will be any hour of the day, any day of the week, any month of the year."

Mars picked up a blanket and wrapped it around his shoulders. "Look, there's no reason for you to stay. We find the bodies, I'll call you. We're not going to do anything with them here, anyway. Impossible in these conditions. We'll just tape the scene, bag the bodies, and bring them back down to you. You can have at them in the comfort of your own morgue."

"Nah," Doc said. "I'm enjoying myself. I wanna be around when the bog people come up in that net."

If Mars and Doc were miserable, they only had to consider what the men in the bog were up against. They wore wet suits with high-power beams strapped around their heads. After the first dive into the bog to set the net, they pulled the beams off their heads.

"Useless," one of the divers said, coming back to the tarp for coffee from the thermoses that sat on chairs. "It's like diving in pea soup. The best we can do is feel our way down."

"Any idea how deep it is?" Mars asked.

"Where we're working now," the diver said, drinking from the thermos cap, green muck from his lips dropping into the coffee, "there's about six, seven feet of water. Maybe another three feet of mud on the bottom. It would be easier to do this when the weather had been cold for a while. The bottom would be firmer. We're just gonna have to hope whatever's down there will snag the net when we drag. Anything more than a foot below the mud line, we're gonna miss."

The net was dragged from two high-torque ATVs that were positioned on the opposite side of the bog. They moved slowly, spitting back mud and vegetation as the wheels dug in, the net shifting forward as they pulled, causing black lines to form across the top of the bog, black lines that melted back to green within seconds.

Minutes after the drag had begun, the net strained.

"Hold it!" one of the divers shouted. He'd been paddling to the side of the net as it moved. He dove down, was under for moments, then surfaced. He pulled the face mask off, shaking his head. "Can't tell," he called. "Keep moving, slowly."

The net inched forward, resisting from time to time, but after forty-five minutes, reaching the opposite side of the bog. All the water patrol staff gathered round to pull the net to shore. Mars and

Doc left the shelter of the tarp to join them, as much out of impatience to see what was in the net as to be helpful.

Old tires, logs, a lawn chair, part of what looked like an oil barrel, and—this was the best part—half of a porcelain kitchen sink.

"Everything except the socks that have gone missing from my laundry over the past fifty years," Doc said.

"Everything except your socks and John Sater and Paul Tanney," Mars said.

It took another half-hour to reposition the net for the drag across the middle of the bog. Then, halfway through the second drag, the net stuck and stayed stuck. Two divers went down repeatedly, resurfacing every few minutes to orient themselves, then diving back down.

The third time up, one of the divers pulled off his face mask and called out, "Got something. Think it'll be easier to get it out of the net and bring it up separately, than continue to drag."

Both divers treaded water next to each other before plunging back into the bog in a synchronized dive. When they came up again—maybe two minutes later—they carried something between them. It was impossible to tell from where Mars and Doc stood what the divers had, and they headed to the shore where the divers were headed.

As they struggled out of the muck, dragging their find between them, one of the divers gave a thumbs-up and called out, "One down, one to go."

Mars and Doc spent the next forty-five minutes looking over the body. Mars had seen snapshots of both men and knew roughly what body types they were. Doc had been right about the bog's preservative effect. The body was in remarkably good physical shape for an organic object that had been dead in water.

"I'm guessing this is Tanney," Mars said. "From what I remember of the photos. Can't see any injuries—can you?"

Doc was on his knees alongside the body, delicately prodding, lifting fabric, pushing the body to the side.

"Oh, my God," he said.

"What?"

"His hands were bound behind his back—the rope's broken, so the arms are free now. But the rope is still on the other wrist, and there's trauma on both wrists." He lifted the pant legs off the ankles. "And the legs were tied. Whoever did this threw the guy into the bog alive. He drowned. We open him up, he's gonna be full of bog. Nasty way to die."

Nasty needs a reason, is what Mars thought. T-Jack didn't have a reason—or time—to be nasty.

They were still by the body when the divers called out again. They were halfway through the third drag, just the other side of the bridge. Mars and Doc walked again to the bog edge, waiting for the divers to bring in what they'd found.

"Well done," Mars said as the divers rose from the bog, a second body between them.

"Better than well done," gasped one of the divers. "There's another one out there. Just couldn't manage two at once."

When all three bodies were lined up along the bog, Doc and Mars took their time looking them over. Of the three, two had been bound at the wrists and ankles with no visible wounds or injuries. The third—the smallest of the three—had been shot through the temple, a bloodstain visible on the bandanna tied around his head.

It all came together for Mars at once. He knew how it had worked. Knew how T-Jack had made it work.

The water patrol guys were wrapping up, stowing gear, starting to remove wetsuits.

"Sorry, guys," Mars said. "I'm going to have to ask you to finish dragging the entire bog. I need to be sure there's not a fourth body down there."

Doc looked up at Mars. "You were expecting two, you get three, and now you want four?"

Mars knelt down again by the smallest victim.

"I think I know who this one is," he said. "Vonnie Gerber described one of the guys who roughed her up as short, with a bandanna around his head. He still looks a little like the photo I have of him. If I'm right, if this *is* Matt Weber, then I've got to be

250

sure Lyle Venema isn't in the bog too. I don't think he is, but I've got to be sure."

"If he's not in the bog, where do you think he is?"

"He's either dead or holed up somewhere taping hundred-dollar bills together. But I've got to be sure."

Mars called Nettie as soon as he'd gotten out of his bog clothes and showered.

"Who's around?" he said.

"Just us chickens. Danny's at his desk—not working the case, of course. He's inputting homicide data on a city map. Totally duplicates my interstate project—on a much smaller scale, but that doesn't seem to worry Clayton."

"Clayton's not around?"

"Was. Looking for you. Wanted to hear all about the three guys you brought back from the bog. Left a few minutes ago. Didn't say where he was going."

"I'm hungry. And I'd like to talk somewhere other than the squad room. Can you meet me for a late lunch in fifteen minutes?"

"Sure. As long as you let me take you to Restaurant Alma. They opened for lunch a couple weeks ago. We deserve a decent meal. And I haven't heard the details on the three guys you pulled out of the bog either. . . ."

Restaurant Alma wore its mantle as one of the city's most sophisticated restaurants lightly. Its staff dressed casually and were uniformly egalitarian in welcoming diners. Located in an unpretentious red brick building on University Avenue near the Mississippi, you didn't know you'd entered a high temple of food until you got the menu.

Wild flower honey, aged manchego, wild cockles, braised chard, and black trumpet mushrooms—on his first visit to Alma's, Mars concluded it wasn't his kind of place. It was after he took a mouthful of Alma's braised short ribs that he fell to his knees in reverence. It was possible to have dinner at Alma's without spending a fortune, but only if you stuck to the top of the menu. And Alma's was the

251

kind of place that did nothing to encourage self-denial. So after one dinner with Chris and Evelyn, Mars had steered clear.

"You can get a really good lunch for under fifteen dollars," Nettie said when their waitress left them with menus. "Salad, an entrée—maybe even a Coke."

"Still rich for me," Mars said. "But you're right. We deserve a good lunch."

Their waitress returned, placing a small bowl of seasoned almonds and olives between them.

"Thanks, Katherine," Nettie said. Pointing at the bowl, she whispered to Mars, *"Free."*

"Katherine?" Mars said. "You're on a first-name basis with the wait staff?"

Nettie shrugged. "I'm addicted. What can I say." Nettie said, "Tell me about the three guys in the bog."

"They explain a lot."

"Really? I would have thought the extra body would have fuzzed things up."

Mars shook his head. "No. Because I think the third man is Matt Weber."

Nettie scrunched her eyebrows together. "One of the guys Yvonne Gerber told you was chasing Paul Tanney?"

"The same. It wasn't just Gerber who said Weber and Venema were looking for Tanney. I think it was pretty much common knowledge. Which means T-Jack could have known...."

"So where's Venema?"

"That's getting ahead of the story. I want to tell you how I think this deal worked. And I want you to tell me why I'm wrong."

"My pleasure," Nettie said, meaning it.

"Okay. You've gotta start with the assumption that T-Jack knew Weber and Venema were looking for Tanney and that Weber and Venema worked for Jerome Hebb. Everyone at Double Ds seemed to know that, so there's no reason T-Jack wouldn't have known."

"Granted."

"I think T-Jack 'paid' Tanney in advance with hundred-dollar bills that had been cut in half, promising to meet Tanney and Sater at the bog with the other half on his way back to the Lake of the Isles house."

"I'm still waiting to hear how Venema and Weber get into this act."

"This is where T-Jack's true genius comes into play. Sometime before the murder, T-Jack stashes the other half of the hundred-dollar bills at the Elouise Butler sanctuary. Then, on the twenty-third, before T-Jack went out to DuCain Industries, he called Venema or Weber. An anonymous call. Used a phone card, a pay phone. Tells them where a pile of halved hundreds can be found at the sanctuary, and tells them they can find the other half of the hundreds when Tanney and Sater show up at the bog. So when Sater and Tanney get to the bog, Weber and Venema are waiting for them."

Nettie wasn't interrupting him, which was a good sign.

"When Sater and Tanney turn up, Weber and Venema appear, hog-tie the two of them, and dump them into the bog."

"Alive? They dumped them into the bog hog-tied and alive?"

"Yeah. Doc is sure that's the way it worked. And it fits. These are mean, nasty guys who were royally pissed at Tanney and Sater for giving them the runaround. And there's no way one guy could hog-tie two guys by himself. One of them was holding a gun while the other was doing the tying. When both Sater and Tanney were tied, Weber and Venema dropped them in the drink. Plus they want all the money, not just what's owed. And they've probably got a real perverted sense of humor. Got a big kick out of dumping the guys in the bog alive. Probably stood around and watched the bubbles come up."

"I still don't know why you think the third body belonged to Weber."

"Two reasons. Number one. Short. Number two. A bandanna around his head, just like Vonnie Gerber said. The lightbulb goes on in Venema's head when he sees the money. Why should he share the money with Weber? So after they've dumped Sater and Tanney, Venema puts the gun to Weber's head. If the third body had been tall, I'd be guessing that Weber put the gun to Venema's head."

Nettie thought and chewed on an olive. "So Tanney owed money to Hebb that Venema keeps?"

Mars smiled. "I saw Venema at Hebb's the day after the murder. Hebb asked him if he'd found Tanney, and Venema started sweating blood. He got out of there with his tail between his legs. Hebb saw the same thing I did."

"So—how do we find Venema? We've been looking for more than a week. . . ."

"We were looking for someone who was alive, Nettie. We need to look for a corpse. My guess is that Venema was a dead man when Hebb figured out Venema was ripping him off."

Nettie stared into space. Mars could almost hear the wheels turning inside her head.

"So you're going to see Doc?"

"You got it." He looked down at the menu. "Right after I eat a green salad with wild flower honey dressing and a corn crepe."

"How does this play in the investigation?" she asked. "I mean, does it get us closer to charging T-Jack or does it complicate the case?"

Always the right question from Nettie.

Mars met her stare.

"What do you think?"

"First reaction? That it's what we were missing. Second reaction? It helps T-Jack."

"You were right the second time. All the circumstantial stuff we've established about Tanney and Sater—except for Sater in the parking lot and the phone call he makes from the parking lot— gets blown away by tying Venema and Weber to their deaths. And I'm going to be real surprised if we can establish any link between T-Jack and Venema and Weber. T-Jack's defense could even make a case that Tanney and Sater went to the Lake of the Isles house to try to get money from T-Jack, that Venema and Weber followed him, there was a confrontation there, and Terri DuCain ends up dead. Then Venema and Weber drag Tanney and Sater out to Elouise Butler and dump them in the bog."

"Doesn't sound half bad. Are we sure something like that didn't happen?"

Mars gave Nettie a look. "You think there's a chance T-Jack isn't responsible for Terri DuCain's death?"

"No, of course not. For one thing, it's a mighty big coincidence that they'd go to the Lake of the Isles house at the same time T-Jack is having the settlement meeting at DuCain Industries."

"Coincidence," Mars said, "is what reasonable doubt is all about. Given the other holes in this case, it just adds weight in the wrong direction." As they finished lunch, Nettie said, "Pretty amazing, when you think about it. Four people dead—maybe five if Venema is dead—and T-Jack hasn't lifted a finger."

"Grace DuCain said it on day one. To understand what T-Jack's done, you have to understand evil." Mars stood up, throwing bills on the table, which Nettie shoved back at him.

"This one's on me. And if you argue, I'll file an affirmative action complaint against you."

"I'm not going to argue. Being a kept man might be one of the few survival options I have left."

"See you later, Mars."

A slow smile passed over Mars's face.

"You've got fifteen seconds: 'Thanks for the warning.' "

" 'See you later,' 'Thanks for the warning'? Oh, God, Mars. This game is getting old. Can we agree that this is the last great-movie-lines game we'll play? I mean, let's make a fresh start tomorrow. You can give up your cigarette pack and we'll both give up the great-movie-lines routine."

"You've got ten seconds."

Nettie's eyes darted back and forth. "I'm going to take a wild guess, based on something I noticed at your apartment the other night. *Alice Doesn't Live Here Anymore* and . . . and—well, it's got to be Ellen Burstyn and that terrific kid who played her smart-ass son. Burstyn says, 'See you later,' and the smart-ass kid says, 'Thanks for the warning.' It's been—I don't know—twenty years at least since I saw the video. I thought when I saw it on your kitchen counter the other night that I need to watch it again."

Mars stared at her. "This is one of those moments when I feel like your talents are being wasted solving murders."

"Tell me something I don't know."

"Tomorrow is T-Jack plus one."

"I knew that too. Tell me Lyle Venema is still alive. That's what I want to hear."

The sun was going down when Mars made it over to the Hennepin County Morgue. Doc was waiting for him, a decaying corpse spread out on a stainless steel autopsy table.

"The tip-off," Doc said, "was when you mentioned the halved hundreds. This guy was brought in three days ago. Found him in the trunk of a stolen car parked at a liquor store on Franklin Avenue."

Mars stared at the remains on the table. "This guy had pockets left to put bills in?"

Doc lifted his eyebrows. With a pristine scalpel and a gloved hand, he repositioned what would have been the object's buttocks. The smell was overwhelming. The gaping rectum appeared to be stuffed with something. Doc used the scalpel to remove fragments of the something.

The fragments were almost indistinguishable. Almost. If you held your breath and got close enough, it looked like currency.

"Stuffed up the rectum," Doc said, "down the throat, in the eye sockets. Proves the point, wouldn't you say?"

"The point being?"

"You can't take it with you."

CHAPTER
21

Mars drove back to city hall too tired to be overcome by depression. But it wouldn't take much to get himself there. Not that his efforts hadn't been productive. He knew a lot more now about how T-Jack had arranged Terri DuCain's death than he'd known when he'd started. The scenarios Mars could construct, based on the accumulating facts of the case, felt right. But the true genius of what T-Jack had done was becoming clearer with each emerging fact. What Mars had was a mass of highly ambiguous circumstantial fact that cut both ways. Every fact—with the possible exception of T-Jack's signal at the window of DuCain Industries—could as easily be used to exonerate T-Jack as to convict him. And T-Jack had exhibited sheer genius in using other people to accomplish his ends, in some cases without their even knowing they'd been used.

Knowing with certainty that T-Jack was culpable at the same time it was increasingly clear that the case was light-years away from being resolved was a heavy weight in its own right. But as the red granite form of city hall loomed ahead, the weight fell on his heart. This was the last time he'd drive back from an investigation to city hall, and in a few hours he'd leave city hall for the last time as a cop. Future cases as a cold case investigator would bring him back from time to time, but it would never be the same.

It was dark outside the mayor's windows by the time Mars was ready to leave, except for a line of light under her closed door. He walked in through the reception area, tapped on the door, and walked in.

She didn't look up at him as he entered. She remained at her desk, glasses down on the end of her nose, writing on the margins of papers as she read.

"Just thought I'd say good-bye. Sorry I didn't deliver on T-Jack...."

With her usual indifference to sentimentality, Alice Geff shrugged.

"They were going to try and charge T-Jack with what we've got. You aware of that? Glenn put his job on the line to keep it from happening."

She kept writing, making a small, dismissive gesture with her hand. "McDoanagh runs the department. If he can get the case past the County Attorney's Office, more power to him."

Mars's voice tightened. "And it doesn't bother you that if they did take the case to trial, as it is, that T-Jack would walk, that jeopardy would attach? Not to mention that the department would look like a bunch of jackasses...."

She looked up at him, taking her glasses off. "You know what Shakespeare said. 'Truth will out.'"

He stared at her. "You'd go that far. Just to get back at the union for forcing you to appoint McDoanagh?"

She thought about his question for a moment then said, in a voice devoid of guilt, "Running the city—including the police department—is like keeping score. Sometimes you're ahead, sometimes you're behind. Sometimes you have to miss an opportunity to score to accomplish a higher objective. That's how I see this situation, Mars."

"You can actually define a higher objective than putting T-Jack behind bars?"

"Oh, yes. Absolutely. Two years of McDoanagh is more than this city can take. He'll do untold harm if he serves out his appointment. I'm a realized eschatologist, Mars. I believe people make their own heaven or hell right here on earth. T-Jack will make his own hell. Count on it."

She gave him a small smile. "If you'd stayed—like I'd asked you to—none of this would have happened. I would have made you head of Homicide, and I wouldn't have let McDoanagh touch you."

"You couldn't have gotten away with that."

"We'll never know, will we? I'm just saying, to a certain extent, all of this is your choice."

"And McDoanagh was yours," he said as he walked out of her office.

Leaving city hall for the last time with the case unresolved made breathing painful. There'd been a time when he'd thought he could carry on with the investigation sub rosa, using the case files Nettie had duplicated. But without Danny on the case, that wasn't an option.

He walked down the steps from the mayor's office to the atrium. The full lights were out, leaving the Father of the Waters to glow dimly in the semidark. Mars walked to the base of the statue and put his hand on the cool marble.

Now, he thought to himself as he left city hall, *I'm an orphan again.*

CHAPTER

22

Karen Pogue had returned to the city early, and her dinner invitation spared Mars the misery of returning to his apartment on a night when his apartment was, more than ever, the last place he wanted to be.

Dinner at Karen's was the perfect option: a comfortable house that reeked of its owners' intelligence and taste, good food, and Karen's conversation and company.

Karen and Mars had met professionally when she had been hired on a contract basis to conduct a series of in-service training seminars for the police department on the psychological origins of sexual deviancy. For the first couple of years, their contacts had been defined by professional demands. Gradually, they began spending time together when work didn't demand. It was an important relationship in Mars's life that was primarily limited by the time demands of their work, in Karen's case a small clinical practice, and a faculty appointment in the Psychology Department at the university. The other limit on their friendship was Karen's husband, Ted. As much as everyone liked Karen, few liked Ted. He was a tax attorney at one of the city's largest firms and fulfilled, with no apparent effort, any and all expectations regarding a tax attorney's personality.

Not that Mars wanted more from his relationship with Karen than the option of spending more time with her without the constraints of work and a demanding husband. He'd wondered from time to time if she wanted more from him. But she'd assiduously avoided discussions of her marriage in general and Ted in particular, and Mars was comfortable leaving it at that. His only concern in that regard was the occasional suspicion that Karen was deeply unhappy in her marriage. If that was the case, Mars would have liked to offer her the same solace of confession that she'd so often provided him.

Nettie being included in the dinner invitation was unusual, but welcome. It would take a bit of the social pressure off Mars on a night when he was running on empty emotionally. And it might be interesting to observe the two women—both of whom had spent time together professionally and liked each other at that level—in what for each of them would be a new setting.

The cooler weather that had begun with a gentle rain at the bog had held. The first wave of a seasonal change was always hard for Mars to take. Nettie said he wasn't good at handling any kind of change. She probably had a point.

It couldn't have been any colder than the low 50s, but Mars turned the heater on in the car and cranked the fan. The car had just become cloyingly warm in the way he needed when he arrived at Karen's Kenwood house. The moist cold grabbed at him as he jogged quickly from the curb to the front door. Did he smell burning wood in the air? Karen could be trusted to know what you needed when you needed it, and a wood fire would confirm that she knew exactly where he was this night.

Mars could see the wood fire burning in the living room from the entry hall. But clearly Karen had failed the test of knowing what he'd needed tonight. The door had been opened by a strange man holding a wine bottle and a corkscrew. The last thing Mars wanted tonight was an evening of social small talk with a guy who, on sight, Mars doubted he'd like.

"Mick Witz," he said, holding the door open. "I'd offer to shake your hand, but both mine are otherwise occupied. C'mon in. Karen's in the kitchen."

Karen immediately appeared in an apron large enough to cover all of them.

"Is the fire all right? I know August is pushing it, but this *is* Minnesota—and it just felt like what we needed tonight."

"You're right about that," Mars said, "the *fire* is perfect." He hoped she didn't hear the implicit, unspoken words that followed: *Mick is the problem.*

Nettie appeared from around the corner. "Karen won't let us in the kitchen. We're supposed to sit in front of the fire until she calls us to the table."

Mars took his place in front of the fire, thinking how luxurious it would be to sit here with Nettie, Karen in the kitchen making something wonderful to eat, if only Mick—who looked like a Mick, shiny black hair slicked straight back, still in suit pants, jacketless, tie loose, big red suspenders holding up the pants—wasn't there, offering a discourse on the changing rules of wine drinking.

"Tonight is a perfect example. I told Karen I'd bring wine, and she started to tell me what she was having, and I told her, it doesn't matter. I'll bring a great wine and it won't matter what you're serving. That's the whole thing. The secret is a good wine. If the wine is good enough, it doesn't matter if it's red, white—whatever." He looked at Mars. "Do you have a preference—between red and white?"

"He prefers brown," Nettie said, saving Mars from having to sound interested in the question and his answer. "He only drinks Coca-Cola. . . ."

"Classic," Mars said.

"Ah," Mick said, switching focus effortlessly. "Classic Coca-Cola. Excellent choice. But you're still going to have taste this wine I brought. It's absolutely—"

"How do you know Karen?" Mars said, hoping his question would put an end to the wine discussion.

"I'm a partner in Ted's firm. Not the tax division. I handle family law cases. It's not a big part of the firm's business, but as there are a lot of high-end clients that do business with the firm, they want one-stop shopping. So, if they need a divorce, and we already handle their tax and estate business, we can offer a full range of service."

The light had gone on. Karen's early return was a strategy—probably instigated by Nettie. And Karen did know what he needed tonight. Karen had an agenda that was designed to meet Mars's most pressing need.

The discussion started at the dinner table.

"Mars—I asked Mick to come tonight because Nettie called and let me know what's going on with your ex-wife and Chris."

"That's good of you, Karen." Mars nodded at Mick as well. He felt obligated to make at least a token protest against Karen and Mick's generosity "And good of Mick to come. But I wouldn't be comfortable asking someone for legal advice in a social setting. Particularly if it's someone who probably gets a couple of hundred an hour if I was sitting in his office, instead of at a dinner table."

"Three hundred an hour," Mick said with a self-satisfied smile. "But I have—the firm has—a policy of providing an initial consultation at no charge. That's how I view this: an initial consultation. Karen's told me something about your situation, and I must say it sounds to me like you're in a very strong position. I'd just like to ask you a couple of questions. . . ."

The questions were straightforward. Did the stipulated divorce agreement specify a time limit on the level of Mars's child support commitment? Did the agreement include a stipulation that the custodial parent could not remove the dependent child from the non-custodial parent's community of residence? Had Mars made child support payments on a timely basis? What other forms of support had Mars provided in addition to the agreed-to child support payments? How much time did Mars spend with the dependent child on a monthly basis? Had he participated fully in such events as school programs, doctor appointments, parent-teacher conferences? Would Mars's work allow him to responsibly meet the child's future needs?

It was the last question Mick asked that posed problems. "Has your son had any problems while he's been in your care?"

Mars started to say no, then caught Nettie looking at him. Mars hesitated. "Nothing serious. He and a friend were on the skyway a few days ago and his friend was picked up for shoplifting. They both ended up in the juvenile division, but there never was a question that Chris had been involved—"

Mick interrupted him sharply. "Who gave the kids permission to be on the skyway on their own?"

"I did," Mars said. "They were going to have lunch and meet me back at city hall. It was the middle of the day, for crissakes. Chris is almost eleven, James is a bit older than Chris. . . ."

Mick made a face that looked like he had a gut ache. "This is exactly the kind of thing the court hates. One other thing. At his age, your son is going to be asked what he wants. Is he gonna say he wants to be with you?"

It was the question Mars knew was coming, the question that made everything they had been talking about moot.

"We've talked about it. He would prefer to stay, to live with me. But he doesn't want to hurt his mother. He won't say to anybody but me that he wants to stay."

Mick shook his head slowly but firmly. "Without the kid weighing in on your side—well, I think the court is going to see it—at best—as a draw. It hurts us that your divorce agreement doesn't explicitly prohibit the custodial parent from changing domiciles without your permission. And your ex has been a good mother, the kid has been thriving under her custody, we've got the problem on the skyway that occurred on your watch—all things being equal, that's going to work in favor of your ex. The only shot you've got—your son needs to tell a judge he wants to stay with you."

"He won't do it," Mars said. "And I won't ask him to do it. The way he explained it to me was exactly right. He has a lot of ways to show he loves me. The only way he can show he loves his mother is to go with her. She'd feel rejected if Chris chose to stay with me; I won't feel rejected if he chooses to stay with his mother."

Karen and Nettie started arguing about needing to do what was best for Chris, even if it meant it was hard at the outset.

"He'll get over it," Karen said. "He'll find ways to make it up to Denise. He's a smart kid, Mars. It'll work out."

"I can't go against him on this," Mars said. "I have to respect

264

his judgment. It's up to me to make sure that his making an unselfish choice works out for him in the long run."

The room went silent. Mars said, "It's like where we are on the DuCain murder. We have almost everything we need to know to charge T-Jack. But the one thing we don't know is the essential piece. What you're telling me is that I have everything I need to get custody, except my son expressing his choice. And that one thing means I won't get custody."

Everyone around the table looked the way Mars felt.

The drive back to his apartment took him closer to what he saw as a bleak future. His mind churned options. What if he moved to Cleveland? Went to work for the Cleveland police?

It was a nonstarter from the get-go. Assuming they were hiring, there wasn't a chance he could go in at anything like his current salary. And he'd lose his retirement vesting in Minnesota. It wasn't just that he needed money for himself, his future. He needed money for Chris and Chris's future.

What he was left with was the need to visit Chris frequently. How was he going to afford that? With his child support payments at current levels, where was he going to get airfare and expense money to fly once a month—even once every two months—to Cleveland? Chris could come to Minneapolis, and if he did, that should be on Denise's dime. But he knew she'd hassle him on that. And Chris would bear the brunt of that hassle.

It was hopeless. He parked in the lot, walking slowly from the car into the back entrance. He hesitated, considering whether to check the mailbox or go up the back stairs to the apartment. The big risk with going to the mailbox was that it would be empty. A final, almost unbearable blow at the end of a tough day.

Even a possibility there'd be postcard from Evelyn outweighed the risk. He went to the front hall, opening his box with breath held.

It was there, solitary, standing on one end, slanted against the side of the box. A golden image of a male statue, standing alone, eyes down, looking at something held in his raised hands. The man was confined, surrounded by reflecting water. The way it looked to Mars, a man without choices. The perfect image for Mars on this day.

Mars flipped the card over. It was an image from a crypt at Winchester Cathedral. There was more on the back of the card than Mars's address. They'd agreed she'd send cards—just the cards, no words—and she'd not broken that agreement. There were no words, just the numbers:

8.31

Meaning she knew what this day meant to Mars, that she'd been thinking about him all day today. He felt the connection like a physical touch.

It got him up the stairs, and kept him from thinking about the fact that tomorrow would be T-Jack plus one.

CHAPTER

23

He was on his way back from Granite Falls when Danny Borg called.

Mars had gone to Granite Falls on his first cold case, investigating the death of a young woman who'd been abducted from a convenience store fifteen years ago. Of all the cases he could have started with on the CCU, this one had the most appeal. Gas station and convenience store violence was, in Mars's judgment, largely the result of station and store owners' negligence in protecting their employees. Anything he could do to document that fact, to draw public attention to the negligence, was worth doing.

The Granite Falls victim, who would now have been older than Mars, was survived by only two relatives, her father and a brother. Both still carried a burden of deep sadness at what had happened to their daughter and sister, but it was like looking at that sadness through a mirror clouded with dust. Their emotions were blurred, unclear. They had no expectation of justice and their memories had been shrouded by a protective swaddling of forgetfulness.

Worth doing or not, it didn't change the fact that Mars was finding the cold case assignment difficult for all the reasons he'd anticipated. He missed the immediacy of police homicides. To put it crudely, and not to his credit, he missed warm blood, fresh grief, and the chaos and energy of recent death.

He'd asked himself: If he'd come over to the cold case unit after charging T-Jack, would it have made the transition easier? Impossible to say for sure. But he guessed it would have helped. It would have helped him to focus on the cases at hand, rather than the one that got away. And Grace DuCain's grief wouldn't have haunted his idle moments and sleepless nights.

In contrast, and just as predictable, Nettie was at home within minutes of occupying their new office. If Alice Geff had got it right—that you made your own heaven or hell right here on earth—Nettie was in heaven. She was grateful to be removed from the daily presence of warm blood and the chaos of death. Her job— the work of the cold case unit in general—was to deal with old evidence, long-established facts. And she took to the task with a kind of joy. Already, when their office phone rang, nine times out of ten the call was for Nettie.

Then Mars's cell phone rang. "I just talked to Glenn," Danny said. "The District Court has ruled that the Timberwolves have to let T-Jack play. He'll be on the court at the first home exhibition game. Four weeks from now."

Mars thought about Danny's news all the way back to his office. Why the hell did T-Jack want to play, anyway? He didn't need the money—not now, not with the settlement money. There was only one answer. The rage he'd face from fans when he took the court was something T-Jack wanted. It only confirmed that T-Jack wasn't wired emotionally like anyone else. He thrived on people hating him.

Walking into their new office, Mars was reminded that of all the things he didn't like about his new job, what he liked least was the office. The state had leased space in a plain, precast concrete four-story building that housed a number of functions for which there was no longer space in the state's capitol complex. The building looked like it had been built by a bureaucrat to house bureaucrats. And as soon as you walked into the building, you felt like a bureaucrat.

Mars and Nettie's office "suite" was on the third floor. There was a reception area—sans receptionist—at the front of their space and they each had an office behind the reception area. The private

268

office should have been a plus, but it wasn't. Mars missed the casual interaction of the squad room, of being able to see Nettie as soon as he walked into the squad room, being able to talk whenever a thought or question popped into his head.

The way things were set up here, a thought crosses your mind, you've got to get up and walk down the hall to Nettie's office. Half the time, you got down there and she was on the phone, and by then you couldn't remember what you were going to say anyway. Hell, he couldn't even hear Nettie smash the bottom of her partially frozen Evian bottle on her desk every morning. Most of all, Mars missed the employee lounge they'd left behind. No place to kick back, talk things over, turn on a decrepit black-and-white TV to see what was going on in the real world.

A few weeks after moving to the new office, Mars had suggested that he and Chris do a late afternoon garage sale run. It was the kind of thing this job allowed him to do that hadn't been possible when he'd been in the police department. He needed to take advantage of the job's upside, given how he was feeling about the downside.

Thursdays offered prime pickings as they gave you a jump on weekend shoppers. Chris's increased involvement in soccer camp had meant they'd done fewer sales during the summer than in previous years and the season was running out on them without Chris having made any major purchases.

It felt hollow as soon as he'd picked Chris up. Chris was making an effort to appear in good spirits, but it didn't cover what his true feelings were. Mars felt more anxiety every time he saw Chris.

Mars realized that their garage sale shtick really didn't work very well when what they considered buying would occupy a future they weren't sharing. The other thing, Chris was reluctant to do things that meant leaving the kitten he'd brought back from Denise's parents' farm after Labor Day. Mars recognized that the kitten was Denise making a bribe of sorts. It annoyed Mars on several levels—as a bribe and as a cheap bribe, at that. If Denise was going to try to bribe Chris into being happy about the move, she could have at least gotten him a dog, which was what Chris had been wanting for more than a year.

Mars liked the kitten more than he'd expected to. It was a feisty little gray tabby with stripes on its front legs, which earned him his name, Sarge. What troubled Mars was Chris's increasing obsession with the kitten. It didn't take a degree in psychiatry to see what was going on. Chris was transferring all of his anxiety, all of his sense of loss, to his care of the kitten. It was good to see him enjoy Sarge, to see him take responsibility for having a pet. But in his gut, Mars felt what was going on with Chris and Sarge wasn't healthy.

On their third garage sale stop, with Chris moving aimlessly through an array of stuff that weeks earlier would have captured his complete attention, Mars had an idea.

"You know what I need to look for?" he said.

Chris looked up at him, uncertain. Their garage sale treks really weren't about Mars buying stuff.

"I want to find some really comfortable furniture for the reception area in the office. All the state's budget gets us is those two metal and plastic chairs and the side table that's the size of a checkerboard. I want something we can sink into, stretch out on if we're working late."

Chris was immediately interested. "How much can we spend?"

Mars thought about it. Anything was more than he could afford. But comfortable furniture in the reception area would make a difference in how he felt about the office. So spending a few bucks would be a good investment.

"My limit is thirty-five dollars," Mars said. "And that has to cover a TV. I want a TV—a black-and-white TV—a couch, and a comfortable chair. If the chair has an ottoman, that'd be a plus. All for thirty-five dollars."

It took them six more stops before they found everything they were looking for. They got a used, cable-ready thirteen-inch TV for five dollars. Mars had to settle for a color TV as there weren't any black-and-whites to be found and because he realized that if he did find a black-and-white, it wouldn't be cable ready and they wouldn't be able to get reception in their bunkerlike building. They bought a plaid armchair, with matching ottoman, that was so cushy you had trouble getting out of it once you sat down. The chair was fifteen dollars, bargained down to eleven dollars, which left them nineteen dollars for a couch.

On their last stop before dark they found exactly the couch they wanted except for two things. The floral-print couch was priced at forty-five dollars—and the owner wasn't prepared to bargain on the first day of the sale. The other problem was the couch was missing one of its cushions.

Chris had a solution for the second problem. "The other couch we saw—the one that just had two cushions so it wasn't big enough, and it had a stain on one of the cushions and a big tear across the back—I think the cushion from that couch would fit this couch, if you don't care that it doesn't match."

"Not matching is a plus. What this office needs is stuff that doesn't match. Problem is, that couch was five bucks, and this couch is already more than our budget. I can't afford to buy both."

"Make him an offer," Chris whispered, impatient. "Offer him fifteen bucks. Tell him to call you when the sale ends on Sunday if the couch hasn't sold. He'd probably pay you to haul it away, then. He's not gonna sell a couch without a cushion, Dad. Then we'll go back and offer three bucks for the couch we don't want and just take the cushion."

Denise's genes in action. Chris had always been, would always be, a better deal-maker than Mars.

So at the end of the day, having spent a total of nineteen dollars, they had a TV, a chair with ottoman, and a spare couch cushion. If they got the couch on Sunday for fifteen bucks, they'd come in one buck under budget. Which pleased them both no end.

Best of all, their transactions had pulled Chris out of his funk and into something like his normal self by the time Mars dropped him off.

*   *   *

271

"What the hell is this?" Glenn Gjerde said, standing in the reception area of Mars and Nettie's office the afternoon of the Timberwolves' first exhibition game.

He held his bicycle at his side. There were tire tracks on the carpet behind him to where he stood.

Nettie was stretched out on the couch, head propped up, watching Oprah. Mars was in the chair, feet up on the ottoman, drinking a Coke. They both turned their heads simultaneously to look at him.

"Shhhh," Nettie said. "We're in the last five minutes of Dr. Phil on Oprah."

"I don't mean what's on TV, I mean where did you get this furniture? It doesn't match."

A statement which caused both Nettie and Mars to let out a whoop.

"That," Nettie said, "is the pot calling the kettle black. Since when have you become a decorating maven?"

"You don't have to be a maven to know that you've got a plaid chair and a couch with flowers on it—wait, a couch with flowers on most of it but stripes on one cushion. This is state-issued furniture?"

"Garage-issued," Mars said. "Right up your alley."

"And it smells," Glenn said. "At least I hope it's the furniture that smells. Either that or the two of you have started to go sour."

Glenn was right. They'd noticed that the furniture smelled the first time they'd come back to the office after being out over the weekend. As far as Mars was concerned, the smell was a soul-substitute for the office.

"I missed the end of the program while we were discussing interior decoration," Nettie said, clicking off the TV as she sat up. "You rode your bike all the way over here?"

"It's only three miles," Glenn said. "Approximately." He leaned his bike against the unmanned reception desk, then sat down on the couch. "I miss you guys. And you never write, you never call." He looked at Mars. "I wanted to find out if you're going to the game tonight."

272

"It may be my only chance to see T-Jack get justice," Mars said. "Of course I'm going."

He picked Chris up before the game. Did Chris really want to go? Hard to say. The only thing Chris showed any real interest in was Sarge. And that interest, in Mars's judgment, continued to border on the obsessive. Chris was still doing well in school, but he spent little time with friends, didn't show much interest in cooking, and was looking thinner and paler each time Mars saw him. There'd been a small, positive blip in his spirits when Denise had announced they wouldn't be moving until the end of the school year. But passing time only brought that deadline nearer and Chris's spirits lower.

The warm, humid air of the arena was a startling change from the cool October evening as they walked into the Target Center's street-level entrance—or, expressed in terms of Mars's aesthetic judgment of the arena—through the butt end of the elephant.

Even at this level they could hear—could feel—the deep, pulsating amps of the pregame music. The crowd was immense. You had little choice about which direction you went or how fast you moved. You got carried. Mars held on to the collar of Chris's jacket, and when Chris was almost pulled out of his jacket at one point, Mars took his hand as well. It was a bit of a shock. How long had it been since he'd held Chris's hand? However long, it was no longer a boy's hand.

"Why is it so crowded for just an exhibition game?" Chris shouted at Mars.

A guy to the front of them turned his head. "Have you been living under a rock? People are here to see a murderer shoot hoops."

It's why I came, Mars thought.

Mars had broken his budget and bought tickets from a colleague with season tickets who was out of town. They were good seats that got them close enough to really see T-Jack. He wanted to see T-Jack's expression when the crowd booed him. He wanted to see T-Jack's Adam's apple bob when the crowd threw beer cups on the floor. And Mars didn't doubt that was how people were going to react.

It was the first Timberwolves game Mars had been to, so he didn't know if it was standard procedure to have the teams take the floor en masse rather than being individually introduced by position. But tonight the opposing team took the floor as a team, then stood, observably tense, as they waited for the Timberwolves.

The tension in the arena was extraordinary. Already a cup or two had come out of the crowd and landed near the playing floor. For the first time, Mars noticed uniformed police officers taking positions around the perimeter of the playing floor. They stood facing the crowd.

A low rumble started and the Timberwolves came onto the court. In moments the smattering of cheers had been overtaken by the low, powerful boom of booing. T-Jack had moved into his position on the court where he stood, relaxed.

It wasn't touching him. Not in terms of his body language, not in terms of the expression on his face. If anything, Mars would have said how T-Jack looked confirmed that T-Jack thrived on hatred.

The crowd read T-Jack the same way. The booing increased, punctuated by sharp cries: *Murderer! Wife-killer!* The less he reacted, the stronger the crowd's reaction. More beer cups flew, this time landing on the floor, some near the feet of players. Some people started to spit, which caused people in the crowd to start fighting with each other.

"Ladies and gentlemen!" The electronic voice of the announcer could barely be heard over the crowd. Referees walked the court, lifting their arms and pulling them down in a signal for quiet. You could tell they were blowing their whistles by their puffing cheeks, but the piercing shrill went unheard.

"Ladies and gentlemen! The game will be forfeited and the arena will be cleared if order is not restored!"

The threat was repeated twice before it took hold. Gradually the booing subsided and an uneasy order was restored.

"Like a quiet day in Jerusalem," Mars said out loud, to himself.

Three minutes into play, T-Jack faked a pass to a teammate,

then moved in an opposite direction, causing his teammate to stumble.

The crowd erupted again, booing and hissing overtaking all other sounds in the arena.

"He does shit like that all the time," the guy next to them hollered. "Fakes out his own teammates. Not hard to believe he'd murder his own wife, is it?"

Play was stopped twice before halftime when T-Jack brought the crowd off their seats with yet more examples of poor sportsmanship. "This is bad even for him," their neighbor said.

Bad sportsmanship didn't keep T-Jack from scoring nineteen points in the first half, and being booed every time he scored. Nor did his nineteen points give the Timberwolves the lead. The score was 41 to 38 at the half, with the Timberwolves trailing.

It was as T-Jack was leaving the court at the half that Mars noticed the woman for the first time. He noticed her at first because she was in the premium seat section, sitting in a chair directly on the court, near a rabid fan who reacted violently to everything that went on during the game. Mars couldn't see her face, but what he could see was that T-Jack was giving her hard and interested looks every time he came off the court, turning to look back at her when he wasn't on the court.

From the back it looked like she was responding. Mars was curious about what kind of woman would be fool enough to get involved with T-Jack. What was even more curious was why she looked familiar. He strained for a better look, but couldn't really see her face.

The half had taken some of the steam out of the crowd's response to T-Jack. The Timberwolves had probably been smart to have T-Jack play and let the crowd work out their emotions. Not that tonight would be the end of it. T-Jack would face this reaction every town he played for the first time in the coming weeks.

T-Jack's shooting arm had also cooled over the half. He missed three consecutive three-point shots and it bothered him. He could stay cool when more than twenty thousand people were booing him, but when he started missing baskets, he became surly. He purposely tripped an opposing team player guarding him, and when the ref called the foul, T-Jack gave him the finger behind his back. It brought the crowd to its feet again and one fan broke through the police perimeter and went after T-Jack on the court. As the police pulled him back, T-Jack's antagonist held up a fist in victory, which brought the first solid cheer of the night from the crowd.

Then Mars saw it again. T-Jack's eyes moving to where the woman sat. Her head was turned slightly toward T-Jack, giving Mars a partial profile. Where had he seen her before? From where he sat, he guessed she was Hispanic, but it was impossible to say for sure with what he'd seen.

The rest of the game was more of the same, except the Timberwolves were dropping further behind. T-Jack went to the bench at the two-minute buzzer and the fans rose in unison to mingle jeers and boos.

From the bench, T-Jack kept looking back at the woman in the crowd. It was obvious she was watching him, not the game. Mars reached down and tapped Chris's shoulder. "It's all but over. Let's get a jump on leaving," he said.

They threaded their way down from their seats. When they were level with the row where the Hispanic woman was sitting, Mars turned to look at her. Other people were standing to leave now, so he still didn't have an unobstructed view. But he saw enough to be shocked.

It was Melanie Gonzales-Robb.

Mars's breath caught at the recognition. What the hell did it mean? Did it matter? He froze in place. Chris turned and looked at him. "Dad! What?"

Mars motioned Chris to keep moving to where he could get a better look at Gonzales-Robb. He wanted to see her reaction when she noticed him. Then she turned, to take a coat off the back of her chair, and Mars got his first full-face view.

He broke into a self-mocking laugh. It wasn't Melanie Gonzales-Robb. It was a Hispanic woman, but not a woman he had ever seen before. He remembered Gonzales-Robb's explanation for how T-Jack's double had fooled people into believing he was T-Jack.

"All they see is the color," she'd said. Which was exactly what Mars had just done.

His mistake stayed with him after he'd dropped Chris and gone back to the apartment. It was unbelievably stupid. A mistake he'd thought he was long past making. If he'd learned nothing else from this case, he'd gotten a big dose of humility.

Mars turned the television on for a while, but immediately hit coverage of the Timberwolves game, which he really didn't want to see again. He went to the fridge for a Coke, and on his way back to the living room, picked Evelyn's postcards up from the counter. He went through each card slowly, looking at the image, then turning it over. He'd gotten a couple more cards since the card he'd received on August 31, but he kept that card on the bottom of the pile, looking at it last, looking at the numbers 8.31 for a long time.

He dropped the stack of cards down on the floor, holding on to the 8.31 card a bit longer. Then he dropped it on top of the others, the image of the solitary man with no options still feeling too close for comfort.

He couldn't have said how, but within seconds, the two images came together. His image of the Hispanic woman at the basketball game and the confined, solitary man with no options melded into a single idea.

An idea that for the second time that night took his breath away.

All they see is the color.

Frantically, he scrambled through the DuCain case boxes that he'd had stacked up against the wall for the past couple months. He wanted the medical examiner's report. The idea that had just come together in his consciousness could begin or end with what he found there. Pulling the ME's report out of the third box he'd opened, he said a silent prayer. He didn't know to whom he prayed, but if there was a god, he wanted to cover all his bases.

He turned the pages with shaking hands. When he'd gone through the whole report he closed his eyes in relief.

He was still in the game.

Then he forced himself to sit down and work through the unanswered questions that had existed since August 23. Why had Terri DuCain been on the porch with someone who looked like Paul Tanney minutes before she'd been murdered? Why hadn't there been any evidence that she'd been chloroformed? What had happened to the roses? Mars considered each question against the idea that had come to him through the merged image of a Hispanic woman and the solitary man. Each question was answered. Beyond those original questions, the merged image gave rise to other questions—and the answers to those questions. Mars was a long way from proving to anyone else that his idea was right, but his gut was telling him he now had *all* the answers.

All the answers and one huge, compelling possibility that meant he wouldn't sleep until the idea had solidified into fact.

It was after midnight when he called Nettie.

"I need you to get hold of Danny Borg and Glenn Gjerde, and I need the three of you to come over to the apartment right away."

Nettie didn't say anything for a minute. It was clear he'd wakened her.

"*Now?*" she finally said.

"Sooner, if you can."

"Why?"

"I'll explain when you get here."

"Mars, I'm not leaving my warm bed in the middle of the night to go into your crappy neighborhood unless you give me a good reason."

Mars couldn't think where to start.

"All I can say now is that I don't think Venema was the last witness to what happened on August 23. There was somebody else. And I think there's a chance our last witness is still alive."

*   *   *

278

Mars didn't start with how he'd put the facts together. That would have addled their sleep-deprived brains. Instead, he started with his conclusion.

"I'm going to propose a case theory that's going to be hard to accept right off. But let me walk you through this. Then, I want your best shots at why what I'm thinking is wrong."

Nettie, Danny, and Glenn looked ready for the challenge, in spite of the fact that they'd all arrived in sleep gear covered by coats. Coat off, Nettie was in black flannel pajamas populated by white polar bears. Danny was wearing sweats that should have hit the rag drawer years earlier. And Glenn was wearing a ratty terry-cloth robe over what appeared to be boxer shorts and a tank top. Nettie and Danny were wearing slippers. Glenn had on brown wing tips with black dress socks.

"Let me start," Mars said, having pulled up a straight-backed kitchen chair in front of his bed where the three sat, "with a mea culpa. What is the mantra that I've been spouting since August twenty-third? *Base the case on facts, not assumptions.* Jeez, I even sat right here and lectured Chris on the primary importance of knowing what it is you don't know. . . ."

His audience's expressions showed no sign of a pending epiphany.

"So," Mars said, "what is the assumption I made on day one that's thrown the case off?"

More blank stares.

Mars drew a breath, knowing what he was going to say next would hit them like a lightning strike.

"I assumed," Mars said, "that the red-haired woman lying on the kitchen floor in the Jackman house *was* Terri DuCain."

CHAPTER

24

They'd sat dumbfounded for moments after Mars had presented his conclusion. He took advantage of their silence to begin at the beginning.

"This is the way I think it happened. Tanney was waiting near the Jackman house for Sater's call. But he wasn't waiting alone. He had a woman with him. A woman who'd been picked because she was the same body type as Terri DuCain. A woman whose hair had been dyed to match Terri DuCain's hair . . ."

"Who's the woman?" Nettie said.

"My guess is it was Gail Pearce. She would have been a sucker for this kind of deal. Tanney could have promised her money or Terri's clothes—anything. He could have said that T-Jack wanted to meet her. Her roommate told me Tanney was always telling Gail what to wear, how to look. And it would explain why we haven't been able to find any trace of Gail."

Danny said, "So the woman on the porch with Tanney—the woman our jogger saw—it wasn't Terri DuCain. It was a woman tricked up to look like Terri."

Mars nodded, waiting to see if they'd start finding holes.

Danny said, "The chloroform. We didn't find any trace of chloroform in the body because Tanney'd used the chloroform on Terri, and the body wasn't Terri."

Nettie was looking off in the distance. Still thinking hard, she started to talk. "And she was hit in the face with the frying pan.

We thought that was random violence. But it was strategic."

"Yeah," Danny said, "but I've seen a lot of parents who could identify their kids when the bodies were in a lot worse shape than the body we found."

"Think about it," Mars said. "The cases you've seen where parents identify barely recognizable bodies. There was a question about the victims' identities—wasn't there? Duke and Grace never questioned the body was Terri. None of us did. None of us were looking at her to establish identification. And her parents hardly saw her. Duke went in first, tried to hold Grace back when he realized what had happened. Then he collapsed, and Grace was focused on Duke. And if you go in assuming the victim is your child, and see that amount of trauma, your natural reaction is to look away. They saw what they were supposed to see. What we all saw. A young woman who, at a glance, looked like Terri DuCain. The red hair being the focal point of their response. A young woman who'd been an abuse victim. They'd known for years that T-Jack had been violent with Terri, and they'd always worried that violence would become more serious. What they saw on the kitchen floor on August twenty-third just fulfilled that suppressed expectation. What they'd dreaded happening had happened."

Glenn got up and started walking around the limited space of the living room. Eventually his movement became a slow orbit through the living room, around the wall that separated the living room from the kitchen, and back through the living room.

"Okay," he said on his second pass through the living room. "They chloroform Terri. Where do they take her?"

Mars shifted his eyes to Danny.

Danny returned the look.

"There was no bathroom in the basement," Danny said.

Mars waited for him to say more.

"And when I think about it," he said, "the end of the basement—the end where the bar was. The room was shorter than it should have been, given the space above—*Jesus*. He's got her in a safe room in the basement? Jesus, Mars. We were—what?—ten feet from that wall on the day of the murder? You're saying she was behind that wall when we were down there on August twenty-third?"

Mars said, "I spent a half hour down there while T-Jack played pool. When I went to talk to him about Davon Els. Don't think I haven't been thinking about that."

"And Gail Pearce—if that's who the body was," Nettie said. "Tanney killed her after he took Terri to the safe room."

The words hung in the air. They required no response.

"The ME's report," Glenn said. "Did Doc do any kind of verification on the identification?"

"Of course not," Mars said. "He had a victim identified by both parents, dead in her own house, and she'd been involved in a violent relationship." He got up, took the ME's exam from the kitchen table and handed it to Glenn. "I checked it out before I called Nettie. Nobody can blame Doc for accepting that the vic *was* Terri DuCain."

It was taking all of them time to accept the enormity of what Mars was saying. Almost at the same moment, the slowness started causing them to panic.

"God, Mars," Nettie said. "She's still alive. We need to get over there. It's too awful to think about—that T-Jack has kept her as a prisoner all this time. Who do we call? What do we do next?"

Mars held up both hands.

"I know how you're feeling. It's what I've been feeling ever since the possibility occurred to me an hour ago. I wanted to slap the flasher on the dash, turn on the siren, and get on over to T-Jack's. But here's what makes this deal really dicey." He looked at each of them in turn. "First, Terri DuCain might not have been the woman lying on her kitchen floor on August twenty-third. In fact, I'm willing to stake my pension that she wasn't—but that doesn't mean she's alive now. T-Jack may have set up the safe-room strategy as a means of providing himself an alibi for the period of time when 'Terri' was murdered. Then, at his convenience, when he's confident he's not under surveillance, he murders Terri and disposes of her body. It would be an easy thing for him to do. He's got an underground garage. He could load the body into the trunk of the car in the dead of night without any risk of anyone seeing him and dump her anywhere."

Danny said, "You think that's the most likely scenario?"

Mars didn't think that was the most likely scenario. But he was making it up on the fly, so he talked out loud while he thought about why he didn't think that was the most likely scenario. "It's what Grace DuCain has been saying all along. She couldn't believe T-Jack would give Terri up. She thought what was important to him in the relationship was control. He kills her—in a way, he loses control. . . ."

Mars shrugged. "It's a soft argument. But it feels solid to me. I think T-Jack gets the whole ball of wax if he keeps Terri alive. He gets the money, he's duped Grace and Duke—killing Duke in the process—and he's duped us. And Terri is his to do whatever with. Everything I know about him tells me that's the way he'd want this to work. And except for one possibility, that's why I think she's still alive."

"The one possibility being?" Nettie said.

"This is the dicey part. If T-Jack gets any clue that we know that Terri's alive, that we suspect she's still alive—she's dead. At the end of the day, T-Jack will take care of himself, even if it means giving up Terri. And consider this. No one in this room has the authority to pursue the line of reasoning we've developed tonight." Once again Mars paused and looked at each of them. "I also assume that no one in this room trusts Chief McDoanagh or Clayton Freize to investigate the possibility that Terri is alive without screwing it up. Bearing in mind that a screwup means Terri dies."

Nettie placed her hands in a prayer position in front of her face.

"What about Keith Narum?" Danny said. "I trust him. He's between a rock and a hard place running Homicide, because Freize is doing end runs to the chief all the time, but Narum's an honest guy."

Mars nodded. "Agreed. But it's just too risky to put this investigation anywhere near the chief and Freize. Narum is too close.

And Narum is just not the guy to carry on an undercover operation. He's competent—but undercover isn't his thing. And what's needed here is an undercover investigation."

"So?" Nettie said. "Where does that leave us?"

"Not in a good place. But we don't have a choice. I'm going to have to talk to the mayor. Get her to authorize us to put this thing together outside of the department." Mars looked at Danny. "Except for you, Danny. You're our inside guy if the mayor says go. You okay with that?"

Danny thrust one hand forward, giving a thumbs-up. He looked happier than Mars had seen him look in weeks.

"I'm serious, Danny. If I'm wrong about this—or, I'm right, but we can't prove it—you're out of Homicide. Probably out of the department. Of the four of us, you're the one with the most on the line."

Danny thrust two hands forward, giving a double thumbs-up. "I'm good to go."

Mars turned to Glenn. "What we need from you is information. What's it gonna take for us to get a search warrant on T-Jack's house?"

Glenn took his time answering. "Number one, something that establishes reasonable probability that the body found at the house on August twenty-third wasn't Terri DuCain. Better yet, reasonable probability that the body found is somebody else. Like Gail Pearce."

"Anything else?"

Glenn nodded. "Yeah. There's a probability that when you go in, you're going to have to tear down walls or whatever. No judge is going to give you a blank check to go in and start ripping stuff up. You're going to have to have something that establishes there is a safe room in the house. If T-Jack had something like that built, there must be plans on file in the City Building Permits Office."

Nettie looked skeptical. "You think we can trust the mayor?"

"It's going to be up to me to give the mayor an incentive to be trustworthy."

"And you've got an idea how to do that?"

"Maybe."

"So what's next?" Danny said. "How do we get what we need for the warrant?"

"I've been thinking about this. I can't emphasize enough how important it is that nobody—and especially not McDoanagh and Freize—finds out or suspects what we're doing. As hot as this case has been, all it will take is somebody thinking we might be working the T-Jack case off-line. That kind of rumor would spread like wildfire. If T-Jack finds out, and if Terri is still alive, it would be a death sentence for her...."

"So?" Nettie said.

"I need to talk to the mayor first. Make sure she's behind what we need to do. Without her, I'm not sure there's anything we can do. For one thing, we're not going to get a warrant on our own. We need the mayor's authority before a judge is going to give us a warrant. And if it comes to that, if we get the warrant, we're going to need someone from the city engineer's office to help us find the safe room and get in with minimum risk of injuring Terri. For all we know, T-Jack may have booby-trapped the room.

"Then I want an ambulance on the scene—and I want Alex Gage on the ambulance—and a couple officers to go in with us. All of that, the city engineer, the ambulance, the police support— that's got to be put together at the last moment. Not more than an hour before we go in."

Danny said again, "Where do we start? What can I do?"

"The first thing Glenn said—that we need probable cause that the body in the kitchen on August twenty-third was not Terri DuCain. I've been thinking about how to do that. The easiest way would be to have Terri's body exhumed and do a match...." Mars shook his head. "Not an option. Grace can't know there's a possibility that Terri's alive—or that Terri may not have been the body we found on August twenty-third. She can't be subjected to the trauma of an exhumation. Not until we know for sure, either way. More to the point, an exhumation would be sending up a rocket that we think there's a question about who it was that died."

Nettie said, "But if it's the only way. . . ."

Mars shook his head. "It's not the only way. I'm going to take another shot at Gail Pearce's sister in Northfield."

"Fine," Nettie said, impatient. "So you get DNA material through Gail Pearce's family. The blood evidence from the scene hasn't been preserved for that purpose. Maybe it'll still be good, but what if it isn't? What do we match against? We're back to doing an exhumation."

"First off," Mars said, "we need the DNA match for criminal prosecution. But we can't wait for DNA typing to get the warrant. For the warrant, I'm hoping we can use blood types to exclude Terri DuCain as the victim at the scene. If we get the warrant, and we find Terri, we've got all the time and source material we need to establish the DNA typing."

"Which means," Nettie said, "that you're assuming you're going to be able to identify Gail Pearce's and Terri DuCain's blood types. How are you going to do that without sending up a rocket?"

"My problem," Mars said. "I've got some ideas. Danny, if you could find a way of getting the evidence box from the case—without anyone knowing why you're doing it—I'd like to have a piece of the hair found at the scene tested to see if it was chemically treated. Terri was a natural redhead, Gail wasn't. Get it to Nettie, and she'll have it checked out from our office at the BCA. It's not a lot, but we need every bit of supporting evidence we can come up with to get the warrant."

Danny glowed. "Consider it done."

Mars turned to Nettie. "It's too risky to have Danny get what we need from the City Building Permits Office. I need you to figure out how we can get construction permit filings on the Lake of the Isles house without tying the request to the DuCain investigation."

Nettie nodded. "Permit requests and floor plans, right?"

Mars could see her already starting to figure it out. "Okay. We meet back here tomorrow. Let's say six o'clock. Glenn, I need you here then too. I'm hoping we'll have what we need for the warrant. But that's going to be your call."

Danny and Glenn left together, Danny turning back toward Mars in the hallway. "The roses, Mars. We're going to find the roses in the safe room, aren't we?"

Mars said, "That would be my first guess."

As Nettie was leaving, she said, "You never did say how this came together. What made you realize it wasn't Terri?"

"Remember what Melanie Gonzales-Robb said about people believing Davon Els was T-Jack?"

Nettie paused for a moment.

"They only see color."

Mars nodded. "And tonight . . ." He looked at his watch. It was almost three o'clock in the morning. "*Last* night. At the Woofies game. I thought I saw Melanie at the game—thought I saw T-Jack eye-fucking her. When I got a good look, I realized it was a Hispanic woman—but not Melanie. I was only seeing the color. So that was on my mind. Then, when I got home, I was looking at a postcard I got from Evelyn. . . ." Mars walked into the kitchen, bringing the card back to Nettie. She held it in two hands, staring down at the solitary statue in the crypt below Winchester Cathedral.

"So I was looking at the figure in the crypt, 'they only see color' still kind of on my mind—and the two things just came together. Seeing Terri's red hair fanned out on the floor at the scene, the figure in the crypt. It didn't take any time after that to see how Terri not being the victim explained everything."

He held both hands up in a gesture of powerlessness. "Basically it was what I said before. I based the case on an assumption. As soon as I went back to facts. . . ."

Nettie had turned the card over, reading what Evelyn had written.

She looked up at Mars, the beginning of an insolent smile on her lips.

"You got this card in August. And you were looking at it tonight?"

Mars could feel color rising from his neck, toward his face. He gave her a push toward the door. "Tonight hasn't happened yet, Nettie."

She didn't say anything, but before she shut the door behind her, she gave him a broad smile.

CHAPTER

25

Mars was in his car outside the mayor's residence shortly before 6:00 A.M.

Her driver pulled up at 6:20. The mayor was out of the house before the car had come to a full stop. Mars let seconds pass before he pulled away to follow the navy blue Crown Victoria as it headed toward downtown Minneapolis.

There was just enough traffic to provide cover, without his losing sight of the mayor's car. The Crown Victoria wasn't taking the mayor to city hall. Instead, it headed north over the Hennepin Avenue Bridge, circling a couple of one-way streets to pull up in front of Essentials4Fitness on the corner of University Northeast and First Avenue North.

Alice Geff got out on the passenger side, bending down to talk briefly to her driver before she pulled out a gym bag, slammed the car door, and headed for the front entrance.

Mars parked and caught her just as she was stepping into the elevator that would take her to the second-floor exercise facility.

"I've never understood," he said, "why somebody going to exercise would take the elevator instead of walking up the stairs."

She was startled to find someone behind her, then surprised when she recognized Mars.

"You belong here?"

"Probably should. But, no. I'm here to see you. Where can we talk in private?"

The elevator doors closed behind them and the car started moving up.

"Can't talk till I finish my session. I work with a trainer for a half hour, then do a weight-lifting circuit on the machines for another half hour. I've got to be back at city hall by eight-thirty, so . . ."

Mars held the door back with one arm after it opened on the second floor.

"You're going to miss your exercise session, Alice. I've got to talk to you now."

The yoga studio was a walled box set in the southwest corner of the exercise facility. There were big windows in the front wall of the studio facing the weight-machine room. Mars had locked the door behind them, and they dropped down on mats under the window. Anyone looking through the windows wouldn't have seen them. Not that there was much chance of anyone recognizing Mars. But caution was the order of the day.

"I think Terri DuCain is alive," he said.

For the second time in less than five minutes, he had succeeded in surprising the mayor. All the more remarkable because he couldn't remember surprising her even once while he'd been in the police department.

She stared at him. "You've been working the case?"

It was a practical question. But not the first question Mars would have asked if Alice had just told him that the city's most famous homicide victim was not dead.

"No," he said. "Something happened that made me rethink what we already know. Other than you, the only people I've told are Nettie, Danny, and Glenn. I talked it through with them to be sure I wasn't completely nuts."

"And you're not?" She was giving herself time to process what he'd said.

Mars shook his head. "They agree." Then he told her why he thought there was a chance Terri was still alive.

She listened without showing any emotion. Her great strength had always been that she knew exactly what it was she needed to know and when to let details hang. All she said after he'd stopped talking was, "And you're telling me because ... ?"

"Because if I'm right, and T-Jack has any reason to suspect that we know—if Terri isn't already dead, she will be in short order."

Alice Geff looked away from him. When she looked back, she asked the relevant question. Except she didn't ask it as a question, she made a statement.

"And you can't trust McDoanagh and Freize."

"Do you?"

"No. Of course not. I suppose what you want is for me to authorize an undercover operation outside the police department. I'm not sure if the city charter gives me that much latitude—but I'm prepared to worry about that later. Tell me what you need."

"I'll need you to talk to the judge we go to for the warrant. To explain how it is the warrant is coming from people not directly involved in the investigation. Then, when we've got the warrant, I need you to pull in the people we'll need to execute the warrant and conduct the search. Somebody from the city engineer's office, a couple uniforms to assist, emergency medical personnel. I'll get you a list of names. The important thing is, we've gotta pull these people together on short notice. We can't risk any leaks that we're going to be conducting a search at T-Jack's."

"And you're sure that's where she is? In the house?"

Mars shrugged. "Like I said. I think there are two possibilities. That she was alive after August twenty-third, but that T-Jack killed her later. If she's still alive, she's in the house. The one thing I'm sure of, the body we found in the house on August twenty-third wasn't Terri."

She shivered. She was quiet then, still thinking.

"Alice—don't even think about using this to make McDoanagh look bad. It's too risky. What you do after we've completed the search is your business. But until then, you try to use this to your political advantage and I will—"

"You think I'd do that? Risk that woman's life just to get back at McDoanagh? What have I ever done to make you think so little of me?"

Mars drew a deep breath. "You weren't all that concerned that they'd charge T-Jack with no hope of a conviction."

"Not the same thing," she said. "This is altogether different. If you're right, there's a life at stake here. I don't play politics with death, Mars. Death scares me."

Mars got up, suppressing a smile. "I'm not afraid of death, Alice. I'm afraid of murder." Going down in the elevator alone, he said, half out loud, "Gene Hackman, *The Conversation*."

"Northfield," the billboard read. "Home of cows, colleges, and contentment."

The "colleges" part was certainly true. St. Olaf, on the west side of town, stood on a hill, looking down on the town and across the Cannon River at Carleton College. St. Olaf had the most dramatic site and better architecture, but it was Carleton that had the more distinguished academic reputation.

As for cows and contentment—well, maybe once upon a time. But over the past decade, the thirty-five miles between the Twin Cities and Northfield had become a prime target for urban sprawl.

Glancing at the dashboard clock, Mars saw that he'd made it from the Cities to Northfield in just over thirty minutes. He held the slip of paper with Marta Rockwell's address in his right hand as he gripped the steering wheel. He'd counted on Northfield being small enough to make finding St. Olaf Avenue easy. But new housing developments with twisting, cul-de-sac streets had started six miles out of town.

Damn. He might have to stop at a gas station and look for a town map. Every minute it took him to do what needed to be done, every delay in doing what needed to be done, made his heart race.

Then he saw a sign for St. Olaf College. Could St. Olaf Avenue be far off? He swung up a steep hill that took him to the western edge of the campus. He circled on a perimeter road, past a dozen Gothic-style buildings uniformly constructed of glowing golden limestone. The campus was guarded by towering oaks, a few surviving elms, maples, and pines.

There was a dissonance between Mars's mission and the bril-

292

liant sunlight. Better that the day had been dark and stormy. A stormy day would have established a connection in Mars's imagination between what he needed to do and an imprisoned Terri DuCain. That he should be driving through sunlight while Terri was confined was intolerable. That this drive might also be a waste of time made his gut twist.

He'd made it to the eastern edge of the campus without finding St. Olaf Avenue. He gave up and headed down a hill toward town. Stopping at the bottom of the hill, the first street sign he saw read "St. Olaf Avenue."

Marta Rockwell's address was a couple of blocks down. Mars pulled over on the opposite side of the street from the Rockwells' house. He'd thought about how to approach her on the drive down. Thought about the man who'd answered the phone, who'd stayed on the line after Marta Rockwell had picked up. Thought about the tension in Rockwell's voice when she'd told him she wouldn't—couldn't—talk about her sister. What you'd hear when you were dealing with a family member who'd been pushed beyond limits by a relative was weariness. Resignation. Defensiveness. There was some of all of that in the way Rockwell had sounded, but there was something else. Mars was betting the something else was knowing that her husband was still on the line. And that her husband had been the one to prohibit further contact with Gail Pearce, Marta Rockwell's black-sheep sister.

If Mars was right, his only shot at getting Marta Rockwell to cooperate was to catch her alone. He'd have to call the house, and if Marta answered, ask to speak to Mr. Rockwell. If Mr. Rockwell answered, he'd have to think of something else. Eating up time on the clock in the process.

Then, from the rear of the Rockwell house, a tall, bespectacled guy appeared, lugging two black plastic trash bags. He dropped the bags at the curb, disappeared toward the back of the house, then reappeared carrying a rake. Mars groaned. The guy must have been on the faculty at St. Olaf, with a schedule that allowed him to be home in the middle of the day. It would take the guy another hour, at least, to rake the front yard.

There was a small café almost directly across the street from the Rockwells'. Mars decided he'd draw less attention having a Coke at a window table than he would sitting in his car watching the guy rake.

Mars picked up the remnants of a day-old newspaper from a rack just inside the front door. He sat at a table with the newspaper open in front of his face, his eyes turned toward the window, fixed on the guy raking the lawn. Mr. Rockwell was not going to win any prizes for speed raking. An hour had seriously underestimated the time he'd be at the job.

Mars was beginning to feel conspicuous. Not to mention restless. He rose, walked slowly to the cash register, took his time paying, then headed for the front door. He'd positioned himself in the café's entrance, feigning interest in months-old postings on the wall, sneaking the occasional glance at the house across the street. Having exhausted the time any human being could spend reading notices about used dormitory lofts and ride-sharing, Mars left the café. At the same time, the front door of the Rockwells' house flew open. A brindle mastiff and a yellowish-brown mixed-breed dog blasted out onto the lawn, tearing into the pile of leaves Mr. Rockwell had been gathering at one corner.

"Otis! Rocket!" yelled the woman who followed the dogs.

"Marta! For God's sake. Get the dogs on their leads, will you? They're undoing all my work."

"I'm taking them over to the arboretum," she said. "They're going crazy in the house with you out in the yard."

"Good idea," he said.

"*Great* idea," Mars muttered.

Mars forced himself to walk back to the car slowly. By the time he slid behind the wheel, Marta Rockwell was a block away. He fumbled with something on the seat of the car, wanting her to have a jump of a couple blocks before he followed.

She went all the way down the hill, crossed a bridge over the Cannon River, and turned left, skirting the Carleton campus. A half-mile from the bridge, she turned down a path that led through

294

a woods, back toward the river. Mars parked, then jogged slowly after her.

She was maybe fifty feet ahead of him when he caught sight of her again. She was standing near the river, calling to the dogs, who were mucking around with sticks along the shore.

She must have heard him, because she turned abruptly, shading her eyes with a raised hand, as if in a salute. She started at the sight of a lone man, coming toward her rapidly, then she moved to the dogs, as if for protection.

Mars reached into his pocket and pulled out his badge. She was still facing him, holding both dogs by their collars. When he was within voice range, she called out, "What do you want?"

He held up his badge before he was close enough for her to recognize what it was. He called back to her, "I'm Marshall Bahr, an investigator with the State Bureau of Criminal Investigation. I spoke to you on the phone last August. . . ."

Her face relaxed with relief, and she let go of the dogs. They both came toward him at a run, barking for attention. Her anxiety had worked to his advantage. If he'd knocked on her door and introduced himself, he was sure her expression would not have been one of relief.

Relief was followed by puzzlement. "How did you find me here? How did you know who I was?"

"I saw you leave your house," Mars said. "I thought it might be easier to talk if your husband wasn't around."

Her face collapsed in an expression of dread and thin resistance. She ran her fingers through her dark blond hair and turned away from him. "If you want to talk, you're going to have to do it on the run. The dogs are here for their exercise."

He followed her along the path, the dogs running ahead, then back toward them, stopping often to shove their faces deep into the weeds along the trail. The river moved slowly to their left, muddy and uninviting. Mars watched Rockwell, catching quick glimpses of her face as she turned to call the dogs. He was looking for a resemblance between Marta Rockwell and Gail Pearce. More than that, he asked himself if Marta and Gail resembled each other, did Marta resemble Terri DuCain?

Marta was shorter than Terri, but her frame was slight, like Terri's. Mars pushed his imagination. He tried to imagine Marta with red hair, lying facedown. If he could merge his memory of the body they'd found on August 23 with this woman, it was one more piece of evidence supporting that the victim had been Gail Pearce.

"You look like your sister," he said, wanting to know if she thought they'd looked alike.

She turned toward him abruptly. "You've seen her?"

"Only pictures. I couldn't say for sure how much you look alike. Maybe it's just that you're both slender. The photo I saw—your sister was wearing a lot of makeup. And her hair was very blond."

A short, harsh laugh followed Mars's observation. "I don't doubt it." She stopped walking. "You *frightened* me," she said sharply, her anger at being followed catching up to her.

"Didn't mean to," Mars said. "I was just waiting for the right time. Like I said, I had the impression your husband didn't want to be part of the conversation."

"What you said before was, you thought it would be easier to talk if he wasn't around. Meaning, easier for you."

Mars nodded. "Just how it seemed after talking on the phone." Mars came alongside her, and for the first time, they walked next to each other. He didn't say anything for a while, sensing that pressing just now would cause her to hold back.

He drew a breath, and conscious of trying to sound casual, said, "What I told you before was that I was looking for a man named Paul Tanney. We found him—found his body. . . ."

She stopped again. "Paul Tanney is dead?"

Mars didn't say anything. He stood next to her in silence.

"So if he's dead—why do you need to talk to me?"

He spoke softly, slowly. She was a smart woman, she knew what his tone meant. He could see anxiety gathering behind her eyes.

"When I called last August, I was hoping your sister could tell me something that would help me find Tanney. Now, the way things have turned out, I need to confirm that your sister is still alive."

Her face crumbled. She clenched both fists and held them hard against her forehead. Something garbled came out of her mouth.

"I'm sorry," Mars said. "I didn't hear what you said."

Her hands fell down from her face, still clenched. Her face was blotched pink and white, streaked with tears.

"I said I didn't get a birthday card this year. No matter what, Gail always sent me a birthday card on September tenth."

A wind had come up, making the cool air cold, clouds breaking the sun's warmth. They moved into a copse of small trees, sitting with their backs against three large rocks. The dogs eventually settled down, bored with their surroundings. Otis, the mastiff, rested his huge head on Marta Rockwell's lap, long strings of spittle spread out on her pants leg. Rocket shoved himself against Mars and fell asleep.

She told him what she knew about Gail and Paul Tanney, confirming that Gail had been in Northfield for three days early in August, with Tanney. They'd come to see Gail and Marta's parents who'd moved into an assisted living facility north of town.

"That's why she said they'd come," Marta said. "The truth was, Gail needed money. Gail always needed money." She shook her head. "She always had some story about how her big break was just around the corner. The thing about Gail was that she really believed that. Every time she asked for money, she meant it when she said she'd pay it back. With Paul, it was a con from word one. When they came down in August, she told me Paul had some big deal going. She just needed something to tide them over until that came off."

She sighed. "You know that Sheryl Crow song, 'All I Wanna Do'? That was Gail. She'd go anywhere, do anything, with someone who offered her a good time. Tanney played Gail like a fiddle. She broke up with him more than once, but all he had to do to get her back was promise her a good time. Not that she had many good

297

times with him. He was physically abusive. While they were here in August, he told her to go out to the car to get something for him. She didn't go right away—and with me sitting right there—he punched her, punched her hard, in the arm."

Mars said, "Do you remember which arm he hit?"

She thought for a moment. Mars could see her reconstructing the scene.

"The left arm. He punched her on the left arm. I can still see it in my mind—where each of them was standing, the look on Gail's face. . . ."

The bruise on the body's left arm. The last shoe had dropped.

"And you haven't seen or heard from her since?"

Rockwell teared up again, shaking her head, but not speaking for moments. Then she repeated what she'd said before. "I always— *always*—got a card from her on my birthday. No matter how bad things were."

Her eyes rose toward Mars. "Tell me what's happened."

Mars took time before he spoke. He reached over, putting a hand on Rockwell's jacket sleeve. She closed her eyes at his touch, her face tightening defensively against what was coming.

He knew from experience that being simple, being direct, was best.

"I think Gail is dead," he said. "I think Tanney killed her."

She flinched, not opening her eyes, her face getting tighter. Once again she drew up clenched fists, knocking them slowly against her forehead. She rocked back and forth gently.

"Damn Gail," she whispered.

He let her cry until she stopped. When she spoke, her voice was hoarse, but steady.

"You need me to identify the body, right?"

"Sight identification isn't an option," Mars said. Which was nothing more than the truth. "I need two things from you—and from a parent, if possible. Right now I need evidence that will get me a search warrant. If I can establish Gail's blood type, that should help with the warrant. If the warrant results in a criminal charge—"

"But you said Paul Tanney was dead. That Paul killed Gail. Why would there be a criminal charge ... ?"

Grief hadn't fogged Marta's brain.

"It's more complicated than that. I'm sorry—I can't explain everything now. If I get the search warrant, and the search works out the way I think it will, I'll be able to explain more then."

She sagged, exhausted. "Say again what it is you need."

"I need to confirm Gail's blood type. That's the piece that I need for the search warrant. Then, on the chance there will be a criminal prosecution, I need tissue, fluid samples from you, from a parent, so we can do DNA typing to confirm Gail's identity."

"Why not just do the DNA tests? Wouldn't that be better?"

Mars nodded. "More precise, sure. But DNA tests take time. I need to move on the search warrant as soon as possible. I'm concerned that the evidence we're looking for could be destroyed."

"What do you need me to do now?"

"Do you have anything that documents Gail's blood type? Hospital surgical records, blood donations?"

She thought hard. "Gail had her tonsils out when she was thirteen. The hospital here must have some record of that ... you know what? My mother had hip replacement surgery just before they moved into assisted living. Both Gail and I were typed before the surgery because Mom has a rare blood type." Marta made a face. "I *paid* Gail a hundred dollars to get typed. Turned out she and Mom were a match. We never did have to donate, but I bet Mom's care center still has the record. I know they keep both Mom's and Dad's blood types on file."

Mars called Doc D at home from the car as he drove back to the Cities.

"Can I meet you in your office in a half-hour?"

Doc didn't show any particular curiosity when Mars showed up after dark.

"To what do I owe the pleasure?"

So Mars told him the story, leaving in the parts about the Hispanic woman at the Woofies game and the postcard of the statue in the crypt at Winchester Cathedral, because that was the kind of thing Doc enjoyed.

"Great inductive reasoning," Doc said. "Problem is, with inductive reasoning, it doesn't necessarily follow that your conclusion is valid."

"Which is why I need your help, Doc."

"Figured as much."

"And it has to be confidential. If I'm right, and T-Jack figures out . . ."

"Say no more," Doc said, still looking unperturbed. He drew his index finger across his lips, then leaned back in his chair. "What do you need?"

"I can't have Gail Pearce's body exhumed. Too big a chance it would draw attention to what we're doing. Not to mention it would kill Grace DuCain. She can't know about any of this until we're sure. . . ."

"Understood," Doc said.

Mars hesitated, afraid of how Doc might answer his next question.

"What was the blood type at the scene?"

"Hang on." Doc got up, left his office, and walked out into the administrative section. He fiddled in his pocket for keys, opened a file, found what he was looking for, and walked back to his office.

"You've got statistical probability working for you," he said when he came back. "Blood at the scene was AB. Only about four percent of the population is Type AB. So, if what you're thinking is, you want to use blood type to rule out that the victim was Terri DuCain, you've got as good a shot as you're going to get with AB." Doc stood for a moment before sitting down, then said, "I'm starting to feel real uncomfortable about this. I should have done a better job of documenting the victim's identity."

"Tell me the last time you had a victim found dead in her own house, identified by her parents, who met the victim's description—and you asked for further ID?"

Doc made a dismissive gesture. "Doesn't make you feel better on a deal like this. The woman you think was the victim—Gail Pearce, you said?—she was Type AB?"

Mars held up the copy of the blood typing card he'd taken from the Northfield Senior Care Center. "Bingo."

"What else can I do on this?"

Mars shoved a sealed nine-by-twelve envelope across Doc's desk. "Hair follicle, blood, and saliva samples from Gail Pearce's sister and mother. Can you get DNA typing started on an expedited, anonymous-donor basis?"

"Consider it done. Anything else?"

Mars nodded. "This is the tough part. To make the search warrant as strong as it needs to be, I need to rule out that Terri's blood was also AB. For the reasons I've already said, I can't exhume the body or go to Grace to ask for Terri's blood type—not unless there's absolutely no other way. Can you check hospital records for Grace's and Duke's blood types? If we can establish that they couldn't have produced an AB offspring, that would help a lot. And it goes without saying—you can't raise any eyebrows by looking for their records."

Doc's eyes shifted as he thought about what Mars was asking. His lower lip extended and he nodded slowly. "I assume you're thinking DNA typing is too slow for the purpose of the warrant— what with the DuCain girl possibly being imprisoned. . . ."

Mars nodded.

Doc folded his hands over his midsection, his index fingers tapping slowly. "It's been long enough since Duke was brought in, his record should be filed in Records by now. Provided the doc who did the surgery is up-to-date on his dictation."

"You're saying it's possible Duke's surgeon hasn't done the dictation yet?"

Doc made a guffawing sound. "We've got docs who are *years* behind on their dictation. Does wonders for the quality of the final record. Administrators are tightening up. But it's still a problem. What you've got going for you is they would have typed Duke for sure, what with all the blood he lost. With his wife there, they probably would have typed her too. Just in case."

Doc sat up straight. "I'll start with Records. They won't think anything about my asking for the file. Do it all the time, especially when I was involved at the crime scene. If it's in Records I can handle that easy. If the doc hasn't done his dictation yet, I'm gonna have to go through surgery. That won't happen until tomorrow. We'll just have to leave it like this: best case, I'll be back to you tonight. Worst case, tomorrow."

Mars hadn't thought he'd be able to sleep until after they'd conducted the search. But leaving the Medical Examiner's Office, he was overwhelmed with fatigue. His coordination was sloppy, his eyelids were dragging. Back at the apartment, he kept himself awake long enough to check his phone messages. Danny and Nettie were on track, but had nothing in hand as yet.

He had just sunk down on the bed when the phone rang.

"Statistics did the job for you," Doc said. "Grace and Duke DuCain were both Type A, which isn't surprising. Forty percent of the population is Type A. Only blood type their offspring could have would be A or O. Not an AB in sight."

When he did sleep, Mars's dreams were fragmented, crazy. The only consistent image was Terri DuCain in her wedding dress, staring out at him, her eyes filled with sadness and dread.

CHAPTER

26

Donald Rupp had been an assistant supervisor in the Minneapolis Police Department Property Room for eleven years. It was a job that exceeded the expectations of his youth. Handling the bags and boxes filled with intimate, telling relics of dead and injured people—people whose lives often became the stuff of daily newspaper and television coverage—never ceased to thrill him.

"You know the girl who was raped and bludgeoned to death on River Road?" Donald would ask a date as he stuffed a Red Lobster cheddar cheese biscuit into his mouth. "It was on Channel Four last night. Special Investigative Report. I personally logged in her—well, intimate apparel. Lots of blood and I wouldn't want to tell you what else. Not over dinner, anyway. Maybe later."

Donald especially enjoyed his contacts with cops. He was always looking for the inside story on cases, the details you couldn't read about in the paper, see on TV. Some cops enjoyed talking about their cases, others wouldn't give you the time of day.

The young guy signing out a box on a six-month-old robbery case was new. Didn't seem real talkative, but from what Donald heard, the guy wasn't on the fast track. Probably didn't work any of the real interesting cases. Word in the department had it that Danny Borg had tied his wagon to the wrong star and got left out in the cold.

Borg had signed for what he needed and started out of the property room when he stopped and came back.

"Hang on one second," he said. "I was supposed to pick up something for ..." Danny fished around in his pockets, pulling out a scrap of paper. "Shit. All I've got is the case number. I don't think I need the whole box—hell, better take it, find out what he wants."

Donald looked at the case number and grinned. "You working the Terri Jackman case?"

"Me?" Danny said, looking surprised. "That's the Terri Jackman case number? Don't I *wish* I was working that one. One of the other guys, when I said I was coming down here, asked me to pick it up."

"What's new on that one, anyway? Haven't heard anything in weeks."

"Damned if I know," Danny said. "Nobody ever tells me anything."

"Well, if you're willing to give me your John Henry, I'll get you the box."

When Donald brought the box back, Danny Borg said, "You know what? Lugging both these boxes up to the third floor is gonna be a pain. If you'll give me just a minute, I'm gonna go through the box inventory real quick and see if I can remember what it was he wanted. Then I'll just sign out the single item, if it's all the same to you."

"Not a problem," Donald said. "Just move over to the side here. Officer Thorstenson behind you needs some assistance."

"Sure thing," Danny said, sliding the box down the counter.

"So, Vic," Donald said, "what's new on that meth lab case you charged last week?"

Donald and Vic were still talking when Danny slid the box back down the counter.

"Thanks anyway. Think I'm gonna double-check what it is he wants before I sign anything out."

"Whatever," Donald Rupp said, giving a dismissive wave as Danny left the property room.

To Vic Thorstenson he said, "What I hear is, that guy's going nowhere fast. Which isn't hard to figure. Guy doesn't even seem to know there's such a thing as a telephone."

304

Scott Menker was Donald Rupp's opposite. There was nothing about Menker's job as supervisor of the City Building Permits Office that he found satisfying or interesting, least of all the salary. Which was why he didn't see anything wrong with taking a little extra from contractors now and again—provided he was getting paid for services above and beyond standard services available from the permits office. Expediting approval of a permit, giving a builder a heads-up on problems he might have with an application. Value-added service, really, nothing wrong with that. Moonlighting was how he liked to think about it. He didn't let it bother him that he did his moonlighting during normal business hours.

Not that he ever made big bucks from his little sideline. Sometimes it would be Vikings tickets. A nice steak dinner at Manny's. One guy got a buddy to replace some defective cedar planks on Scott's deck. Nothing big—except maybe for the five hundred dollars he'd gotten from Tommy Hopper, the general contractor on the Tayron Jackman renovation.

Damnedest thing about that five hundred bucks was all he had to do was check every week to see if the permits office had received any requests involving Jackman's property identification number. Which was easy enough for Scott to do when he was putting together the fucking office productivity numbers every Friday. Took him maybe an extra five minutes. The way Scott figured it, five minutes a week added up to less than five hours in a year. So he'd make a hundred dollars an hour if he did it for a year.

If the number ever showed up, he was supposed to give Hopper a call. But in the eight months Scott had been scanning the weekly numbers, T-Jack's number had never turned up. Which was too bad, because Hopper told him it would be good for a little extra if Scott passed on anything about an information request on Jackman's property.

"He's paranoid," Hopper had said. "Not that I blame him. A star basketball player like T-Jack, some nut could get ideas."

"So what happens if we do get a request?" Scott had asked. "T-Jack throws whoever asked for the information off a bridge?"

Hopper had shrugged. "Not my problem. All I've gotta do is pass on whatever you tell me to T-Jack."

So, every week, Scott ran his index finger down the list of property identification numbers on which the office had received permit information requests for the past week, a job he always did on Fridays. If he was out on Friday, or it was a holiday, he'd do it first thing Monday. After the first couple weeks, he knew the number by heart.

21–003–23 23 0267

But the number never showed up, not even after his wife was murdered in the house, and T-Jack had become a major celebrity.

"I need to talk to you," Renae Roberts said. She'd been hanging outside Scott Menker's office door the whole time he'd been on the phone with his buddy planning their deer hunting trip.

"What," he said, sitting up with a jerk, giving Renae a short, hostile look. Of all the things about his job he hated, Renae Roberts was right at the top of the list. She had this sign on the wall in her cubicle, "If it is worth doing, 'tis worth doing well." Probably some shit she heard somebody say on Oprah. Whoever she copied it from, those words pretty well summed up most of her problems. She drove him frigging crazy with all her picky little problems, most of which had to do with something she decided Scott hadn't done right. If she was so sure he'd screwed something up, why didn't she just fix it and get on with her life? *Because* what she really wanted to do was make his life miserable. God knows she was doing one hell of a job on that.

"This," she said, holding out a fax request. "I got this request from the BCA this morning. Rush request, high priority. Blah, blah, blah. They want permit activity on these four properties, going back to 1990, including blueprints on permits granted. . . ."

"So," Scott said. "That's your job, right? Responding to permit information requests. Why do you need me to tell you how to do your job?"

"We have guidelines," she said, in a voice that made clear she was telling him something he should know that she assumed he didn't know, "about the number of requests we'll fill for one person and the time within which we respond. Because it was a state agency request, I went ahead and pulled the information, even though it was outside guidelines. It was picked up by messenger just before noon. Then I get a call. They want *all* permit activity and blueprints for one of the properties, going back to the original building permit. Which was 1923. And they want it this afternoon. No way I can do that and get my application processing done by deadline. . . ."

"So don't do it. I'm still waiting for a question that's my problem."

For the first time, Renae looked vaguely uncertain. "It just seems, because it's a state agency request, and all—I told them I'd have to ask you to approve overtime."

"Fuck the state agencies. You already did more than you had to. They can wait. Like the rest of the world has to wait to get what it needs."

She hesitated again. "The thing is, the woman at the BCA who made the request said they were getting the information for the FBI, and what with what's been going on with the U.S. Attorney's Office and all . . ."

The hairs rose on the back of Scott Menker's neck. There'd been a number of indictments over the past year involving city council members and the building inspections department. Those problems had precipitated a series of subpoenas from the U.S. Attorney's Office to various city departments. Did this request mean the permits office was about to become the target of an investigation?

Shit. The key question was, had Scott's moonlighting drawn someone's attention?

"Lemme see that," he said, taking the fax request from Renae Roberts. It didn't make sense to get worked up about anything if it didn't involve properties where Scott had a relationship with the contractor. He scanned the request quickly.

Double shit. Tayron Jackman's property ID number jumped out at him. The prickly feeling that had hit him when Roberts first mentioned the Feebies and the U.S. Attorney's Office had been replaced by intense warmth. Roberts was staring at him, noticing that he was upset. He shoved the request back at her, his mind racing. Scott Menker might have been lazy and dishonest, but he wasn't dumb. He knew that stonewalling on the request would come back to bite him on the butt. The best thing for him to do now was to cooperate. To look like he didn't have anything to hide.

"Give them what they want," he said.

Renae Roberts stared at him. "You're approving overtime, then?"

"Do whatever the fuck you need to do!" he heard himself shouting. Lowering his voice, he said, "Just get it done, okay?"

Menker sat in his office with his hand on the phone for minutes after Renae had left. He didn't have any doubt that approving the fax request was the smart move. He just wasn't sure what his next move should be. He thought through a number of scenarios that could have prompted the request from the BCA. The scenario that scared him was that the Feebies had something on Hopper and Hopper was telling the Feebies that Menker had extorted him. Menker had been around long enough to know that a U.S. attorney appointed by a Republican president would be more than happy to nail a public employee in a city administration dominated by Democratic-Farmer Labor officials. And he knew Tommy Hopper was smart enough to figure that out for himself.

He had to talk to Hopper. Maybe the guy wouldn't tell him the truth, but Menker was pretty sure he'd be able to tell something about what was going on just by listening to his voice.

"I'm going out for a while," he said as he walked past his administrative assistant. Scott Menker knew not to make this call from a phone that could be traced to him. He walked through the tunnel that connected city hall and the Government Center, stopping at a pay phone near the cafeteria.

Just after 2:00 p.m., Menker dialed Tommy Hopper's phone number.

Tommy Hopper sat with his hand on his phone after assuring Scott Menker that if the Feds were looking for trouble, they hadn't come his way. He didn't know what the Feds' request meant, but he was pretty sure it didn't have anything to do with him. Other than the chicken feed he'd given Menker to let Hopper know about any requests regarding T-Jack's property, Hopper hadn't done anything the Feds would care spit about. The arrangement he'd had with T-Jack—well, that was private. All T-Jack had said was he wanted to know if anyone came around to ask Hopper about the renovations at the house. T-Jack hadn't said anything about the City Building Permits Office. That had been Hopper's idea. Gave him another shot at getting the five thousand bucks T-Jack had promised Hopper if he tipped T-Jack on anyone snooping around.

What Hopper was thinking about was whether it was worth the time and aggravation to call T-Jack to let him know about the request. Hopper was pissed at T-Jack for all the trouble T-Jack had given him on the renovation at the Lake of the Isles house. T-Jack had reneged on countless commitments and verbal agreements during that project—why would T-Jack honor this commitment?

Hopper pulled his wallet out of his inside jacket pocket, sliding the little card that had the Timberwolves' schedule. No out-of-town games for the next few days, then the second exhibition game of the season. Which meant T-Jack was probably in town.

He picked up the phone to make the call just as his secretary buzzed him. His 2:30 appointment was early.

It was after 5:30 p.m. when Tommy Hopper cleared off his desk to head out of the office. He noticed the Timberwolves' schedule lying where he'd left it. He sighed. He didn't make the call, there was no chance of picking up the five thousand. He makes the call, and there's a chance.

Chance or not, it would have to wait until later. The Gophers basketball team was playing the University of Wisconsin Badgers. Maybe he'd have time to call T-Jack at halftime.

CHAPTER

27

Nettie had a near miss.

They were all back at Mars's apartment by 6:15, pretty much on schedule. Nettie came in last, breathing hard, taking her coat off as she entered, carrying an outsized manila envelope.

"It was almost over before it started," she said.

Mars, Danny, and Glenn looked at her, tense.

"It worked out," she said, enjoying their anxiety. "But for a while this afternoon, I thought what we were thinking about the safe room was wrong. Or that we weren't going to be able to *prove* that it existed, if it did."

She sat down, cross-legged on the floor, taking things out of the envelope. "What I did was send the permits office a request for construction permits and blueprints on four properties going back to 1994—which was before T-Jack bought the Lake of the Isles house. There's a woman in the permits office—Renae Roberts? Short, dark hair? Smart. Worked with her before. She's great. She had everything ready for me before noon. Problem was, when I got the stuff back here, there was nothing that showed T-Jack had put a safe room in the house. The renovation work that was done prior to Terri and T-Jack's separation showed a new wall at one end of the lower level, but that was it."

She drew a deep breath. "So, I thought about it. I remembered my grandmother talking about all the civil defense exercises that went on back in the sixties—bottom line, it occurred to me the safe room could have been built before T-Jack bought the house. I knew there was no way I could ask Renae to go back to the 1960s on all four properties and still get what we needed today. I had to zero in on T-Jack's house. Which I covered by kicking up a little dust. Told Renae that the information wasn't for us, that the Feebies wanted it. That I *had* to have it this afternoon. And bless her anal little heart—she did it."

"Did what, Nettie?" They all stared at her, barely breathing.

Nettie pushed herself up, tipping her head toward the kitchen. "Let's do this at the table."

"This is off microfiche," she said, spreading black-and-white sheets of paper out on the table. "So the quality isn't great." She tapped her finger on a page in the center of the table. "Lower-level renovation circa 1962. The house was owned by somebody named Donus. They had a bomb shelter built at the end of the room where—" She reached over for another page. "Where the bar is now." She pointed at one end of the renovation plan for the lower level of T-Jack's house. "There'd been a half-bath there. The Donuses expanded the space around the bath, put in a sally-port entrance—"

Glenn said, "A sally-port entrance—you mean like we've got in the jail? You open one door, go into, like a holding tank, until the first door locks behind you—?"

Nettie shrugged. "Something like that. The point is, it's a double entrance." She looked at Mars. "I had to ask someone in the State Facilities Office to help me look at the plans." Anticipating his concerns, she said, "I dummied up a copy that showed another property ID. But I couldn't figure out why you'd go to the trouble of doing a sally port on a bomb shelter, and I wanted him to look at the T-Jack renovation to see if there was any way we could tell how you'd enter the room now that the bar wall has been put in. . . ."

"And?"

"He said the sally-port entrance was unusual, but people who were going whole hog on bomb shelters back in the sixties sometimes did a sally port." She pointed again at lines on the microfiche that surrounded the sally-port entrance. "This is a return air vent.

312

You'd enter through the first door, then through the second door. When the second door closed, you turned on a vacuum device that essentially drew the air out of the sally port and sealed the second entrance. The guy I talked to had never seen one installed, but he said he thought the idea was that if there'd been an atomic attack, the vacuum device prevented radioactive contamination." She shrugged again. "Doubt if it was worth spit, but the point is, the sally port is a great way for T-Jack to get in and out of the safe room with minimum risk of Terri getting out."

"How about how you'd enter the safe room now that the bar has been installed?"

Nettie made a face. "There just isn't enough detail that you can see on the microfiche copy to be sure how that works. The facilities guy said it probably works like a pocket door on an electric switch. You push a button and half the wall slides sideways behind the other half of the wall. Then you'd have the first door into the sally port. . . ."

Glenn hissed in frustration. "Damn, Nettie. I've gotta have something that I can take to the judge that says there's a safe room behind that wall."

Nettie held up one hand. "Oh, ye of little faith. I had the facilities guy do measurements on the Donus floor plan and on the floor plan after T-Jack's renovation. The structural footprint for the house doesn't match the lower-level footprint on T-Jack's floor plan unless you add the dimensions for the safe room from the Donus floor plan. The facilities guy gave me a written statement that, in his judgment, the Donus safe room is still in place behind the T-Jack bar."

Glenn got up from the table and began to pace. "It'll have to be good enough. What else? Where are we on the blood evidence?"

Mars handed over the blood-type documentation for Gail Pearce and the DuCains. "Gail Pearce was AB—a blood type consistent with four percent of the population. The DuCains could have produced offspring with A or O blood types, but no possibility of an AB offspring. And here's the statement from Doc. Only blood type at the scene was AB."

"And what've we got linking Gail Pearce to Terri?"

It was Mars's turn to get up and pace. "Dammit, Glenn. We shouldn't need that for the warrant. We've gotta just focus on the point that the victim at the scene couldn't have been Terri DuCain. And tie that conclusion to the existence of the safe room. All we need, Glenn, is to find Terri. Then the rest of the case builds itself."

"The roses," Danny said. "We know that less than an hour before the murder, T-Jack had roses delivered to the house. But when we got to the house, there were no roses—not in the house, not in the trash. . . ."

"Oh, great," Glenn said. "I'm gonna ask for a warrant to search for a bunch of dead roses."

Mars said, "It's what you always say, Glenn. No detail is too small to be ignored. And it adds bulk. Gives the judge another thing to think about."

"What else?" Glenn said.

Danny said, "The hair I got from the evidence room. It tested out as being chemically treated. Terri was a natural redhead."

"Dribble, dribble," Glenn said. He let loose with another big sigh. "Okay. I'm gonna go back downtown. I wanna work on this in my office. I'll call you from there when—and if—I think we're good to go."

After Glenn left, Mars turned to Danny.

"What you said, Danny. About Terri's hair. You said Terri was a natural redhead."

"Yeah?" Danny said.

"She *is* a natural redhead, Danny. We've gotta keep believing that."

Glenn's call came at 8:15 P.M. He sounded genuinely tired and worried. "It's gonna be a close call. If Penner is still in signing mode, we've got a chance it'll fly. If not . . . Hell. Go for it. Make your call to the mayor. Tell her to call Penner and explain why it'll be you and me coming over."

* * *

314

The mayor called Mars back within minutes of his call to her. "Penner is hosting a reception at her house. She can't leave, so you're going to have to go over there. And it had better be worth her time, or she says she's going to have words with the county attorney first thing in the morning."

"There'll be lots of people to have words with in the morning if we miss our mark on this one. You going to stay at this number?"

"I'll be here. By the phone."

"I'll get back to you as soon as we have a signed warrant."

Penner took them into a study, the noise of her guests close at hand as Mars and Glenn stood beside the desk while she read the warrant. She mouthed the words as she read, her finger tracing her place.

Then she stopped abruptly, removed her glasses and stared at them.

"Are you serious? How can this be?"

Glenn pointed at the warrant before her. "It's all spelled out in the warrant, Your Honor."

She held her glasses up to her face without putting them on and read rapidly. Her eyes still fixed on the warrant, she said, "It's thin. You're asking me to sign off on a search warrant on the basis of evidence that blood at the scene doesn't match the identified victim's blood type. And this highly speculative conclusion that the identified victim has been imprisoned in a safe room in the house—a safe room that doesn't exist on . . ." Her hands riffled through the supporting documents attached to the warrant. "The safe room isn't shown on the Jackman house floor plan. I simply can't—"

Glenn stepped forward quickly. "Your Honor, if you would note that a state building facilities supervisor has compared the footprint of the house structure with the footprint of the lower-level renovation on the Jackman house. . . ."

Penner waved him off. "Yes. I saw that. If there were a clearly established reason to support your supposition that the existence of the safe room is a priori evidence that the identified victim was in fact a hostage, that would be useful. I can't justify issuing a search warrant without that evidence. What I'm going to have to insist on is DNA evidence that the victim is this woman—what was her name?—here it is. I need to establish that the victim is Gail Pearce. Then what you have here regarding the case theory and the involvement of Mr. Tanney creates reasonable cause to suspect that Mr. Jackman may have substituted Ms. Pearce for his wife...."

Something welled up within Mars and erupted before he knew it was coming. His anger was so intense that in spite of the emotion behind his words, his voice was low and hoarse.

"Do you have the remotest idea what's at stake here? We're not talking about abstractions of the law. We're talking about a living, breathing person who has been subjected to the grossest violation of human rights imaginable. To be completely honest, Your Honor, I don't give a flying fuck if you sign the warrant or not. I can't get another night's sleep knowing that a monster is holding an innocent victim captive. You don't sign? Fine. I'm going into the Jackman house tonight—with or without the warrant. And when I do that, and when I come out with Terri DuCain, it won't be me that's not sleeping nights."

"Mars!" Penner's voice was as steely as her expression. "All I have asked for is reasonable documentation of the identity of the victim. I'm already stretching to accommodate you—asking for something as trivial as that is *not* unreasonable. And please bear in mind that I am an officer of the court with a sworn responsibility to prevent the commission of crimes. You may retract what you just said, or I will have to act on my responsibilities and have you taken into custody...."

Mars shook his head violently. "You're just not getting it. You say, 'all I'm asking for is reasonable documentation.' I'll tell you what you're asking for. You're asking that we extend torture for several more days. You're asking that we continue to expose the victim's child to the deprivation of her mother's care and love. You're asking that we increase the risk that our victim will not survive the due process of law."

316

Penner was hearing him, but he could tell just by looking at her that she wasn't where he needed her to be.

In a soft voice, Mars said, "Your Honor. In the past, when we've come to you with a search warrant, what's been at stake has been our ability to charge and prosecute a case. In my sixteen years as a law enforcement officer, I don't ever remember a situation where we were executing a search warrant to save a life. But that's what's going on here. If I had to make a choice between successfully prosecuting T-Jack and saving Terri DuCain's life—well, it's not a choice. I'd like to think we can do both. If not . . . ."

"And you're telling me that if I sign the warrant, you're one hundred percent certain you will save Terri DuCain's life? I'm asking you, Mars, are you one hundred percent certain Terri DuCain is in that house? I don't think either one of us has to worry about the consequences of your executing the warrant if she is in the house. But I hate to think of what happens if she isn't there. Given the unusual circumstances—the mayor authorizing an investigation outside the chain of command in the police department—you, the mayor"—she nodded at Glenn—"the County Attorney's Office—all of you will be in deep trouble if you're wrong about Terri DuCain. This isn't just about covering *my* ass, Mars."

Mars thought for seconds before answering Penner. It finally came down to the only answer that made sense.

"I can't be one hundred percent sure of anything. All I can tell you is that I've been investigating murders for a long time. I've made mistakes, I've been wrong. But I've learned to trust my gut. And my gut is telling me that Gail Pearce, not Terri Du-Cain, was the homicide victim. Everything I know about T-Jack tells me the only reason he'd fake Terri's murder is to maintain control of her. And the one thing we do know is that Terri's murder was faked. We know with certainty that her blood was not at the scene."

Penner kept looking at him, waiting for his answer.

"I'm willing to stake my career—no, I *have* staked my career—on Terri DuCain's being in the house. And a lot of other people

317

have put up big chips on that bet too. That's the best I can give you."

Penner picked up a pen.

"I'm going to amend the warrant in one respect," she said as she wrote.

Mars held his breath. It was already a difficult, complicated search; any restrictions and the whole thing could fall apart.

"I'm . . . going to require . . . ," she said, speaking the words as she was writing, "that I be advised . . . as soon as is practicable . . . of the outcome of this search." Then she signed the agreement with a flourish and passed it back to them.

As they left, Judge Penner said, "Mars . . ."

He turned back to her.

"Godspeed," she said.

Outside, before he and Glenn got in the car, Mars called the mayor.

"We've got the warrant. Make the calls to the search team. We'll meet at your house."

It was just after 9:00 P.M.

An HCMC ambulance and an unmarked squad that belonged to Danny Borg were already outside the mayor's house when Mars and Glenn pulled up. Another car pulled in behind them, and Reilly James, the city engineer, followed them up the steps to the mayor's front door.

"What the hell is going on?" he said.

"All will be revealed," Glenn said.

Alex Gage looked startled when he saw Mars and Glenn. While Mars and Glenn were taking off their coats, he approached Mars. "Look. I don't know what my role is going to be here, but I've got to tell you that I'm uncomfortable handling the ambulance on my own. If we have anything like a real medical emergency, I'm not going to be able to do my job properly. . . ."

Mars put a hand on Alex's shoulder. "It has to be this way. Until we arrive at the scene. You'll be able to call in a chase car as soon as we get in at the scene. But for now, trust me."

318

Alex winced, but turned back to where the others were sitting. The mayor kicked things off.

"I've exercised my authority under the city charter to initiate a special investigation outside the normal chain of command within the police department."

Glenn gave Mars a quick side glance that told Mars he had some doubts about how the mayor was defining her authority under the city charter.

"I've personally asked Marshall Bahr to lead this investigation until we have completed a highly sensitive operation tonight. I think when Mars explains your mission, you'll all understand why confidentiality and surprise have been a high priority." She paused for only a moment, and then said, "The only other thing I have to say is that any fallout from your participation in this operation is my responsibility. Mars . . ."

He stared at the mayor before he said anything. It had been, in his experience, her finest moment. She was putting her political and professional neck on the block and doing it heroically.

It left him with a lump in his throat, partly out of gratitude to the mayor, partly because the emotions that had been accumulating since August 23 were about to be released.

Talking fast to get past the emotion, he said, "I don't have time to tell you all the facts that led us to initiate this operation. What you need to know is that we have concluded that the woman who died at Tayron Jackman's house on August twenty-third was not Terri DuCain Jackman. . . ."

His words hit them with physical force. They were too surprised to formulate questions. He pushed on. "We believe there is a strong possibility that Terri is still in the Lake of the Isles house, secured in a safe room."

Mars looked at each of them in turn. "It is also our belief that if T-Jack were to become aware of our suspicions, that Terri DuCain's life would be in immediate danger."

They were like zombies awakening from a deep sleep. They began to move, to look at one another, to form incomplete sentences.

Mars said, "We'll have time later to talk about the whys and hows. For now, you need to understand the operational plan and your roles in that plan. Danny, start with the floor plan."

It was 10:10 when they left the mayor to drive to the Lake of the Isles.

CHAPTER

28

It was wrong from the moment T-Jack opened his front door.

Over the past two and a half months, Mars had come to understand the subtle nuances of T-Jack's face. He'd learned not to expect a change of expression. He'd learned to pay attention to T-Jack's eyes, and what was going on behind T-Jack's eyes.

T-Jack's eyes, as he opened the door to Mars, Glenn, Danny, Reilly James, and Alex Gage, were defiant. They glimmered with arrogance.

Looking at T-Jack's eyes, Mars knew that T-Jack had been expecting them.

"You again," T-Jack said, casually.

"Mr. Jackman," Danny said, "we're here to execute a search warrant—"

"You'll have to wait in the hallway while I call my lawyer."

The words gave Mars the opportunity he needed. He moved between T-Jack and the phone.

"We don't have to wait for your lawyer to show up to begin the search," he said.

"Let me see that," T-Jack said, grabbing at the warrant. He read quickly, his eyes scanning the two-page warrant. "It says the search is limited to—what do you call this, anyway?—the 'safe room' on the lower level of the house?"

"More or less," Glenn said. "We're limited to looking for evidence that your wife, Terri DuCain Jackman, has been held in the so-described safe room since August twenty-third. We're free to move beyond that area if what we find there gives us reasonable cause to suspect she may be held somewhere else in the house."

T-Jack sneered, moving away from them. Dressed in black silk pajamas, his long, narrow feet shod in black leather mules, he looked like the devil, if the devil had been dressed by *GQ*.

"Craziest fool thing I've ever heard," he said. "This had better fly with my lawyer, or you all will have cause to regret being here. You're gonna do this, you damn well better be quiet while you're at it. My daughter's sleeping upstairs. I don't want her waking up to this nonsense."

T-Jack moved ahead of them going downstairs. Mars took Danny aside, and in a low voice said, "Check the call log on the phone. Get the numbers of anyone who called today." He gave Danny a slap on the butt as Danny moved quietly back upstairs.

Once downstairs, T-Jack switched on the lights and picked up a phone to call his lawyer. Then he made a convincing display of being more interested in playing pool than he was in what the search team was up to.

Danny came up behind Mars. "A call from Hopper Construction at eight-forty tonight. Nothing other than that." Danny looked over at T-Jack, and still whispering said, "He's not acting like I thought he would."

"He's acting," Mars said, "like he was expecting us."

Danny's eyes widened. "How?"

"The call from Hopper Construction. Somebody in the permits office tipped the construction company and they tipped T-Jack. But right now I'm less worried about *how* he found out, than what he's been up to between the time he found out and us showing up."

Reilly James approached T-Jack at the pool table. "We're interested in inspecting the room behind the bar." James held the floor plan out to T-Jack who, concentrating on his next shot, ignored it.

"I'd prefer not to have to take down the wall to get to it. You know how to get in?"

T-Jack took time to make his shot. Then, without looking at

James, he straightened up, dropping his cue stick on the table. "All you have to do is ask," he said.

"*Shit,*" Mars whispered.

T-Jack moved slowly toward the bar. "Don't use the room, but it was cheaper to leave it there when I did the renovation than to take it out. Besides, never know when something like that might come in handy." He shot a quick, triumphant glance toward Mars.

Mars's stomach sunk. He no longer had any doubt that when the room was opened, Terri DuCain wouldn't be there. All that was left for him to wonder was what T-Jack had done with Terri between the time he got the call from Hopper Construction and the time the search team had arrived. It was roughly an hour and a half. T-Jack would have had to restrain Terri in some way and remove any evidence that she'd been living in the room for more than two months. That hardly left him time to take her any great distance from the house.

An appalling idea struck Mars: that Terri could have been sedated, restrained, and moved to another part of the house. She could be there now. Within seconds of where he stood, just as she had been within seconds of where he'd stood the two previous times he'd been in the house. She could be lying on a bed upstairs, in a closet, behind a locked door. And their warrant gave them no authority to confirm that possibility.

Mars knew then what he'd have to do if the safe room yielded no clues to Terri DuCain's whereabouts. He'd have to go through the rest of the house on his own. He'd have to violate the warrant, compromising T-Jack's prosecution for what he'd done to Terri and for his role in Gail Pearce's death. There'd be personal consequences as well. He'd damage his credibility at the BCA and Danny Borg would be tarred by his association with the illegal search. It would hurt the mayor, it would hurt Glenn.

None of which meant that Mars had a choice. If the safe room told no stories, Mars would have to become a rogue investigator. There was no leaving this house, this night, until he knew, beyond doubt, that Terri wasn't here.

T-Jack stood behind the bar, facing the wall, his right hand feeling under a shelf. He was making a good game of it, appearing uncertain of what he was doing.

"Here it is," he said, stretching a bit farther. There was a clicking sound, and the bar wall split in half, each side retracting. With a double thunk the wall stopped. Recessed perhaps three feet behind the wall was a door. T-Jack stepped forward, pulled the door back, turning toward Mars.

"This what you wanted to see?"

Mars and Danny moved forward, passing through the door into the sally port. When the door closed behind them, they moved forward, opening the second door.

Danny scanned a flashlight around the safe room until he found a wall switch. It was the only light source in the room. It didn't feel like enough light to sustain a small plant, much less a human being. The room was approximately eight feet by ten feet, maybe something less than that. There was a sink against one wall, a single bed frame and mattress to the side of the sink. A toilet was at the opposite end of the room. It was a brutal environment.

"I'm going to want the Crime Scene Unit guys to go over this room and take out every speck of dust, every hair. . . ."

"What good will it do us?" Danny said. "Even if we find something that proves Terri was down here—it was her house. She lived here."

Danny was, of course, right. The best Mars could do now was to separate the others from what he was about to do.

"Danny," Mars said. "I need you to leave. Take Glenn and Reilly with you."

Danny wasn't paying attention to him. He was down on one knee, his flashlight focused on something under the wall sink.

He turned back to Mars with a grin on his face. "The warrant," he said. "Did it include the shit about the missing roses?"

Mars stared at Danny.

Danny held something small and dark between his thumb and index finger. When he shone his flashlight on the fragment, it became almost translucent. It had an unmistakable reddish hue.

324

"I'm no florist," he said, "but I'd bet my shield this is a dried rose petal."

"Your shield *is* what you're betting, and . . ." Mars took the petal into the palm of his hand. He grinned back at Danny. "I think this is a bet you're gonna win."

"If there's one, I bet there're more," Danny said, frantically flashing the light across the floor. They found two petals in the opposite corner from the sink, and when they moved the bed frame, there were another half-dozen petals. Danny shot snaps of each of the locations, and they moved back into the sally port.

Two more petals were stuck under the frame of the door.

"What do you think?" Danny said, trying to read in Mars's face what they needed to do next.

Mars stood in the center of the sally port, hands on his hips, thinking.

"Two possibilities. That T-Jack has been tracking rose petals out of here before today. He's such a neat nut, I'm betting if he tracked petals out earlier, he would have noticed them by now. I think what's more likely is that when he took Terri out today, some petals got dragged out with her. Maybe he wrapped her in a blanket or something and picked up the petals in the blanket. He wouldn't have had a lot of time to get the room cleaned up after he took her out—and we would have missed seeing the petals if you hadn't had the flashlight."

"Is it enough?" Danny said. "Does it give us probable cause to extend the search?"

Mars said, "I want to have a little confab with Glenn."

They opened the sally-port door into the bar area, and Mars signaled for Glenn to join them.

"What?" Glenn said when the door closed behind him.

Mars said, "We've found rose petals. In the sally port and in the safe room."

Glenn clapped his hand to his forehead.

"Holy Mary Mother of God, if you knew how close I came to excluding that nonsense about the roses. I was worried it would expose that we were grasping at straws. . . ."

"Grasping at petals, as it happens," Mars said. "What we need to know, Glenn, is finding the rose petals down here gives us probable cause to extend the search beyond the safe room."

"You found petals outside of the safe room itself? In here?"

Mars nodded.

Glenn's tongue slid back and forth across his lower lip while he thought. "Okay. We stated in the warrant that roses delivered within an hour of the victim's death were not found in the house immediately following the death. The search has yielded evidence that the flowers may have been in the search area, along with evidence that they had been taken beyond the search area. . . ."

"Yes!" Danny said, pumping one arm in the air.

"Look," Glenn said. "Just to be on the safe side, I'm going to say we'll extend the search to the remainder of the lower level. . . ."

Danny's face crumpled. "What does that get us? There isn't any place out there she could be hidden."

Glenn said, "All we have to do is find one petal on the stairs going to the next level, and we can extend from there. What I'm trying to do here is preserve the legal integrity of the search results. . . ."

Mars thought back to when he had considered that T-Jack might have confined Terri in the safe room until it would be safe for him to murder her, toss her body in the trunk of the car, and remove her from the house.

Mars said, "Am I remembering right that the garage is just the other side, on this level?"

Fritz Mercer was waiting with the others when Mars, Danny, and Glenn emerged from the sally port.

He held the warrant in his hand. He was, as always, calmly arrogant.

"If you've completed the search of the designated area, gentlemen, I'd appreciate your leaving my client's house at your earliest convenience. Mr. Jackman has already stated his concern that his young child may be disturbed by your presence, and as Mr. Jackman has cooperated in every way possible to allow you to complete your business—"

Glenn stepped forward. "Based on evidence found within the area specified in the warrant, Fritz, and on items specified as objects of the search, I've approved an extension of the search to the remainder of this level of the house . . ." He paused only a moment before adding, "Including the garage area."

T-Jack exploded. He turned on his attorney with a ferocity that stunned everyone in the room. "You fucking asshole! Why the hell do I pay you five hundred dollars an hour to let these bozos come in here and abuse me like this." He pushed Mercer to the side and moved on Mars. "I told you once before not to come back here. I let you in tonight just to show good faith. Now I want you gone. And you can take your two-bit warrant with you. Get out of here!"

T-Jack's performance was all Mars needed to be sure where they'd find Terri DuCain. Now that he was sure, he couldn't move fast enough to get to her.

"Danny, Alex, I need both of you in the garage, now."

Mars and the others started toward the door that led into the garage.

T-Jack came after them like a banshee. Danny saw him a split second before T-Jack was on them. Danny stuck out a leg, causing T-Jack to fall forward, his head knocking against the side of the bar. The blow stunned him momentarily, giving Danny time to clap cuffs on his wrists and ankles.

Danny looked at Mercer and said, "Your client moves from there, and he's gonna have an assault-on-an-officer charge along with everything else."

The doors and the trunk of the Jaguar sedan were locked. Mars took a spade hanging from the wall and smashed in the driver's side window. He found the trunk release in seconds.

Mars saw her hair first. Just like he had on August 23.

No longer smooth and shiny, but still red. She was wrapped in a blanket, her mouth covered with duct tape. Her skin was pale, blue-tinged, her eyes closed. As they lifted her out of the trunk, limp, they saw that she'd vomited under the tape.

"Shit!" Alex said. He was holding her wrist, his head to her chest. "He must have drugged her. Her breathing is shallow and she's hardly got any pulse—I've gotta get her to the truck—I don't want to go all the way upstairs and then down the stairs. Danny—I'm gonna start working on her here. Go out to the truck and drive it up to the garage, then we'll move her from here. And call me a chase car while you're at it."

"There's a gate," Danny said, "and it's locked. T-Jack isn't gonna lift a finger to get us in . . ."

Alex turned his head away from Terri, toward Danny, for only a second.

"So drive the truck through the gate if you have to! We need it here yesterday! I'm in load-and-go mode. And the sooner the better."

To Mars he said, "She's shocky and it's cold in here. Take her out of the blanket and spread it over the floor, then go inside and get something to cover her with."

With Terri lying on the garage floor, Alex ripped the duct tape from her face. Terri gave a slight moan in response to the pain, her lips and the skin around her mouth immediately reddening.

Alex, who was breathing hard and sweating, gave Mars a quick look.

"A moan is good, that's a start. But her pulse is braidy, not even forty. She's *so* cyanotic. . . ." He paused, shining a pencil-thin pocket flashlight into Terri's eyes. "Her pupils are nonreactive—all of which means her heart and brain cells aren't going to last much longer if I can't get her tubed." He nodded at a blue canvas medical bag he'd brought into the house. "Drag that over. Inside, there's an airway bag . . . yeah, hand me that."

"What do you think he's done to her—"

"Not now, Mars. I've gotta work on her airway."

Breathing heavily, he said, "Hear that gurgling? She's aspirated vomit. I'm going to have to do a finger sweep to clear her air passage. . . ." Alex manipulated Terri's jaw, simultaneously pulling

328

on a clean latex glove before he angled two fingers down her throat. In moments, he brought his fingers out, shaking a glob of vomit onto the garage floor.

"Ohhh-kay," he said. "I've got a decent airway. I'm going to intubate—move over some, will you? I need all the light I can get."

Mars held his breath. He'd been at enough emergency medical scenes to know that intubation—even in ideal conditions—was one of the most daunting procedures to undertake. He'd seen experienced emergency room doctors fluff intubations at the cost of patients' lives.

With Alex it happened in less than ten seconds. The result was immediate. Mars saw Terri's first breath inflate the bag, heard a fine whistle of air pass through the pop-off valve, saw a rise in Terri's chest.

Alex gave Mars a grin. "I think we've got her back." Then he frowned. *"Where's the truck?"*

From outside the garage door, they heard a crash, then the wail of an alarm.

"I think," Mars said, "the truck has arrived."

The ambulance was followed by a jeep chase car that had quickly assessed the situation, driven over the smashed gate, and come up directly behind the ambulance. With a second paramedic on the scene, Terri was in the ambulance in moments. Standing outside the ambulance's back window, Mars could see Alex start an IV and put Terri on a monitor.

Mars leaned against the van, closing his eyes. "We can't lose her now."

"You've always said Alex can bring people back from the dead." Danny hesitated, then said, "Mars, there's a crowd gathering down on the street. It's probably only a matter of minutes before news crews start showing up. If Grace DuCain . . ."

Mars straightened up. "Jeez. She can't hear about this on the news." He looked at his watch. "What we've got going for us is it's after eleven o'clock. But my guess is Grace doesn't sleep well. If she turns on the radio or TV . . ." He shook his head. "I can't go out there until we know whether Terri has a chance or not." He thought about telling Grace that Terri hadn't died on August 23, but she was dead now. It just wasn't a possibility.

Alex came out of the back of the ambulance. He looked wrung out. When he saw Mars look at him with alarm, he smiled.

"She just opened her eyes. We're going to whistle her in. She's probably gonna have one hell of a case of aspiration pneumonia." Alex's grin widened. "But that's not my problem."

Mars closed his eyes and wrapped an arm around Alex's neck.

"This isn't the time to slow me down, pal," Alex said, pulling away.

"I'm going out to get her mother. If there's even a chance—the smallest chance—that Terri might not make it, I need to know before I see her mother. I need you to tell me Terri's going to make it."

"Aspiration pneumonia is serious, Mars. And she's been through a lot. . . ." Alex turned to climb back into the truck.

Mars called after him, "Can I tell her mother she's going to be okay?"

Alex called back as the ambulance pulled away.

"Slam dunk *yes*."

Linda Burnet answered the phone and at first said Grace wouldn't be able to take Mars's call. Her voice was low, guarded.

"Linda," Mars said, "tell Grace it's urgent. I need her to be ready to go when I get there—which should be in less than half an hour. And Linda—have you spent time with Tam? I need someone who knows Tam to pick her up at the Lake of the Isles house and take her back to Grace's. . . ."

"Bring Tam here? Of course I can do that—but Mars, what's happening?"

"I'll tell you when I get there."

For the second time in as many months, Mars drove from the city to the DuCains' Lake Minnetonka house with his siren wailing and

330

the flashers rotating, cutting through the black of the night. He didn't need the siren and the flashers to get through traffic—there was no traffic. He needed the sound and the light to assure himself he was getting to Grace as fast as was humanly possible.

When he pulled up in the driveway, Grace DuCain was standing in the doorway, Linda Burnet just behind her.

Mars got out of the car without turning the engine off, without shutting the door behind him. He was so focused on Grace that he wasn't aware that tears were streaming down his face.

"Terri's alive, Grace. She's going to be fine."

It was dawn before Mars made it back to HCMC from the county jail where Danny and Glenn had completed filing charges against T-Jack. He walked the stairs to the Women's Medical Ward, checked in at the nursing station, was told Terri DuCain was in Ward Room 318, then went back to a large room meant for four patients.

Only one of the four beds was occupied. Terri DuCain slept, her skin flushed, her breathing regular, her red hair fanned out over the pillow. Grace DuCain was on a chair next to the bed, her head lying on the bed, her arm extended over her daughter's arm.

Sensing him, Grace raised her head. When she saw Mars, she stretched out her hand.

He walked over to her, taking her hand, touching his lips against the back of her hand. She lifted his hand to her cheek, holding it there. Then she turned her head back toward Terri, fixing her eyes on her daughter's face.

Mars stared at the two of them for moments. Then he turned and left. He stopped briefly at the nursing station.

"Terri DuCain, Room 318," he said. "No roses. I don't care who they're from."

CHAPTER

29

"You've got to come over right away," Denise said. It was the week after Christmas. She sounded like she'd been crying.

Mars's heart stopped. "Chris," he said. "Is Chris okay?"

"Yes," she said, "I mean, not exactly. Sarge is sick. Chris is beside himself. You need to come right away."

Chris and Sarge were in Chris's room, on Chris's bed. Sarge was lying on his side, breathing heavily, an eerie, humming purr coming from his partially opened mouth. The cat's eyes were mattered.

Sarge isn't sick, Sarge is dying. Mars could tell that at ten paces.

Chris was lying next to Sarge, on his side, gently stroking the cat. Chris's eyes were hollow with grief.

Mars sat down on the bed next to Chris. "When did this start?" he said.

"Last Thursday," Chris said, his voice hoarse from crying. "He just gets worse and worse."

"What did the vet say?"

Chris shook his head. "We didn't go to the vet. *Carl* said it was stupid to spend money on an animal. It'd be cheaper to just get another cat."

Mars was off the bed and out of the room before he knew he'd moved.

Denise and Carl were standing in the kitchen. Both looked guilty.

332

"It would be cheaper to get another cat?" Mars hissed, staring at them both.

"It's my fault," Denise said. "We should have taken him. I know that. I just thought he'd get better."

"It *would* be cheaper to get another cat," Carl said, trying to sound belligerent, but not quite pulling it off. "It'd cost less in gas to just drive out to the farm and get another kitten. These vets charge an arm and a leg—"

Mars moved on Carl, slamming him back against the kitchen counter. The force of the impact caused the cupboard above the counter to creak, then crash forward, dishes falling out and shattering on the floor.

Mars and Carl stumbled backward, the disaster stopping them all in their tracks. Denise stepped between Mars and Carl.

"Stop. Both of you. Right now. Carl," she said. "I don't ever want to hear you say anything like that again. If you do, I won't go to Cleveland."

"I'm just trying to save your money," Carl started to say.

"It *is* my money, Carl. It has nothing to do with you, and you have nothing to say about how I spend it." She turned, took her purse from the counter, and taking out her wallet, handed it to Mars. "Take him to the vet, will you? Chris is going to need you there, or I'd do it myself. I don't care what it costs, Mars. You don't have to give me any money next month if that's what it costs to save the cat."

They rode in silence to the vet, Sarge, wrapped in a towel, on Chris's lap.

"I'm never going to love anything again," Chris said, his voice just above a whisper.

Mars flinched. He reached over and put a hand on Chris's shoulder.

"Chris," he said, "we'll do everything that we can to save Sarge. Your mom and I don't care how much it costs." He hesitated. "But if the vet says there isn't anything that can be done, then the best

333

way you can love Sarge is to put him down. He's suffering. And if he can't get better, he shouldn't have to suffer any more."

Which was what the vet said. He said it gently, putting his hand on top of Chris's hand, which was on Sarge.

"Your kitty has feline leukemia, Chris. We could have vaccinated him against this when he was younger, but once a cat has it, there isn't anything we can do. He's suffering. The kindest thing to do would be to let him die as peacefully as possible."

Tears started down Chris's cheeks. After moments of silence, he said, "If we do that, if we put Sarge down, what happens to his body?"

The vet gave a small shrug. "This time of year—it's going to be what tonight, twenty below?—I'd recommend cremation. It would cost a little extra, but we can have an individual cremation done, and you'd get your kitty's ashes back...."

Chris shook his head, hard. "No," he said. "I want to take him with me after."

The vet looked up at Mars.

"We'll take him when you're through," Mars said.

"How much do I owe you?" Mars said just before they left.

The vet looked at him. "You're the guy that arrested T-Jack, right?"

"One of the guys," Mars said.

"We don't charge for euthanasia," the vet said, avoiding Mars's eyes.

"What *are* we going to do with Sarge, Dad?" Chris's voice was small, but calm. He held Sarge's limp body, swaddled in the towel, in his arms.

"I've got an idea," Mars said. "We need to stop at the Cub on Lyndale that's open twenty-four hours."

"They're all open twenty-four hours," Chris said.

Chris stayed in the car with the engine running while Mars went in. He bought all the twenty-pound bags of charcoal the store

334

had. In December, in Minnesota, that was six bags.

He wheeled the bags in a cart back out to the car, which wasn't easy. The snow had frozen into deep, icy ruts in the parking lot, and moving 120 pounds of charcoal over those ruts took effort.

Chris looked at the bags as Mars loaded them into the trunk.

"Is Mom gonna let us do that on the lawn?" he said, figuring out what Mars had in mind.

"Oh, yes," Mars said. "Mom is going to let us do this."

"Just try not to make a mess," Denise said, not even putting up a fight. She was still sweeping up broken glass from where the cupboard had fallen.

"You do that on the lawn," Carl said, "and it's gonna look like hell in the spring. Just when we're putting the house on the market—"

"*Carl,*" Denise said, and Carl turned away, his hands jammed in his pockets.

They cleared a four-by-six-foot patch of snow first. It was at the far side of the back lawn, on a bit of a slope, facing east.

"Sarge always liked to lie in the window in the sun in the morning," Chris said. "This'll be perfect."

With the snow cleared, Mars and Chris emptied the bags of charcoal, heaping it in a mound. They used a whole can of lighter fluid, then lit the mound. It made a glorious blaze, with heat so intense that it pierced the below-zero cold.

Chris went into the garage and brought out lawn chairs. They set the chairs up and sat down in a comfortable silence, their fronts warmed by the glowing coals, their backsides still cold. Somehow, the contrast was comforting.

"How long do you think it's going to take?" Chris said.

"This is the first outdoor, below-zero burial I've done," Mars said. "I don't have any idea how long it'll take to get the ground thawed. I do think we'll want to put Sarge down pretty deep, or critters might try to dig him up."

"Damn raccoons," Chris said. Then, "Maybe until it looks like the coals are starting to lose heat."

"Sounds like a plan to me," Mars said.

An odd peace came over them as they sat, silent, before the glowering mound of coals. It was as if the elemental forces of nature—fire and ice—had joined to heal their grief. Just after midnight, Mars stood and stirred the coals with the fire iron he'd taken from the fireplace, causing Denise, standing at the back door, to open and close her mouth without saying anything.

"Get the spades from the garage," he said. "I think it's soup."

They had made two critical miscalculations in their burial plan. After they'd removed the coals and started to dig into the pudding-soft dirt, the cold air and the warm earth erupted into thick steam, blinding them. That and the slope above the grave site had become slippery and their feet had become mired in mud with sufficient suction to hold a rhino in place.

Their reaction to their dilemma was to collapse in laughter. Partially collapse into laughter. They were up to their knees in rapidly solidifying mud which prevented their falling horizontally.

"Dad," Chris gasped through his laughter, "what do we do now?"

"That's just what I was going to ask you," Mars said, which sent Chris into a second fit of laughter. Mars wouldn't have cared, at that moment, if the two of them froze to death, knee deep in mud. This was as close to normal as they'd been in months.

"Oh, shit," Chris said. "I just peed in my pants."

"That's good," Mars said, "it should slow down the mud from freezing."

More laughter.

Eventually they had to take their situation seriously. Mars started making mud balls to throw against the house.

"Mom isn't going to like that," Chris said.

"She'll like it better than having two garden gnomes rotting in the backyard when the thaw hits," Mars said as he lobbed the first ball against the side of the house.

After two solid hits, the backyard light came on, and Denise stuck her head out the back door.

"What's going on? Aren't you done yet?"

"We're stuck!" they yelled in unison.

"Get Carl to get the tire chains out of the garage. He's gonna have to pull us out."

It didn't work. Carl couldn't get enough traction on the icy slope to pull them out.

"Goddamn," he said. "I'm gonna have to get the pickup to pull you out. There isn't going to be anything left of the yard by the time we're through."

Most of what had been the yard spat back on Mars and Chris as the truck's tires spun on the ice. But after a couple of false starts, Chris came out with a loud crack, followed by a whoosh. Minutes later, Mars was out. Seriously cold at this point, they clumped to the back door, into the immaculate kitchen hallway, where they stood, hunks of mud falling from them. As Denise walked into the hall, Chris tripped trying to pull a boot off, knocking both Chris and Mars into the wall. They left a long trail of mud on the yellow and white wallpaper as they slid to the floor.

"You always said you wanted a house with a mud room, Mom," Chris said.

Mars and Chris couldn't stop themselves from another paroxysm of laughter. Denise stood, staring at them, somewhere between rage and disbelief, until she gave way and began laughing too.

"You're crazy, the whole bunch of you," Carl said.

Mars stopped in Chris's room after they'd both showered. He was wearing Carl's clothes, which was a surreal experience.

Chris was seconds away from sleep, his eyes barely open, his face still red from the heat of the coals.

Mars pushed Chris's hair back from his forehead.

"Dad?" Chris said. "I feel better. I mean, better about everything."

"Me too," Mars said.

337

*　*　*

Mars fell asleep immediately when he was back at the apartment, something he hadn't done for a long time. He couldn't have said how long the car horn had been beeping before he was fully awake. He looked at the clock. It was after 3:00 A.M.

He got up and split two slats of the blinds, looking into the parking lot. Denise's car was just below his window. He could barely make out her face, peering up at him from behind the car's windshield.

Mars put on his pants, stuffed his bare feet into his boots, and pulled on a jacket. Then he went out to the parking lot.

"I'm sorry about the honking," Denise said, "but I don't dare get out of the car in this neighborhood in the middle of the night." She drew a deep, wobbly breath. "I don't want you to say anything. This is hard, but I know it's the right thing to do. It's always been the right thing to do, but I just couldn't face it before. I'm going to give you custody of Chris—I said, don't say anything. It just hit me tonight. He does love me, or he wouldn't give you up. He loves me enough to do that—even though he knows, I know, he belongs with you. I'm the adult, I'm his mother. I've got to do what's best for him. Watching the two of you together tonight—well, I just can't take him away from you. I'll tell him in the morning."

They both sat, crying, Mars with his hand on her shoulder, for minutes before Denise started talking again.

"It was when you started seeing Evelyn that it got hard for me. I always felt I was important to both of you before Evelyn. But after Chris started spending time with you and Evelyn, I just felt like I didn't have a place anymore. Chris was always saying, 'Evelyn does this,' and 'Evelyn says that.' "

She took a tissue out of her purse and blew her nose hard. "I know Carl isn't good for Chris. He's not a bad man, Mars. He's good to me. We're good together. In a few years, Chris will be gone. Then what do I have? With Carl, I'll have a life. Until tonight, I felt like if I gave Chris up, it would mean I was choosing Carl over Chris. Until tonight, I didn't have the confidence to stand up to

338

Carl. Now that I have—this just feels like the right thing to do, for all of us." She sighed deeply, staring blankly out the windshield. "Now I need you to leave. We can talk more later."

As Mars got out of the car, Denise called out to him.

"Mars? One other thing. On the floor in the backseat. The bag. Take it with you. Don't ask what it is. And don't open it until you get upstairs. I want you to have it."

It felt solid as he lifted the towel-covered object out of the bag. But he didn't realize until he folded the towel back that, after everything, they never had buried Sarge.